New York Times and *USA TODAY* bestselling author **Cathryn Fox** is a wife, mom, sister, daughter, aunt and friend. She loves dogs, sunny weather, anything chocolate (she never says no to a brownie), pizza and red wine. Cathryn lives in beautiful Nova Scotia with her husband, who is convinced he can turn her into a mixed martial arts fan. When not writing, Cathryn can be found Skyping with her son, who lives in Seattle (could he have moved **any** farther away?), shopping with her daughter in the city, watching a big action flick with her husband, or hanging out and laughing with friends.

Alexx Andria is a *USA TODAY* bestselling romance author who writes about bad boys with a tough exterior but a soft, warm heart deep down. She loves sweet but dirty romance with lots of witty banter and, of course, sizzling scenes in the bedroom (or kitchen…or wherever they happen to end up) and a guaranteed HEA.

If you liked *On His Knees* and *Decadent*
why not try

Untamed by Caitlin Crews
Mr One-Night Stand by Rachael Stewart

Discover more at millsandboon.co.uk.

ON HIS KNEES

CATHRYN FOX

DECADENT

ALEXX ANDRIA

MILLS & BOON

First Published in Great Britain 2019
by Mills & Boon, an imprint of HarperCollins*Publishers*
1 London Bridge Street, London, SE1 9GF

ISBN: 978-0-263-27376-2

MIX
Paper from
responsible sources
FSC™ C007454

This book is produced from independently certified FSC™ paper
to ensure responsible forest management.
For more information visit www.harpercollins.co.uk/green.

Printed and bound in Spain
by CPI, Barcelona

ON HIS KNEES

CATHRYN FOX

MILLS & BOON

To my husband, a true romantic at heart. Love you.

CHAPTER ONE

Tate

"You can't be serious."

My grandfather curls knotted fingers around his crystal snifter, and holds the glass up in salute. Time-ravaged lines deepen around mossy eyes as he smiles at me. "As serious as a heart attack, son," he says, his Adam's apple bobbing as he takes a long pull, draining the rich, amber liquid with one easy swallow.

I push from the ebony leather chair, shocked at the real reason my granddad asked me to stop by after a long week setting up my new office. Here I thought we were going to catch up, shoot the shit, reminisce about old times after I moved my law practice from Boston to Manhattan to be closer to him. But instead I find myself alternating between sitting and standing, pacing and pausing as his unexpected request pings around inside my brain.

Change my property title and deed half my billion-dollar Manhattan estate to Summer Love.

"She's quite the looker, this one," Granddad says,

and picks up the Polaroid picture sitting on the mahogany side table in his study, one of the many nostalgic pieces he salvaged from the bygone gentlemen's club where he once networked. I glance at the picture in his hand. Christ, he's been grinning at it like love-struck teenager since I arrived thirty minutes ago.

Could he really be in love—with Summer Love?

And what kind of name is that anyway?

"What do you think, son?"

What I think is she's a third his age. For Christ's sake, she's young enough to be his granddaughter. What the hell is going on inside that brain of his? I shake my head, as arthritic fingers hold the photo up higher for my inspection. I glance at the Polaroid, which showcases the left half of my grandfather's face, and Summer Love from the chin up. I study her full pouty mouth, makeup-free face, big brown doe eyes and caramel hair piled haphazardly on the top of her head. Yeah, okay, she's gorgeous in that fresh-faced girl-next-door way—which probably opens many *affluent* doors for a gold digger like her.

And who the hell takes a selfie with a Polaroid anyway?

I shove my hands into the pockets of my black dress pants, and walk around Granddad's monument of a desk. Incredulous at what he's asking me to do, a garbled sound catches in my throat—a half laugh, half snort. I pace to the window and look out. On Sixty-Fourth Street below, dozens of people bustle about. A robust, early December breeze ruffles their clothes and pushes them along the sidewalk.

"Come on, have a celebratory drink with me, already," Granddad says again, his once syrupy voice now broken and gravelly.

Agitated, I remove my hands from my pockets, and swipe one through hair that desperately needs a barber. I just haven't had a lot of time lately. After moving back last week, I've put all my energy into getting my Manhattan apartment in order as well as the new firm—we're set to open for business after the holidays. My other hand smooths down my tie, a habit I picked up from my granddad even before I began wearing suits.

"Yeah, okay," I finally concede. The truth is I need a drink, something to help me swallow and digest this troubling news. But I'll be damned if I'll drink to my grandfather losing his mind and signing over half his estate to some con artist. I won't let that happen. Not in a million fucking years. I walk to the bar, pour a generous amount of brandy into a glass and throw it back in one motion. I welcome the burn as I slam the glass down on the bar harder than necessary and turn around to regard my grinning grandfather.

"She's lovely, James. Don't you think so?" he asks, using my middle name. He always preferred James to Tate. Probably because James is his first name, too. He loved the idea of his grandson carrying his name into the next generation. My mom, however, insisted on Tate as my first name, after her late father. But thinking of my mom ties my stomach into knots. She left when I was a child, accepting a big payout from Dad to leave me behind. Acid burns in my throat to think she chose money over her son. I guess she knew how to get around the prenuptial, and in the end I'd rather be with a parent who wants me.

Pushing those ugly thoughts to the recesses of my mind, I pace for a moment, then perch on the arm of the chair opposite Granddad. With my hands braced on my thighs, I take a deep fueling breath and let it out slowly. "Granddad," I begin, then clamp my teeth together with an audible click. How the hell can I tell him this woman is a con, out to bleed millions from his bank account, without hurting him in the process? This is a man who worked hard his whole life, dragged himself up from the gutters and turned thousands into billions on Wall Street. He's a man of morals, one who led by example and taught me and my father—not to mention my aunts, uncles and cousins—the value of hard work. Nothing was ever handed to any member of the Carson family. Sure, I was given a top-notch education at the finest schools, but Granddad always made me hold down part-time jobs. At Harvard, I worked the dish pit at the campus pub, eventually climbing my way up to bartender. I owe this man so much, and the last thing I want is to slap him with reality when he thinks he's in love with some…fraud.

The picture falls from his rickety hand, and his

frailty hits me like a punch to the gut when he bends to retrieve it. His big, gray cardigan hangs a little looser on his shoulders as he sits back up. He adjusts it, but there is nothing he can do to hide his ill health. Goddammit, I should have come home sooner, should have been here to prevent this woman from ever digging her claws into a dying man.

"How did you two meet?" I ask, choking back the emotions crawling up my throat.

Chuckling, he gives me a wink. "At the clinic."

"The clinic?" Restless, I stand, drawing myself up to my full six feet. "What was she doing there?"

"She held the door open for me."

"That's it?" I really don't like the sounds of this. I put my hand on the back of my head, apply pressure to the dull ache beginning at the base of my neck as every muscle in my body tightens, goes on alert. "That's how you met?"

"Yes."

I angle my throbbing head, my gaze raking over my grandfather's face as I take in his body language. There's something he's not telling me. The grandson in me senses it, the lawyer in me knows it. "What was she doing at the clinic?"

Granddad hesitates and I pinch the bridge of my nose, envisioning Summer Love hanging out at the geriatrics clinic, scoping out her next target. If it's money she's after, and obviously it has to be, she definitely scored big-time with Granddad. But Jesus,

what kind of a woman would do something so rep-
rehensible?

A conniving one.

"Does she work there?" I ask.

Gnarled fingers swat the air, like I'm an annoying
fly, buzzing with too many questions. "What's with
the interrogation? You're going to love her, James.
I'm sure you two will hit it off as soon as you meet,"
he says, pivoting the conversation.

Doubtful.

Anger prowls through my blood, a hot burn that
nudges my temper. In the past Granddad always had
an ironclad prenuptial drawn up. Why doesn't he
want one this time? Christ, he's not even married to
the woman, yet he wants to sign half his estate over.
He has to be losing his mind. What other explanation could there be?

"How long have you known her?"

"Long enough to know I want her to be part of
the family." He averts his eyes for a moment, glancing over my shoulder to gaze at the floor-to-ceiling
bookshelf behind me. Why the hell is he being so
cagey?

I stand, walk to the bookshelf and run my hand
along the aged bindings. The musty scent of old
paper, combined with its vanilla undertones, takes
me back to my days spent in the Harvard library.

"What does Dad think of this?" I ask, turning
back around to square off against my grandfather.
No way can I let this go.

His bony collarbone jumps as he gives a shrug. "He thinks it's a brilliant idea."

My head rears back in disbelief. No way would my father give consent to this, unless he's losing his mind, too. Not that I can call him and have a chat to gauge his mental capacity. He's out of reach, off to Bali on his fourth honeymoon with a girl half his age. Both Dad and Granddad have a history of marrying younger women—although this time Granddad is really widening the age bracket, horrendously so. At least Dad still had enough wits about him to draw up a prenuptial before he said I do.

My gaze rakes over my grandfather. I take in his winter-white hair, the thinning of his face. Heavy lines bracket milky blue eyes that have dulled with age as he turns his gaze back to the Polaroid. Christ, I don't want to burst his bubble, but no way can I let him sign over his life's work. I'm not just his grandson, I'm his power of attorney, in charge of his affairs and sworn to keep his best interests at heart.

"When can I meet her?" I ask.

His head lifts, and for a brief second I catch a sparkle of something in his eyes—a reminder of the youthful man who was as sly as he was strong. He briefly shuts his eyes, and when he opens them again, the sparkle is gone. His face pulls into a sad grimace when he says, "She's on vacation, in St. Moritz. Won't be back for a week."

Of course she's on vacation in St. Moritz. Why wouldn't she be, considering Granddad owns numerous hotels and chalets in the Alpine resort town? I spent a lot of days on the slopes during my school breaks and holidays, and a lot of nights working the bar. Like I said, Granddad wanted me to understand the value of hard work.

"Is she staying in one of your hotels?" I ask, holding no punches.

"Enough with the questions, son." He climbs to his feet to refill his glass, but his nonanswer says it all. She's staying in one of his hotels, and he likely footed the bill for the whole trip.

I dig my phone from my front pocket and do a quick search for Summer Love. I scan all the social media sites and come up with nothing. How can a woman in her late twenties have zero online presence? I'm on Instagram and Twitter, even though I rarely post, but I at least have an account. She has nothing. I guess she's smart enough not to leave a trail behind after she cons people out of their money.

Agitated, I push from the bookshelf and pace. *This*. This is the reason I don't get emotionally involved with women. Between my father, and my grandfather, I've seen enough "aunts" come and go over the years to realize it's not the men themselves these women want. It's what they have in their bank account. My own mother was no different.

Christ, is there not one decent woman left in the world, one who cares about love, life and people over money? If she's out there, she's certainly not traveling in any of my social circles. Not that I'm looking to settle down. I prefer a revolving door, sex for sex and no commitment. Those are the rules I live by, rules that protect me. But right now I have much more important things on my plate. Things like worrying about my grandfather's state of mental health and exposing Summer Love for the fraud she really is. I will not stand back and let her cheat my family out of millions.

"How long will it take for you to draw the papers up?" Granddad asks, settling himself back into his leather chair, that hint of a spark back in his eyes. "I want to surprise her when she returns."

I scrub my chin, a stall tactic as my mind races, a plan forming in the depths of my brain. I lift my eyes to his as the idea takes shape, becomes lucid. It might be ludicrous, but extreme situations call for extreme measure. "It will take about a week," I inform him. Just enough time for me to go to St. Moritz, seduce Summer Love and take her to her knees.

CHAPTER TWO

Summer

"HERE GOES NOTHING," I say, unable to hide the nervous edge in my voice as I look at the towering ski hill and wonder how I'll get down it without breaking my damn neck.

"It's just the bunny hill," Amber says, as she tugs at her glove with her teeth, adjusting it around the cuff of her coat. "You'll be fine. You did great during the lessons." She nudges me to set me into motion, and I nearly tip over in my sturdy ski boots. Oh yeah, hurtling down the mountain on two waxed-up sheets of plastic is going to be so much fun, especially when I can't even stand in my damn boots. Amber points to the ground. "Now get those skis on so we can catch up to Cara."

I glance up to see Cara skiing toward the gondola, and resist the urge to throw my pole at her as she effortlessly glides across the snow. I love my girlfriends, I really do. They both grew up in the Hamptons and were best friends when I met them at Harvard. They brought me into their small circle when I arrived alone and nervous my freshman year—my first time being away from my father, and our Brooklyn apartment—and we've all been tight ever since. I'd do anything for them, which is why I'm currently standing at the foot of a very big ski hill in St. Moritz, one tumble away from concussion…or worse.

I glance around at all the other mountains. "Can we go tobogganing instead?"

"No," Amber says, then slips her booted feet into her skis and snaps them in place.

"Why did I let you two talk me into this when I could be relaxing on a Caribbean beach?" I mumble as my breath turns to fog in front of my face.

Amber laughs. "Because our entire trip here was free." She winks at me. "Compliments of your boyfriend."

"James is not my boyfriend," I say, and plant one hand on my hip, even though I know she's teasing. It's just that James is generous, and exceptionally good to me, always trying to lavish me with gifts and trips to show his gratitude for my care. Odd really, considering he'd gone through a slew of doctors, firing them for one reason or another. He took an instant liking to me, but I flatly refused this trip when he suggested it. My God, I still have so much to do to build my practice, and my new website was recently hacked. I cringe to think of the picture on display, that of my face sitting on top of a fake—naked—body. How mortifying. Thankfully Dan, the guy I hired to fix it, was able to wipe all the info from my site until he can get the picture down, so future clients won't associate me with it. I should be home dealing with all those things. Then again, I can answer Dan's questions from here as easily as I can from New York. So when James pushed, and pushed—even at ninety, the man is damn stubborn, his mind still sharp as a scalpel—and the girls begged me to say yes to this trip of a lifetime, I finally caved. I've been under so much stress lately— trying to build my practice, working part-time at the geriatric clinic and taking on private patient care for the extra money—that getting away was just what the doctor ordered, and since I'm the doctor...

"He's my patient," I say and stop to consider his ill health. I hated to leave him, especially after his last bout of pneumonia, but he assured me his grandson James was moving back home and would be there to care for him in my absence. Still, I asked a colleague to check in on him once a day.

"I know, I know, now come on. Let's go pop your cherry. Like sex, skiing is fun once you get used to it." Laughing, she takes off toward Cara, who is waving us over from the gondola line. I glance over my shoulder and consider sneaking back to the lounge. It's only ten in the morning, but hey, it's five o'clock somewhere, right? I exhale a defeated sigh, about to join my friends for my death ride, but stop when out of my peripheral vision I catch a movement, the shadow of a man running toward me. Catching me completely off guard, he grabs me from behind, and lifts me clear off the ground.

"Ohmigod," I cry out as strong arms tighten around my waist, practically squeezing the air from my lungs. "What do you…" My words die an abrupt death when he spins me around, going faster and faster until I'm dizzy and completely disoriented. My brain wobbles inside my head, and I briefly close my eyes as he laughs, his breath warming the side of my face.

"About time you got here," he says.

What the hell?

When he finally stops twirling me, and my feet are on solid ground again, I slowly turn around, my breath catching in my throat when I come face-to-face with the hottest guy I've ever set eyes on.

"I…um…think…"

I struggle to find my words when he steps back, and blinks thick lashes over gorgeous blue eyes that could melt the panties right off my hips, despite the cold temperatures here in the Swiss Alps.

"You're not—" he begins, his brow furrowing as he gives a hard shake of his head.

Shocked, intrigued…aroused—despite my spinning brain—I work to focus in on the six feet of pure testosterone standing before me. A wide smile splits his lips, showcasing perfect white teeth as he grabs a fistful of hair, and takes another measured step back to give me space. My gaze slides downward, lingering over broad shoulders that fill out his ski jacket nicely, to jeans that cradle his package to perfection. I study the curved outline of an impressive bulge. I've not been with many men, but my guess is this guy won the man lottery in more ways than one.

Stop staring at his crotch, already.

"I'm so sorry," he says. My gaze jerks back to his as he holds his hands up, palms out, a nonverbal gesture that communicates his mistake. "I thought you were someone else."

Still wobbly from the spin, I widen my feet to brace myself, and reach for something to hold on to before I face plant in the snow—in front of the hottest guy on the planet. I stumble a bit, and once again his arms are around me, invading my personal space and securing me to his firm body. Only this time we're face-to-face. And oh, what an incredible face he has.

I lift my chin until we're eye to eye. Damn I wish I was the someone he was looking for. "Sorry to disappoint you," I say, surprised I can form a coherent thought as my lust-hazed mind struggles to work.

"Who says I'm disappointed?" he asks, his rich, low baritone curling through my body and arousing all my neglected girly parts. I take him in, my shaky gaze going from unruly dark hair that I want to run my fingers through, to a sculpted jaw covered in a light dusting of stubble—stubble that would leave burn marks on my naked body, if I ever found myself beneath him in bed.

And oh, how I want to.

His grin is back, doing the most ridiculous things

to the needy juncture between my legs, when he says, "I'm Tate, by the way."

Tate. The perfect name for the epitome of male perfection. As I think about that, wind gusts around us, blowing my hair across my face. I catch a few strands in my mouth. I sputter a bit, and swat at them with gloved fingers. How attractive must that look to him? Ugh.

He holds his hand up again and cocks his head. "Mind if I…"

Our gazes latch, hold, and the air around us charges with enough electricity to keep the gondolas running in a black out—for a month straight. I take a breath, work to keep it together, but everything about this man reminds me I'm a woman with needs, which shatters my ability to present *composed*.

"Please," I say quietly. He pauses for a split second, like that one word means something entirely different, then he's back in the moment, his rough fingertips brushing my cheek, lingering a second too long, before he pulls the strands free and tucks them into my hat.

Come on, knees. Keep it together. Just because six feet of sex-in-ski-jacket is touching you, doesn't mean you have to weaken.

"I… I'm…"

Okay, Summer. You're a Harvard educated physician. Find your words, already.

He angles his head, those astute blue eyes moving over my face, assessing me, as my body flushes.

Heat curls through me and climbs up my neck. No doubt turning my cheeks a darker shade of pink. Will he think my flesh is wind-burnt, or will he realize it's my body's way of telling me it needs to get laid? Right now. By him.

I inhale, and little lightning bolts of electricity zing though my body when I catch his scent. Sun. Outdoors. One hundred percent hot male. Every bone in my body wants him. I honestly can't ever remember reacting so strongly to the opposite sex before, but this guy, holy hell, he has me rethinking my stance on one-night stands. Or maybe one-week stands. Something tells me one night wouldn't be enough to sample everything he has to offer. My mind races, the vision of him warming my currently chilled body beneath the sheets stirs the desire within me. I hadn't planned to have a vacation fling when I arrived here two days ago, but now…

"Summer," I say on a breathless whisper.

Tate frowns, and glances at the snow-covered hill. Then he turns back to me and gives me a look that suggests I'm a snow bunny with little going on upstairs. "Could have fooled me."

"No," I say. "That's my name." I don't bother telling him my last name. While on vacation, I just want to be Summer, not Doctor Love. Ironic really, since Doctor Love can't find love. But seriously, when guys find out I'm a doctor, it somehow intimidates them, scares them off. Just once in my life I want a guy to look at me as a woman—the way Tate is looking at me right now. Although there is something about him, something confident and powerful that says he wouldn't be intimidated by anyone or anything. A fine shiver moves through my blood and settles deep in my core at that thought.

He takes my gloved hand in his bare one, and shakes it. "I know it's probably a little late for a proper introduction," he says, that sexy grin tugging at the corner of his mouth again.

I lift my chin. "You mean because of the groping?"

He laughs, and the sound awakens all my dormant parts. "I'm not sure I'd call it groping."

"Then what would you call it?" I ask, surprised at my flirting. I was never very good at it.

He looks up to the left, like he's thinking, then gives me a wink. "Maybe copping a feel?"

This time I laugh, but then I mentally kick myself for missing my chance to cop my own feel when he had his arms around me.

"I really am sorry." He frowns. "I shouldn't have touched you." The sincerity edging his voice relaxes me.

"Don't worry." I give a wave of my hand to dismiss the incident. "I'm not going to report you." Not only because it was an honest mistake, but because I damn well liked it.

He blows out a relieved breath. "Good. I need this job." He lets go of my hand, and it falls to my side.

I glance at him again, admire his too longish hair, and athletic frame. "Ski instructor?"

"Nope."

"Oh, I would have thought…" My words fall off as I let my gaze travel the length of his long, hard body. What would it feel like to have all two hundred pounds of him on top of me, or better yet, beneath me?

"Would have thought what?" he asks, his voice snapping me back to the present. *God, girl, get it together. You're acting like a sex-starved idiot.* While that description might be fitting after meeting Tate, I certainly don't have to act it.

"You're just so fit and athletic." Head tilted, I hold my hand out, wave it down the length of him. "I mean you look like a professional. Not that I know what a professional skier looks like," I say. "This is my first time on a slope." I glance toward the bunny hill, catch sight off all the children conquering it. "Those kids are going to put me to shame. Honestly, I don't even really like heights. Couldn't even look out the window during the plane ride."

Okay, Summer, stop rambling.

"You've never skied before?"

I shake my head. "You seem surprised."

"It's just that…" His eyes narrow as they move down my body, a slow inspection that sparks something low and needy in my stomach. "You're so fit and—"

"You can't tell that," I blurt out, and glance at my puffy white coat and snow pants. "I look like a big marshmallow."

He grins, takes a small step closer, his scent once again surrounding me as blue eyes lance mine. "I love marshmallows."

Omg, he's flirting with me, too.

"And I would have thought you were a ripper, given your top-of-the-line gear," he says.

"Ripper?"

"Ski slang for an accomplished skier." He nods toward my clothes. "You're dressed like one."

I frown at the skis, boots, poles and clothes I'm wearing. They were in the penthouse suite waiting for me when I arrived, compliments of my generous patient. "A friend bought them for me."

"Nice friend."

"Very nice," I say, and glance around. "So where's this friend you were looking for?" Before I can stop myself, my gaze goes to his left finger. He's smiling when my eyes move back to his, totally aware I was checking on his marital status.

Subtle, Summer. Real subtle.

He glances around. "I guess she's not here yet." With a nod he gestures toward my friends, who are staring at us. "Looks like your friends are waiting for you."

I let out a slow breath. "They may have to get used to waiting for me this week."

He grins, then says, "Listen, I really am sorry about grabbing you. Why don't I make it up to you?"

The needy girl in me perks up, ready to suggest all kinds of ways he can make it up to me.

"I work the bar at Diamond's Peak." He jerks his thumb over his shoulder. "Just across the road. Come on by tonight, let me hook you and your friends up with a drink. It's the least I can do."

The least.

I twist to see my two friends grinning. "I, ah, should probably go. My friends."

He holds his hands up, like he's ready to grab me again if I should fall.

Oh, how I want to fall.

"No more dizziness?" he asks.

"I don't think so."

"You'll be okay?"

"Yeah," I lie. The truth is, after being in his arms, being subjected to that sexy, panty-melting grin of his, I'm not sure I'll ever be okay again.

CHAPTER THREE

Tate

I GLANCE AROUND the busy bar, the thick scent of cigar and perfume clogging the air as I take in the sea of people milling about. Most are talking about the trails they skied today, or worrying about the storm that's supposed to hit midweek. I'm hoping I'll be out of here by then, back in Manhattan, no longer worrying about my grandfather getting taken advantage of by Summer Love.

I may have put this plan together quickly, but before following through with it, I tried calling Granddad to ask once more about Summer. Again, I didn't get any straight answers from my grandfather, who has swung between acting like a moony teen and being purposefully evasive on this topic. This isn't like him, and if I can't rely on him for information, I need to get it myself.

Honestly, he's always been a generous man, always loved younger women, but something about this whole situation just isn't right, and I'm not so sure I can blame it entirely on his mental deterioration. I visited him last summer, before he got sick. Since getting pneumonia last month, he lost his sharpness but two days ago, when he dropped this bombshell on me, there were times when he seemed like his young self, quick with a response, his mind as bright and agile as I remembered.

Truthfully, when I was little, I thought he'd live forever, but I guess age and frailty catch up with all of us, eventually. Guilt niggles at me for up and leaving him, right after returning home. I fibbed and told him I had some urgent out-of-town business. I guess it wasn't that much of a lie. He waved me off like he wanted me to go, telling me he was fine, that he had in-house care every day and didn't need me fussing.

I reach into the fridge behind me and grab an imported beer, then glance at the door to the bar. I've been watching it for the last hour, but Summer has yet to arrive with her friends. Maybe she changed her mind and isn't going to come. Disappointment takes up residency in my gut. Not because I want to see her again, to continue our flirting and easy banter from earlier, but because I need to get close to her, get her into my bed, prove she's only after my Granddad for one thing. Not that I plan to carry through with the seduction. No, I just need to strip her bare and expose her for the con she really is.

I uncap a beer and slide it across the smooth mahogany bar top, before turning my attention to the next customer. As I take his order, I glance over his head to keep one eye on the door. I can definitely see what Granddad sees in Summer Love. She's gorgeous, and has a sweet, almost innocent quality about her. It might be all an act, but dammit if that doesn't bring out the protectiveness in a man— at least in the Carson men. Since Dad is okay with the arrangement, it sounds to me like he's fallen for her charm, too.

I, of course, am not about to be lured in by her, not in a million years, but Jesus, when I put my arms around her, felt her soft body against mine, I almost got derailed and forgot why I'm really here. But when it comes to her, there's a line I have no intention of crossing. Not even when she whispered the word *yes*, all sultry and seductive like—okay, it's possible I imagined the sultry and seductive part. My mind drifts once again, envisioning that one word on her lips when I have her naked, beneath me in bed, my cock sliding in and out of her hot, sweet body.

Get your shit together, Tate.

You're not here to sleep with the woman, you're here to prove she's not who your grandfather thinks she is. With that last thought pinging around inside my brain, and steering me back on track, I finish making a Manhattan, then glance at the door in time to see Summer enter. Her caramel hair is piled haphazardly on her head, and she's dressed in tight jeans and a snug sweater that showcases one hell of a hot body.

My dick twitches.

I track their path to the back of the room—and I'm not the only one—to a coveted window table that just opened up. Once she and her friends are seated, I turn to Henry, the older gentleman who runs the place. The two of us go way back, to when I used to come here during my high school years. He's much older now, a little rounder, with thinning hair. After explaining the situation to him when I arrived yesterday, he jumped at the chance to let me work the bar. Granddad was always good to Henry, was always a generous tipper, and gave Henry's wife a damn good job managing one of the hotels. Most people around here would bend over backward for Granddad.

Would Summer bend over for me?

Shit. Don't go there, dude.

"Hey, Henry, you want to take over the bar for a bit? I'll take the floor."

"Sure," he says, and gives me an understanding nod.

I tug the cloth from my shoulder and slap it onto the counter, giving it a little scrub as I plot my next step with Summer. A drink is a great icebreaker, and since I promised her one, it gives me a reason to go to her and start up a conversation. If I could turn back time, I never would have grabbed her by the waist and spun her around. I shouldn't have put my hands on her like that. It was a snap decision, a stupid one, because now, I can't help but want my goddamn hands on her again. I clench down on my teeth, and whip up three strawberry daiquiris, taking a chance it's their drink of choice, like most other snow bunnies, and set them on the tray. I wipe my hands on my apron and carry the drinks across the room.

"Hello, ladies," I say, and all eyes turn to me. I hand Summer the first drink. "On the house, as promised." She smiles up at me, and it messes with my equilibrium. My hands shake and the drinks on my tray wobble. I make a quick adjustment, and I'm able to rebalance before making a damn fool of myself. I hand the other drink to her blonde friend, and catch the way the men at the table beside me are staring at the three ladies, most focusing on Summer. Not that I can blame them, she's the hottest girl in the room.

Her friend accepts the drink, and takes a sip, then nibbles on the straw. I hand the third woman a drink, and her lips twist into a grin.

"A daiquiri for copping a feel," she says, and leans a little toward me in a conspiratorial way. "What would you give her if…you know…" She holds both hands out, and cups them. "You got an actual, full-on feel."

"Amber," Summer says, and whacks her friend. The slap reverberates through me, settles into my balls.

"Ouch." Amber pulls her hand back, and her other friend laughs. Summer's face is as red as her drink when she glances up at me. Something inside me softens as dark lashes blink rapidly over big mortified eyes.

"It's okay. I hear lots of comments working in a place like this," I say, brushing it off to put Summer at ease.

Amber looks me over. She must like what she sees because she bobs her head and makes a lip-smacking sound. Does Summer like what she sees?

Jesus, Tate. It doesn't matter. You're not here to sleep with her.

Why do I have to keep reminding myself of that?

"I bet you get lots of offers for lots of things," Amber says, pointing a finger at me, and running it up and down.

I grin, and Summer clears her throat. "Tate, this is my friend Amber. Amber is obnoxious and doesn't have any filters." She points to her other friend, who is still nibbling on her straw. "This is Cara. She's the nice one."

"Hey," Amber says. "I'm nice, too." Without missing a beat, she turns to me. "So this friend you were looking for earlier. Was she your girlfriend?"

Summer opens her mouth, no doubt to yell at her friend again, but I hold my hand up to stop her. I turn to Summer. "No, just a friend."

"Well then, I'm not so certain a drink for a grope is quite enough," Amber announces.

"You're right," I say. I brace one hand on the table and lean into Summer. I catch her floral scent, and breathe her in. "Have you eaten?"

She sits up a bit straighter, my offer taking her off guard. "No, not yet. But I had plans—"

"I think I'm getting a cold," Amber says, and nudges Cara as she fakes a cough. "I think I caught it from Cara."

Catching on quickly, Cara coughs, too, and I can't help but grin at her friends' antics. If the circumstances were different I would probably really like them. "We're going to skip dinner, and just get soup delivered to our room." Amber takes a big sip of her daiquiri. "After I finish this delicious drink of course."

Summer is staring at her two friends like she's going to kill them. I touch her arm, to bring her attention back around to me, and she nearly jumps out of her chair.

"Sorry," I say. "No touching. I get it."

"No…no, it just surprised me."

"I get off in a few, why don't you let me buy you dinner."

"You don't have to buy me anything, and we can pay for our own drinks, Tate. Seriously, today was just an accident."

She wants to pay?

Okay, I totally didn't expect that. Then again, Granddad's probably set her up with a nice bank account by now.

"What if I want to?" I ask. Summer's breath comes a little faster, as she reaches for her drink and takes a long pull from the straw. "There's a really nice restaurant at Raydolins with a great view of the mountains and lake."

"I've passed by it," Summer says. "We're staying at that resort," she adds.

Of course she's staying at Raydolins. My grand-dad owns it.

"We got in late two days ago, so we haven't had too much of a chance to explore the resort or visit the shops." She reaches into her purse, her hand rustling around for something.

"Good, I can be your tour guide. So yes to dinner?"

"Um…sure." She glances at her watch, dropping a ten-dollar bill onto my tray. I stare at it, confused for a moment. Ah, she's tipping me. Surprise number two. "I can meet you there at eight, but do you think we'll get in without a reservation?" she asks, her nose crinkling.

I give her a wink. "I've got a few connections, and I'll pick you up at your door."

She holds her hands up, palms out. "You can pick me up, as long as there's no spinning involved this time," she says, and I laugh. I have to admit, she does have a great sense of humor. Probably has Granddad laughing all the time.

"What room are you in?"

"301."

"Penthouse Suite," I say.

Why the hell would Granddad put her in the one place we always stayed, and never rented out. He must be more serious about her than I ever thought. Damn, this is going to crush him. But what choice do I have? I have to protect him. He's not just fam-ily, he means the world to me.

"You know it?" Summer asks.

I nod, and push a rebellious lock of hair from my forehead. I'm normally clean cut, and it's driving me crazy. I really should have visited the barber before I bolted to the airport. Then again, I guess the disheveled look works better with my ruse. "I know it."

"Summer's friend owns it," Cara informs me.

I nod. "Like I said before, nice friend."

"Don't worry, he's not her boyfriend, or anything," Amber says and aims a wink Summer's way, as if to say, *not yet.*

"After dinner, maybe we can hit the slopes?" I say, banking my anger and putting myself back together.

"Once on the hill today is enough for me."

I glance outside, take in all the hiking trails. "Okay, I'm sure I can find something else for us to do."

"Oh, I'm sure you can," Amber says, laughing.

Summer shakes her head at me. "Ignore her, please."

Please.

What is it about her saying that one word that gets to my dick? I look at her lush mouth and for a brief second, I envision it wrapped around my thickening cock. Goddammit, the vision is ridiculously hot.

"Can I get you ladies anything else?"

Summer smiles up at me again. "No, thank you for the drinks. You didn't have to do this, but I really appreciate it."

I nod and walk away, thinking about all the other things I could give her that she just might appreciate.

Stop it, Tate.

I step back to the bar. Henry has a thin sheen of moisture on his forehead, and his breath is a little more labored as he gestures with his chin, and lowers his voice. "That her?"

"Yeah." Worried that he's been working too hard, I grab the glasses from the dishwasher and stack them on the bar, taking over for him.

Henry shakes his head. "Your grandfather must be having a midlife crisis."

"If that's the case than I guess he's going to live to one hundred and eighty."

He laughs. "At least he has good taste."

"That he does."

And therein lies the problem. Summer is breathtakingly beautiful, a girl I plan to expose, except suddenly exposing her—her clothes, that clip in her hair, her inhibitions—is playing out all kinds of wrong in my head.

CHAPTER FOUR

Summer

I PACE INSIDE my suite, hardly able to believe I'm about to have dinner with Tate the sexy bartender with a body made for sin. He never did give me his last name, and I never gave him mine, which is A-Okay with me. If I'm going to have a hot affair with a man I never plan to set eyes on again, the less I know about him the better.

Wait.

What?

I'm going to have a hot affair with Tate?

My blood races faster, heating my flesh and no doubt turning my cheeks a deeper shade of pink. God, am I really going to do this? I mean, there is no denying the heat between us, the insane, off-the-charts attraction. As soon as he approached our table, crowded my personal space, we created a volatile bubble of sexual energy that even my friends felt to their cores. Off course, after he left, they suggested I jump his bones and have a little much needed fun while I'm on vacation.

Should I?

I walk to the patio window and glance out at the slopes. Honest to God, I have the nicest view in all of St. Moritz. James spared no expense, giving me this suite and setting my friends up in their own rooms. Guilt tightens my stomach. I'm not one to take from people, not at all. I've always paid my own way in life, and went without when I couldn't.

For most of my life, I've had my own preconceived notions about the wealthy, thanks to many childhood incidents with the rich boys at my school. Spoiled, entitled, mean boys who bullied me, and set me up for disaster. Growing up in New York and going to Harvard, I've met people from all walks of life, most of them kind. But after what those boys did to me when I was a kid, I was never able to shake the feeling of distrust I get around rich people. And, honestly, several summers spent working at an upscale steakhouse in Boston did little to help with that. The tips were great, some of the diners... not so much. But James is kind, compassionate, fair and generous. In the world of the rich, he may be one of a kind.

The knock on my door startles me, and my heart jumps into my throat as I turn around. I glance at myself in the mirror. Am I dressed appropriately? I only packed a few nice dresses. I had no idea I'd be dining with anyone other than my girls.

I check my clipped hair, take a deep breath and walk to the door. I open it and my pulse leaps when

I find Tate standing there, hands in the pockets of his dress pants, and a suit jacket that fits him to perfection. He must have had it professionally made to fit those shoulders. Then again, probably not. Not on a bartender's salary anyway. I give him another once over. Tate in jeans is one thing, but damned if he doesn't clean up nice.

His gaze leaves my face, drops to take in my little black dress. "You're beautiful," he says so low, I almost don't hear him.

"You are, too."

He grins as his eyes lift to mine. "I've been called a lot of things before, but beautiful was never one of them."

"Well, it's fitting," I say. "You look amazing. I'll be the envy of every woman in the restaurant tonight."

He steps into me, captures my chin with his thumb and index finger, lightly brushes the soft pad back and forth, and my mind takes that moment to envision him using the same movement, on a different part of my body.

"Thank you for the compliment," he says. "But you're the one who's going to turn heads tonight."

His intense gaze sets my panties on fire, and I resist the urge to run to the bathroom to change my damp thong. My God, the man sure knows how to sweet talk a woman.

His hands drop. "You all set?"

"I am." I grab my purse from the table, and let the door click shut behind me. Silence ensues as we walk to the elevator and I steal a few glances at him as we wait for it to arrive. It's empty when it opens and Tate puts his hand on the small of my back to lead me in. Breathless, I move to the back wall, and grip my purse tighter.

"How long have you worked here?" I ask him as he presses the button for the lobby.

"Long enough to know my way around the place. Are you up for a tour later?"

"I'd love a tour." I glance down at my little black dress and heels. "I'll have to change though."

"Of course. We can't have you going outside in that dress."

The doors open and he leads me into the exquisite lobby. Raydolins is a pretty top-notch resort, so I'd imagine the fine dining restaurant must be pricey. He puts his hand on the small of my back again and guides me across the wide expanse of marble flooring. Heat sizzles through me at his touch, and I try not to appear as flustered as I feel.

We step through the doors to the restaurant, and I take in its opulence. "Tate," I begin quickly. "We don't have to eat here." Jeez, how do I say this without offending him? He wants to take me out to dinner to a nice place, but I don't want it to empty his bank account.

"You don't like it?" he asks.

"No, it's beautiful, I just…" To be honest it's a little out of my element. Deep down I'm just a simple girl from Brooklyn and I don't want this man to think he has to wine and dine me to impress me. I'm good with a cheeseburger and Coke. I might even prefer it.

He leans into me, puts his mouth close to my ear and whispers, "If you don't want to stay…" he says, looking and feeling far more comfortable in this swank restaurant than I do. He actually looks like he belongs here, like he *wants* to be here.

"No, I do," I say. If he wants to stay, we stay.

"Anything you want, Summer. Just say the word."

What would that word be, please?

My brain spins, buzzing like a fine wine, as his low, sexy voice travels down my body, hitting every erogenous spot along the way. I tremble. Almost violently.

Tate's brow furrows. "Maybe we should run back upstairs and grab you a sweater."

"No, it's okay, I'm fine," I lie. I'm far from fine because the thoughts of running upstairs with him sounds appealing. Except I don't want to go back to my room to put more clothes on. Quite the opposite, really.

When the hostess arrives, Tate says something I can't hear. The waitress laughs, and her face lights up in admiration. She touches Tate's arm, and I sense the familiarity between them. I guess working here, the staff all know each other and probably hang out. Heck, they probably all live together in the staff's quarters.

We're led across the restaurant, and a few heads turn to Tate, give him a nod of acknowledgment. I guess he's well known, even with some of the guests.

The hostess takes us to a table with a spectacular view of the mountains, as nice as my penthouse view. I stare at Tate, and wonder how exactly he managed to arrange this.

"You're right, you do have some pull," I say as we're seated.

He grins, and smooths his hand over his tie. I angle my head, the gesture so familiar to me. James does the same thing, even when he's not wearing a tie.

"Told you," he says, but not in a show-off way. Just then the server stops by.

"I'm Justin. I'll be your server tonight. Can I start you both off with some drinks?"

Tate turns his attention to me. "Summer, what would you like?"

"White wine, please."

The muscles along Tate's jaw twist, and he goes quiet, like he needs a minute to compose himself. He scrubs his chin, and the bristling of his fine hair is like silk being dragged across my nipples.

"A bottle of your best," Tate says.

The waiter nods. "Thank you, Tate. I'll give you a minute to look over the menu, and I'll be right back with your drinks."

"Does everyone here know you?"

"Pretty much," he says, and opens his menu.

I do the same, and nearly swallow my tongue when I see the prices. Even on a new doctor's salary, these prices are a bit steep for me. Fortunately, the salmon costs the least and sounds the most appealing. I close my menu and glance at the crystal chandelier above us, take in the amazing view outside. The hill is lit up under the star-studded night sky, and off in the distance I hear children laughing. The sound brings a smile to my face.

"Something funny?" Tate asks, and I turn my attention back to him as he sets the menu down.

"No, I just… I love this view. I've never seen anything like it actually."

"No? Where's home?"

"I'm originally from Brooklyn," I say, an invisible band tightening around my heart as my thoughts go back to the old apartment I shared with my late father. God, I miss him. If it weren't for Amber and Cara, I'd be all alone in this world. Sure, I have my patients, but that's not quite the same. "How about you, where do you call home?" When he arches one eyebrow, I laugh. "Right, St. Moritz."

"I used to live in Boston," he says.

"Ah, I spent time in Boston, too. Maybe we crossed paths a time or two."

"What were you doing in Boston?"

I open my mouth, not wanting to lie to this man, but not wanting him to know too much about me either, especially the fact that I'm a Harvard grad and a doctor. Just then the waiter returns with our drinks. He pours a small amount into Tate's glass and he tastes it.

"Perfect," he says, and the waiter fills our glasses. We put in our order and once he's out of earshot,

Tate leans toward me. "You never did tell me your last name."

I hesitate for a second. "It's just Summer."

He leans back and nods, a flicker of a smile on his face. I expect him to call me on it, ask why I'm not giving up more information, but he doesn't, and for that I'm grateful.

"What do you do, Summer?" He lazily waves his hand toward the view of the mountains. "Besides vacation in St. Moritz."

I chuckle. "Right now I'm between jobs," I say. Not a lie. I do run between the geriatric clinic and James's mansion on Sixty-Fourth Street. Not to mention my own clinic that I'm trying to build. I look out the window. "This was all compliments of a friend."

"A very generous friend."

Averting Tate's gaze, not wanting to flaunt the fact that I'm here living in luxury—and feeling guilty about it—I pick up my napkin and place it on my lap. "Very generous indeed."

When I don't elaborate, he lifts his glass, redirecting the conversation. I reach for my wine and we clink crystal.

"What are we toasting to?" I ask.

"Mistakes."

I crinkle my nose. "Mistakes?"

He laughs. "Yeah, me groping you by mistake."

"So, you admit to the groping?" He laughs harder and I arch a challenging brow. "I'm beginning to wonder if it was a mistake," I say, fully aware I'm leading this conversation elsewhere.

His blue eyes deepen, little flecks of honey sparkling under the chandelier lights. "Believe me, Summer. If I was touching you on purpose, you'd know it," he says, his voice full of promise and heat. My breath rushes as he stares, his eyes latched on mine, not letting me go.

The waiter returns to top our wine glasses, and Tate expels a breath, long and slow…tortured. A thrill goes through me, to know I can do this to him. I'm not being totally honest about who I am, but it's the woman in me he wants, so it's the woman in me he's going to get. The bottom line is, I want this man, and dammit, before the night is through, I plan to have him.

A loud group of middle-aged men gets seated next to us, and I shift my chair a little closer to the window. The hostess hands them their menus, and when they start making inappropriate comments to her, every muscle in my body stiffens. My heart goes out to the girl who stands there quietly and smiles. Having been in her position, I know just how she feels. If she says something, puts a complaint in about their behavior, she'll be out of a job before the night is over. Men like the ones beside me, ones with impressive pedigrees, well, they think they can get away with anything—and they usually can. I lift my eyes to find Tate watching me, his gaze narrowed, zeroed in on me.

"Summer."

"Yes?"

"Would you excuse me for a minute?"

I nod. "Of course."

Tate slides his chair back, and stands to his impressive height. "I'll just be a moment." He turns from me, and I expect him to disappear down the hall, to the little boy's room. What he does instead surprises me.

I study the way his hair flirts with his collar as he bends down, puts his hands on the backs of two chairs and says something to the table of men, his voice low, for their ears only. A moment of silence, then he straightens and smooths his hand over his tie as he walks back to me. My jaw is practically on the table, as the men give their apologies to the girl, then go deathly silent. The hostess smiles after Tate, but his attention is back on me.

"Want to get out of here? Go somewhere a little quieter?" he asks.

"But we ordered."

He smooths his hand over his tie again. "I'll take care of it. What's important right now is if you want to leave."

I hesitate for a second, not wanting to ruin this date, but not wanting stay here a minute longer either. "Yes, please."

CHAPTER FIVE

Tate

I PUT MY hand on the small of her back as I lead her out of the restaurant. I stop to talk to Katrina, the hostess I just stood up for, and tell her to put the food on my tab, package it up and take it back to the dorms for her and her boyfriend. We step into the lobby and Summer gives me a grateful smile. I smooth my hair back and lead her toward the elevators, both of us momentarily lost in our own thoughts.

Here I thought she would have been more comfortable in a room full of wealthy people, seeing as she's soon going to own half my grandfather's estate if I don't do something about it. But she wasn't relaxed at all. Sure, she maintained her composure, was poised and beautiful the whole time, but her body language spoke volumes. She wasn't comfortable. Why would a con out to steal millions be out of place in a classy restaurant? Oh, maybe because she was afraid to run in to some other rich guy she bamboozled in the past.

"What just happened in there?" she asks, her voice low, a bit strained.

"You didn't like the way they were treating the hostess, and neither did I." Anger burns through my blood. I've worked in the service industry trenches for years, and I know what it's like to be treated poorly.

"I used to be a waitress," she tells me, and from the way she's scrunching up her face, it's clear she's been in the hostess's shoes before. "I'm sure as a bartender, you get your fair share of unruly clients, and unwanted advances."

"Yeah," I say. As a powerhouse lawyer I do, too, but I keep that to myself.

"What did you say to those guys?" She pulls her bottom lip between her teeth, and it draws my attention as she worries her teeth over it. "If you don't mind me asking."

"I told them they were being a bunch of assholes to the hostess, and if they kept it up, I knew a hot-shot lawyer who would make a public mockery of them." The corner of my mouth turns up in a grin. "Then I told them if that didn't scare them, I knew where their wives were."

Her small laugh curls around me, through me, warms me from the inside out, and I take a sidelong look at her, in time to see her put her small hand over her mouth, looking so damn adorable as she tries to quiet her laugh, it's all I can do not to drag her to me and kiss the hell out of her.

"Then I told them to apologize."

She puts her hand on my arm, and her touch stops me in my tracks. I turn to face her and the sincerity in her eyes hits me like a double shot of tequila, making me a bit unstable.

"Thank you," she says softly, glancing at her feet. Her mouth turns down, so soft and lush, I ache to feel it under mine. "I'm sorry it ruined our nice dinner."

"Dinner's not over," I announce sharply, shaking thoughts from my head that shouldn't be there.

"Oh," she says, and looks at the elevators I just led her to. "I thought—"

"As much as I like you in this dress, you're going to your room to take it off." Her eyes widen, and my cock jumps as I envision her taking it off for me, slowly, seductively. "You'll need jeans and a sweater for where we're going."

"Where might that be?" Her inviting gaze rakes over me, and a groan of pure torture catches in my throat.

"You'll see." I could take her to her room and seduce her. She looks about as ready for it as I am. I'm not slowing this seduction down because I want to spend a bit more time with her. No, that's not it at all. I'd rather do it in my chalet, on my turf. That way after I take her to her knees, and out her for the con she really is, she can think about how much she hurt my granddad on the walk back to her penthouse, which I plan to have packed up before she even gets there.

"What about you?" Her eyes linger on me. "Are you going to change?"

"Yes."

She glances toward the front sliding doors where three doormen stand waiting. "Where are the staff quarters located?"

"Not too far from here," I say. Not that I'm staying in them. No, I'm in one of Granddad's private chalets just down the road from this hotel, and that's where I plan to take her, right after I grab us some take-out. The sooner I get this seduction under way, the sooner I can get away from her…from temptation.

Shit.

"I can make my own way back to my room."

"I—" Granddad pounded manners into me, and letting her walk back to her room unaccompanied on a date isn't something I'd normally do. Then again this isn't a real date, but still.

She puts her hand on my chest, and my heart pounds fast. Can she feel it? Feel what her touch does to me?

"I'm a big girl, Tate. Go ahead and run back to your quarters and get changed," she says. I'm about to protest again, but she looks like she needs a minute to herself after the incident in the restaurant. It obviously shook her up. I can imagine a beautiful girl like her has been the subject of much taunting during her waitressing years. I might be trying to take her down, but I'm not a total asshole—not all the time anyway.

My gaze moves over her pretty face. "You sure?"

"Yes, we can meet in the lobby, say thirty minutes?"

"I can be fast," I say and step into her. Like I said, the sooner I get this done the better. Being fast has nothing to do with wanting to get back to her as quickly as possible. I touch the sleeve of her dress, run my fingers over it. A low whimper catches in her throat. Yeah, I'm getting to her as much as she's getting to me. That much is obvious. "But if you want thirty minutes, I can be slow," I say, and she blinks up at me, like she's trying to figure out whether I'm talking about sex or not.

"Fifteen…" she says on a breathless whisper. "Fifteen is good."

"Okay," I say, and usher her onto the elevator when it arrives. I watch her, and before the doors shut, I say, "Keep your hair up."

I grin as I walk away. Oh yeah, I love seeing the long column of her neck, and I want to be the one to pull that clip free to let her mess of curls fall over her shoulders. I grab my coat from the bellman who took it earlier, and step outside, the cold air like a punch to my throbbing dick, knocking some sense back into me, thankfully.

The wind blows as I hurry to my chalet, the snow crunching beneath my shoes on the winding pathway. I hurry inside, turn the heat up a bit more, wanting it warm for when we arrive, and check the logs in the grate. The perfect setup for a seduction. I change into a pair of jeans and a sweater, and then I tug on my Sorels and ski jacket.

I check the time and hurry back outside, wanting to keep my word that I'd only be fifteen minutes. I enter the lobby and find Summer dressed in a different coat, one that reaches her knees, and a big pair of boots with fur peeking out of the tops. Goddammit, how she can make that look sexy is beyond me. Her eyes are searching for me, like she can't wait to be with me again. A wave of need builds inside me at that realization. Why the hell do I like the idea of her needing me so much? I stare at her slightly parted lips for a moment, and resist the urge to stalk over there, grab her and plunder her mouth already. I exhale slowly to get myself together.

She turns her back to me and I hurry toward her. I bend to put my mouth near her ear. "Fifteen minutes," I say, as her scent teases and torments my senses. "I'm a man of my word."

She spins and the smile that lights up her face fucks me over big-time. Her eyes drop to take in my casual wear, and her smile widens as she taps her chin. "I can't decide which I like more, the dressed-up version of Tate or this dressed-down version."

"Once you see me naked, there will be no competition," I tease, and wonder if I'm going to get a punch to the nuts for my crudeness.

"Cocky much?" she teases in return.

"Cocky? That's one way to put it." She stares up at me like she doesn't know how to respond, so I lean into her again and say, "But that'll cost you more than a drink."

She whacks me. "I told you, you didn't have to buy me a drink."

"I wanted to." My stomach takes that moment to rumble. I put my hand on the small of her back, and lead her to the door. I hand the doorman a couple bills as she pulls a hat and mitts from her pocket.

"Is it far?"

I point to the lodge down the road. "Right there. You up for the walk?"

"Absolutely," she says, and I kind of like that she's a trooper, not one of those pampered women who needs to be shuttled everywhere.

She pulls her sleeve back and shows me her Fitbit. "Every step counts."

I laugh. "You don't need to count your steps," I say as we head toward the lodge. "You're perfect just the way you are."

She glances down, averts my gaze. What is it with her? Does she not know how to take a compliment, or is she never complimented? A girl like her should always be admired.

Shit. What am I saying? She's a con and you'd be wise to remember that.

Our breath fogs in front of our faces as we hurry along the busy path, people coming and going all hours at the bustling resort. We reach the big log-built lodge and I usher her in. In the center of the room, a fire burns in the hearth, and tons of people are around it playing board games, cards or just sitting and chatting. Off to one side a group of teens are laughing and playing some sort of rope game that requires them to contort their bodies. At numerous tables, people are eating cheeseburgers, hot dogs, chili dogs, French fries and onion rings.

"Not quite as classy, but the food is amazing," I say. "I used to eat here all the time." Not a lie. When I was a teen this was my favorite hangout.

Her eyes widen as she takes it all in. "I can see why, it looks so good."

"Go warm yourself by the fire and I'll put an order in for us."

She nods, and I watch her walk away, unable to tear my gaze from her, until someone at the counter asks me if I want to order. I make my way over, and since I don't know what Summer will like, I order a bunch of everything—to go—then hand over a stack of cash.

After I pay, I turn back around, and go ramrod straight when I see the group of teens, four guys and four girls, dragging Summer into the game they're playing. Looks like she chose the wrong table to sit at—the one right next to theirs.

"Tate, save me," she says as they try to persuade her to join them. I have no idea what's happening, so I wander over to check it out.

"What's going on?" I ask, as I step up to them.

Summer glances at me with pleading eyes. "They want me to play some rope game."

I look back at the group of friends, the grins on their faces telling me they're having a great time. Probably on a winter break from school and making their own fun for a night. Reminds me of when I used to come here as a teenager.

"Here's how it works," a blonde girl around seventeen says as she holds out two ropes, both looped at the ends. "You put your hands in here—" she slips her hands in the loops to demonstrate "—and then you thread the other rope through, and your partner…" She turns to face a guy I assume is her boyfriend from the way he looks at her. "Loops his hands through his like this." She smiles at us, holding her hands up to show us the ropes. "Now you have to get out of it." The two start twisting, and climbing through the rope, and everyone laughs as they fall to the floor, all tangled up.

Summer is laughing with them. She seems to have a natural way with the teens… What the hell, we have some time to kill while we wait for our food. And more importantly, this might be a good way to further break the ice with Summer, get up close and personal before we go back to my place. "Should we give it a try?" I ask her.

"Come on, everyone who's come in here tonight is trying it," one of the teens tells me.

"Has anyone ever figured it out?" I ask as I shrug out of my coat.

The blonde who demonstrated shakes her head as she continues to try and free herself. After a few minutes she gives up, slides her hands from the loops and hands both ropes to us. "Come on, it's fun."

I take the ropes, and we both loop our hands through. I glance at Summer and try to strategize our first moves. "How did I ever get roped into this?"

"Ha-ha. Aren't you clever?"

"I'd like to think so."

Smiling, she rolls her eyes at me, then, when she puckers up that cute little nose of hers, I sense the competitive side to her. It matches mine.

"Okay, I think I have an idea. Sit on the floor," she says.

"Bossy much?" I mumble, and she grins at me.

"Depends on who I'm with."

I sit on the floor, as she takes charge. Goddammit, who knew a take-charge Summer would be so sexy? "Okay, I think I got it," she says, and crawls over my lap and through the loop. She twists, and her damn ass is nearly in my face. I swallow. Either that or I'm about to bite my tongue off.

"Ah, what are you doing?" I ask.

"Did I get it?"

We hold our hands up, and we've only managed to make matters worse. "Well darn," she says. "Now we need to reverse it."

If she puts her ass in my face again, it just might be the end of me.

She puts her ass in my face again.

And it's pretty close to being the end of me.

"We're back to where we started," I say.

She glares at me. "Do you have any ideas, Einstein?"

The group laughs, and Summer grins at me. "Yes, I have an idea."

"Let's hear it, then."

"Stand up and turn around," I say, and we both climb to our feet. "Arms above your head."

She lifts her arms, and holy fuck, I love how she takes a command. Would she be so obliging in the bedroom? "Turn around."

She turns, and I put my arms around the front of her. She leans into me, tucks that sweet little ass against my growing cock. "Try to pull your arms down as I pull up."

We both make a move, only to find out our ropes are still twisted together.

"That didn't work for me either, man," the guy who demonstrated it a minute ago says. I glance at him and he gives me a lopsided grin. "But it sure was fun trying." His girlfriend laughs and bats him in the stomach. He lets loose an oomph of air and bends forward.

"Any other bright ideas?" Summer asks.

Oh, plenty.

"Arms up," I say. She lifts her arms. "Now turn back to me." She does as I say, and there is a sexy pink flush on her face when her eyes meet mine. Her hair is a tumbling mess, coming out of the clip and falling over her shoulders. Goddammit, I can't wait to release it all, grip it tight as I bring her mouth to mine. Kiss her until she's begging for me, pleading with that one sexy word…*please*. A tremor rips through me, and zaps my aching balls as I picture her sprawled out on my bed, mine to do with as I *please*.

Fuck, maybe I should sleep with her. Take from her the way she's taking from Granddad. Talk about logical reasoning at its worst. I shake my head. Yeah, I could justify it any way I want, but what it boils down to is this—I want to do dirty, wicked things with her. I want my mouth on her, my hands, my tongue. I want to spread her legs wide-open, and bury myself between her legs until morning. A week from tomorrow.

But that would make me a complete asshole.

"What if we step over it?" she asks, breathless.

I think about that for a minute, anything to get my mind off the way she's wiggling against me, her scent teasing my senses, playing havoc with my restraint. Agreeing to this game is having the intended effect, but it was supposed to be only on her, not both of us.

"It's worth a try." She bends first and steps over the rope, putting both our hands behind her back. She's flush up against me, trying to get free. "It's impossible," she says.

"Do you give up?" the blonde asks.

"No, I don't give up, but we have to call it quits," I say, and gesture toward the counter holding our take-out bags. "Our order was just called."

The girl unhooks our hands, and tosses the rope over her shoulder. "That was…fun," Summer says with a laugh as she bundles her hair back up, and clips it. I glance at her slender neck, as energy arcs between us. She touches her throat, like she's well aware of the way she affects me.

"Thanks for playing with us," the girl says. "Come back tomorrow night, see if you can do it then. We'll probably have other games, too."

"I'll come back right after I look online," I murmur, and Summer narrows her eyes at me.

"That's cheating."

"No, that's called playing to win," I say, and give her a wink. I grab our coats and hand hers over before we head toward the pickup counter.

She shrugs into her coat. "Do you always play to win?"

"Always," I say, and step up to the counter to grab our food.

"So do I," she says, her voice holding all kinds of promises, but her attention gets diverted when she sees the three big bags in front of us. "What did you order?" She goes up on her toes for a better look.

"I didn't know what you liked."

"So you ordered one of everything?"

"Something like that."

"You're crazy." I'm beginning to believe so, too. I should just seduce her and end this now, before I do something I can only regret later. "Here, let me help," she says.

I hand her one of the bags, and she gives a finger wave to the teens before we head back outside.

"Wait, why didn't we eat inside?" she asks, stopping on the steps.

I nudge her to set her into motion. "We're going to my place."

She stops again, her big eyes round and curious. "You want to take this back to the staff quarters?"

"Nope," I say, and start walking. She hurries to catch up.

"Then where are we going?"

"Right over there." I point to the private chalets at the base of the mountain.

"Oh." Curiosity morphs to confusion. "How…"

"A friend lent it to me," I say. Not a lie. "Come on. Let's hurry before all this food gets cold."

We pick up the pace, and we say hello to a handful of guests headed toward the shopping district. A few minutes later I'm standing on the stoop of my granddad's chalet, which will one day become mine. I just hope that's a long time from now. Beside me Summer is shivering.

I open the door, usher her in and drop my bags on the kitchen counter. "I'll get a fire going."

"This place is gorgeous," she says as she slowly spins around to take it all in. I've been here so many times I rarely stop to admire it. This time I look around the chalet, take it in from her eyes. On the main floor, there are two bedrooms, a four-piece bathroom and a big fireplace with a TV mounted over it. There is a full kitchen, but the one thing the eye is drawn to is the loft upstairs. I glance up, admire the stars from the overhead skylight. Many times I've fallen asleep under those stars.

"Why don't you grab us some plates and I'll get the fire going?" She nods and walks to the kitchen. Dishes clang and cupboards bang as I bunch up old newspapers then arrange dried kindling and a few bigger logs over it. I light the paper on fire, and the wood sparks.

She comes into the room with two plates, both loaded with food. "If I eat all this I won't fit into my coat tomorrow."

"Doesn't matter. You already look like a big marshmallow in it," I tease.

"Hey," she says, and glares at me.

Why do I keep doing that? Why do I keep teasing her like this? Oh, because I love the reaction it pulls from her. She is so sexy when she's pretending to be mad.

"What?" I say, feigning innocence. "I already told you I like marshmallows."

"I saw some in the cupboard. Maybe we can roast some later."

I climb to my feet just as she settles herself on the shag carpet in front of the fire. My gaze goes from her to the kitchen table back to her again. "I thought we were—"

She taps the floor. "Come, let's sit in front of the fire. This is such a luxury for me."

I drop to the floor beside her and we both cross our legs, the flames gaining strength, and creating a romantic ambiance.

She eats an onion ring. "I can't believe you bought all this food."

I pick up my cheeseburger and take a big bite. I chew and swallow. "So good, right?"

"I think this is the best burger I've ever had," she says after swallowing a bite of her own.

"Food always tastes better after a day on the hill." I jump up. "I need a drink. Do you want one?"

"What do you have?"

I go to the kitchen and open the fridge. "I have beer, wine, soda or water."

"What are you having?" she asks, then slides a French fry into her mouth.

Shit.

Keep it together, Tate. Don't imagine that's your dick she's drawing to the back of her throat.

"Beer," I say. Is that my voice? I sound like I'm strung out on painkillers. I clear my throat. "Beer," I say again.

"I don't have a hearing problem," she says, and grins at me, like she's well aware of what she's doing. Christ, I'm the one who's supposed to be seducing her, taking her to her knees, but she's somehow taking charge of this situation and turning this around on me. "I'll have a beer, too."

I grab two beers, uncap them and hand one to her as I settle back onto the floor next to her. She slides another fry in, and my pants grow two sizes too small. *Get yourself back in control, and get her out the door, already.*

Easier said than done.

I take another big bite of my burger. "So how is it you're still single?" I ask after swallowing.

She averts my gaze, takes another few fries and chews slowly like she's considering my question deeply. She swallows, then takes a big swig of beer. "I could ask the same about you."

I shrug. "I just don't believe in long term, or marriage," I admit honestly. "I've not had great role models in my life." My mother walked out on me, and none of my stepmothers had any interest in bonding. No, they were only in it for the money and stature. I remember Dad's second wife, or was it his third? She absolutely despised the sight of me. Oh, she'd pretend in front of Dad, even went to a few parent-teacher meetings, but when it was just the two of us, she gave me scathing looks that let me know I was a nuisance. At least Dad didn't ship me off to boarding school like she wanted. Yeah, I learned early on no one wanted a real relationship with me. Now, well, now I'm not about to set myself up for that kind of disappointment.

Summer nods but doesn't probe any deeper. "I'm not the marrying type," she says, so quietly, so softly…with such gut-wrenching sorrow, the protector in me comes out full force. Why wouldn't she be the marrying type? Hell, my granddad wants to marry her. At least I'm pretty sure he does. He said he wanted to bring her into the family. Thoughts of Granddad help me get myself back on track. I give myself a two-second mental lecture and remind myself why I'm eating cheeseburgers with this girl in my chalet. "I'm just…" Her head lifts, and she almost looks like she wants to make a confession. "I'm not…" Her words fall off and she pushes her plate away. "I'm full," she says, redirecting the conversation before she takes another big pull from her beer.

I shove my plate away, too, as she settles on her stomach, braces her elbows on the floor and cups her face in her hands. She bends her knees, points her feet toward the loft, and the sight of her like that is almost more than I can bear. I drain half the contents in my bottle with one easy swallow, hoping the liquid will cool the blood racing through my veins.

"Why do you think you're not the marrying type, Summer?" I push, wanting to know more about her, even though it shouldn't matter. After tonight I don't plan on ever setting eyes on her again.

She rolls to her back, meets my gaze straight on as she spreads her arms, her fingers fluttering over the shag carpet. "You want to know what I think?" she asks, as dark lashes fall over lust-imbued eyes. Pink invades her cheeks, everything about her body language telling me what she wants—and that she's playing to win.

I am so screwed.

"What?" I ask anyway, my gaze trailing the length of her lush body as she sprawls out in front of the fire. The sexy sight is torturous, and I must be a damn masochist, because I can't seem to tear my gaze away.

"What I think is, I don't believe in long term either, Tate." She goes up on her elbows, and the fire in the hearth behind her flares, the light glistening off the caramel highlights in her hair. Goddammit, I want to kiss her. Need to kiss her. Need to taste every inch of her body. Okay, I'm in trouble here. "But tonight… well, I don't believe it's about thinking. It's about taking what you want, and what I want is you."

"Summer," I begin, and take a deep breath, then another, working to keep my head on straight as all the blood rushes south. This dangerous pull toward her is messing with my ability to think straight.

She gestures with a crook of her finger, and my resolve loosens. How can she tear me apart so easily, make me forget who I am and why I'm here?

"Come here…" she says, her voice a low, throbbing murmur I can't ignore.

Shit.

Unable to help myself I fall over her, press her into the plush carpet. Now that I got her right where I want her, I should call her out, expose her. But in this moment, as her soft, sexy body moves beneath mine, teasing my cock and arousing me in ways no other woman ever has, only one thought drives me: getting her naked and getting my cock inside her.

I dip my head, my lips crash over hers. I kiss her like a man starved, a man taking his dying breath. I ravage her mouth, pillage it, thrust my tongue inside to taste the depths of her. When I realize I'm going at her like an animal—a fucking caveman—I tear my mouth away, look at her kiss-swollen lips, note the way she's panting beneath me, as lost in me as I am in her.

"Summer," I say, pushing her hair from her face, desperate to get myself together. Her clip falls out, and her hair tumbles free. I grip the long strands, roll them around my hand three times and tug. Her lips part, a sexy, whimpering noise catching in her throat. She's the most beautiful woman I've ever set eyes on.

"Tate," she whispers, and somewhere in the back of my mind, where one working brain cell still exists, a warning light flashes.

End this, Tate. End it now.

"Please," she begs again, her soft hands sliding around my back, palming my muscles and pulling me harder against her lush body. As images of us fucking infiltrate my brain, I spread her legs wider with mine, and she wraps them around my back, centering my hard cock on her sex.

My lips go to her throat, desperate to taste her skin…between her legs. Yeah, this is all kinds of messed up. I'm not just crossing a line with her. I'm stomping on it, chewing it up and spitting it out, but holy shit, after one sweet taste I'm too far gone to turn back now.

"Yes…" she murmurs, and I hesitate for a brief second, trying to remember why this is wrong when she once again whispers, "Please…"

And just like that, I'm done for.

CHAPTER SIX

Summer

"TATE...YES," I murmur when he kisses my jawline, his breath like fire on my skin. His hands roam my body, explore my curves and I arch into him, wanting him to brand every inch of me. If I only have one night with this guy, I plan to make the best of it.

I tug at his sweater, and he goes back on his heels. In typical man fashion, he reaches over one shoulder, grabs a fistful of the material, and in one smooth motion peels it over his head. Firelight glistens off his gorgeous frame and I take my time to stare at his hard body, and abs I could play a game of Plinko on. He's absolutely breathtaking, better than I could ever have imagined.

"Like what you see?" he asks, a small grin curling up the corner of his mouth, making him look so damn sexy. My God, I definitely won the man lottery tonight.

"Love what I see," I say, holding nothing back. It's been so long since I've been with a man—and never with a man quite like this one—that I plan for this night to go out with a bang. I haven't been completely honest with him about who I am, but I've been honest about everything else, and right now, in this moment, there is no room for anything but the truth.

"Keep going?" I say.

He grins. "It's your turn."

I sit up and slowly pull my sweater over my head, then shake my hair out. I catch the heat in his eyes, and while I sense he wants to tear my clothes off, get me naked sooner rather than later, it's easy to tell he's struggling for patience, holding it together by a fine thread so he can watch me undress for him. I'm anxious to have him naked, too, to put my hands all over him, but right now he wants a show, so I'll snap that thread later.

His eyes drop, latch on to my breasts as I slide my hand around my back and with agonizingly slow movements, unhook my bra. I let it fall into my lap, and his breathing changes. Intense blue eyes slowly lift to mine again, and my heart lurches. Good God, I've never seen a man look at me with such unchecked need, such ravaging hunger. He's going to eat me alive—wreck me.

There's nothing I want more.

I work to speak, to sound like I'm in a little more control than I actually am. "Like what you see?" I ask.

"You're beautiful," he says, and a little thrill goes through me. I like the way this man looks at me, like he's going to worship every inch of my body as soon as he gets his hands on me.

"Your turn," I say, and point to his pants, to the bulge pressing hard against his zipper, specifically.

He angles his head. "You want me naked, Summer?" he asks, his voice so deep and gravelly it's almost unrecognizable.

"Yes, please…" I choose my words carefully, getting the sense he likes hearing *please* on my lips.

He pulls himself up to his full height, and I stare, mesmerized as he unhooks his pants and drags them, along with his boxers, down his legs, completely uninhibited. Not like he has a reason to have any hangups. The man is drop-dead gorgeous, in a suit, in jeans…especially naked.

"You were right, you know," I say.

"About?" he asks, as he points at my pants, a gesture for me to get rid of them.

"There is no competition." I wave my hand the length of him. "And I'm going to owe you more than a drink."

He laughs at that, but it comes out a tortured groan when I stand, and slowly wiggle my pants down my legs, leaving only my lace thong in place.

"Jesus," he murmurs.

"Something wrong, Tate?" I hook my fingers into the thin strap of my panties, and just move them around on my hips, a vicious tease, despite the fact that I'm so damn delirious with need, I can barely form a coherent thought.

"No, Summer, everything is just about right."

He steps toward me, slides his hand around my back and drags me to him. His lips find mine again, and I taste the beer on his tongue when he slides it into my mouth. I whimper, sag against him and skate my hands over his hard body, palming all his sculpted muscles.

He grips my ass, kneads it with his fingers, then inches back. Without warning, he slowly slides his big hand inside the front of my soaked panties. He moves his fingers along my folds. Unable to help myself, I buck against him shamelessly.

"God, you're so wet for me," he murmurs.

"I've wanted you since I first set eyes on you," I say honestly.

He sinks to his knees, drags me down with him, and then he takes his time to just look at me. Nearly naked and wide-open, I let him look his fill, never having been the object of a man's affection quite like this before. A log in the fire snaps and it does something to him.

"I need my mouth on you," he murmurs.

A second later, I'm on my back, and he's on top of me, pressing me into the carpet as his scorching mouth goes to my marbled nipples.

He licks, nibbles, draws one into his mouth, sucking so hard little hollows form in his cheeks. He cups my other breast, then treats it to the same hot tongue massage.

"Yes, Tate, just like that," I say, and rake my hands

through his hair, holding him to me. "That feels incredible." He moans, his cock like steel against my thigh. I move under him, tease and torment his erection as he eats at me. His breathing is labored, his breath falling over my naked flesh, turning me on even more.

I tug at him, wanting my mouth on his body, around his cock, but he has other ideas. He kisses a path down my center, and my skin tingles everywhere his mouth touches. The growth on his jaw abrades my flesh, and his fingers press into my hips. Tomorrow I'll be bruised and chafed, a beautiful reminder of this one-night affair. He goes to his knees, grabs both of my legs and lifts them, until my feet are pointing at the high ceiling.

"Keep them there," he commands in a soft voice, as he grips the lacy straps on my thong and pulls them up over my legs. He tosses them aside, and brings my legs back to the floor, spreading them. His gaze latches on my sex, exposed and ready for him. The muscles along his jaw clench and his nostrils flare as he reaches out and lightly strokes me.

My body practically convulses at the first sweet touch. I move, writhe, trying to force his finger to where I need it the most.

"Such a needy girl," he whispers, but from the way his muscles are bunching, it's easy to tell he's still hanging on by that thread, one I'm ready to break.

"How could I not be?" I murmur. "Have you seen yourself?"

He chuckles, and it vibrates through me. "I could ask you the same question."

"I need you to touch me, Tate."

He widens my sex lips. "Where do you need me to touch?" he asks, and lightly strokes my clit. "Right here?"

"Yes," I cry out, and briefly close my eyes to concentrate on the sensation. I fall back to the carpet, the fire licking at my skin, as he continues to stroke me. My throat dries as I gulp for air. I open my eyes as he repositions himself to lie on his stomach, his gaze latched on my sex.

"You have the prettiest pussy," he murmurs, the look on his face letting me know he's going to ravage me, eat at me until I'm a quivering mess of need. His eyes lift, meet mine as he pets my sex, and in that instant, I realize he's a man used to getting what he wants. "I'm going to ruin your sweet little pussy with my mouth. You know that, right?"

"Oh God, yes." My sex clenches at his dirty words. Need burns through me, amping up my temperature. I go up on my elbows to watch and my gusting breaths ruffle his too-long hair.

"You want that, Summer? You want me to ruin this sweet little thing?"

"Please, Tate," I murmur, and just like that his mouth is on me, eating at my wet pussy, plundering and wrecking me with his tongue. A growl rips from his throat when he comes up for air, and then he's kissing me again, deeper, harder, as he slides one hand out from under me. My throat tightens when one thick finger probes my opening, then finds its way deep inside me, touching me and awakening my body the way no other man ever has.

I exhale, my nails digging into the carpet as he lifts my hips higher, feeding his mouth with my sex. The way he's devouring me is delicious and dirty, so damn pleasurable small pulses begin in my core. He pulls his finger out, then slides two back in, touching me deeper, using smooth steady thrusts that push me over. He strokes along my walls, teases my G-spot. I cup my breasts, run my fingers over my quivering nipples as he expertly wrings an orgasm out of me.

"That's it," he murmurs from deep between my legs. "Come all over my mouth and fingers."

I pulse and clench around him, blindsided by the intense pleasure now ruling my body. He laps at me, drawing out the waves, as I come and come and come some more. I'm a hot trembling mess by the time my body stops spasming. He licks at me and moans, like he's savoring every drop. I've never had a man taste me so deeply, or like what he's doing so much.

"Tate," I manage to get out.

He climbs up my body, and his wet mouth glistens in the firelight. The sight does something strange to me, arouses me all over again. He wipes his mouth with the back of his hand.

"You taste so fucking good," he says. "I could eat you all day."

"Come here." I drag his mouth to mine, and taste myself on his tongue. I've never done that before, but tonight I want to do everything with this man. "Mmm," I moan.

"Like marshmallow," he teases, but his voice is strained, his body in desperate need of release.

I smile, pushing his hair from his face. "I want you to fuck me, Tate."

His eyes turn dark, predatory, and if I was smart I'd run now. "It won't be slow and easy, Summer." His hard-as-granite cock brushes my inner thighs. "Not this time. No, this time I'm going to fuck you hard and fast. I'm going to leave you so wrecked, you're going to feel me inside you for a week."

"No, you're not," I say, and worry backlights his eyes. He takes a breath and lets it out slowly. He thinks I'm having second thoughts, but I'm not.

I'm desperate to have his cock inside me, but first I need it in my mouth. I push him, and he slides off my body. His brow furrows, but then it smooths out when I go to my knees and wrap my mouth around his impressive cock.

"God, Summer," he murmurs, his hand in my hair again, wrapping it around his hand and tugging it so he can watch his cock slide in and out of my mouth. I take him to the back of my throat, wanting him deeper, wanting all of him but knowing it's impossible. I relax my throat, take in another inch. Blood rushes through his veins, his cock growing impossibly thicker in my mouth. I cup his balls, massage gently. He tugs on my hair, dragging me off him.

One look at his face tells me he's close, and while I want him to come in my mouth, I'm desperate to feel his thickness inside me. He's about to position me under him, but I don't want vanilla with this man. I press down on his chest, keeping him pinned beneath me. Taking control, I straddle him.

"I'm the one who's going to fuck you hard and fast, and I'm not about to apologize for it."

"Jesus," he murmurs, the thread holding him together unraveling before my eyes.

"Protection?" I ask. I'm on the Pill, but no way am I about to have unprotected sex with a stranger.

"Pants," he says. I climb off him for a second and grab his pants. I fish the condom from his pocket, and when I turn around he's gripping his thick cock. He pumps his fist, and I gulp for air.

"Like what you see?"

I've never seen a man do that before, and I have to say, it's incredibly hot. "Yeah, I do," I say, and wet my lips, my mouth eager to be back on him as everything he's doing taunts my body. His hand moves steadily, and I tear into the foil. He reaches for it, but I pull it back.

"Let me."

He curses under his breath. "Are you trying to kill me tonight?"

I laugh, but it's full of need and desire. Moving back between his legs, I get ready to slide the condom on, but stop when precum drips from his slit. I lean forward and lick it with the tip of my tongue. "Mmm," I murmur. "I love the taste of you. I could lick you all day," I say, echoing his earlier words.

"Get that condom on me. Now," he commands.

He fists his cock, as I press it to his crown and slowly slide it down. His agonized moan curls around me, and I shimmy forward, my legs on either side of him as I straddle his body.

He grips his cock, ready to feed it to me, and I brace my hands on his chest and I slowly lower myself, taking one glorious inch at a time, until he's seated inside me. I go still, to give my body time to adjust to his girth.

He swallows and places his hands on my hips. "Do you have any idea how sexy you are, how good my cock feels inside you?" he asks, his voice labored, strained. He's struggling to hang on, and I love knowing I can do this to him.

He moves his hips a little, powering upward, and I gasp. "You have the nicest cock, Tate. I love the way you fill me." My lashes fall as I wiggle my hips, move his cock around inside me. Sparks of pleasure shoot through me, taking me by surprise. "I can't believe how close I am to coming, again," I whisper. I open my eyes and look at him. "I never come twice," I admit.

"That's because you've never been with me before," he says, his voice low, intense, deadly serious.

"You're pretty confident."

"Yeah, I am."

With my body shaking, and a new kind of need taking up residency inside me, I say, "Then ruin me, Tate. Ruin me with your beautiful cock." I lift my body, until only his crown remains buried inside me. "Please…"

His grip on my hips tightens, and he pistons upward. Air leaves my lungs as he fills me, sliding in and out, creating heat and friction that fogs my brain. His cock throbs inside me, and I move with him, slamming myself down on his steel rod as he thrusts upward. My clit smashes against his body as we fuck. He presses roughly into me, and my muscles flex around him.

"You are so wet and tight," he growls, his hard flesh pounding inside me, a maddening, punishing pace.

"I… I…" I begin, but my voice falls off as my body lets go a second time, my hot cum spilling over his cock. Why is sex with this man so good? I moan, revel in the swirling heat and pleasure racing through my body.

"Jesus," he murmurs, his thrusts picking up speed as he chases his own orgasm. I lift and come down on him again, and his curses reach my ears as the last of his thread snaps. I cup my breasts, pinch my nipples, and his nostrils flare. We move, crushing our bodies together, each pulling and pushing, giving and taking. He swells even more inside of me and I cry out his name. I lift again, but he pulls me down, his fingers digging in for purchase as he throws his head back and fills the latex with his cum.

"Yes…" I whisper, loving the look on his face as he comes for me.

The only problem is, I said we only had tonight, but now that I've had him, I'm going to want more.

CHAPTER SEVEN

Tate

MY EYES BLINK OPEN, take in the naked woman sleeping soundly beside me. Sometime throughout the night, or maybe it was closer to dawn, we'd managed to make it to the bed in the loft. I stretch out as the late morning sunlight filters in through the skylights, and Summer shifts beside me, the blankets sliding off her shoulders. With a chill in the air, I tug the blankets up and wrap them around her. I take a moment to look at her, the mess of her hair, a satisfied smile on her face, even in sleep. While I'd like to wake her again, put my cock inside her, I inch away, keeping my hands to myself. Last night… well, what can I say about last night? I totally fucked up and lost control.

I give a hard shake of my head. Why the hell did I have sex with the one girl I should have kept my distance from? I was supposed to strip her bare, and take her to her knees. But instead she took me to mine.

Shit.

I inch away a little more, careful not to wake her. I need time to think before we speak. Need time to figure out my next course of action before I do anything else with Summer Love. I slowly climb from the bed and make my way down the stairs. The pile of our clothes on the floor brings back erotic images of the night before. My cock thickens at the memories. Sex with Summer was un-fucking-believable.

I've never met a woman so open or honest, so... bare during sex. The way she gave me her body so freely, and dragged me into a vortex of need and desire, well that's never happened to me before.

I glance at my cell phone on the kitchen counter. I have to talk to Granddad, try a final time to ask more questions about Summer Love before I say or do anything rash. *Yeah, last night wasn't rash at all.* I tug on my jeans and sweater, toss a few logs into the hot embers and grab my phone. New York is six hours behind us, but Granddad will be up. He's always up at the crack of dawn, ever since I could remember.

I step into one of the main level bedrooms for privacy and punch in his number. I'm not sure what I'll say. If he knew I was in St. Moritz checking up on Summer Love, he'd be on his private jet, ready to tear me a new one. Not that he could take his private jet, since I'd already done that, and it's currently waiting for me at the airstrip just outside of town. Seriously though, he would take my actions as a breach of trust, and men like my grandfather don't get over something like that easily. I take a fueling breath, when my call goes through.

"Hello," a woman says.

What the hell, he has a woman at his house? Maybe he's moved on from Summer, and all this was a waste of time. A wonderful, delicious waste of time, but a waste of time nonetheless. "I'm looking for James, my grandfather."

"I'm sorry, he's resting. I'm his health care worker, and it's not in his best interest to disturb him." Ah, right, I remember Granddad saying he would have in-house care. I feel a measure of relief to know he's being looked after. "I can take a message for him."

I hear my granddad cough in the background. "It sounds like he's awake to me."

"He, uh…" She hesitates, then says, "He'll have to call you back."

Why the hell won't Granddad take my call? Does he know what I'm up to? "Can you tell him it's important?"

"Of course I will. Bye for now." And just like that the line goes dead. Son of a bitch.

I shove my phone into the front pocket of my jeans, and step back into the main room, the fire now heating the place back up again. I'm not sure what comes next, but I'm going to need coffee before I can figure it out.

I open and close the cupboards. The place hasn't been stocked in ages. I grab my coat and consider leaving Summer a note. It's not in my nature to bolt without so much as a goodbye. Then again, it's not in my nature to have sleepovers either. I grab a piece of paper, scribble that I'm headed out to get us breakfast and step outside.

I pull out my phone again and open the app that allows me to order from Hauser's, my favorite breakfast spot. Since I don't know what Summer likes, I order a ton of food, then shove my phone back into my pocket after I prepay. I should probably cool it with the big gestures—it might tip her off that I'm not the bartender of modest means I'm pretending to be.

Snow crunches beneath my feet as I follow the path to the café, and monstrous clouds cast shadows over the ski hills. I'm guessing we'll be getting a storm like everyone was speculating. That will really put a damper on Winterfest, which begins tomorrow. It's an annual festival to raise money for charity, so they'll go through with it as best they can, despite the weather. I'd planned to be gone before the storm hits and the place grew busier with the upcoming festivities. But now I'm not so sure that's going to happen. I think I'm going to have to hang around until I hear from my grandfather. And while I'm waiting, I plan to get to know Summer better, to see who she really is and what's really going on with her before I report back to Granddad.

I nod a good-morning at a couple walking by and weave through the path to the restaurant that is famous for its Belgian waffles. Long strides take me to my destination in record time, and when I pull the door open the fresh scent of dark roasted coffee fills my nostrils. I might need two extralarge this morning. I step up to the counter and give my name, then hang back as they seat guests.

From the corner of my eye, I catch sight of Summer's friends as they linger over coffee. Shit. I don't want to make conversation, so I inch back a bit more, but I think they've already seen me. If Summer wants them to know she slept with me it'll come from her, not me. Although one look at me, or her, and it's easy to tell we were up all night partaking in a sex marathon. My order comes out, and I grab it and dash outside. I retrace my steps back to my chalet and when I enter, I hear water running in the bathroom.

I set the food on the counter, and step up to the closed door. Hand on knob, I listen for a moment, all the while trying not to visualize her in there naked, soaping up her perfect body. Too late, I'm visualizing it. I clench down on my teeth, then knock.

"Summer, I'm back and I have breakfast." The water stops running, and I step back, before I do something stupid, like barge in and fuck her in the shower.

"I'll be right out," she says, and I grit my teeth at the sound of her sultry voice. Will things be awkward between us this morning? I never hang around or do morning-afters, so I'm not sure what to expect from her. I back up and stare at the door until she comes out, wrapped in nothing but a big fluffy towel.

"Good morning," she says, her cheeks a sexy shade of pink.

I follow her bright, cheery tone that sets the mood for us. "Hungry?"

"Starving." She looks past my shoulder. "Tell me you have coffee."

"I have coffee." I stand there, unmoving, and she smiles at me.

She blinks up at me. "Everything okay?"

"Ah, do you want to get dressed first?"

"No, I'm okay." She moves past me, and her laugh reverberates through my body, settles in my balls. Did she just give an extra shake to her backside? "Tate, did you order one of everything again?" she asks when she sees the bags.

"I—"

"Didn't know what I liked," she says, finishing my sentence for me. There's concern in her eyes for a brief flash. "This is totally unnecessary by the way…but very sweet of you."

"Sweet?"

She pulls container after container from the bags, and glances at me over her shoulder. "What, another word you've never been called before?" Her teasing voice seeps through my veins, and I'm pretty certain she's playing with me, testing my hard-earned control.

I reach into the cupboard and pull out plates. "What do you take in your coffee?"

"Just milk."

I dump out the bag with the milk and sugar and fix her coffee for her. "How's this look?"

"It looks like heaven." She wraps her hands around the paper cup. She breathes it in, and the small smile on her flushed face is sexy as hell. She takes a small sip. "Mmm."

"Fuck."

Her eyes open. "What?"

Okay, yeah, she's messing with me. "Do you know that's the same sound you make in bed?"

"Well, technically we weren't in bed." Our eyes both go to the spot where we had sex on the floor, numerous times.

"Yet," I say, and surprise myself.

Okay, Tate, you're supposed to be getting to know her better. That doesn't mean sex again.

"Just so you know, I'd take sex with you over coffee any day."

Unable to help myself, I step up to her and slide my hand around her neck. I grip her tightly, sweep my fingers over her soft skin and drag her mouth to mine. She tastes like mint and coffee and everything sweet. I break the kiss and we're both breathless.

"What was that for?" she asks.

"That was for shaking your ass at me a minute ago."

"I'll keep that in mind," she says, and turns her attention to the containers. She opens the waffles and her eyes go wide. "These look amazing."

"They taste better than they look." She divvies them up as I uncover the sausage, bacon, eggs, toast and pancakes.

"I'm going to be fifteen pounds heavier when I leave here next week."

We sit at the table and I take a much-needed drink from my coffee. "You're only here for a week, then?"

"Yep, then it's back to the real world."

"What is your real world, Summer?" I ask, since she opened the door. "You only have a first name, and you're in between jobs. What else can you tell me about yourself? Family, friends?"

"You met my friends."

"I saw them this morning at the restaurant. What do they do, besides hang out in St. Moritz with you?"

"Well, believe it or not, Amber lives in Palo Alto and works in finance for a startup company, something to do with the trucking industry."

"No way."

"Yeah, she's really smart."

"What does Cara do?"

"Cara is an emergency room doctor at Southampton Hospital."

My jaw falls open. "Really?"

"Impressive, right? I have smart friends," she says. "I could never work at the kind of pace Cara does. Which is why…" She suddenly closes her mouth like she said too much.

How can she be so secretive outside of the bedroom, and so open and honest inside it? "Which is why what?"

"I'm not an emergency room doctor," she says, and gives a laugh.

"How did you all meet?"

She averts my eyes, and says, "Oh, when I spent time in Boston, I met them. We've been tight ever since."

How would a con living in Boston get in with two smart, successful women like Amber and Cara? Something really isn't adding up here.

"They like you," she says.

"Well, I'm pretty sure they knew what we were doing all night. Not sure if you're okay with that or not. When they saw me I dodged them. I didn't want to do or say anything that would make you uncomfortable."

Her eyes soften when she looks at me, her gratitude evident. "They're the ones who told me to go for it with you."

"Oh yeah."

She reaches out, puts her hand on mine, and the softness of her skin messes with my thought process. "I don't sleep around, Tate. This," she says and glances around the room, "was my very first one-night stand."

"Oh." Okay, so I didn't expect that. Then again, is it the truth? I study her face, find nothing in it to tell me she's lying, but a good con is hard to read.

"Not that there is anything wrong with a woman

having many different partners. We should own our sexuality. As long as she's sensible and safe, it's okay to have sexual freedom."

Curious to know more about her, I ask, "If you feel that way, then why is this the first time for you?"

She goes quiet, and looks down at her food, giving me the sense that she's trying to choose her words carefully. Last night she was open and honest, but the lawyer in me senses that in the light of day she's hiding something. Just like Granddad was. I should come right out and ask her about him, and why he's signing half his estate over to her. So why don't I? Because I can't risk messing this up before I've learned anything useful at all. For now, I have to keep going.

"I've just…been busy with other things in my life," she says, a vague answer, which confirms my suspicions. "What about you, Tate? You said you didn't have great role models in your life. Tell me more about yourself." She picks up a slice of bacon and nibbles on it.

This time it's me who is choosing their words carefully. "Let's just say, the women in my life turned out to be different than I thought they were."

"I'm sorry." A log in the fire crackles and she smiles. "How long do you have this chalet?"

"The entire week." Not a lie. I dig into my food, hungrier than I thought. No surprise, really. I haven't had a night like last night in…ever. I mean, sure, I've had sex before, plenty of it. But come to think of it, I've been so busy setting up my own practice and worried about Granddad that it's been months. That's probably why last night was so incredible.

Her eyes light up. "Winterfest starts tomorrow. I hear a lot of the proceeds go to the local hospitals, with each event donating to a different department. I think that's wonderful." She takes another sip of coffee, looks at me over the rim. "Are you taking part in any of the festivities?"

"Probably. Staff usually are involved. I'm sure Henry will let me know what he needs."

"Henry."

"My manager at the bar." She crinkles her nose. "What?"

"You like working here?" I nod. I always liked working here when I was younger, but that's not what she's really asking. She's asking if I have any higher aspirations. Summer Love would never settle for a simple bartender. Another clue that she's a gold digger? My stomach twists at that thought, because the more I'm around her, the more I get the sense that she's not that girl.

"I like it," I say.

"I can see the allure. Do you miss the States?"

Just then my cell phone rings. Saved by the fucking bell. Praying it's Granddad, I pull it from my pocket and check the display. Shit, it's my new receptionist, Helen. She's been going over candidates for the law firm. I'm in need of a junior partner. "Excuse me for a minute. I have to take this." I step into the privacy of the bedroom and answer the call. When I'm done, I walk back into the main room and catch Summer texting. She sets her phone down and smiles up at me.

"Everything okay?"

No. Nothing is okay, but being here with her like this, locking the outside world out for a few hours, makes everything better.

I am so fucked.

CHAPTER EIGHT

Summer

I SIP THE STRAWBERRY daiquiri in front of me, my body on hyperdrive, unable to stop staring at the hot bartender as he takes orders a few feet away from me. I shift in my seat, my stubble-abraded body stinging in the most glorious ways. My muscles hurt as I move, but I love the reminder as well as the finger bruises I discovered on my hips this morning.

Two girls sidle up to the bar and take a seat. Tate turns his attention to them, and out of nowhere, a wave of jealously surges inside me when one of the pretty ski bunnies leans into Tate and whispers something in his ear. He laughs, and she slides a napkin across the counter. No doubt her room number. Tate accepts it and shoves it into his back pocket. I have no idea if he plans to meet up with her or not, and I truthfully shouldn't care. I mean, come on, I've only had sex with the man once. Okay, well maybe it was more like four times—but all in the course of one night, which means I have no claim to him, no right to feel jealous.

This is just sex, Summer. Don't go mixing it with emotion.

"So, how was he?" Cara asks, and nibbles on her straw.

"I don't kiss and tell," I say, and give her a coy smile.

"We don't want to know how he kisses. We want to know how he was in bed," Amber pipes in. "How big was his cock?"

I laugh and shake my head. "That is none of your business."

Amber blinks long lashes over pleading eyes. "Come on, Summer. I'd tell you, and since I'm currently going through a dry spell, give me something. You can't have sex with the hottest guy around and not share a few details."

"Okay, fine. We went to his chalet—"

"He has a chalet?" Amber crinkles her nose and I follow her gaze, take in Tate once again. He's dressed in a black button-up work shirt and jeans, his hair falling in his eyes as he reaches for something under the bar. He stands again, and despite the fact that he's not in a tie, he smooths his hand over his chest, in typical James fashion. Such a funny thing that Tate would have the same gesture as my patient. I think about that for a moment, notice the way he carries himself, like a man of great authority. If it weren't for the too longish hair and bartending job, one could easily mistake him for a man who comes from means. I'm just glad he's not. I doubt I'd be able to connect with him the same way if he was—the only rich guy I've found myself able to trust is James.

"How can he afford a chalet?" Cara asks, pulling my thoughts back.

"He has a friend who's out of town and lent it to him."

"How fortunate that it fell on the same week we're here."

"Very fortunate," I say. "But I do have a whole penthouse suite to myself. We could have gone there. Then again, it probably wouldn't look good if he was caught sneaking out of my room every morning. They probably have rules about staff fraternizing with the guests."

Amber's eyes light up, catching on to the one thing I was sure she would. "So this wasn't just a one-night stand?"

"I think I'd like to make it a one-week stand?" I say, my body remembering all the ways he touched me with his hands, his mouth, his magnificent cock.

"Yes," Amber says, and does a fist pump. It catches Tate's eyes and he looks our way. I give him a smile and he grins back.

"You so deserve a week of fun and hot, dirty sex."

"Who said it was dirty?"

Amber laughs. "I saw the way you were walking this morning."

"Ohmigod, Amber," I say, shaking my head.

"What does Tate think about a weeklong fling?"

"I don't know, actually. After breakfast this morning, he had to get ready for work, and I spent the day on the slopes with you girls, so we never really talked about it." I sip my drink and look at my friends. "Besides, it's not talking I want to do with him."

"Talking is overrated," Amber says, and we all laugh.

I steal another glance at Tate, but then my view is blocked when a man steps up to our table.

"How's it going?" he says, a slight slur to his voice as he glances at us. "Can I buy you ladies a drink?"

I hold up my half-empty glass. "Already have one, thanks."

He frowns, and checks in with the other girls, and after we all decline him, he gestures with the beer in his hand to where he's sitting with a group of guys. They're all leering at us, and it makes my skin crawl. "If you change your mind, I'm over there. I'm Bill, by the way."

"Thanks, Bill," I say, never one to be outwardly rude, even to a drunk guy trying to pick me up. Bill stumbles back toward his friends, and suddenly Tate is at our table.

"Everything okay here?" he asks, his eyes landing on mine.

"Everything is great."

He gestures with a jerk of his thumb. "You need me to take care of that guy?"

It's ridiculous how the feminine side of me reacts to his protectiveness. "We already did," I say. "But I appreciate the offer."

He nods, the muscles along his jaw tense. If I didn't know better I'd say he was jealous, about to start pounding his chest and intimidating all the other men in the bar. But that can't be right. We've only had one night of sex, which I'm hoping to rectify shortly.

His eyes flicker to our drink glasses. "I'm just about to go on break, but I was wondering if I could get you ladies anything else?"

As a matter of fact, you can.

"How about another round of drinks," I say, and put my hand on his arm. He takes a breath, and I love the effect I have on him. No man has ever reacted to me like this before. Then again, maybe they have and maybe I ignored it because none of those men were Tate.

"Sure thing," he says on a rasp. I pull my bottom lip between my teeth to stop myself from grinning; but when he turns and I glance at my friends, they're shaking their heads.

Cara fans herself. "I was pretty sure he was about to take Bill down caveman-style."

"The tension between you two is off the charts," Amber adds.

"And I plan to do something about that." I glance at the bar, watch Tate make our drinks. He hands them over to a female server, and his eyes meet mine before he disappears down a long staff-only hall-way—off-limits to patrons. Am I going to let that stop me? Hell no. "You two wouldn't mind excusing me for a minute, would you?"

"A minute? It had better be more like thirty," Amber says, and gives me a suggestive wink.

I climb from my chair and adjust the clip in my hair, piling it high on my head, the way I always do to keep it off my face. As I make my way toward the hall, my heart pounds harder. I can't believe I'm in a bar, in the Swiss Alps, about to have sex in some back room with a bartender. This is so not like me, but holy hell, I've never done anything so brazen, so exciting, in my entire life. I walk by some storage room just as a door opens. I jump, fearing my seduction has been foiled and I'll get kicked out of the place for trespassing, when Tate emerges.

His head rears back, and his eyes widen when they land on me. "Summer," he says as he smooths one hand over his chest again while the other flicks the storage room light off. He glances left, then right. "What are you…"

His words fall off when I give his chest a little shove, sending him back into the storage room, and follow him in. I shut the door, push him against the wall and go up on my toes to kiss him.

"Holy fuck," he murmurs.

"Exactly," I say, letting my eyes adjust to the dark. For a brief moment, he stiffens, like he's having second thoughts. "I want you, Tate. Right here, right now."

His body softens, well, all except for one part,

and his hands slide around my back to capture my ass. He tugs me hard against his erection, and I let loose a little whimper of need. I deepen the kiss, and he moans into my mouth. What we're doing is risky and inappropriate, but I don't care. I want this. I want him.

"I've been thinking about your cock all day," I whisper into his mouth, as my hands rake through his hair.

"You want my cock again?" he asks, his voice changing tone, dropping an octave.

"I've never stopped wanting it," I say, bolder than I ever have been before.

"When I was behind that bar, saw you sitting there all hot and sexy, all I could think about was putting my tongue inside your hot pussy again, and tasting your sweetness."

Oh God!

My entire body quakes, and in the light coming from under the door, I catch his grin. Yeah, he knows how much I love his brand of dirty talk.

"You like the idea of that, Summer?"

"Yes," I say.

"Then you'll let me fuck you with my tongue, feast on you and make you come?"

"Yes…please…"

He growls, low and deep, like an animal ready to attack. "Will you let me do anything else I want to do to you, right here in this storage room, where we could get caught at a moment's notice?"

I'm not sure if it's the risk of getting caught that makes this a hundred times hotter and dirtier, or hearing how he's going to fuck me with his tongue, feast on me. Either way, I'm shaking all over, and eager for him to do just that.

"Yes, but I want your cock in my mouth again."

As if my words unleashed the beast inside him, he tears into my jeans, and the hiss of my zipper cuts through the room. Am I really going to have dirty sex with Tate in a public place. Hell yeah!

His lips devour mine, then move to my neck. "You are the sexiest woman I've ever met," he says, as he presses hot, openmouthed kisses to my flesh. I tug at him, tear at the buttons on his shirt, wanting my hands on his magnificent body. Buttons pop, scattering on the floor, in my haste to get my hands on him.

"Sorry," I murmur.

Not sorry.

"I have another," he says, dipping his fingers into the front of my jeans as I shove his shirt from his shoulders. I lean into him, press my lips to his chest and breathe in his scent. It wraps around me, and hijacks my thoughts. The pad of his finger circles my swollen clit, and I cry out in sexual frustration, eager for him to slide it inside me.

"Tate."

"Yeah," he murmurs.

"Touch me."

"I am touching you," he says, teasing me with slow small circles that come close but never quite hit their mark. "And I have to say, I love finding you wet like this. Christ, you're dripping all over my hand."

I clench his shirt in my fists, and buck forward, but he continues to tease me with those damn barely there touches.

"I can't wait to get my mouth on you again. You're going to taste so fucking good." His finger swirls, slides along my folds, then finally dips into my quaking sex before he centers it on my clit. I whimper, move against him. A needy girl not afraid to show him what his touch does to my body.

"Please, Tate, I want to come all over you."

"You'll come. You'll come so fucking hard, Summer, you won't be able to walk out of here. But when I leave this room, I want your scent all over my fingers and cock. I want your sweet aroma to linger on my skin when I'm back at the bar, thinking about all the things I'm going to do to you tonight when I get off." He chuckles against my flesh, and then his throat makes a grinding sound when he swallows. "You know, I was so goddamn thirsty tonight." His mouth nuzzles my ear, his hot words vibrating through me and taking me to a place I've never been before. "Water wouldn't even quench my thirst, but I know what will." He turns me, puts a hand on my stomach and presses me against the wall. Then he sinks to his knees. I move my hips, eager to get out of my pants.

"Stay still," he commands in a rough voice, and I stop rocking. I take deep shallow breaths and blink in the dimly lit room, as he takes charge of my pleasure—and I let him. The rustle of my jeans reaches my ears as he hooks his fingers through the belt loops of my pants and tugs them down my legs, taking my thong with them.

He nuzzles my sex, his breath like fire on my skin as he breathes me in. "So fucking perfect," he murmurs, then takes one of my legs, lifts it and places it on one of the shelving units beside me. I stand before him, back against the wall, pants somewhere on the floor, my pussy spread wide-open, his for the taking. We're in the dark, but I never felt so bare, so exposed…so worshiped.

He touches me with his finger. "So hot and wet and needy," he murmurs. "Exactly how I like you." He leans in and licks me, a long, languid slide from bottom to top.

"Yes," I cry out, louder than I should. I grip his hair and curl my hips into him. "Fuck me with your tongue," I say rawly—maybe his brazen words are rubbing off on me. He laps at me, slow and gentle at first but then his tongue stiffens, whips my clit, until I'm writhing against his mouth. "That is so goooo."

He treats my clit to a good lashing. I cry out and he pushes his tongue inside me. I quake around him, so damn close to release it's insane. Delirious with need, I buck against his face as he greedily eats at me. He jabs his tongue in and out of my hot core, his thumb pressing against my lust-inflamed clit. I toss my head from side to side, barely able to get air in my lungs.

He thrusts a finger inside me, his mouth and fingers changing position, and when my muscles slacken, grow weak, I hold his hair tighter. He softens his tongue, presses it flat against my clit as his fingers probe deeper. God, that feels incredible. I moan, my throat too tight to pass words.

"I wish I could see you better. I love the look on your face when you come for me," he says, and just like that my body gives in to the pleasure. I stand on boneless legs and suck in a wheezing breath as I clench hard around him, drawing his finger deeper into my body. I concentrate on the pulses of pleasure, as my release drips down his hand and my thighs, hotter, wetter than I'd been the night before.

"Yes, come all over me," he murmurs. I sag against the wall, as his powerful fingers go deeper and deeper, his thumb sweeping my oversensitized clit as he wrings out a second orgasm. I can't believe I'm coming again so fast. This man…my God, the things he can do to my body.

I pant, gasp for air, my hair damp on my forehead. "Tate…that was…" I stop talking. How can I describe what this man makes me feel? He climbs to his feet, his hard cock denting my body as he leans into me.

With nothing soft or tender about him, he presses on my shoulders, and I go to the floor. "Take my cock in your mouth. I want you to take it deeper this time, Summer. I want to bury myself in your mouth."

Goddammit that turns me on. "Yes," I say, and part my lips, wanting him to choke me a little. I lean into him, but he stops me.

"Don't move."

I go still, but keep my mouth open, widening it to accommodate his girth, and in the dim light he grows fatter under my gaze. "See how hard you make me?" He laughs, but it's tortured. "You like making me hard like this, don't you, Summer?"

"Yes. I love your cock like this," I say, open and honest with him, and loving that I don't have to hold anything back in the bedroom—or the storage closet. He brings out the best in me that way, makes me completely comfortable with my sexuality.

He rubs his cock, rougher than the night before as the salty tang of his arousal teases my senses. His hips jerk forward, and he feeds me his length, one glorious inch at a time until his crown hits the back of my throat, and I whimper for more. I shift a little, holding his legs for leverage. The floor is hard on my knees, but I don't care. All I care about is taking as much of him into my body as possible. I relax my throat and lean into him. Footsteps pass by the door outside, but I don't stop. I couldn't even if I wanted to. I actually love it when he fucks my mouth like this.

"That's it, Summer. Just like that. Take it nice and deep, babe. It's the sexiest thing I've ever seen."

We both move, find a rhythm, my breath harder and harder to catch as he fills my throat with his length. He cups his balls and puts his other hand on my head, to follow along with the motion. He thickens even more, and I work my mouth around him harder, alternating between licking and sucking, wanting to make this so good for him, wanting him to fill my throat with his cum.

"If I didn't need to be inside you so bad, I'd come down your throat, watch you drink me in." I moan at the dirty talk, my body heating up all over again. Holy hell, could this sex get any hotter?

He pulls out, leaving my mouth empty and hungry, and I whimper at the loss of him. He helps me to my feet, and I use the wall for support as he shoves the supplies from the shelf to clear it.

"Come here."

Obeying, I push off the wall, and he drops a soft gentle kiss onto my mouth, a kiss so tender and sweet, it takes me by surprise. Why would he kiss me like that? I have no idea why, but I have no time to think about that, because he's turning me around to face the shelf. His big hand grips the back of my neck, and he bends me over the long, wide ledge. I slide my hands along it and grip the rough back edge of the wooden board to hang on.

"I want you like this," he says, and runs his hands down my spine, until he reaches my backside. He squeezes slightly, his thick cock hitting my soaked inner thighs. He backs away for a second, and I go completely still, listen to the rustle of clothes. A moment later, the sound of foil being ripped fills the quiet.

Please hurry...

Restless, I wiggle my hips, but stop when he grips them. One foot goes between mine, gives a little nudge to widen them. I spread my legs, never more open to anyone than I am in this moment. My body is on fire, and if he doesn't enter me soon, I might shatter to a million little pieces.

His cock centers on my opening—*finally*—and in one hard thrust, he's inside me, fucking me with an urgency that makes our sex that much dirtier, darker—intense.

"You feel so good," he murmurs, and leans forward to press a kiss to the back of my neck.

"So good," I repeat, as his voice seeps under my skin and into my brain, until I hear and feel nothing but him. My God, this man is in my head, and in my body, doing such incredible things to me, I'm not sure whether I want to cry or laugh.

His body smacks mine, driving me harder against the shelves. Each hard thrust destroys me a little more, and before I know it my arousal peaks, and I'm coming all around his cock.

"Oh Jesus, Summer. I feel you."

He thrusts once, twice, then stills inside me. I hold my breath, my muscles squeezing around him as he climaxes.

"Tate," I murmur.

"You feel me. You feel me coming inside you?"

"Yes," I cry out, wishing we had no barriers so I could have all his cum inside me. He falls over me, presses hot kisses to my neck, his breathing fast and labored. Then he's laughing, the sound doing crazy things to me again.

I chuckle with him, even though I'm not sure why or what we're laughing at. Maybe it was just the intensity of the moment that's messing with us both. He stands, lifts me and turns me around to face him.

"Summer," he murmurs, and cups my chin, the gesture so sweet and tender, my pulse beats triple time. His finger sweeps my jawline, and his mouth is back on mine, kissing me softly this time. "That was—"

"Fun," I say between his kisses.

"Yeah," he whispers. "Are you okay?"

"I'm not sure I'd use the word *okay*," I say, and we both begin to laugh again. He rests his forehead against mine.

"I might have been a little rough." He puts one hand between my legs and strokes me gently, as if to ease the sting his cock left behind.

"And I might have loved it."

His laugh dies down as footsteps walk by the closet again. "That was insane," he says, his breaths slowly returning to normal. "We need to get you dressed." He holds me to him. "Will you be okay if I let you go?"

I hold the shelving unit, and appreciate his concern. "I'll be okay," I say.

"I need to find something to clean you up. Is it okay if I flick the light on?"

"It's okay," I whisper.

The light flicks on and we both wince. "Damn," he says, as he turns to me. "Summer," he says again, and steps into me, to drop a soft, barely there kiss on my lips. The contradiction of wild Tate and tender Tate messes with my brain…and my heart. I pinch my eyes shut, and try to clear both.

I just seduced the man out of his pants in the storage room. *This is simply sex, Summer. Don't ever forget that.* There was a time in the past I thought a boy wanted something more, and that turned out to be disastrous.

He backs up, searches the shelves until he finds some napkins. He softens them by rubbing them through his fingers, and slides his hand between my thighs. He wipes me clean, tosses the paper into the trash and reaches for my jeans and panties.

"Lift," he says, tapping my leg.

"I can dress myself," I murmur.

He grins up at me, and my heart flutters. "I know, but I tore them off you, so I'm putting them back on." He drags my panties to my hips, and then follows with my jeans.

I fix the clip in my hair as he reaches for his pants, the napkin he'd stuffed in his back pocket falling to the floor. We both glance down and I see a hotel name and room number. I look away. Goddammit, I don't want him to see my jealousy and get the wrong idea about what I want from him. We live completely different lives and this can't be more than a fling to me, albeit a wonderful, hot, dirty fling that will fill my thoughts for the long New York winter I'm going to go back to.

"Hey, Summer," he says, as he bunches up the napkin and tosses it into the garbage.

"Yeah."

"One week," he says as he puts his palm on my face and draws my eyes back to his. "You and me. No one else."

CHAPTER NINE

Tate

My room is still dark when I roll over in my bed and reach for Summer. When my hand comes up empty, I open one eye and stare at the threatening clouds moving across my skylight. A quick check with the clock and I open my other eye. Jesus, I haven't slept in until noon since I was a kid. I stretch out as memories of last night's sex-a-thon, as well as this morning's sweet, sweet lovemaking, infiltrate my brain and put a smile on my face.

Lovemaking?

What the fuck? No, it's just sex. The best sex of my life, but sex nonetheless.

And it shouldn't even be that.

I let out a frustrated breath as it sinks in how far I've strayed from my original plan. I'm supposed to be here for Granddad, not myself. I don't know what came over me when I suggested a weeklong fling. Well yes, I do. It was Summer. Everything about her draws me in and makes it impossible for me to resist her. I can't deny how good it is between us, and I'm starting to give up trying to.

I'm not supposed to be sleeping with her, but a fling could still work in my favor. Keeping her close might be my only chance to figure out what's really going on. Does it make me an asshole, to use her like that? Maybe…but if she's using Granddad, too, does it matter? *Yes, it does*, a small voice in me says.

I run a hand through my hair, sitting up in bed. I flew to St. Moritz for one reason, and one reason only. Protect the family from a con.

She doesn't seem like a con.

While one part of me wants to believe that, there's the other part that reminds me Granddad is signing half his estate over to her. James Carson may be generous but he's also whip-smart in business and money management. He'd never just sign all that away, then give me the run around when I try to find out why—not unless he was coerced somehow…*or seduced*. Add that to the fact that Summer, no matter how nice she seems, is secretive. She has no social media presence and she's been vague about her work, and who she really is. And what did she mean the other night when she said she's not the marrying type? Does she move around a lot? Change identities or something like that? None of it makes sense to me yet, which is why I have to hang out here longer.

But I can't get too involved, no matter how confused I'm getting about who she really is.

I glance over, see the indentation on her pillow

and that's when I remember why she's not snuggled beside me. She had breakfast plans with her friends, and then they were heading into town to do some shopping.

I push from the bed and check my phone. Still no call from Granddad. Worry gnaws at me, but he has at-home care, so I have to assume he's okay. That nurse would've called if he'd taken a turn for the worse…right? Christ, maybe I never should have come here. I think about calling my dad, to see what he knows about the situation. But I don't want to bother him while he's on his honeymoon. I rake my hands through my hair. It's getting so long it's driving me crazy. Maybe I should visit one of the barbers in town this morning and get it trimmed.

I open my messages, answer a few from my receptionist, Helen. Once done, I hit up social media. I should have asked Summer the last names of her friends, to see if I could search them. I do another Google search for *Summer Love*, and numerous women show up. I scroll through them again, but the girl I've been sleeping with is a no-show, and none of these women compare. I continue to scroll and up pops a website. I glance at the link, which has Summer's name, followed by the word *practice* and what looks like a bunch of spam. I click on it anyway and jackknife up in the bed when a picture of Summer pops up. Well, technically it's not Summer, but it *is* her face photoshopped onto a naked body. What the hell? She's obviously been hacked.

I can't imagine she'd do this on purpose, but what do I really know about her, and why would she have her own website? There's no information on the site to explain this, just the picture, I make a mental note to keep checking for updates.

I check the time on my phone again, and punch in Granddad's number. It rings and rings and rings, then goes to voice message. I leave a message telling him he needs to call me, it's important, then slide my finger across the screen to end the call. I jump from bed, bare naked, and make my way downstairs to the main level. The fire is burning bright, and I smile. Summer must have fed it before she left. That was thoughtful of her.

My stomach grumbles, and I'm in desperate need of coffee, so I shower quickly, dress and head outdoors. I stop to grab a bite at my favorite café before I head to the bar. I don't really have to work, now that I've connected with Summer, but I guess I still have to maintain my cover. That, and with Winterfest upon us, it's one of the busiest times of the year. Henry appreciates my help, that's for sure.

I hurry to the bar and find it bustling. "Henry," I say, and greet him as I go down the hallway to the staff's lounge. I pass by the storage room and memories bombard me. I laugh. Summer has a sweet nature about her, so her seducing me here at work, well, that was quite the pleasant surprise.

I shrug out of my coat, tie a bar apron around my

waist and meet Henry, Jaquelin and Luca at the long bar. "Place is packed," I say.

Jaquelin sidles up to me. "Floor or bar?" she asks, and puts her hand on my arm, a suggestive gesture.

"Doesn't matter. Take what you want," I say, and already realize my mistake.

She gives me a coy grin, goes up on her toes, puts her hands on my shoulders and says, "After work, my quarters. I'll show you what I want."

"I, ah… I'm kind of with someone," I say, and glance around the bar, hoping Summer isn't witnessing this.

"I'm into sharing," Jaquelin says.

"I like you, Jaquelin, but I'm a one-woman-at-a-time kind of guy."

She pouts. "I saw your woman. She's a vacationer, Tate. Gone in a week."

That makes two of us.

"Just think about it, okay?" she says.

"Okay," I say just to appease her.

"Bar or floor?" she asks again.

"Neither for him," Henry pipes in, and I look at him over Jaquelin's head. Wait—is he firing me?

"What's going on?"

He tosses a rag over his shoulder, and says, "We all have to do our part for Winterfest. And every year we do a kissing booth. Vacationers love it!"

"You've got to be kidding me."

Luca mixes a drink beside me, and I nod to him. I've only just met Jaquelin and Luca. They don't know who I am, but Luca and I instantly hit it off. I wonder what his story is. He came here from Italy a few months ago, that much I know about him. A bartender is a great job for cash, but the guy is smart as hell, and could probably be doing more with his life.

Henry puts his hand on my shoulder. "Afraid not."

"Please tell me you don't want me to work it."

"I want you all to consider taking a turn," he says forcefully, and points to the wooden booth set up in the corner. How did I miss that? "You'll be helping so many people by volunteering. We do it every year *for charity* and it's a huge success." He winks at me. "I think this year it will be even more successful." His eyes move over my face. "Although you might want to get a damn haircut."

I laugh and run my fingers through my hair. "Where should I go?"

"Go see Luigi, down at Martina's salon, then get back here. You're up first."

"You want me to go to a salon?"

"Luigi has been here since you were a kid," he says quietly. "He'll do a good job."

"I kind of like his hair long," Jaquelin says from behind me, and runs her fingers through it. I flinch and jerk away from her unwanted touch. I'm about to walk back down the hall to get my coat, when she says, "Think about it, Tate."

"Think about what?" I hear Luca ask her as I disappear. I shrug back into my coat and step outside. The clouds are growing darker, knitting together as they move over the mountain. But it's warmer today than it has been. A good day to hit the slopes or go skating on the man-made rink outside Granddad's hotel.

I hurry to the salon, and an array of smells sting my sinuses upon entering. I wince and ask for Luigi. He's currently with a client, so I sit and flip through one of the magazines on the bench. Numerous women glance my way as they come and go. They probably recognize me from the bar. That does raise a bit of concern though, something I should've thought of before. Some of the resort staff know me, but they know not to give me away. Thankfully, I was able to keep my cover the other night at the restaurant—the few patrons who recognized me were too polite to interrupt me on a date. But what if someone else recognizes me as Tate Carson, grandson to billionaire James Carson, and says something? I have enough on my mind to worry about, so I'll cross that bridge when I get to it.

Luigi finally comes to get me. He's an elderly man with a thick Italian accent. He looks me over, narrows his eyes.

"Do I know you?"

Shit.

"I work at the bar, pretty new here."

He nods and says nothing more, but I think he's putting it together. He probably cut my granddad's hair many times over the years. Maybe even mine when I was little.

He sits me in the chair and gets right to it, humming to himself as he cuts, then shaves my neck. I shake my hair out and run my fingers through it, taking in the short, professional style I usually wear, and feeling more like myself.

Will Summer like this look?

What the hell do I care about that for?

Luigi tugs off my cape and says, "Voilà. As handsome as I remember."

I cast him a look, and he gives me a wink, letting me know my secret is safe with him. One of the girls leads me to the counter to pay, and I make sure to give Luigi an extra big tip.

I hurry back outside, the wind cooler on my ears with my hair cut. I glance around, and take in all the festivities. Honestly, I've been working so hard lately, setting up my practice, I forgot what fun was anymore. I miss coming here. Hell, I miss having fun. Granddad told me that on numerous occasions. He worked hard, but he played hard, too. But I work hard because I want him to be proud of me, want to make something of myself, on my own merit. Seriously though, how many times has he told me I need to find myself a nice girl? I scoff. I would if I could, but there just aren't any out there that I trust.

Summer is a nice girl.

Jesus Christ, Tate, get your head on right. You don't really know her at all.

I pull open the door to the bar, and there is already a lineup for the kissing booth. Goddammit, do I really have to do this? Then again, the money raised from the kissing booth goes to help the local children's hospital.

I peel off my jacket and wave to Henry to let him know I'm here. I find Luca in the back room, taking a break.

"Can you believe we're being guilt-tripped into doing this kissing booth?" I ask, looking over at my new friend. There is something about him that reminds me of me. Is he, too, playing a part, disguising himself as something he's not? If so, why?

"All for a good cause."

"Where in Italy are you from?" I ask.

He looks down, grief ripping through his face before he scrubs his jaw and says, "Massara."

"What brings you here?"

He grins. "The great weather."

I laugh. Okay, so he's not going to tell me. "Yeah, same here," I say.

I head back to the bar and take my first order. I twist a cap off a beer and slide it across the counter, then take the guy's money. I turn my attention to the next customer, hoping Henry will forget all about the kissing booth, but no such luck. He taps me on the shoulder, and he grins at me, like he's enjoying this way too much. But it's the least I can do for him, right? He's helping me out, and I should be helping him out in return.

"Nice cut," he says, a little breathless, his skin

paler than it was earlier. He jerks his chin up. "Now go. You got an hour shift."

"What about you?"

"Hell no. No one wants to kiss an old coot like me, and besides the wife would kill me. Now go."

"Shit," I mumble under my breath, and untie my bar apron. I slap it on the counter and head across the room. A familiar scent wraps around me and I turn to find Summer sneaking up behind me.

I grin at her and I don't want to think too much about how happy I am to see her. "Were you going to lift me up, spin me around?"

Her eyes go wide when she sees my haircut. "Tate, what did you do?" she asks.

I rake my hand through my short hair, scrub my palm over it. "Not good?"

"No, it's perfect. I actually really like your hair like this."

"It's usually how I wear it, just got busy."

She goes up on her toes and runs her fingers over my head. "A little less for me to grab on to, but I'll make do," she teases.

"Fuck, Summer. You can't say things like that to me. Well, you can, just not when I can't get you naked," I finish quietly. She laughs and I get how much she loves it when I unleash on her. "I have to work the booth."

She crinkles her cute little nose and I resist the urge to kiss her. "No way."

"Yeah, no choice." I point to the others behind the

bar, as Henry starts organizing the event. "We're all taking a turn."

Something flashes in her eyes but it's gone before I can identify it. She looks away, studies the string of women gearing up for their turn to kiss me as Henry herds them into a straight line "Such a hardship to kiss all those pretty girls," she says, her voice low, soft, and I can't tell whether she's teasing or not.

I cup her chin. "The only pretty girl I *want* to kiss is you, and I'm going to prove that to you tonight, over and over."

She laughs and puts her hand on my chest and from my peripheral vision, I catch the way Jaquelin is glaring at Summer. I don't like it. Not one little bit.

"Well, I'll let you get to your duties, then."

She backs away and grabs a table with her friends, but then I lose sight of her when I take my seat in the booth.

Soon enough I'm lost in a sea of lips—quick, efficient kisses that mean nothing and do nothing to me. I check my watch. Only a half an hour of my one-hour slot has gone by, but for some reason it feels like an eternity. I shove all the five-dollar bills as well as all the phone and room numbers into the cash box beside me and lift my head ready to kiss the next girl.

I shift in the booth, as Summer takes the chair opposite me.

"What are you doing, Summer?"

"Well, this is to raise funds for the children's hospital, is it not?"

I look over her shoulder at the long line of women, some I might have even taken to my bed in the past, but now... I can't seem to think about anyone but Summer, and that is fucked up.

"It is."

"Then I want to do my part." She puts ten dollars on the table.

"It's only five."

"I want to make a donation."

"The thing is, Summer. If I start kissing you, I'm going to get a major hard-on and have to get out of here."

"Well if that's the case, and you can't provide these ladies with what they want, I'll make a big donation in their names. Say..." She turns, does a quick tally of the women in line, then says, "Two hundred."

"Seriously?"

She wants to donate toward the cause? Once again, Summer takes me by surprise.

"I don't think—"

"I do," she says, and leans into me. Her soft lips hover over mine, and I breathe her in, smell cinnamon on her breath. All I can say is I'm glad I'm behind a booth, because my dick is thickening, eager to get back inside her as she slides her tongue into my mouth, and kisses me with unchecked heat. The crowd behind her goes crazy, and when we break apart, there is a little blush on her cheeks. I gesture to Luca.

"Hey, man, you're going to have to take over here for me."

Tray in hand, Luca laughs as he saunters over, and the women don't seem too displeased. He's a good-looking guy, so why would they? I snatch the tray from him and put it over my crotch. He laughs louder, and drops into my chair.

"Henry, do you need me, or can I take off?"

He waves me away. "Go."

"Thanks," I say, and slide my hand around Summer's waist. "You're going to pay for that."

"Can't wait."

"Want to get out of here?"

She nods, and I follow her to her table. "Do you ladies mind if I steal Summer away for a few hours?"

"Hours?" Amber says. "Now I'm officially jealous."

I laugh as Summer shakes her head at her friend— I'm getting used to Amber's antics. *You're not supposed to get used to any of this.*

I'm about to turn away when Ambers asks, "Do you have any brothers, cousins, just hanging around this place?"

"Sorry to disappoint you," I say, and Summer picks up a big bag from the floor before I lead her outside.

"Did you buy everything in town?"

She laughs. "No, I'm not you. But I do have a surprise."

"I like surprises."

"I know you do," she says, and when her eyes dim with desire, I'm guessing she's thinking about the stockroom rendezvous. That was one hell of a surprise, and I'd like a repeat. "But I'm not so sure you're going to like this one," she says, and frowns.

I stop walking. Jesus, is she finally going to confess, tell me she's been conning James Carson? "What is it?" I ask, all humor gone from my voice.

She stiffens and glances up at me. "It's okay, Tate. It's nothing bad."

I relax, and I'm not sure whether I'm disappointed or glad that she didn't confess. "What did you think I was going to say anyway?"

I open my mouth, not knowing how to answer, when a child lets loose a howl of a scream.

"What the hell?" I say. I glance over to the skating rink, where a young boy is lying on the ice and still wailing, one leg bent out severely at an awkward angle. The next thing I know Summer shoves the bag into my chest and darts toward the ice faster than I would have thought possible in her big winter boots. I grip the handle on the brown bag and follow Summer, find her down on her knees assessing the boy, checking his neck and leg for injuries before she'll let him move. She takes off her mitts and gingerly examines his leg, checking where it hurts. Maybe I should run back to the bar and get her friend Cara. She should be able to help. Or I could go to the resort's clinic, but Cara is closer. As I consider that, a crowd forms, and I lose sight of Summer. I stand back, debating on what to do, when the crowd opens up. I spot Summer talking to a man, likely

the child's father, since he has the boy in his arms.
Her nervous glance flickers to mine, and I angle my
head and watch her.

As they come toward me, I hear her say, "I think
it's just strained, not broken. But I'd still take him to
the resort's clinic for X-rays just to make sure there's
no hairline fracture or anything."

The father thanks her profusely, as the preteen boy
wipes tears from his face. "Thank you," he says, and
the two head along the path.

"What's going on?"

She hesitates for a second. "I just reacted."

"I'd say." I take in the flush on her face, the worry
in her eyes. It's kind of nice that she jumped in to
help like that. Most people, especially back in New
York, are reluctant to get involved, but not Summer. She ran like she was being chased by the Devil
himself. This woman confuses the hell out of me. "I
thought about going to get Cara."

"That would have been a good idea, but I think
the boy just strained his muscles."

I nudge her. "Oh, you're a doctor now, are you?"
I tease. If she were a doctor she would have told me
that, right?

"I just…" She pauses for a second. "My dad was
a construction worker. He injured himself a lot on
the job. They didn't have strict safety measures in
place back in his day." Then, almost to herself, she
says, "God, it's a wonder the job didn't take him out."

"Your dad, he's gone?" I ask quietly.

She nods, but I don't miss the water in her eyes as she looks off in the distance, her blurred gaze scanning the mountains. She seems to be a million miles away. I want to ask about her mom, but I'm not sure now is the time.

"I'm sorry," I say.

She shakes her head, like she's trying to clear it, and smiles up at me, but this time there is no light in her eyes. "Anyway, I know a broken bone when I see one." She redirects and points to the bag I'm holding. "About that surprise."

I inch the bag open, hoping to find some sexy lingerie, but what I see instead shocks me. "No way, Summer. Not in a million years."

CHAPTER TEN

Tate

"OH, COME ON, TATE, don't be a big baby." She takes the costume from me and shakes it out so I can get a better look at it.

I back up and hold my hands out. "A big baby? How does refusing to put on a ridiculous donkey outfit make me a baby?"

She rolls her eyes at me and somehow makes it look sexy. "It just does."

"I'm not doing it, Summer. Not in a million years or for a million dollars."

"I don't have either of those, but there is something else I can give you." She steps into me, goes up on her toes and her chilled lips meet mine. She kisses me softly, and our lips create both heat and friction. Forgetting where I am, I slide my hand around her back and drag her to me. We kiss like there is no one in the world but us. In the distance a child's laughter drags me back to my senses. I pull away, and her eyes are slightly closed, dreamy as she stands there, lips still poised. So fucking gorgeous.

"Are you bribing me with sex?" I ask.

A small smile curls up the corners of her mouth. "Me? Now, would I do something like that?" she asks, and blinks thick lashes over innocent eyes.

"I don't know you well enough to know if you're bribing me or not."

"But you'd know if it's working though, right?"

"It's not working."

It's working.

"Oh, come on," she pleads. "It's for charity. Please, Tate…"

"Summer…" I groan, and she grins.

"That groan does not mean I'm wearing it."

It means I'm wearing it.

How the hell can I say no to her when she's gazing at me with those big doe eyes. *Is that how she manipulates men into giving her what she wants?* If that's true, why don't I care more that it's working on me?

"The funds go to the geriatric department at the hospital, and that is near and dear to my heart."

Why, is that where she hangs out to pick up her victims?

Even as I ask myself these questions, they suddenly don't sit right in my brain, or my gut. The more time I spend with her, the less sure I am that she's the conniving gold digger I first thought. But then, what's her relationship with my granddad?

"What's your costume?" I ask, and look into the bag. I pull out a cute little red fox outfit. "How come

you get something adorable, and I have to be an ass?"
I glare at her. "Are you trying to tell me something?"

She laughs. "No, it's just that most of the men's costumes were already rented when I signed us up last minute."

"Wait." I stop in my tracks, and wave my hand, a motion to stop and backtrack. "Signed us up for what exactly?"

"You've worked here long enough. You should know what event has costumes like this."

"Enlighten me, I forget."

"It's the polar bear plunge."

I step back. "Nope. No way. Not happening. I'm not jumping into ice-cold water and freezing my balls off."

She leans toward me. "Not even if I promise to warm them up later, with my mouth?"

"Jesus. How the hell can I say no to that?"

"Pretty sure you can't."

I pinch the bridge of my nose, trying to wrap my brain around this. "So we jump into ice-cold water, with suits on?"

She produces two tickets. "I already bought us the tickets, and we can win prizes."

"Like what? Most Shrinkage? Best Blue Balls?"

She laughs, a deep belly laugh that nearly topples her over. For some strange reason I start laughing with her. I must be losing my damn mind. How can a woman I can't figure out be so easy to laugh with?

"No," she says, still laughing. "Like Best Jump,

Best Costume. Things like that. Some of the kids from the children's hospital are here and they're the judges. That's why we have the costumes on. To make it fun for them." The smile falls from her face, all serious now. "They need fun, Tate."

"Yeah, and I need my balls. I might want to have kids someday."

She puts a hand on her hip, her eyes challenging. "The guy who doesn't believe in marriage wants a family someday?"

"I say a lot of things." I shake my head, flustered. "I can't believe we're paying to jump into cold water." I take the tickets from her and turn them over in my hands. "These were one hundred bucks apiece?"

"Yes."

"That's a good chunk of change." I reach for my wallet. "I'll reimburse you."

She waves a dismissive hand. "No, this is on me. I like donating to hospitals." She takes the tickets back and puts them in her purse. "Come on, this is going to be fun."

"Yeah, it's right up there with skydiving without a parachute."

She laughs and slides her arm through mine, leading me around the resort, like she's already gotten her bearings. Cheers originate in the crowd when we reach the huge pond behind one of the resorts, the ice broken in a large path from the shoreline to the deep middle, to allow us to dunk. People in costume already wait out on the center of the ice, ready to jump.

"Motherfucker," I whisper, and she nudges me.

"Shh, there are children around." She tugs on me. "Let's grab a hot chocolate before things get started." We move through the crowd, and some of the guests are already in costumes. Nice ones, like famous superheroes, not like my damn donkey. Yeah, I'm really going to make an ass out of myself in more ways than one. Children in wheelchairs, covered in blankets, are sanctioned off to one side, their caregivers and parents with them. They look on with bright eyes, and something inside me softens. Despite that the money raised goes to geriatric care, it's nice they invite the kids to be judges. Summer was right, they do need fun, and what could be more fun than grown adults dressed up in costumes dunking themselves in freezing water? When I was a kid, I would have found it hilarious. Summer fills two paper cups with hot chocolate and hands one to me. I take a sip and it warms my stomach. If only I could pour it over myself before I take the plunge.

A woman in her midthirties steps up onto a platform and taps on a microphone to draw our attention. "Okay, folks, those participating, go ahead and get your costumes on. Changing rooms are set up in the conference rooms inside, one for the men and one for the ladies."

"Let's go," Summer says, and we follow the chattering crowd into the hotel. Heat blasts over my body in the main lobby, and I carry my costume into the makeshift changing room. Since my costume has enclosed feet, I kick off my shoes and remove my clothes. Dressed only in my boxer shorts I climb into the suit, and zip it up in the back. I put my clothes in one of the cubbies set up along the wall and head back out to the main lobby. Everyone laughs as they walk by me.

"Okay, have your fun," I grumble, good-naturedly.

Summer finally joins me, dressed in her cute fox costume, with a hoodie and adorable ears. Her legs are bare, save for her knee socks and furry slippers. How she can make that sexy is beyond me.

"You look amazing," she says.

"I look like a manic-depressive donkey," I counter.

She wiggles her tail at me. "Do I look foxy?"

"Of course you do, and now I look like an ass with a boner," I say, and she laughs. Once again I'm laughing with her. Truthfully, it feels good, too long in coming. Granddad was right. I do need to get out more often, inject a little more laughter into my life. But thinking about Granddad brings me back to reality.

"Hey, it's not so bad," Summer says, picking up on my mood.

I tug on my long donkey ears. "I'd better win a prize," I say, and she hooks her arm in mine and leads me outdoors. Hell, I should just come right out and ask her about Granddad. Ask her what her connection to him is, and why he wants to bring her into the family. Maybe Granddad isn't in love with her. Maybe they have a business arrangement. If that's the case, then maybe I can have her all to myself.

What the fuck am I saying?

Even if I am right, and Granddad isn't in love with

her, we could never be together. If she ever found out the real reason I came here, she'd hate me, and I wouldn't blame her. When this week is over, I need to let her go. I'll only hurt her more if I don't. Better to make a clean break.

We reach the pond and line up on the ice. The first jumper half runs and pretty much does a belly flop. He howls and water sprays up and splashes the kids. They laugh and clap. The man swims to shore, stands up and spreads his arms wide, amping up the crowd for more cheers.

"Someone is going to have a heart attack," I say.

"You know, circulation can actually take a boost, going from cold to hot. With the cold the flow is directed inward, with the hot it's directed outward, and it makes circulation move like an accordion." She moves her hands, mimicking the movement of the instrument.

"Where does the hot water come in?"

"My suite. My hot tub."

I stand there, watch a few more people jump in until I'm in the front of the line. Summer tugs on my ears. "Looks like you're up."

"Oh, I'm up all right. I've been up since I saw you in that costume."

I glance at her and her eyes light, her bottom lip between her teeth, the look so adorable and sexy my pulse jumps. It's clear that she loves when I say things like that to her. She loves being the center of my attention. I guess I'm honest enough to admit I like being the center of her attention, too. And in bed, when she worships my cock, fuck, a guy could get used to something like that.

I wave to the kids, who are all cheering me on. "Want to see a donkey do a cartwheel into the water?" I ask, and they laugh. I run forward—the snow-packed surface of the ice isn't too slippery—and demonstrate the world's worst cartwheel as I hurtle myself into the frigid water. Jesus H. Christ. It's cold. I clamp my mouth shut before I shout a string of obscenities. There are children nearby, after all. The cold water sinks into the suit as I dunk. I swim back to shore, find my footing and stand, lifting my arms for more cheers, despite my frozen balls.

From the center of the pond, Summer is laughing, clapping and jumping up and down as I drag myself out of the water, and my pounding heart crashes a little harder against my chest. I love that look on her face, love seeing her so revealing with her emotions like that. I wave my hand for her, and she waves back before letting out a little squeal and cannon-balling into the water. The splash shoots up into the air.

When she comes up the kids are laughing. She swims to shore and runs past me, fast. I catch up with her at a booth nearby where volunteers are handing out blankets. She's laughing and shivering while we warm up as best we can. "Ohmigod, Tate."

"I guess you're rethinking the brilliance of this idea, huh?"

"No, it was fun, and the kids loved you." We hurry

back into the hotel. "I need to change," she says, her teeth clattering.

We both collect our clothes and disappear into our changing rooms, where I grab a towel and wipe myself down after shedding the wet costume. I leave it in the bin where other costumes have been discarded—to be picked up later by the shop associated with the event—and meet Summer in the lobby again. She runs to me, slides her arms around my waist and hugs me.

"I want your heat," she says, laughing, and I snake my arms around her, loving the way she's clinging to me just a little too much.

"Come on, let's get you home."

Home?

Well, technically the penthouse suite isn't her home. It's my grandfather's.

"We need to warm up," she says.

I inch back, grab her coat zipper and pull it to her neck. From her pocket I pull out her hat and mitts and help her put them on. Her entire body is shaking.

"Should we stay for the prizes?" she asks.

"No, I need to get you inside and get you warm."

"I put down my name and room number, so they'll call if we win anything."

"I don't care about the prizes. I only care about you."

But I can't care about her. I barely know her. And all I've done is lie to her. I also know that while we're here together, I can't stay away.

CHAPTER ELEVEN

Summer

I PUT THE key card in my door, and Tate ushers us in. "Come on, let's get out of these wet clothes." He herds me into the bathroom, and that gives me pause. The corner penthouse suite is huge, with numerous rooms leading off the main room. How did he know exactly where to go? Has he been in here before? With other women? Jeez, he's probably been in every room in every hotel here. I've seen the way women look at him, the way his coworker watches him when they're behind the bar. Did he have sex with her in the storage room, too?

Easy, Summer.

I shut down my mind, not wanting to give the jealousy taking up residence in my stomach any kind of power. Tate and I are having sex, are exclusive for the week. Nothing more, nothing less. I've been keeping things to myself, so I can't expect to know Tate's business. I considered telling him that I'm a doctor earlier, after he saw me with that boy—would it be a big deal if he knew? He seems like the type of guy who wouldn't be intimidated by it. But then, why risk changing anything between us? It's not a big deal if he doesn't know either…this isn't going to last beyond the week. I just need to keep things simple and enjoy this while I can.

"Then I'll pour us some brandy," he says, his deep raspy voice curling low in my stomach and arousing things in me no other man ever has. How the hell will I ever be able to go back to Manhattan and live a normal life after experiencing this one with Tate? I'm pretty certain he's going to ruin me for other men. Not that I had time for men back home, building my business, working at the clinic several days a week, and taking care of James.

Lacking any sort of modesty, we both peel our clothes from our bodies and drop them onto the marble bathroom floor. Tate looks me over, and his nostrils flare. Dammit, I love it when he gets all carnal and gazes at me with pure adoration.

"I want my cock inside you again, Summer. But first I need to warm you up in the hot tub." I nod, and a little jolt of pleasure goes through me at the protectiveness he directs my way. I've always been an independent woman—had to be—and I have to say, I kind of like it when this strong, alpha man takes care of me.

"I haven't tried it out yet."

"Why not?"

"I've kind of been…ah, preoccupied," I say, and he laughs.

He grabs a big, fluffy towel and wraps me in it, then scoops me up into his arms like I weigh nothing more than the towel I'm wrapped in. I slide my arms around him, unable to get close enough. He walks to the bar, sets me down and turns over two brand-new glasses. He fills them both and hands them to me. I follow him to the patio door. The latch sticks, so you have to wiggle it just right, something I learned the first time I went to check out the hot tub. I'm about to tell him there's a trick to opening it, but stop when he easily opens the door, like he's done it a million times before. Which of course, he probably has.

Cut it out, Summer.

"This is going to be cold for a second," he warns, and then gives me a wink. "But it's so worth it." He slides the door open, and an angry gust of wind whips through the suite. "Wait here for a second." Stark naked, he steps outside, and I stare at his beautiful ass as he removes the cover from the hot tub. It has a privacy fence, but on the back side of my corner suite, we're facing mountain terrain. The only one he's going to flash is nature's animals. I chuckle but have no idea why I find that so funny. Maybe I'm just giddy because I'm having the time of my life with this man.

He slides the door back open and takes the drinks from me. He sets them in the drink holders then takes my hand. "Careful, the deck is a bit slippery." Strong arms hold me as I walk outside, and I'm grateful. I so do not need to do a face-plant in front of him—with only a towel on. I release the knot holding the cotton together and toss it over one of the Adirondack chairs before I climb into the tub. Warm heat seeps into my bones, pushing back the cold.

"This is heavenly," I murmur, and let my head fall back onto the cushioned rest.

Tate climbs in beside me, and I slowly turn my head to see his beautiful body before he submerges. "Now, this is more like it," he says, then moves closer to me. "Thank you."

My heart misses a little beat at the sincerity in his tone. "For what?"

"I'm glad you made me do the plunge. It was for a good cause and the kids really seemed to enjoy it. My granddad would have liked that. He's geriatric, so…" he says, and lets his words fall off.

I think of my patient James Carson and smile. He would have liked it, too. I can't wait to tell him all about it when I return. I know it will bring a smile to his face to know I had a great time. Of course, I'll probably leave out the part where I slept with the donkey.

Tate hands me the brandy, and I take a sip. The amber liquid burns down my throat and relaxes me even more. I gaze at the rock-hard, handsome man next to me, and admire his new haircut. He now has a young, professional look about him. In fact, he resembles James when he was younger. I think back to the old pictures James showed me. His hair was always short, clean-cut, with a suit that fit him to perfection. I grin when I think about the Polaroid he used to take a selfie of us during one of my visits.

Tate puts his hand on my thigh, and when a soft kiss lands on my forehead, my thoughts shift.

"Warm?" he asks.

"Very." I close my hand over his and our fingers automatically link together, like we've held hands for years.

"Have you signed me up for anything else I should know about?" he asks, his mood as mellow as mine.

"As a matter of fact, I have." I take another sip of brandy as he shifts and brushes his thumb over my temple, pushing my hair back.

"Are you going to tell me?" he asks quietly.

"Not right now," I say, and stretch out, the warm water making me sleepy…aroused.

"I'm an expert negotiator, you know. I can probably find a way to make you talk." His hand slides up my thigh, and slips between my legs. They instantly fall open for him. I swear to God, the man could do anything he wants to me right about now, and I'd happily let him.

"Toboggan races?"

"No, but that sounds like fun," I say, and move in my seat, trying to force him to touch me.

"Chili cook-off?"

"No, I'm not a great cook, but I like the idea of eating the chili."

"Speed skating?"

"No," I say, my breath coming a bit faster. "Tate…" I murmur as he toys with me.

"Tell me, Summer, and I'll give you what you want."

"You don't play fair."

"All is fair in love and war, right?"

My lids open, take in the strained look on his face. Why do I get the feeling that statement is about something else entirely? He strokes my clit, and my thoughts fall off.

"You want more of this?" he asks.

"Yes, please…"

"Then I suggest you tell me what you have planned for me."

"If you really want to know, I was going to throw a blanket and pillow onto the floor in front of the fire and stretch out on it, stomach down."

"Shit."

"The pillow of course will go under my hips, so I can open my body to you."

He rewards me with a caress to my clit.

"Mmm," I moan.

"I love when you make that sound."

"I know," I say, and his chuckle warms me all over.

"So you're a tease, then?" he says, and lightly plucks at my clit.

"Tate…"

"I can tease, too, Summer."

He goes to his knees in front of me, water laps around him as his lips find mine. We kiss, and I revel in the taste of brandy on his tongue. He lifts me a bit, and the wind batters my nipples. They grow hard, and he groans when he gazes at them.

"Put your mouth on me," I plead, and he gives me a look that suggests my openness during sex just might be killing him. He wraps his mouth around my nipple, and my sex clenches, the sensation of hot to cold on my flesh settling deep between my legs. He breaks the kiss, and dips his finger into the brandy. The alcohol pools on his fingertip as he brings it to my nipple. He lets the drop fall and spread over my hard bud, then swirls his fingers around the outer edge of my areola.

"Tate…that feels so good." I let my head fall back, as he bathes my nipple in brandy, then uses the soft blade of his tongue to wipe it away. Dear God the man certainly knows his way around a woman's body.

"Let's go inside. There are things I need to do to you that I can't do out here."

He stands, his cock right there, and I do the only thing I can do. I lean forward and take him into my mouth. He groans as I suck on him, and I go up on one of the steps, the wind whipping over my hot body as I place his cock between my breasts and squeeze them. Tate holds my head and rocks into me, slowly moves his cock between my wet breasts.

With each upward thrust, I lick his crown, and the sensation of him fucking me like this settles deep between my legs.

"I need you inside, Summer," he says, stepping back and lifting me to my feet.

He climbs from the tub first and helps me out. Steam rolls off his body, as he reaches for my towel and wraps it around me. We step inside, and he closes the door, locking the world out and us in, and for a little while longer I want to live in this bubble with him. He grabs one brandy glass and fills it as I head to the bedroom to gather blankets and pillows. I return to find him flicking the switch to the propane fireplace. It goes up in a burst.

My eyes meet his, and warm familiarity moves through me. There is something about our mellow mood, our sleepiness, that wraps around me like a favorite old blanket, and arouses deeper things in me.

"Turn," he says, a soft command as he swirls his finger in the air. I do as he wishes, and stand there for a moment with my back to him. He's upon me without a sound, his body pressing against mine, his erection denting my back as his hands move to my ass. He cups my cheeks, squeezes gently then spreads me. I gasp when he bends his knees and nuzzles the long length of his cock between my cheeks. He slides his hands around my body, and cups my breasts, as my ass cheeks hug the long length of him. I stiffen a little, the position both strange and new to me. Honestly, I've never had anal sex before, never trusted a man with my body like this.

His breath ruffles my hair when he puts his mouth to my ear and whispers. "You are beautiful." Then he's gone from my body, leaving cold where there was once heat, and his departure leaves me aching to my core, a big gaping hole only he can fill.

Oh God, Summer. Be very, very careful with this one.

I take a second to pull myself together. Still not fully composed, I turn to find him picking up the brandy glass. "Come here," he says, and crooks his fingers. I let my gaze drop to his steel erection. I crave him, need him inside me more than I need my next breath. Good God, what have I gotten myself into here?

I step up to him, let the blanket and pillows fall to the floor. His knuckles brush mine, then slowly move up my sides, reintroducing them to my quivering body. There are no hurried fingers this time, no frenzied rush between strangers, just a slow exploration that rocks me to my core. I draw in a quick breath, and it comes out as a shuddery exhale. Never in my life have I felt so open and vulnerable…adored.

I blink, realizing he's asked me a question.

"What?" I ask.

"Why can't I seem to get enough of you?"

Do I dare tell him I feel the same way? That sex has never been like this with any other man before?

"I think it's the mountain air. Makes a person light-headed." It's the only explanation I can come up with.

His soft, barely there chuckle falls over me, and brings on goose bumps. He turns, grabs the glass of brandy and hands it to me. "Drink."

I tip the glass and swallow. When I'm done, he takes the crystal from me and finishes it. We've had sex numerous times, so why does drinking from the same glass seem that much more intimate? He turns to pour another splash into the glass, and I go to my hands and knees, to spread out the blanket and arrange the pillows.

His growl wraps around me, and in that instant, I realize I've offered up my ass to an ass man.

"Summer," he growls.

Still down on all fours, I swallow past a tight throat and say, "Yeah."

"What are you doing?"

"I'm just arranging the pillows," I say, but that's not entirely true. I'm down here on purpose, enticing him because I want him to take me this way. Want to create something special, some lasting memory as I seduce him into marking me the way no other guy ever has.

"Lay down," he instructs, his voice a low, soft command. "On your back. Legs spread."

Relinquishing all control, I do as he says. Honestly, I love when he takes over during sex as much as when he takes care of me outside of the bedroom. He's being as open about his needs as I've been about mine. He stands over me for a minute, his eyes drinking me in. He settles himself on his knees, glass of brandy still in his hand. He dips into it, and then runs his hands over my stomach, between my legs, painting my flesh with the alcohol. Silence ensues as he continues this for a long time, his eyes latched on me, the muscles along his jaw tight. I practically convulse beneath him and his eyes dart to mine. This pull between us is insane.

"Are you on the Pill?" he asks.

"I am."

He turns his attention back to my body, and his wet fingers widen my sex lips. His tongue snakes out, swipes over his bottom lip like he's preparing his mouth for a feast.

Yes.

"I'm clean, Summer," he says, his eyes still latched on my sex, as he lightly pets me. "And I always use a condom."

"Me, too," I say. As a doctor, I have to worry about sexually transmitted diseases, so where is my intelligence now, and why do I trust this guy enough to believe every word coming out of his mouth? It's not like me.

"I want my cum inside you," he says, and eases a finger into me. My breath catches and a sound squeaks out of my throat. "I want you to feel it dripping out of you when we're done." His eyes slowly move back to mine. "Tell me you want that, too?"

"I want that, too," I say honestly.

He backs up, slides out from between my legs. "Roll over." I do as he says. "Pillow beneath your stomach." I adjust the pillow, and the next thing I know he's on his back, pulling me down until my sex is hovering over his mouth. His tongue is murderous against my clit, swirling, striking, hitting its mark like a bull's-eye. His hands slide around, grab hold of my ass and hold me to him. I widen my legs even more, and a little cry gurgles in my throat. He thrusts his tongue into me, and I pant like I've just run a marathon, three times. He groans and sucks and kisses me, dragging his teeth over my clit until I'm a trembling mess.

Heat chases through my body as my climax builds, and I cry out, but for what I'm not sure. As he owns my sex, possesses it, I surrender to the pleasure. My lips part, but no sounds emerge as I come all over his mouth. Heated curses reach my ears, as he continues to lick me, his rough tongue prolonging the pleasure between my legs. After a long time, I stop spasming, and he climbs out from under me.

My nails rake the blanket beneath me, and while I want to touch him, I'm not certain I can get my legs to move. He caresses my back, drags rough fingertips over my spine, and I shake all over. "I'm going to put my cock in you now," he says, his voice low and even, like he's about to order a cup of coffee. Such a strange mood we're both in. The aftereffects of the polar bear plunge? Or something else entirely.

He adjusts the pillow, moving it to my hips, so my ass is in the air. He leans into me, presses kisses to my flesh. I shake beneath him, my sex wet and ready for all he has to offer me. His cock slides between my legs, and he slowly inches into me, dropping his mouth to my shoulder, where he lightly grazes my flesh with his teeth.

He moves in and out of me, and my body vibrates, clenches around his hard length. He falls heavily over me, pinning me beneath him as he continues to glide in and out of me. Moisture breaks out on my body as he moves, strong determined strokes that make me *feel*, in more ways than one. A moment later he shifts positions, like the previous one wasn't letting him get deep enough.

I glance over my shoulder, take in his tight face as he puts another pillow under me, lifting me higher. He goes up on his knees, and when he glides in, he reaches untouched parts of me, and awakens more than just my body.

He runs his finger along my back crevice, his cock moving steadily inside me. He parts me, and presses the tip of his finger into my hot core. I stop breathing, stop thinking as he does things to my body, delicious things that never seemed right before, but with him, they suddenly do.

"I want all of you," he whispers, his words, the way he wants me teasing all my senses.

"Tate…" I cry out.

"Summer," he says, and seeing him like this,

hearing my name on his tongue, pushes me over the precipice. I come hard and fast, a firestorm of need centered between my legs. My vision goes fuzzy around the edges, the room closing in on me. I try to breathe, see past the edges but I'm gone, lost in a haze of lust and Tate.

"Holy fuck," he murmurs as I keep coming and coming, my hot release dripping all over him. He pushes deep, this time the thrusts are for him as he chases his own orgasm, and my sated body quakes, eager for him to fill me when he comes.

He grunts, pants, drives into me so hard and deep, I slide on the floor, my hard nipples chafing on the blanket below.

"Summer," he says again, and his fingers dig into my hips as he goes perfectly still. I hold my breath, turning my head to steal a glance at his face as he splashes high inside me. His muscles are tight, his face beautifully contorted. My eyes travel over him, memorize every sculpted inch of his body. I continue to watch him, lost in the moment.

His eyes open, latch on mine, and the corners of his mouth turns up in a smile. I smile back and his deep rumble reverberates through me as he collapses on my back. He kisses my shoulder, my neck, my hair, but I get the sense he's not done with me.

A moment later he pulls his cock out of me, and I whimper at the loss. Strong arms scoop me up and carry me to the bed. He's inside me again, our bodies tired and lazy, but that doesn't stop us from taking more, everything, from each other. Eventually our eyes close, sleep pulling at us.

I wake to a warm room, and when my eyes open it's still light outside. I glance at the clock, shocked that I slept the afternoon away. Well, mostly. After making love in front of the fire, Tate carried me to this bed, and we spent the next hour or so messing up the sheets.

I stretch like a lazy cat, my body sore but so damn satisfied. I turn to the window and examine the dark clouds. The storm will likely shut down the festivities, keep us all inside.

"Hey," I hear from the doorway, and turn to find Tate leaning against my doorjamb, dressed in nothing but his jeans. I let my gaze move over him, indiscreet about how much I like to look at him.

"Hey yourself," I say, and he walks to my side of the bed. The mattress dips as he sits. He touches my face. "How long have you been watching me?" I ask.

"For a few minutes."

"Creeper much?" I tease.

His soft chuckle curls around me like a warm blanket. "You're beautiful when you sleep."

"Did you get any rest?"

"I did."

"I had no idea how tired I was." He glances at the clock, and his brow furrows. That's when it occurs to me he has a life outside of having sex with me, and probably has to be somewhere. "Do you have to go to work?" I ask.

"No, I'm good. I don't need to go back."

"Oh, then do you have somewhere you have to be?"

That troubled look appears for a brief second, and then his brow is smooth again. "There is only one place I have to be, Summer," he says, and slides his hand under the blanket. He lightly touches my sex. I moan, and it mingles with a grumbling stomach.

He grins. "Hungry?"

I nod. "Starving."

"Do you want to go out to eat or order in?"

"How about we stay in, unless you want—"

He silences me with a soft kiss, even less hurried than earlier. His mouth lingers, our breaths merge. "Oh, I want," he says, as he pulls back and produces his phone. He runs his fingers across it, then sets it on his nightstand. "Food will be here in about thirty minutes."

I race my fingers through his hair. How is it I want this man again? We've been having nonstop sex, and yet I still crave him.

"Can you take me again, Summer?" he asks, his eyes the deepest shade of blue I've ever seen them. He slides a hand under the blankets again, and with the lightest caress, he strokes my clit. "Or are you too sore?"

Never too sore for him, I open my legs. "I'm already wet for you."

He stands, and makes quick work of his pants. Without a word he falls over me, his cock pushing into my body, as his lips find mine. He moans into my mouth and I murmur with him as he penetrates me. We move together, our bodies in sync, the dance of intimate lovers. Needing him closer, I wrap my arms around him, and hang on because what we're doing here, what we did in front of the fire hours ago, has awakened something in me, something I fear there is no coming back from. Something that could destroy me when I leave here in a few days.

CHAPTER TWELVE

Tate

I FLICK THE TV ON, turning to the news station tracking the storm, and then sit cross-legged in front of the fire with Summer. Outside the wind is howling, the festivities shut down for the night. I have nowhere to go, and neither does she. Her friends are at the restaurant bar downstairs, finding their own entertainment as Summer and I hang out in her suite. We're eating the pasta and salads I had delivered, as the flames flicker in the hearth.

My mind travels back to earlier today, when she went down on all fours, offering me her ass. I nearly lost my shit then and there. If I do take her like that, then I'll have been inside her everywhere, claimed and marked every inch of her body. Only problem is, having sex without a condom really screwed me up. Taking all of her just might do me in. Guilt stirs in me. I want all of her, yet I'm lying to her. And I haven't completely abandoned my plan to learn more about her and her situation with Granddad. I know I shouldn't want her this badly, but I can't help it.

"It's kind of cozy in here," she says, her honeyed hair piled high on her head as she digs into her food like she's starving. I suppose she is after all the exertion she's been through. That brings a smile to my face, despite my inner turmoil. I like seeing her all soft and comfortable like this, dressed contentedly in her yoga pants and T-shirt, the marks on her body a sweet reminder of the things we did to each other over the last couple of days.

Thunder rumbles overhead, and I think back to the dog I had as a child. He was terrified of storms. "You're not afraid of thunder and lightning, are you?" I tease.

"No, I actually love it." She grins. "Especially here in the mountains. I've never seen the sky light up quite like this before." Her smile falters and she crinkles her nose. "It's too bad it shut down Winterfest for the night though. I'm sure a lot of people who came here for it will be disappointed."

I take in her frown, the sincerity in her eyes. Summer Love cares deeply about others, of that I'm certain. "Let's hope they're making the best of it, like we are," I say.

She twirls her pasta and puts it into her mouth. "This is delicious, Tate." She glances at me, her brown eyes sated and sleepy. "How did you know pasta was my favorite?"

"Carbs," I say as I stab my fork into a big meat-ball. "You can't go wrong, right?"

She shakes the arm sporting her Fitbit. "Oh, you can go wrong," she says with a grin. "I'm going to have to double my steps after this."

"I told you, you're perfect. But if you want to work off the calories, I can think of better ways." Thunder rumbles again and the lights dim for a moment. The TV flickers off and I leave it that way. "I had a dog growing up. He used to hide under the bed when it stormed," I say, guiding the conversation to a more personal level.

"Poor thing." She breaks a meatball in half, and it hovers over her mouth when she asks, "What was his name?"

"Arlo."

She laughs. "What a cute name for a dog."

"Dad named him after his grandfather. Did you have any pets growing up?" I slide a forkful of pasta into my mouth and lean back against the sofa to stretch my legs out.

"No, we weren't allowed pets where I lived. I would have loved to have one though."

I tap the floor, and she shimmies back to join me. Lightning zigzags across the sky, and with the floor-to-ceiling glass windows on two sides of the suite, we have perfect spot to enjoy the storm as we ride it out.

"Let me guess, cat person," I say.

I reach out, wipe the sauce away from her chin. "Nope," she says.

I put my finger into my mouth. "You're kind of a messy eater."

"I am not," she says, and grabs a napkin.

"You snore, too."

She whacks me and I laugh. "Dog person?"

"Nope."

"Please don't tell me a guinea pig or anything like that." I feign a shiver. "Those things always freaked me out a little."

"You don't strike me as the kind of guy who freaks over anything." She shakes her head, and a few strands of hair fall to her neckline. "And no, not a guinea pig person."

A smile plays on her lips. She's being coy with me. "What then?"

"I'm partial to donkeys," she says, and bursts out laughing.

"I'm going to have to pay you back for making me wear that."

"Come on, the kids loved it. You were adorable," she says, and leans into me to place a soft kiss on my mouth. She pulls back and reaches for her wine. She takes a small sip and hands the glass to me. I drain the sweet wine, then grab the bottle to refill it.

"So you weren't allowed to have pets in your Brooklyn apartment," I say, curious to know more, for many reasons.

She angles her head, worry lingering behind those astute eyes as they move over my face. "How do you know where I grew up?"

"You told me." I tap my head. "I don't forget anything."

She nods. "As a bartender I supposed that's a good trait to have. You can remember people's problems when they come back in."

"Do you want to tell me your problems, Summer?"

She smiles softly. "Vacations aren't for talking about problems. Vacations are for fun and relaxation."

"And sex. Don't forget sex," I say.

Her cheeks turn a pretty shade of pink. "Lots and lots of sex."

I laugh. "Any brothers or sisters?" I ask.

"No, it was just my dad and me growing up. How about you?"

Acid punches into my throat as I think back to the day Mom walked away from me. So we were both raised by our dads. "Only child, too."

"What?" she asks, and puts her hand on mine, obviously picking up on my tension.

"I...uh...always wanted siblings though." That's not a lie. It was a lonely existence in the big mansion with no other kids. I get that I had it good, and I hate to lament on that when others had it way worse.

"Me, too."

"You didn't have a mom?" I ask.

Her chest expands as she draws in a fast breath, and there is a new kind of sadness about her. "Mom died due to complications after my birth."

Shit, I hadn't expected that. "I'm so sorry."

She toys with her noodles, running her fork through them, almost absentmindedly, like her thoughts are a million miles away. "I don't usually talk about this, Tate."

"Bartender," I say, and lean in to give her a little nudge. "Good listener, remember. We have a confidentiality oath."

She rolls her eyes, goes quiet for a moment, then begins, "It's just… I'm sorry I never got to know her." Her shoulders touch her ears, and then she relaxes again. "According to Dad she was an amazing woman."

"If you're anything like her, I can believe that." She forces a smile and puts her plate down beside her. I hand her the wine. She takes a sip, and leans into me, using my body for support. "It was just your dad raising you, and he was a construction worker?"

"You're right, you don't forget anything, and yes, it was just Dad and me. He never remarried. He said he couldn't. Mom was the love of his life." She smiles up at me. "It's sad, but it's so sweet, too." I go quiet as she opens up to me, telling me something painful and private. "People aren't like that anymore. Marriages are way more disposable today."

"You're right. After Mom left us, my father had dozens of women come and go. He's off in Bali on his honeymoon with his fourth wife. She's not much older than you." Why am I telling her this? I must be losing my fucking mind. I never open up, to anyone. Not even my college buddies that I still keep in touch with. But the truth is, her opening up to me makes me want to be honest with her. Out of guilt, or something deeper? Either way, it feels good to get that off my chest.

"Oh, Tate. I'm sorry. That can't be easy."

"I'm fine with it, I guess. I want him to be happy, you know." And protected from gold diggers, too. Though, I was too far away to intervene when he started dating wife number four. I set my plate aside and put my arm around her. We go quiet for a moment, lost in thought. I curl her hair around my finger, and she snuggles in closer. Who knew that outside of our compatibility in the bedroom, we'd have something else in common.

"Neither of us had a mom growing up," she says quietly, her thoughts obviously on the same track as mine. "Tate."

"Yeah."

"I'm sorry your mom left you." She puts a comforting hand on my thigh and gives a squeeze.

"It's okay."

"Do you have any other family members?"

"I have some aunts, uncles and cousins. But I'm really close to my granddad," I say. "He's a good man. The best. He was always there for me, for all his grandchildren, actually." I pinch the bridge of my nose. "He's not well. I can't even imagine the void I'm going to have in my life when he's gone."

"I'm sorry." A pause and then she asked, "How old were you when your mom left?"

My breath hitches when my mind rewinds to the day she stood in the doorway with her suitcase. She smiled at me, told me to be a good boy, and just like that she left, never to be heard from again. "Six. Old enough to understand I didn't matter to her."

"Damn." She leans into me. "You matter, Tate. This is on her, not you, but believe me, I get how we blame ourselves." I'm about to ask what she blames herself for when she says, "For as long as I can remember, I always wanted to make something of myself, get a good education, a high-paying job and become a responsible member of society."

"Yeah?"

"My dream was to move Dad from our Brooklyn apartment to a luxurious home in Manhattan." She gives me a wobbly smile. "I think he would have liked that. Would have been so proud to see me succeed in life."

"And?" I ask, encouraging her to elaborate. Her throat makes a choking little sound, and I look at her. My heart squeezes at the sadness on her face, the water pooling in her eyes. Goddammit, these memories are hard on her. I feel like a prick for prying, but what choice do I have? I'm so close to getting some real answers, and I still feel protective of Granddad. "He died of a heart attack before I could ever make that happen. I wasn't even with him at the time, couldn't do anything to help him." She chokes on a sob, and I run my hand up and down her arm.

"So you wanted a mansion for your dad," I say, a statement, not a question, as I try to digest everything she's telling me.

"Not a mansion, not really." She puts her fingers into the corners of her eyes, and squeezes her lids shut. "My whole life he worked hard to provide for me, to give me everything he could, but I didn't need 'everything,' I only needed him. And believe me, he was there for me." She rubs her nose. "Every Saturday he took me out for snow cones, spent quality time with me. I didn't really need anything more than that from him, but he thought I needed things, you know. I guess it was his way of trying to be both the mom and the dad."

"That couldn't have been easy." At least I had nannies and servants. Not that I can tell her any of that, and I suddenly feel so shitty about keeping secrets from her. Because she's wide-open.

"And..." she begins, but her voice trails off.

"What?"

She averts her gaze, stretches her legs out. "Maybe I said too much already."

"Go ahead, Summer. Bend the local bartender's ear."

A long pause and then, "Is it strange that I feel survivor's guilt? That my mom died because of me? That Dad spent an existence alone, because of me?"

Jesus Christ. "It's not like that. You have to know that."

"I know." She taps her head. "You can beat that into my brain all you want, but it doesn't change the fact that in my heart I feel that way. Just like I can tell you it wasn't your fault for your mother leaving, but you're never going to believe that."

She's right. I do blame myself. I wasn't enough for her.

Would I be enough for Summer?

She touches my face, her hand lingers on my cheek, like she needs the contact. I get that, I totally do because I can't stop touching her either. "I know it's crazy, but…"

"It's not crazy," I say, and close my hand over hers. I give it a kiss, and bring it to my lap.

"I guess that's why I wanted to do so much for my father. To make up for what I'd taken from him and his lonely existence."

So, she's conning my grandfather to make up for some misguided belief that she owes her father? Doing all the wrong things for all the right reasons? Which I'm having a hard time even wrapping my brain around now.

"You're wrong, you know," I say.

"Wrong?"

"Your father didn't have a lonely existence. He had you, and from what you're telling me, you were the world to him and he wouldn't have changed a thing."

"My father never said it, but there were hints of it," she says so quietly I have to strain my ears to hear her.

"Hints of what?"

"That during labor it came down to the baby or my mom. Mom chose me."

I hug her tighter, and her arms go around me. "And he died before you could become a millionaire and buy him a big home."

"I didn't really need a million dollars," she says, and then laughs, but it holds no humor. "I don't even like rich people."

What? Seriously? "That's kind of a blanket statement, don't you think?"

"Yeah, I suppose," she says, and then drifts off like her mind is elsewhere. What is going through that pretty head of hers?

"You must like the guy who sent you here."

"He's different."

"Different how?"

"He's...nice."

"You think most rich people aren't nice?"

She shrugs. "I'm sure some are, I've just happened to meet many who aren't." She lets out a sigh. "When I was a girl, there were these self-entitled boys. They were bullies and used to tease me, throw things at me, and...well, let's just say they thought they could get away with anything, and they usually could."

"Fuckers," I say under my breath, anger burning through me. "They threw things at you?" I look her over, to check for scars. "Where do they live? I'll pay them a visit."

She chuckles. "I can fight my own battles today, Tate."

"I know," I say. Summer is proving to be a strong, independent woman, yet everything in me wants to protect her. "Did they hurt you?" I ask quietly.

"Yes."

That one simple word, so soft, so low, so full of raw pain, rips through me. "Summer," I whisper, my stomach clenching so hard I feel sick. "What did they do?"

"I was the poor kid, you know, and when we reached high school, one of the boys said he liked me." She shakes her head. "I was so stupid to think a guy like that would ever go for a girl like me."

"A girl like you?"

Her throat gurgles. "From the wrong side of the tracks. But I believed it." She pinches her eyes shut and gives a shake of her head, her fine hairs falling over her shoulders. "Oh, did I ever believe it."

She shifts in my arms, and lays her head on my lap. I smooth my hand over her hair and tuck it behind her ears. "He invited me to his house one day."

"Did you go?"

"Yes. But when I passed beneath a window, I could hear him and his friends inside talking."

"About you?"

She sniffs, and her voice is low when she says, "They were talking about the things they were going to do to me." Her voice cracks. "Really awful things, Tate. They were going to take turns."

"Summer, I'm so sorry," I say, the words tight in my throat.

"I ran though, before they could touch me or hurt me."

I let loose a slow breath. "Thank fuck."

"He lied to me, tricked me into thinking he was something he wasn't."

I swallow. Hard. Guilt niggling at me. No wonder she doesn't trust privileged guys. When it comes right down to it, I'm lying to her, too, tricking her into thinking I'm someone else. Is that why she thinks she's not the marrying type, because they did that to her? That guys only want one thing from her?

"You were young. You thought you could trust him and it wasn't your fault you couldn't, Summer."

"I never told anyone that story, Tate. Back when it happened, I was too embarrassed."

"Hey, you have nothing to be embarrassed about. That was on them, not you."

"I know that now, but it took me a long time to realize that. I have no idea if they planned to go through with what they were saying, but it was wrong either way… I'm not even sure why I'm telling you." She gives a small sigh, her voice low and tired. "Must be the bartender in you that's able to drag the stories out of people."

"I know they never put their hands on you, but they still hurt you. I'm sorry they were such assholes, and they should be held accountable for their actions," I say, the lawyer in me coming out. I want to tell her she should have called the cops, but I don't. Going through that was hard enough on her.

"It was shortly after that I went to Boston, putting it all behind me."

As the storm pummels the mountains, Summer's breathing changes, becomes softer and slower as she falls asleep on my lap. My heart pounds against my chest, her stories playing over and over in my head. How could this sweet, tortured girl from Brooklyn be the same girl who's conning my grandfather?

CHAPTER THIRTEEN

Summer

I WAKE UP in bed alone, and unease moves through me. I go still, and listen for noises in the main room, but when I hear only the flames in the hearth, I berate myself. No wonder he left. Last night things became personal, too personal. Why the hell did I open up to Tate like that? This is just an affair. A sex-only weeklong affair, where emotions have no part. Tate didn't need to know about my father or mother or what those stupid boys did to me. I crossed a line, didn't follow the rules of a one-night, or rather one-week, stand, and I don't blame Tate for leaving. This wasn't what he signed up for. Although I do have to say, I liked the insight into him, learning more about his childhood. He doesn't want my pity, just like I don't want his, but when he told me about his mom leaving, my heart ached for the six-year-old boy still in him.

I put my arm over my forehead and stare out the window beside me. The storm might have passed, but deep in my gut, there is still one going on. Maybe I should be happy that he left, end this affair before I get in too deep. Oh, how I wish it were that easy. A noise at the door draws my attention and I go up on my elbows, my hair a tumbling mess over my face. I shake it free and zero in on Tate as he reaches above his head to stretch his body.

My eyes widen. "I thought you were…"

"Thought I was what?" He arches a brow, and my gaze rakes over him. He looks like sex in jeans as he watches me, his bare feet crossed.

I shrug. "Gone, I guess." He gives me a puzzled look, and I hurry out with an explanation. "Tate, about last night. This is an affair and I shouldn't have told you any of those things. I get it if you want to leave."

"I don't want to leave."

A little thrill goes through me. "You don't?"

"No." He points to the window. "The storm passed, and it's time for payback."

I look at the man who has been doing the most glorious things to my body, and there is a change in him. I can't quite figure out what it is, but his mood is different. "Payback?" I ask, not sure what he's getting at.

"Yeah. For the donkey costume. I told you I was going to pay you back for that."

He has a mischievous grin on his face, and I can't help but admit I'm intrigued. I sit up and the blankets fall from my body. That's when I realize I'm naked.

"Where are my clothes?" I ask, and pull the sheets up to my neck.

He pushes off the door frame. "Why are you covering up?"

"Because I'm naked."

His eyes go dark as he stalks toward me. "Are you forgetting that I've been inside you?"

A shiver moves through my body, igniting my insides. I'll never forget that for the rest of my life, and I'm sure that's going to be a problem. "No," I say. "It's just that I don't normally sleep in the nude."

He gestures to the chair and I see my yoga pants and T-shirt. "You fell asleep on my lap last night, and I undressed you for bed."

"I don't normally sleep in the nude," I repeat.

"When you're with me you do."

I laugh at that. "Oh, is that how the rest of this week is going to play out?" As soon as the words leave my mouth, I realize just how little time I have left here, with him. Sadness seeps under my skin, settles around my heart. God, Summer, what did you go and get yourself in to?

My phone rings in the other room. "I'll get that for you," Tate says.

I grab his arm, a little too aggressively, and he goes still and looks at me. "I'll get it," I say, and jump from the bed. I tug the sheet around myself and hurry to my purse. I pull my ringing phone out and see that it's from my web expert. I've been so distracted with Tate I've barely had time to think about my online hacker. "I have to take this." I dart into the bathroom for privacy and slide my hand across the screen.

"Hi," I say, keeping my voice low.

"Hi. We're still working on things." Dan's voice booms loudly and I'm glad I excused myself for this work call. I still feel bad for lying, but I've already decided it doesn't really matter at this point.

"Is the image down yet?" I ask.

"These hackers are good. A lot of our clients have been hit."

"I know but none of them got the boob job I got," I say, and Dan laughs.

"Anyway, I just wanted to give you an update. We're close. Any day now. Just keep checking the site."

"Thanks, Dan," I say, but hate the thought of checking the site to see my head on a ridiculous body.

I end the call and step back into the other room to find Tate scrolling through his phone. "Everything okay?" His brow arches as he glances up at me.

"Yeah, just some things I needed to deal with back home." I shove my phone in my purse, but feel his eyes burning through me when I reach for a glass of water. "What are our plans for the day?" I ask.

Our plans. Oh, how I like the sound of that.

"First, I'm going to feed you, then we're going to go bungee jumping off the mountain."

I gasp and turn around fast. "Tate, I'm afraid—"

"I'm kidding," he says, stepping toward me, his

knuckles brushing mine. "I know you don't like heights, and I'd never ask you to do something you're uncomfortable doing."

"Thank God."

"There's a game of snowshoe softball going on. I thought we'd check in with your friends, see if they want to play." My heart melts a little.

"That's really sweet."

"I've been keeping you all to myself, and I'm not sure that's fair. I already bought four tickets."

Dammit, I hate how he's putting so much money out for me, but I don't want to insult him and bring that up. "Let me text them." I grab my phone, and shoot off a text. Cara instantly answers that they're both in, and we agree to meet later for the game.

"All set," I say.

"Tonight though," he says, and rubs my nipples through the sheet, "I want you all to myself again."

My body warms. "I want that, too." He gives me a little tap on the ass to get me moving, and I hurry to the bathroom for a quick shower. Tate is fully dressed in his boots and coat when I emerge, and I quickly get myself ready, pulling on the bomber-style jacket I brought with me, and my boots, and we're out the door in less than fifteen minutes.

I breathe in the fresh morning air—there's nothing like a new day after a storm. We go to the café in the center of town, and after we put our order in, he stands.

"I have to run an errand. You okay here for a minute?"

"Sure."

He walks toward the door, pulling his cell phone from his pocket as he does. He goes still for a second like he's reading a message, and then he disappears out the door.

I sip my coffee, and glance around at all the happy vacationers. I have no idea what Tate is up to and when it comes right down to it, it's none of my business. Less than ten minutes later he's back, and he shrugs out of his coat.

"Sorry about that," he says, no explanation.

"Just in time." I look up to see our food has arrived.

I dig into my pancakes and consider his whereabouts. Maybe he was trying to get someone to cover his shift. "Do you work today?"

"No," he says. "I have a couple days off."

"Tate," I say. "I really hope you're not taking time off on my account. I wouldn't want to do anything to jeopardize your job."

He stops eating, and leans toward me. His hand touches my chin. Instead of answering, he drops a soft kiss onto my mouth, one that leaves me breathless and confused when he breaks it. My head is swimming as I refocus on my food. Honest to God that kiss, it felt more emotional than physical. Tate digs into his food, but suddenly I no longer have an appetite. I nibble a bit, and when we're done, Tate pays the bill and we head outside.

"Come on," he says, and captures my hand. He hurries me to the frozen lake, where the game is being held, and I give myself a good hard lecture about what is real and what isn't, when I see my friends picking up their snowshoes. Tate asked my friends to join us because he's been monopolizing my time, not because he wants to get to know me better through my friends, and that kiss, well, I'm just fooling myself into thinking there could be more to us, right?

Stop it, Summer.

"For the record, I've never played snowshoe softball before," I say to Tate.

"That makes two of us, but the money to play goes to a good cause."

My heart misses a beat. Donating like this is so sweet of him.

"Summer," Amber says, and waves me over to where everyone is putting on snowshoes.

"I'm going to break my neck," I whisper to myself, and Tate puts his arm around my back and guides me over. The sounds of a ball hitting a bat cracks the air, and I turn to see the batter warming up.

"This was a great idea," Cara says, moving easily in her snowshoes. She's obviously worn them before, natural athlete that she is.

Tate and I are each handed a pair of snowshoes from the coordinator. "How do you even put these on?" I ask as I drop them in front of myself.

"Sit," Tate demands, and I lower myself onto the

bench. "First, you have to figure out which is left and right." He picks mine up and switches them, as he goes to his knees in front of me and opens up all the straps. I grin at him, liking him in this position, and from the heat in his eyes when they lift to mine, he knows where my mind is going. "Slide your foot in." I do as he says, and he positions the toe of my boot before he tightens the straps. He reaches for the heel, and uses some sort of ratchet to tighten it. "Easy," he says, and fits me with the other.

I glance up to see Cara and Amber grinning at me. Then Amber says something sexual about getting to all the bases and Cara laughs. A whistle is blown, and we're all given positions on the snowy field. The bases are marked with bright orange rubber-covered bags, easy to see in the snow. They put me in outfield, and Tate plays shortstop. Amber is on second base, and Cara is catcher.

The first ball is hit, and I let out a surprised squeal as it comes my way. I run in the shoes, and my feet tangle. Within seconds, I'm facedown in the snow, and Tate is picking me up. His expression is worried as he brushes snow from my cheeks; but then he's grinning when he sees I'm okay.

"Are you hurt?"

"Just my pride."

"Maybe you'll get a prize for best face-plant," he teases, and I scoop up snow and throw it at him. Being with him, in this place, makes me feel like a kid again. He helps me to my feet as the runner moves around the bases and the guy in left field searches for the ball. It's all hilarious really, and I can't help but laugh, my insides warm and happy. My God, when was the last time I was ever this happy?

We all position up again and for the next fifteen minutes we play. Now that I've figured out how to move in snowshoes, I'm doing pretty darn good, and I love how Tate keeps looking over his shoulder to check on me. After three strikes, we come off the field and take our turn hitting the ball. I strike out, naturally, but stand on the sidelines with Cara and Amber as Tate makes it to second base.

I clap, and can only imagine I'm beaming, because Amber elbows me. I turn to her, and my smile fades when I find her eyes narrowed, worry backlighting her eyes as her gaze moves over my face.

"What?" I ask, my heart beating a little faster in my chest.

"You like him."

"Yeah, I like him. I wouldn't be sleeping with him if I didn't like him."

"No, Summer. You like him, like him. It's written all over your face."

"It's not like that," I say, not about to admit it to my friends, since I'm not about to admit it to myself.

"I'm afraid it is." She takes my hand in hers. "He's a bartender at a resort in the Swiss Alps. You're a physician from the US."

"It's just sex," I say, my stomach tight, as I search the field to find Tate watching us carefully. I look him over, take in his expensive-looking boots and coat. He puts his hand on his chest, brushes away the snow. Something niggles in the back of my mind. I reach for it, but can't quite grasp it.

"Are you sure about that?"

"Yes," I lie, even though I know she can see right through it.

"I can see why you're falling for him." Amber follows my gaze to the field, and she expels a heavy breath. "But do you really even know each other?"

He's fun, kind, easy to be with, amazing in bed and so protective of me. But I don't say any of that.

"Does he even know who you are, Summer?"

"He doesn't know I'm a doctor," I say, and glance at her.

She frowns. "You've been lying to him."

"I know."

"We leave here in two days. I don't want to see you going home with a broken heart," she says quietly as she gives my hand a squeeze.

My gaze falls over Tate as he runs the bases, and I know Amber is right. I am falling for him, goddammit. How could I not? As my heart pinches and my throat tightens painfully, I know what I have to do.

"I'll end it tonight," I say under my breath. "Before I get in too deep," I add, fearing that I already have. But before I end this affair, I'm going to gift myself with one more time in his bed. It's not a want, it's a need, and that scares the living hell out of me.

Tate reaches home base, and the crowd goes crazy.

He's breathless when he steps up to us, unaware of our conversation. His knuckles brush mine through my gloves. "Who's up for snow cones?" he asks, and my heart squeezes more. He's right, he doesn't forget anything.

Amber checks the time. "We have a spa appointment," she says. "But that was fun. Thanks, Tate," she says, and loops her arm in Cara's.

As they head off, Tate dips his head. "Everything okay?"

"Yeah, why?"

"You guys looked like you were having a pretty serious conversation." He runs a hand through his hair. "Want to talk about it?"

I take a breath, and let it out slowly. It turns to fog in front of my face as I think about returning home to the States, back to my real world. This is a fantasy. A fun, real-life fantasy, but that's all it is or can ever be. Right? "No, actually I don't. I just want to enjoy this day."

"Okay." He bends and unlatches his snowshoes, and turns to do mine. He holds my arm to balance me as I step out of them.

"Now, what was it you said about snow cones?" I ask.

"I saw a cart going by. Let's go find it," he says, and hands our snowshoes over to the guy collecting them.

Another team makes their way out to the field for a game as I follow Tate, feeling treasured when he puts his arm around me and drags me to him. We follow the winding path leading around the resort, and up ahead Tate finds the cart, a little girl munching happily on her ice as her parents pay. I take in the child's blond curls and get an ache in the center of my chest. The truth is, I always wanted a family of my own but never saw that happening in my future, after my bad track record with men. But with Tate, I feel closer to that dream than before…is that crazy? But even if I wanted a future with him, how could I possibly have it? I can't uproot my life in New York and the practice I've been working so hard to build to be with him.

When we reach the cart, he fishes his wallet from his back pocket, but I stop him.

"This is on me," I say, and take off my mittens. "You got the tickets to the game."

"No," he says firmly. "That's not how it works when you're with me."

I put one hand on my hip and purse my lips. "Are you always this stubborn?"

"Yes."

I roll my eyes. "What is it with the stubborn men in my life?" I say, and he goes stiff beside me, the muscles along his jaw tightening as he clenches.

"What men?"

"I just mean…the guy who lent me his place here. He's a stubborn man. You remind me of him in a lot of ways."

"Yeah?" he says, and turns from me, like he

doesn't want to carry on this conversation. Wait? Does he think James is my boyfriend or something? Amber was kidding about that. Surely he realized.

"What flavor would you like?" the man asks, as he slides the lid open and scoops ice into a white cone cup.

I look over the flavoring bottles. "Blue raspberry."

"Same," Tate says, and I feel a new chill in the air, one that's coming from him.

Tate pays for our treats, and the cart moves on, disappearing around one of the buildings.

I touch his arm to bring his attention back to me. "The man who lent me this place, he's—"

A loud cry cuts my words off, and I turn. The outburst is coming from the little girl standing over her snow cone, a blue mess spreading on the ground. "Mommy, it fell," she wails.

I glance up, but the cart is long gone. Since my own snow cone hasn't been touched, I walk over to her and crouch down. "Here, have mine. I haven't even touched it."

The little girl wipes her face with the back of her mittens. She blinks up at her mom and dad. "Mommy?" she says.

"We can't take yours," the mother says.

"Of course you can." I glance at Tate. "He's pretty good at sharing."

"Are you sure?" the dad asks.

"Positive."

"That's very kind of you. Let me pay for it." The father reaches into his back pocket.

"No need." I hand over the snow cone, and the little girl smiles at me. I stand and go back to Tate. He's staring at me, strained blue eyes moving over my face. He's looked at me in a lot of ways, but never like this. What is going on with him? I'm about to ask but stop when he speaks.

"He's what?" he asks.

For a second I have no idea what he's talking about. "Oh, he's…a friend," I say, not a lie. I do think of James as my friend. "Not a boyfriend, or anything like that."

"Does he know that?"

My back starches, surprised by the question. What a strange thing to ask. "He's fully aware of that, Tate. Believe me."

Heavy lashes fall slowly over his eyes, and he opens his mouth like he wants to say something, but when a horse-and-sleigh comes down the lane we're walking on, his lips pinch tight, and he holds his hand up. The driver stops, and I stand there for a moment, confused. I have no idea what he was going to say, but every instinct warns, it was something serious. I fight the impulse to ask, but I'm not sure I want to know.

CHAPTER FOURTEEN

Summer

IT'S LATE AFTERNOON by the time we finished our sleigh ride tour of the gorgeous town, mountains and quaint shopping district. It was a breathtaking journey, and I'm so glad I got to experience it with Tate, even though he was quiet for the most part. Then again, so was I. I'm not sure what's on his mind, but I do know what's on mine.

"That was a lot of fun," I say to him, and he nods in agreement. "Do you have any other surprises?" I ask.

"I might have one or two," he says.

"Yeah?"

His steps are fast, determined, as we walk the snow-covered path toward my suite, but he turns down the lane leading to his chalet, then casts me a quick glance. "Don't worry, it's something you want," he says, and I catch a flicker of heat in his eyes. I push back the emotions twisting inside me, a storm of need and desire. One more night, and then

I'll make a clean break, get my head on straight before I go home.

We hurry along the path, and he lets us inside. I keep my coat on, my body chilled from being out in the cold for so long. Tate pulls something from his pocket before he shrugs out of his coat. He kicks his boots off, sets whatever he took from his pocket on the mantel and works quickly to start a fire. He turns to me, and holds out his hand.

"Come with me," he says.

I have no idea where he wants to take me, but I remove my boots and blindly follow. He guides me to the bathroom, and sits on the edge of the tub. I stand before him, and he unzips my coat and slides it from my shoulders.

"I want to get you warm."

"I've never showered with a guy before," I admit.

"No?" he asks, but he doesn't seem all that surprised.

"I'm doing lots of firsts with you, Tate."

"Good," he says, and pulls me to him, his strong arms around my waist as he puts his face to my stomach and breathes me in. He's acting strange, different, his touch less physical. No matter how hard I try to fight them down, emotions stir within me, wrap around my damn heart. But I don't say a word, instead I let him undress me. Once I'm naked, he takes off his clothes, turns the shower on and adjusts the spray.

"Tonight you're mine," he says. "All of you. Everywhere."

I tremble as he guides me into the shower, the hot water warming my chilled body. In seconds his hands are on me, touching me all over. His hard cock presses against my back when he turns me and places my hands on the ceramic tile. "Don't move," he commands.

My heart is beating double time as he lathers his hands, and runs them all over me. The smell of his soap fills my senses, and I stand on wobbly legs as he cleans me, skating his big palms over my breasts, stopping to linger on my nipples. His teeth scrape the back of my neck, and I nearly break beneath his touch.

My eyes slip shut and my breathing changes. Everything in his touch is soft, sensual, the harsh sound of his breath in opposition to his tenderness. He slides a hand down my belly, between my legs, cups my mound and just holds me for a moment. Then he rinses the soap from his hand and two stiff fingers are inside me. My body quakes, and I move my hips, needing depth, friction, but he pulls out of me. He brings his fingers to his mouth, and tastes what he's done to me. I whimper, desperate for more, to get his cock inside me…everywhere. I gulp at that thought. Wait, did he mean—

"Turn," he orders.

I push off the wall and face intense eyes, and my heart nearly stalls. His nostrils flare as he hands me the soap. I lather up, and the second I put my hands on his body, his eyes pinch shut. I caress him, palm his hard muscles and take his thick, heavy cock into my hands.

"Fuck," he says, his voice an agonized whisper. "That feels good."

Once I have him entirely soaped, I walk into him, curl my arms around his body, and we back up until we're under the spray. His heart pounds against my cheek, and the fast beat matches mine. The spray washes us clean, and then Tate turns the tap off. He helps me out, and wraps me in a towel before knotting one around his waist.

The fire is blazing by the time we make our way to the front room, and Tate runs the backs of his fingers along my cheek. "I want you right here, like we did that first night." He gestures with a nod. "Why don't you go get some blankets and pillows. I'll pour us a drink." I hurry to the main level bedroom, tug the sheet off the bed and grab some pillows. I find Tate sipping brandy, his cock tenting the towel when I come back.

"Lay them out," he says.

I drop the blankets and go down on all fours. He growls and that's when I realize what he's up to. A little jolt of pleasure goes through me as I take my time, crawling around on the blankets, my ass in the air, wide-open and vulnerable, giving the ass man the show he clearly wants.

He drops to his knees behind me, slides one powerful arm around my stomach and lifts me. My back hits his chest, and he puts the glass in front of me. "Drink," he says.

I take a small sip, and love the way it burns, and warms me from the inside out. Warm hands slide over my breasts, one flattens on my throat and I tilt my head back, until my head is lying against his shoulder. His other hand goes to my sex and he slides a finger in. He swirls it around, and I grow wetter for him.

"I've had you here," he murmurs into my ear. I cry when he pulls his fingers out and runs them over my breasts. "I've had you here." He slides his hand up farther, puts his fingers into my mouth to allow me to taste myself. "And I've had you here," he says, as I suck on his fingers. He pulls out with a plop, and those deft fingers go to my backside. "But I've not had you here," he growls, his hand sliding over my ass. He runs his finger along my crevice.

"No one has had me there," I admit.

"I know."

"How do you—"

"I just do, but I love it when you're honest with me like this."

Guilt weaves its way into my thoughts, and I push them back. I never told Tate the truth about me for a reason, and after tonight, after we part ways, none of it matters. We'll both have erotic memories to draw on, and the truth won't matter. Right?

"I'll always be honest when I'm with you like this, Tate. And right now, I want your cock in my mouth."

"Tonight, I give the orders," he growls in my ear. "Now lie down." I set the glass of brandy down, move away from him and position myself on my back. Tate grabs a pillow and places it under my head. He's on his knees, his hands on his cock, stroking himself, and my throat dries.

"I want you to tell me exactly what you want," I say, gazing up at him.

"Spread your legs."

I surrender to his orders, and he climbs over me. In one quick thrust he's pounding into me. I briefly close my eyes.

"Open your eyes. I want to see you when you come all over my cock. I want you to get it all nice and wet for when I flip you over, and give us what we both want."

My heart pounds double time in my chest as my lids flicker open. My vision goes fuzzy, the only thing I can see is this man, the tightness on his face as he joins our bodies as one. I wrap my legs around him, squeeze my sex around his magnificent length and he growls. Eyes locked, we fuck. Each taking and giving, his wet slick crown gliding easily in and out of me. I've not had anal sex before, and while I should be terrified, I'm not. I want this, need, in some unfathomable way, for him to mark all of me. I haven't known Tate long, but I know enough to understand he'll take care of my body.

His lips close over mine, and our tongues play as he brings me higher and higher, and before I know it, he's pulled another orgasm from me. My fingers curl into the sheets, and I make a whimpering sound as pleasure bursts inside me.

"That's it, Summer. You are so wet and hot, it's killing me."

I touch his face, splay my fingers and he leans into me as I ride out the waves. "I've never come so much in my entire life," I say. "I'm going to miss this."

Instead of telling me he's going to miss it, too, he pulls out of me, and flips me over, his breathing changing, becoming harsher against my skin. "Lift your hips," he orders, and I do as he says. He slides two big pillows under me. "Comfortable?"

"Yes."

He stands and walks to the mantel, grabs a box. He tears into it and produces lubricant.

"You had this planned," I whisper.

He drops down behind me and I can no longer see his face. "Last night, I wanted this. From the way you were crawling around on the floor, it seemed you wanted it, too. But no way would I ever take you like this until we were properly prepared." My throat squeezes at his thoughtfulness. "Do you still want to try this with me, Summer?" He presses his finger between my cheeks, curls it around my opening.

"Yes," I cry out.

A second later cold lubricant is being poured on my ass. "Sorry, it's cold," he says, sounding like he's just eaten a box of nails. "I promise to warm you up."

He slowly, lightly runs his fingers over me, and I

close my eyes to enjoy the sensations. "How do you feel?" he asks.

"Good. Really good."

He inches a finger into me, and I gasp. "Try to relax for me," he whispers, and drops soft openmouthed kisses to my lower back. A tingle goes through me, settles deep between my legs. What we're doing seems so elicit, so deliciously naughty, it arouses me even more. I move against his finger and he laughs.

"In a hurry, are we?" he teases, but behind his words, I hear the urgency. He wants to mark me like this as much as I want to be marked.

"Tate," I whimper, and move some more as he works another finger in, stretching me, preparing me for his girth.

"You want my cock in here?" he asks.

"You know I do," I manage to get out.

"You need me to touch you everywhere, Summer. Brand every part of your body."

His fingers stroke, massage, an urgency in them, but a tenderness, too. Oh God, I'm fighting a losing battle when it comes to this man. I don't answer. Instead I pinch my eyes shut at this emotional journey he's taking me on, and will the tears back.

He falls over me, and every part of my body feels swollen. I catch the tang of his arousal, and breathe him in, wanting it in my lungs and memory for years to come.

"Please…" I say to taunt him, and he gives me an inch. I curl my fingers into the sheets, but then his hands are right there, on top of mine, curling with me like we're in this together—like it's affecting him as much as it is me.

Is that possible?

I exhale a sharp breath, concentrate on relaxing my muscles as he inches in. Pain rips through me, but I honestly don't care. I need this. Need him. Even if it's going to destroy me in so many ways.

"Tate," I murmur into the pillow.

"I've got you," he says, and kisses my neck. "I've got you, Summer."

"I want you." He goes a little deeper and his moan curls around the ache in my chest. I gasp for breath and he goes still, giving me time to catch up. I take a few minutes, and then my body expands to accommodate him, and he's deeper inside me.

"You're perfect," he murmurs, and with slow steady strokes he moves inside me. The sensation is so new to me, yet it's powerfully erotic knowing the pleasure I'm giving him, knowing that we're doing this for the first time together. It heightens everything, and I let out a moan. I glance at him over my shoulder, see the restraint all over his face. It tells me he cares about my comfort and while I appreciate it, I need Tate unleashed.

"Fuck me, Tate," I cry out, and his thrusts grow faster as my body trembles around his cock. I lift my hips for him, and he slides back inside my body. Our groans merge and our hands grip tighter as we push boundaries and take each other to a whole new realm.

"Mine," he says, as our shaking bodies slap together, the noise a beating drum in my head, where my emotions are at war. He slides one hand between my body and the pillow, and there is possession in his touch as he applies pressure to my clit.

"Yes," I shout, my body burning up, spiraling out of control in a way that's almost scary. I revel in the dark depth of his penetration, the way he needs this as much as I do. My body lets go and he rides me through the tremors, never stopping, never letting go of my hand. Honest to God, this is the most intense experience of my life.

"You feel that, Summer? You feel my cock getting big and fat inside you? See what you do to me?"

His dirty words thrill me, instantly heighten my arousal. "Yes," I cry out around a second mind-blowing orgasm. I move, buck and my sex shudders as he slams harder, driving oxygen from my lungs. Need intensifies, vibrates against my quaking nipples, the world outside ceasing to exist as we move together.

"I'm coming," he growls. His body tightens, then goes slack, as he surrenders to the pleasure and fills me with his cum. Each pulse amps up the things I feel for this man, and when he falls over me, I lie beneath him raw, stripped to the bone, spent.

"Holy fuck," he finally says when he gets his breathing under control. He pulls my hair back, kisses my neck, my cheeks. "Shit," he says when he looks at me. I must look pretty dazed right now, stunned even, by the emotional intensity of what just happened. He slowly eases his cock out of me. "Did I hurt you, Summer?"

"No."

"What is it?"

"We need to talk."

He exhales slowly, and rolls off me. "Yeah, we do," he says. "Let me clean you up first."

"No." He stills, and I prepare to tell him this is over, but there is a small part of me that doesn't want to be done. A stupid, hopeful part of me that has visions of grandeur. Maybe Tate could move to the States, and we could have a real relationship. I've never believed in love at first sight before. The doctor in me knows it's a quick release of chemicals such as dopamine that give a fast high, a euphoria, the feeling of falling in love. But my heart is definitely telling me something different. The way he touches me, kisses me, the possessive way he makes love to me…has to mean he cares for me, too, right? But what if it doesn't?

What if he does?

"Summer." He scrubs his chin, his brow furrowed, like he has something to say, too, but I want to go first.

I hold my hand up. I have no idea what words are going to come spilling out, but I have to say something. I open my mouth, but his ringing cell phone abruptly cuts me off.

CHAPTER FIFTEEN

Tate

I GRAB A bottle of beer from the fridge and glance around the busy bar. Summer and I need to talk, of that I'm certain. She was about to tell me something when my cell phone went off. I wasn't going to answer but reached for it anyway, hoping it was Granddad. It wasn't. It was Jaquelin asking me if I could come in because Henry isn't feeling well.

My body is still reeling from that afternoon lovemaking session. Jesus Christ, to think she'd give herself to me like that, put that kind of trust in me. It was the most intense, profound moment of my life, and I'm pretty sure I'm going to have to cash in my man card just thinking that thought.

My heart speeds up when I see Summer and her friends enter and grab a seat near the window. My gaze meets Summer's and she gives me a shaky smile. I look her over, and I swear she has sex written all over her. I'm guessing I do, too.

I have no idea how I'm going to be able to work,

concentrate on anything tonight. I've yet to hear from Granddad, but no way do I believe she's conning him. She's full of humanity and compassion and no way could she do something like that. Unless she's conning me, too, but I don't—can't—believe it for a second. Summer and Granddad must have some sort of business arrangement. It's all I can come up with.

But what's she going to think of me when the truth comes out? How can I prove to her I'm one of the good guys, after coming here and crossing a line with her while pretending to be someone else so I could get close to her? I scoff. Crossing a line? Yeah, more like stomped the hell out of that line. Talk about a fucked-up situation.

She's going to hate me.

Bile punches into my throat, and Jaquelin shimmies up beside me. She puts her hands on me, and I try to back away from her unwanted touches.

"When does your girlfriend leave?" she asks, and follows me until I'm pressed against the counter. I lift my hands, not wanting to put them on her, or give her any kind of encouragement.

"What are you doing, Jaquelin?"

"Come on, Tate. Don't be such a douche."

"Douche?"

She pushes her breasts into me, and I shake my head.

"Hey, Jaquelin, sexual harassment works both ways, you know," Luca says, as he slides in beside me, his arms crossed. "He can file a lawsuit."

"What the hell?" Jaquelin says, and turns a venomous glare Luca's way.

"Why don't you leave Tate alone? I think he made it pretty clear he's not into you."

Her face turns beet red, and she glares at us for a minute, and then she storms off into the back room.

I let out a low whistle and turn to Luca. "Thanks."

He shakes his head. "Sometimes my law degree comes in handy."

My brain stalls. "You're a lawyer?"

"Yeah," he says, and goes back to mixing drinks.

I spread my arms. "What are you doing here?"

"I could ask you the same question."

"Shit. How did you know?"

"That case you won last month in Boston. I was following it."

I nod. "Can we keep this between us?"

"Yeah, sure. I figured as much anyway." He gestures with a nod to Summer's table. "By the way, I overheard your girl telling her friends she really likes you." I take a look at Summer, find her watching me in return. "You might want to put a ring on that one," Luca says with a laugh.

That would mean telling her the truth—and she'd never forgive you.

I hand Luca my business card, and he glances at it before he puts it into his pocket.

"I'm looking for an assistant. If you're ever in Manhattan," I say, half my thoughts on him, the other half on Summer and what I'm going to do about this situation we're in.

"What's going on here?" Henry asks, and we turn to him. "You two making a date?"

I take in his pallor, the thin sheen of moisture on his skin. "What are you doing here? Jaquelin called me in because you were sick."

He waves a dismissive hand. "I've worked through worse."

"Henry, really, I think you need to lie down." I exchange a look with Luca, and his dark eyes are narrowed, as worried as mine.

"Come on, let's get you in the back room so you can lie down and I'll arrange for a car to drive you home."

"I'm fine," he says, but then clutches his chest.

"Shit." He falls into my arms, and he's gasping and clawing at his throat.

"Is there a doctor in the house?" Luca yells, to be heard above the crowd.

I seek out Summer, hoping her friend Cara will jump in, but both Summer and Cara come running around the counter.

"Set him down," Summer instructs, and my head is racing, spinning, as she takes control. She looks him over, checks his eyes. "He's having a heart attack," Summer says as she loosens the collar of his shirt.

Cara looks right at me. "Call for an ambulance, ASAP." I back up as Summer and Cara work on Henry, giving him CPR.

"I'm not getting a pulse," Cara says after a moment.

My heart is racing in my chest as I grab my phone, but Jaquelin is back behind the bar, and is already one step ahead of me. As she gives directions, I glance up to see a crowd gathering. I instantly start pushing them back. "Clear out. I'm shutting the bar down. The doctors need space to work."

Doctors?

I usher everyone out of the bar, and go to the front doors to wait for the ambulance. It arrives quickly, they're always on call here at the ski resort.

"This way," I say. "He's having a heart attack but there is a doctor performing CPR. No pulse." I hurry the men into the room, and both Summer and Cara work until the first responders take over. They get him onto a gurney, and hook him up to some type of machine as they get him into the back of the ambulance.

"I'm going with him," I say. I turn to Jaquelin. "Call his wife, tell her to meet us at the hospital."

The first responder nods when I start following him, and I climb into the back of the ambulance then move out of the way so they can do their work. I catch Summer's eyes, note the worry lines on her face, before the door slams shut and the sirens sound. Five minutes later we're at the hospital, and people are running about as they wheel Henry in.

Is Summer a doctor?

I'm not sure, but I can't think about that right now. I need to be here for Henry. I follow the first responders, until a nurse stops me.

"You can't go in there, sir."

"Oh yeah, right," I say, and run a shaky hand through my hair.

"You can have a seat out there." I turn and in comes Marion, Henry's wife. She rushes to me.

"Tate," she says. She either recognizes me from a couple years ago, or Henry filled her in on my ruse. I put my arm around her, and guide her to a chair in the waiting room.

"He's going to be okay," I say. "I know it."

She cries against my chest. "I told him not to go in to work. Stubborn man."

My thoughts travel to my granddad, an equally stubborn man, and grief tears through me at the thought of losing him. I work to pull myself together, and offer Marion my strength. "We were lucky there was a doctor at the bar." *Or two.* "She worked on him until the ambulance arrived."

I hold Marion in my arms, and seconds turn into minutes. We wait quietly, the TV droning in the corner but I ignore it. A few more patients are rushed in, accidents on the ski hill. Time ticks by, and I grab us both coffees from the vending machine. We sip them, and when we reach the bottom of our cups, the doctor finally comes out. I stand, help Marion up, and she leans on me for support.

"How is he?" I ask.

"Unstable angina," he says.

"How bad is it?" Marion asks, and clutches the front of my shirt.

"Tomorrow we'll do a stress test. If he passes that, we'll send him home with nitro, to be taken as needed. If he doesn't, we'll have to do a cardiac cath and check for blockage."

"Can I see him?" Marion asks.

"Of course, he's awake and asking for you."

Marion holds on to me and I guide her down the hall to his room. Her legs give a little when she sees her husband hooked up to so many machines.

"Henry," she says, and rushes to him. I stand back to give them a minute. Henry hugs his wife, and looks my way. "Thanks," he says to me.

I nod, and knowing they need time together, I excuse myself. I go back down the hall, and give the nurse my number so she can keep me updated. Shaken up from the ordeal, I step outside and hail a cab. Since I took off without even putting a coat on, I can't walk back to the resort.

The cab comes. I slide into the back seat, and give directions to Granddad's hotel, hoping to find Summer in her suite. The driver cranks the heat and I'm grateful. As I freeze my nuts off, I pull my phone out, checking for messages, when it rings.

Granddad.

Heart racing, I run my finger across the screen. "Granddad," I say quickly. "You haven't been answering my calls, are you okay?"

"I'm perfectly fine, son."

"Then why haven't you called me back?" I ask,

and pinch the bridge of my nose, impatience thrumming through me.

"I didn't want to ruin your ski trip," he announces, an almost triumphant tone in his voice.

What?

"How did you know?"

"My jet doesn't go anywhere without me knowing, son."

"Shit."

"Did you meet her?" he asks, a new lightness in his voice, a burst of excitement. You'd never know the man was sick, or losing his mind.

"Did I meet who?"

"Summer Love?"

What the fuck is going on?

"You knew she'd be there, I straight up told you, even showed you her picture so you'd know who she was." Ice clinks against a glass, and then I hear Granddad swallow. "What do you think of her? Do you like her?"

What the hell am I supposed to say? Oh yeah, I liked her so much I spent the week fucking her.

"I knew you wouldn't be able to resist her," he says, and lets loose a laugh.

What the hell?

"What are you talking about?"

Granddad laughs some more, and I can hear him slapping his leg, like he always does when he's victorious about something. "Summer is my doctor. Didn't she tell you?"

So, Summer *is* a doctor.

"No." My mind spins out of control and I shut my eyes to let my thoughts catch up. Summer is a doctor. I think about the clues. They were all there, I just hadn't put it together but now everything makes sense. Except for why neither Granddad nor Summer told me.

"I knew you'd go after her. I wasn't kidding when I said I wanted to bring her into the family. I knew you two would be perfect for each other. Do I hear wedding bells, son? And I still plan to sign half the estate over to her, and the other half over to you as my wedding gift. I'm not going to live forever, you know. I'll be going in the ground someday."

It might be sooner than you think.

I work to rein in my anger, reminding myself this is my ninety-year-old granddad, who only has my best interests at heart, but he's gone too far this time. Way too far.

"Why didn't you just tell me about her, see if I might want to go on a date like normal people do, instead of setting up this elaborate story, and forcing me to fly to St. Moritz when I have work to do?"

"Would you have listened to me? Asked her out on a date?"

"Probably not, but—"

"Exactly." He claps his hands loudly and hoots. "Summer wouldn't have let me set her up either, without a little push. Probably too concerned about mixing business and pleasure. I knew that if I wanted you two to get together, I'd have to force you into it. But I also knew it'd all work out in the end. You've fallen for her, I can tell. I can hear it in your voice."

"Granddad," I say slowly. "I might have fallen for her, but now everything is all messed up."

"Then go fix it, James."

The phone clicks dead and I stare straight ahead, not realizing the driver has stopped in front of Ray-dolins.

I stare at the lobby and realize I have two choices here. One, I can leave without her ever knowing who I am, because the last thing I want to do is hurt her with the truth; or two, come clean and find a way to make her mine…forever.

CHAPTER SIXTEEN

Summer

CARA CALLED THE HOSPITAL, got the latest information on Henry, and I'm relieved to know he's going to be okay. What I'm not relieved about is the way Tate found out I'm a doctor. Is he going to hate me for keeping that from him? Or will we just laugh it off? I'm not sure, but I do know we need to talk, which is why I'm heading to the lobby of my hotel, hoping he's back at the bar by now.

The elevator stops and I step out. From across the wide expanse of marble, I catch sight of Tate rushing inside, dressed only in his work shirt, jeans and shoes. He took off so fast with Henry, he had no time to grab his winter gear. Our glances collide, and we hurry toward one another, but suddenly someone else gets to him first.

"Tate? Tate Carson—it *is* you. I knew I recognized you from the bar earlier. Hell of a thing to happen to that man, I hope he's all right." Tate looks at me over the man's shoulders, and his face has gone pale. "How have you been? How is James? Still as sharp as ever at ninety, I bet."

My feet stop moving, and my breath catches in my throat.

Tate Carson...is James's grandson?

Wait, James told me his grandson was also a James, and that he's a powerhouse lawyer. If that's the case, why is he going by Tate, and bartending at the resort? The room spins before my eyes, and I grab the edge of a chair to hold on for the ride.

Since he didn't go by James, or tell me he was a lawyer, there was no way I could've put this together. And yet, the signs were all there. Everything from the way Tate knew his way around my suite, knew how to open the latch, to the way he smoothed his hand over his tie, whether he was wearing one or not. Those things should have tipped me off, and in a sense they did, but it was too ludicrous to think they'd be related. But now, when I really look at him, the resemblance between him and James as a young man is crystal clear.

So why didn't Tate tell me who he was? Was he slumming it with some random girl, having a little fun on his vacation? Is he even on vacation if he's taking shifts at the bar? I am so confused.

He finally excuses himself from the man and stalks toward me. "Summer, it's not what you think," he says quickly.

I shake my head. Honestly, I have no idea what to think.

"I never knew you were my grandfather's doctor when I came here looking for you."

I falter a little at that. "You came here looking for me?"

He reaches for me, but I jerk my arm free. "Yes, let me explain—"

My mind trips back. "When you picked me up and spun me that first day, it was me you were really looking for?"

"Yes."

"You…you lied to me?"

He rakes an agitated hand through his hair. "Yeah, but I want to be honest with you. I want to tell—"

"We slept together, Tate. Or is that your real name?"

"It's my name. James is my middle name, and that's what my grandfather calls me, and I know your name is Summer Love—"

My head rears back. "So you knew my last name all along." I shake my head, and strands fall from the clip.

"Yes, but I didn't know you were my granddad's doctor. Granddad showed me this Polaroid of the two of you." He tugs on his hair and takes a few fast breaths. "Look, he set this all up. He was matchmaking. Some weird twisted way of trying to get us together."

A sound gurgles in my throat. "I guess it worked, because yeah, were we ever together." I laugh and it sounds almost manic. "Over and over again." My stomach knots, twists, and I'm pretty sure I'm going to be sick.

He reaches for me again, and I shake my head no. His hand drops and he drives it into his jeans.

"He told me he wanted to sign half his estate over to you. I thought you were conning him. My mother was a gold digger..."

"And you just assumed I was, too. That's great, Tate," I say, doing my best to stay calm, when tears are pressing hard against the backs of my eyes. "And after you met me, you still believed it?"

"I didn't know what to believe, but I had to do what I had to do to protect my grandfather."

"And sleeping with me? That was to protect him? Or was that just an added benefit?" I draw in a shaky breath. "Get a little action from the bad girl gold digger from the wrong side of the tracks. Because that's who you thought I was, right?"

He pounds his forehead. "Yes, no..."

"You're no better than the self-entitled rich boy who lied to me, tricked me into thinking he was something else. Yeah, I'm a real cliché, but maybe that's better than being an asshole." I give a humorless laugh. Why did I go and fall in love with him? "You'd think I would have learned my lesson the first time, but nope."

"None of this is coming out right, Summer."

I blink repeatedly to prevent the tears from spilling. Never in a million years did I think Tate had come here with an agenda that involved me.

"No, I pretty much have it all figured out," I say.

"I'm so sorry, Summer."

"So am I."

He puts his hands in and out of his pockets, and paces. "Why didn't you tell me you were a doctor? I wasn't the only one keeping secrets."

"No, you weren't, and I do apologize for that. But I kept the truth about my career from you because I liked the way you looked at me. Most men are intimidated when I tell them what I do. I wasn't being mean or malicious, Tate. Every other thing I told you was true. I was always honest and open during sex. I planned to tell you after we made love this afternoon. I mean after we *fucked*." He winces at the cruelty in my voice. "But you got called into your fake job."

"It wasn't a fake job."

"So the hotshot lawyer is a bartender now?"

"Why were you going to tell me, Summer?" He moves toward me, but I can't be close to him right now, so I match his steps backward. "Why were you going to tell me this afternoon who you really were?"

"Because I thought we... Never mind, it doesn't matter."

"I wasn't going to sleep with you that first night. I really wasn't. But when you seduced me, you were so sexy and beautiful, it took me to my knees."

"Well, that's good to know. It thrills me that you couldn't resist my body, while you were trying to prove I was a con. That obviously changes everything, and maybe I should get on my knees for you, as a thank-you."

He pinches the bridge of his nose. "Wait, please, none of this is coming out right."

"No, I get it. I really do." I look him straight in the eyes and it takes everything in me not to run to my room and cry. I square my shoulders, collect myself. "Everything between us has been a lie. I get it."

He angles his head, the fine lines around his face tightening when he says, "Not everything, Summer. You know that."

My knees wobble. "I never want to see you again." I turn and walk away, and it takes all my concentration to place one foot in front of the other. I'll be damned if I stumble in front of him. I climb into the elevator and when the doors slide shut, I sink to the floor, a quivering mess of tears and grief as the elevator ascends.

CHAPTER SEVENTEEN

Tate

I PACE GRANDDAD'S STUDY, those astute blue eyes of his burning into my back as I walk around his desk and go to the window, a restless energy inside me that I just can't shake. I scrub my face, the bristle scratches, and I glance down at my wrinkled dress pants and crooked tie. Christ, I'm a fucking mess.

"Stop moping," Granddad says, the ice clinking in his glass as he takes a drink of brandy and then carefully places it back on the coaster.

"I'm not moping." It's been almost two weeks since I've returned home, and I've not heard a word from Summer, not that I expect her to take my calls, or come running to me with open arms. I hurt her, made her feel used, like those bullies from her youth. God, the last thing I ever meant to do was hurt her. She's the kindest, sweetest, most compassionate woman I've ever met. Here I thought women like her no longer existed, and when I finally found one, I did everything wrong. I could be the poster boy for screwed-up good intentions.

"Come have a drink with me."

"I don't want a drink." I look out on Sixty-Fourth Street below, search the crowd hustling down the sidewalk, their coats bundled as snow falls and dusts the ground. Many have boxes and bags as they shop for Christmas, but I'm dreading the holiday. The only one I want to kiss under the mistletoe is the one woman who hates me.

Well done, Tate. Well fucking done.

I step away from the window and stab my hands into my pockets as I walk to the bookshelf. The books bring my mind back to my years at Harvard. I scoff. Summer and I were probably there at the same time, for Christ's sake. If only I had met her then, under different circumstances.

"I'm glad Henry is going to be okay," Granddad says, changing the subject. "Good thing Dr. Love and her friend were there to take care of her," he adds with a laugh.

Okay, so maybe he's not changing the subject at all.

"Yeah, good thing," I agree. A call from the nurse let us know there was no blockage. Henry will go on nitro as needed and after some much-needed rest, he'll go back to work. Personally, I'd like to see him retire, but he actually loves what he does, and he treats us all like family.

Luca called me after I returned home, and he's going to stay on and help Henry until they hire more staff; then he's thinking about taking a trip here. I still have no idea why a man with a law degree is working behind a bar, and when it comes down to it, it's not my business. I just know he jumped in when I needed him, and we hit it off. Upon my request, he emailed his résumé to Helen, and I think he'd be a good fit at my office.

My phone pings and I fish it from my pocket, but disappointment settles in my gut when I see it's a text from one of my old college buddies. I swipe to dismiss it, not in the mood to talk about the upcoming reunion.

"That her?" Granddad asks, even though he knows it's not. He just likes keeping her name on his lips and in my head.

"No," I say.

Granddad coughs, and I eye him. He glares at me. "I'm fine," he says, but I worry about his health so much. I love the man, despite his damn meddling, but I get why he did it. He's been telling me for a long time now that I need to enjoy life more—because it's short. I ignored him, so I guess he figured out a way to *show* me instead. And boy oh boy did he ever show me. At least Summer hasn't totally given up on Granddad. She arranged for in-house care with a colleague, who relayed the message that Summer would return after she'd taken care of some things. She's as pissed at Granddad as she is at me, but deep down she cares greatly about him, and in the end she'll find forgiveness for him.

Deep down she cares about you, too, Tate.

Does that mean she'll ever find a way to forgive me, too? Do I dare hope?

"She's a real looker, isn't she?" He holds up that beloved Polaroid he has of her and smiles at it.

"What were you thinking?" I ask, for the hundredth time. "Why didn't you just introduce us like normal people do?"

"Where's the fun in that, and you know you wouldn't have given her the time of day outside the sack. I know what you're like, son. You've got quite the reputation."

I cringe. Jesus, I am so not about to talk about my bedroom exploits with my grandfather.

"This one's a keeper though."

I tug at my hair as I drop to the arm of the chair across from Granddad. "Yeah, well I screwed that up, didn't I?"

Grandad's head lifts slowly, and one corner of his mouth turns up in a coy grin. "You think it's too late?"

I shake my head and smooth down my tie. "Of course it's too late."

"The man I raised isn't one to give up so easily. Where the hell is he right now?" He laughs and says, "Maybe he froze his balls off in the Alps."

Weary, I say, "I'm still that same man, Granddad, and my balls are just fine." I take a breath, and try not to think about the day I froze them in the polar bear plunge and how Summer warmed them up afterward.

He waves gnarled fingers at me. "Then go get her, already."

"She hates me. Thinks I'm an ass."

"An ass, huh? Then that's where you start."

I glance at Granddad, and he has the sparkle in his eye again. What the hell is he up to now?

"You know what you have to do, son."

I think about that. Honest to God, I've been miserable without Summer. She's the best thing that has ever happened to me, and what I was to her was—an ass.

A total fucking ass.

My brain comes to a resounding halt and I pull myself up to my full six feet. That's it. Grandad is right.

That's where I start.

CHAPTER EIGHTEEN

Summer

IT'S BEEN TWO long, grueling weeks since I returned home from the Swiss Alps. Life is back to normal, but I swear I'll never be normal again. I fell in love with a millionaire, one who was pretending to be something else. Okay, I get that I kept my identity a secret, but that's different, right?

Don't go soft now, Summer. He hurt you.

I push away from my desk and think about something else. I glance at the stack of files that need sorting. Friday afternoons at the clinic always seem to be the busiest time of the week for some reason. No wonder I'm drained by now, as we're about to close up. I guess the elderly want their checkups, so they can go into the weekend worry-free. Unable to help myself, my thoughts roam to James and my heart pinches. He's called a few times but I'm not ready to speak to him after what he did. I'd never leave him high and dry though. My colleague is still caring for him until I'm ready to face him again. I just pray his grandson is nowhere around when I make my house calls.

I spin in my chair, ready to call it a night. I have a good book and a bottle of wine waiting for me when I get home. A sudden pang of loneliness hits. Dammit. How will I ever find my normal again after Tate Carson? I miss him. Goddammit, I love him. Heartache sets my chest on fire and I try to breathe past it, try not to think about all the fun things we did in St. Moritz. Despite myself, a smile tugs at my mouth when I remember the polar bear plunge. I glance at the brown envelope holding Tate's badge for Most Entertaining. They gave it to me upon checkout and for some reason I can't seem to throw the damn thing out.

My mind goes to the rope game we played, the way our bodies touched and teased, to the first night he took me in his chalet. Or rather James's chalet. My lips tingle, remembering his sweet kisses, the mellow mood we were in when we made love in my suite after the hot tub. Warmth moves through me. Was I too hasty in walking away?

Forget him already.

I close my eyes, and memories of the kind, sexy, hot bartender play out like a slide show. He said not everything was a lie, but how can I believe that? Oh, maybe because of the way he touched me, cared for me and worshipped my body. Desire and need like that can't be faked, right? When he took me that final night, he needed to brand me as much as I needed him to do it. How could any of that be a lie?

Have I made a horrible, horrible mistake? Letting past hurts haunt me, lumping Tate in with the likes of those cruel boys. Do I think he was as vicious? No, I don't. More important, do I think he meant to hurt me? Maybe at first, when he thought I was something I wasn't...but later on, after we'd gotten to know each other, no, I don't think he would purposely hurt me.

Should I have given him another chance? When it comes right down to it, he was trying to protect his family, and that's admirable. Can I really hold that against him?

The truth is, Tate fucked up. But so did I. I mislead him about my identity. Is an omission the same as lying? Maybe it is. It certainly might be to the lawyer in him.

I pinch my eyes shut, unsure of my next move. But there is one thing I do know, Tate and I need to have a conversation.

"Oh. My God!" my receptionist shrieks from the other room.

Fearing there's someone in need of medical attention, I bolt from my seat and hurry into the waiting area.

"What?" I ask, when I find her backing away from the window, her jaw slack.

My stomach flips as I follow her gaze. I slap my hand over my mouth, when I see Tate's face pressed against the glass. No wonder he frightened Tamara.

Making of fool of himself, he waves at us, and I

take note of what he's wearing—the same costume I forced him to wear in St. Moritz.

"He's gone crazy," I whisper.

Tamara looks at me and blinks. "You know this guy?"

I nod. "I know him."

"You'd better get him off the street, then, before he gets arrested for loitering."

"I don't think they would, unless we called them," I say, making no move to let him in. "I think we'll let him sweat it out a bit longer."

Tamara eyes me. "What did he do to you anyway?"

"Long story."

Tate walks up to the door and puts his hand on the glass. I stare at him, my heart in my throat. All the love I feel for him wells up inside me when I see the pain in his blue eyes. Tate is hurting as much as I am.

I back away, and Tamara says, "He looks like he's in agony."

"Let him in."

Tamara rushes to the door and opens it. Tate walks in, his presence overwhelming the place, overwhelming me.

He pushes his hoodie off, and his donkey ears flop onto his back. "I'm an ass," he says.

"Yeah, you are." I fold my arms and perch on Tamara's desk.

As tension arcs between Tate and me, Tamara grabs her purse. "I'm heading out early," she says and disappears out the door.

Tate turns and sets the bolt, locking us in. Then his eyes meet mine and my stupid heart wobbles.

"A big fucking ass," he says.

"Not disagreeing."

He exhales slowly as he looks at the floor, and then his eyes slowly lift to mine. "I've never believed in love at first sight," he says. I open my mouth, but he holds his hand up to stop me. "Can I please just get this all out? I've been practicing, and I don't want to screw this up like I did last time."

I hide my smile and nod.

"I think I fell for you when Granddad showed me that Polaroid. Your sweet smile, the light in your eyes. I don't know. All I know is I was drawn to you. Then when I met you, put my hands on your body, well, let's just say that was a total mind fuck. I thought you were a gold digger, Granddad sort of led me to believe that, and I've seen so much of it in my life." A pause and then he confessed, "It's hard for me to trust anyone, Summer."

"I know."

He taps his head and says, "Just so you know, that old man is on the ball, as sharp as ever."

"I know that, too," I say quietly.

"He misses you."

"I miss him."

"Well, anyway. The plan was for me to seduce you. It was messed up from the start, I know. But I thought if you went for me, I could report back to Granddad that you didn't love him and were just using him for his money. But when you opened yourself to me, Summer, so honest and giving, I lost it. I truly lost it. I never meant to cross the line, but after we made love the first time, there was no turning back for me." He takes a small step toward me, gauging me. I don't move so he comes a bit closer.

"There was a part of me that couldn't believe you were a con. After a while, I thought maybe I didn't want to believe it because I wanted you for myself. But that last night in front of my fire, when you put your body and trust in my hands, opened yourself to me completely, I finally had to admit to myself that I was head over heels in love."

A little gasp pushes from my lungs, and he takes a measured step closer, but I hold my hand up and he stops. "You hurt me, Tate. You made me feel small, used, all alone in the world. Like I did when I was a girl."

"I'm sorry, Summer. I never in a million years wanted to make you feel that way. If you'll let me I'll spend the rest of my life worshipping you."

I look down, take my time to sort through the matter, the extent Tate has gone through to get my attention so he could apologize. "I do like the way you worship me."

As if those words were all the encouragement he needed, he steps up to me, opens my legs to stand between them. I glance up at him, take in the scruff on his cheeks. When was the last time he shaved?

"I'm miserable without you, Summer. I can't sleep, I can't eat. I can't work. All I can do is walk through the streets like this, so I can let all of Manhattan know I'm the biggest ass in the world. Please forgive me."

"You're not like those boys from my childhood, Tate. You're admirable, kind, sweet and protective. I apologize for saying you were no better than them, because you are. Your grandfather set you up, and I plan to have words with him about that. But you were doing what you thought you had to do to protect your family. James went about this matchmaking the wrong way, and you went about *everything* the wrong way with me—well, maybe not everything—but I understand why you did what you did."

"I'm in love with you, Summer. Lost in you."

My heart soars, and my throat grows so tight it's hard to speak. "I'm in love with you, too, Tate."

He exhales heavily and I catch mint and coffee on his breath as he cups my face and presses a hungry, needy kiss to my mouth. "Can we start over?"

I nod, and grab a tissue to dab at my eyes.

He holds his hand out. "I'm Tate Carson, my granddad is a sly son of a bitch matchmaker, and he set me up with the most beautiful woman in the world, a woman perfect in every way. A woman I plan to worship from the top of her head to the tips of her toes every single day if she'll let me."

I sniff. "I'm Summer Love. I'm James Carson's

doctor, and that sly old matchmaker is going to get an earful from me, and then a big thank-you."

Tate wraps his arms around me, lifts me clear off the desk and spins me. His lips find mine and he kisses me long and hard, and with such passion and love my heart fills with a kind of joy I've never felt before. Dad would have liked this one. I know he's up there smiling down at us now. Tears slide down my cheek, and when Tate sets me down, I'm light-headed, but I think it's more from the barrage of emotions swirling around my heart.

"Just so you know, Granddad wasn't kidding when he said he wanted to sign over half of his Manhattan estate to you."

I put my hand on his chest. "No, Tate. I can make it on my own in this world. I don't want his money or yours."

"I know that and that is just one of the many things I love about you. But in this case, you have no say. He's doing it as a wedding gift."

I crinkle my nose. "A wedding gift?"

Tate drops to one knee, pulls out a velvet box and opens it to showcases the biggest diamond ring I've ever seen. "I haven't known you for very long, Summer, yet I feel like I've known you my whole life. I love your kindness, your generosity, your humility and compassion. I love everything about you." He grins up at me. "And I love all those things about you more when you're naked for me." That pulls a chuckle from me. "Will you make me the happiest man in the world and marry me?"

As I glance at Tate, one knee on the floor, dressed in that silly costume as he proposes to me, I'm not sure whether to laugh or cry. "No," I say, and Tate falters, the sadness in his eyes like a knife to my heart.

"Summer?"

"I just mean no, not like this. I can't tell our children that you proposed to me in a donkey costume, now can I?"

He lets loose a relieved laugh. "So the answer is yes."

"Yes, Tate. Yes, a million times over."

He slides the ring onto my finger. "And yeah, you can tell this story to the kids, if it'll keep them from making an ass of themselves when they grow up."

"I like your ass." I reach around him and grab a handful of donkey tail.

He touches my chin, his face serious. "Tomorrow night, we'll get dressed up, and I'll take you somewhere nice to celebrate."

"Speaking of clothes, let's get you out of this costume and into something else."

"Shit, I didn't bring clothes."

"That's okay," I say, grabbing a fistful of his costume and dragging him into the examination room. I shut the door, locking the world out and us in. "Because right now, the only thing I want you to get into…is me."

The blue in his eyes deepens, and his nostrils flare.

"Please..." I murmur quietly, as I settle myself on the examination table.

And just like that, Tate Carson, my sexy fiancé, has once again been taken to his knees.

* * * * *

DECADENT

ALEXX ANDRIA

MILLS & BOON

My deepest gratitude and appreciation goes out to Pat and Lori Dodd, for their gracious help (and lovely hosting of our Italian dinner) in building the foundation behind my fictitious winery, Castello di Baroni. Your help and expertise in both the wine industry and the Italian way of life was invaluable in crafting this book. You provided a treasure trove of information that was tactile, tasty and educational that I will never forget.

Any mistakes are my own, and no reflection of the generous information shared.

Thank you so much!

"Inside my soul a treasure is buried.
The key is mine and only mine.
How right you are, you drunken monster!
I know: the truth is in the wine."

("The Unknown Lady")
—Alexander Blok

CHAPTER ONE

Dante

"You came a long way for nothing. As I told your father previously, Castello di Baroni isn't for sale, nor will it ever be." Alessandra Baroni, sole living heir to the centuries-old Tuscan winery, wasn't pleased. But out of courtesy, she sat stiffly through my requested meeting.

"In my experience, everything and everyone has a price," I returned, undeterred. I wouldn't back down. I was leaving Italy with the deed to this historic winery, one way or another.

The green-eyed beauty narrowed her gaze. "Your presumption that my position might change with a face-to-face was a waste of both our time. I am a busy woman, Mr. Donato. I do not have the luxury of idle conversation."

I took my time before saying, "For a winery steeped in tradition and generational heritage...I am surprised a woman is at the head of the business table."

Her eyes flashed but whatever temper flared, she kept reined in. A slow smile followed, which seemed far more dangerous. "Careful, Mr. Donato... one might accuse you of being a misogynist."

He'd been called worse.

Her Italian accent flavored her impeccable English, giving an otherwise sharp rebuke an exotic flair.

I smiled with amusement. Even with the influence of modern thinking, the wine business remained stubbornly patriarchal—particularly in Italy. The majority of wineries privileged enough to earn the right to place a Chianti Classico label on their vintage were controlled by men. That black rooster seal was an exclusive membership with rigid rules.

The fact that Alessandra had managed to find her footing among those in the Good Ol' Boys Club was a feat not lost on me. In another time, I might've enjoyed watching Alessandra square off against the old men, pressing for change, but I didn't have the luxury of such entertainment.

I came for business and a win.

"My father is a stubborn man and he's set his sights on Castello di Baroni, not that I can blame him now that I've made the trip. The property and the working vineyard are exquisite." Much like Alessandra herself. "You should be proud."

"Flattery is a waste of your time, too. We are not selling."

The woman was intractable. I liked it. A flare of excitement started in my gut. It'd been a long time since I'd had a worthy adversary. Boredom had a way of dulling the edge. I'd have to be on my game with Alessandra.

As stunning as she was—green eyes and dark hair always caught my attention—she neither flaunted nor flirted. She simply held her ground with quiet, if not annoyed, confidence.

Definitely a worthy opponent, even if she had no idea that Donatos played to win.

"I'm sure you're aware my family built this very castle you call home," I said, drawing on personal history, showing that I'd done my homework before arriving. I'd always known, in a peripheral manner, that my family's roots were firmly planted in rich Italian soil and that at one time, we'd been premier winemakers before branching off into different fields. Since my father's retirement, he'd been keen to return to his roots.

Thus, his interest in the winemaking business.

Of course, he wanted Castello di Baroni back in the family fold, seeing as this old castle had given birth to our legacy.

If only our ancestors hadn't sold sometime in the seventeenth century.

"Yes, I am aware," Alessandra said, her tone cool. "Many *centuries* ago. Much has happened between these old walls since your family was a part of its existence."

"I'm sure you can understand how my family would feel that it rightfully belongs with the Donato name."

"I do not."

I smiled. "Although I feel it's more than the property is worth, we are prepared to double our original offer." I jotted an exorbitant number on a piece of paper and slid it toward her, chuckling as I said, "My father is *very* keen to have this property back."

Alessandra didn't even look at the offer as she slid the paper back toward me. "And as I already stated, *numerous* times, it is not for sale, no matter the amount you scribble on your little paper," she said, her lip curling with subtle scorn. "Americans think that everything has a price—but what you have forgotten is that some things have no price. They are, indeed, priceless."

I disagreed. "Nothing is priceless. Everything has a price. The question is, how far is one willing to go to find it?"

Her jade eyes darkened as her gaze narrowed. "You are an arrogant man."

"Confident," I corrected with a small smile.

She shrugged. "Semantics. Whereas you self-evaluate and come up with confidence, I see arrogance." Alessandra took a moment to carefully pour a glass of wine from her Riserva vintage. "You see, Mr. Donato, you are not the first businessman to approach Castello di Baroni with an offer to purchase and you won't be the last. We have survived lean years and we have thrived in fat years, but always we prevail. The quality of our wine is unsurpassed. Our wines have graced the tables of royalty and dignitaries. We are not quick to boast but our success speaks for itself. While others might be flattered by your persistence, I am irritated by your refusal to listen. The answer is an *emphatic* no."

I carefully lifted the wineglass to my lips to savor the full-bodied red, rolling it around on my tongue for a brief second before agreeing that the wine was superb. However, I said, "You think highly of your product but perhaps you overestimate its appeal. While Castello di Baroni *may* have been a favorite of the royals for a time, it is my understanding that Antinori Tignanello has been the most recent royal favorite as of late."

She laughed. "You imply that we have fallen out of favor? Nonsense. Our labels remain on the aristocratic preferred list. Truly, is that your big play? To prey upon our vanity?" Alessandra tsked as if disappointed. "I had thought that someone of your business acumen would bring more of a challenge. I see I was wrong." She rose, looking the picture of fire and grace in all of her petite stature. "Please enjoy your glass. Before you leave, perhaps you'd like to visit our gift shop to bring home a lovely bottle for your beloved father as he loves our wine so much."

Alessandra left me in the great hall of the historic castle to attend to business more pressing than mine. Not by accident, I was given a knuckle-biting view of her near-perfect heart-shaped ass as she exited the room. The woman was sharp and cunning, which was an intriguing and welcome surprise.

Clearly, my father had underestimated Alessandra Baroni when he'd sent me to a castle in the middle of Tuscany to retrieve his latest interest.

I took the time to enjoy the wine while I surveyed the rough-hewn yet solid craftsmanship of the great room, silently appreciating that it'd stood the test of time this long.

The financial burden of the castle's and vineyard's upkeep was probably substantial. It didn't seem as if the Baroni family was struggling to keep the lights on. The keep was well-maintained and there didn't seem any overt signs of financial distress, which would explain why Alessandra hadn't blinked an eye at the ridiculous sum of money my father was prepared to offer for this place.

So, if money wasn't the carrot I needed to dangle in front of her…what bait could I use to entice her to take the offer?

I needed to do more research. I'd broken my own cardinal rule: never come to a negotiation without knowing everything about your opponent.

I'd wrongly assumed that I could persuade Alessandra with a little charm and a lot of money.

I rubbed my chin. A man would have to be blind to miss how stunning she was but I saw no ring on her finger. Even the prettiest face and hottest body was no match for a sharp-tongued woman. My interest in being nagged at for the rest of my life was dimmer than a dying bulb, but most men weren't as smart as me. My brothers, for example, had already lost the battle when they'd married, ceding defeat with smiles on their faces. That wasn't going to be my fate. But I did find it interesting that Alessandra remained unspoken for in a country that still observed a definite edge in favor of the men. The battles she must face on an everyday basis…I mused with reluctant fascination.

Which is likely why she shut me down so quickly and without batting an eye. I grinned in spite of my embarrassing fail. Talk about an inglorious smackdown of epic proportions.

No worries. I welcomed the challenge. It'd been a long time since I'd felt useful or needed. My older brother, Luca, had the family business, Donato Inc., well in hand, which left me to trot after him, suffocating in his shadow.

Father had given me this opportunity to bring home something of great personal value to the Donato family and I wouldn't fail.

Alessandra…get ready to see what tangling with the Donato family will get you.

I chuckled as I exited the great hall.

She was going to wish she'd taken the offer.

CHAPTER TWO

Alessandra

THE NERVE OF AMERICANS.

Dante Donato reeked of arrogance like a smoking jacket smelled of cigar smoke. Of all the offers thrown our way to purchase the winery and its operations, none had been as condescending as Donato's.

He thought he could walk into my house, smugly throw down a wad of cash and walk away with my family's legacy as easily as shipping a case of wine.

I smirked at the raw audacity. He had balls, I would give him that.

Handsome as the devil, too. Hair as dark as sin and eyes that sparkled like the ocean after a hard rain, he was built with all the thick swagger of his Italian ancestors but he carried the height of a Viking. Although I stood only to his chest level, he did not intimidate me. I'd faced off with worse than Donato men and I was still here.

It was too bad Dante was such a prick. I think I would have enjoyed him in my bed. It'd been a while since I'd taken a lover and by the looks of him, Dante could satisfy the appetite growling inside me. I sighed with disappointment and a little frustration as I headed for the business office.

In the past I'd invited Como to my bed but I'd stopped when I realized he had difficulties separating feelings from simply satisfying each other's needs.

And we worked together, so that further complicated matters that I didn't need right now. So much was riding on our newest Chianti, Uva Persa, that I didn't have time to entertain distractions of any kind.

Made from *tenerone* grapes, a lost variety that had only recently been brought back from oblivion, lovingly and carefully cultivated from ancient vineyards, Uva Persa was my baby, my triumph, and I couldn't allow anything to stand in the way of my success.

I was funneling every dime I personally had into the launch of this wine but it was much more than simply a new venture. I was taking a huge chance, risking not only my personal finances but also my family's reputation as classic vintners with a name that went back for generations.

Our wines remained under the Chianti Classico label, adhering to the strict criteria that 80 percent of the blend was from Sangiovese grapes—though I was one of the more vocal advocates for expanding the criteria—but sales were static and barely holding steady.

That would all change as soon as I launched Uva Persa.

But innovation came slowly, particularly with the old guard. When I'd first broached the subject of purchasing land to plant the *tenerone* grapes, my father, Sergio, had shut the idea down quickly.

"It's a risk we don't need to take," he'd said, rubbing chopped garlic on his bread before dipping it in the fragrant olive oil. "There's no need. The Classico Riserva remains strong. We should stick to what we know, safer that way. Why take risks when we don't have to?"

"But, Papa, the future is in the lost grapes. Resurrecting the ancient varietals will give us that edge we need in the coming market," I'd insisted, frustrated by my father's lack of vision. "Please, one small investment is all I'm asking for. The Castello di Baroni brand can withstand the hit but we need to make the leap now. I have the opportunity to purchase—"

"No."

"Papa! You are being stubborn and pigheaded! I'm looking toward the future of Castello di Baroni and you're content to live day to day. That's not how to sustain a business in this new market. It's not like it was when you were young. Please trust me in this and let me make the purchase."

My father dusted his hands on the linen napkin, shaking his head, not willing to budge.

We argued for hours but he'd only dug his heels in harder. I wasn't going to convince Sergio Baroni to change his mind, and at the time I couldn't make the purchase without my father's approval.

If it hadn't been for my nonno, I might not have taken the chance.

With my grandfather's help, I'd made that small investment but it'd taken everything I had. If I failed…I not only risked my father's respect after going against his wishes and making a decision he'd been dead set against, but I could lose my seat as Castello di Baroni's CEO.

I swallowed the sudden lump in my throat and smoothed the nervous jitter in my stomach.

Dante had touched on a small truth. Baroni wines hadn't been selected for any recent dinners with heads of state and country, but these things were fluid and at any given moment we could be back in the most prestigious cellars. I tried not to worry that my predictions for our brand had come to fruition, but my fears added to my heightened anxiety. Donato showing up with his frivolous offer was an irritant to my already raw nerves.

I rounded the corner to find Como scowling behind his desk. "Is he gone?" he asked.

I didn't pretend ignorance. "I left him in the great hall. I have no idea if he has left the premises. I have work to do. I cannot spend all my time sparring with an arrogant American."

"Is it true his family built these walls?"

I shrugged. "So he says."

"And why now? Why is he sniffing around right

when we are about to launch our biggest accomplishment? Perhaps he is a spy for another winery."

I laughed at Como's suspicion. "He is no spy. He is an entitled American who feels he can throw money at any problem or challenge. I disabused him of this notion."

"I do not trust him. He has shifty eyes."

I disagreed. Dante's eyes were magnificent—they smoldered with cool heat. The stormy blue was mesmerizing but I didn't share my observation with Como. The last thing I needed was Como getting jealous. "How are we on production?" I asked, going straight to business.

"We are on track," Como said, but he was still grousing about the American. "You don't take this threat seriously. I sense he is not one to give up easily. You should've thrown him from the property to send a stronger message that he is not welcome."

What Como found most threatening was that where Como was long and lanky in build with a strong hawk nose, Dante was built like a soldier, molded with muscle and brawn. Even that designer suit couldn't hide that hard form. I smothered a shiver. I was willing to bet that in bed, Dante was an animal. Just the kind of lover I craved. I returned my attention to Como, snapping my fingers with irritation. "Stay on task, Como. Just because we operate out of a castle does not mean we keep medieval ways. We don't toss the distasteful from the ramparts. We send them on their way with our compliments. Better for business."

Como nodded, grudgingly admitting I was right. "You do your family proud. You are so smart and wise. And beautiful." Como's gaze warmed and I exhaled with a slight shake of my head.

His last comment only cemented my decision to keep things professional between us. Como had been a competent lover but mostly convenient. In spite of ending our sexual relationship more than a year ago, he still held out hope that I would change my mind about wanting more—which I wouldn't—and he followed me like a puppy.

Bad judgment and sexual frustration make for terrible bedfellows. Como's endless unrequited-love sorrow was annoying, but out of deference for our long friendship and business relationship, I tolerated his overtures while avoiding any physical contact.

However, my patience was at its end. I turned to face him, my expression stern. "Como, we are no longer lovers," I reminded him. "We agreed that we were better as friends."

"No, I never agreed," he said with a frown. "You made a decision and expected me to simply fall in line. I understood your reasoning, and with the strain of Uva Persa hanging on your shoulders, I realized it was better to go along with your decision. But soon we launch and the stress will no longer weigh you down, freeing you to see that you and I are a perfect team. I am a patient man and you are worth waiting for."

My stomach knotted, not for the first time, at Como's self-assuredness of his belief, which was wrong on so many levels. I glared with frustration. "You are not patient. You are stubborn."

"You will come around," Como said with a cockiness I found unattractive on him. "No one knows you as I do."

"You do not know me as well as you think if you believe I enjoy being patronized," I said coolly, and Como stiffened at the rebuke. "You are a valuable member of my staff and I appreciate your talents on a business level but do not mistake me. If you continue to pursue this dangerous line of thinking it will not only ruin our friendship but our working relationship, as well."

"You would fire me?" Como asked, surprised.

"If you continued to force my hand."

Como held my gaze as if trying to ascertain whether I was serious or bluffing. If he knew me as well as he claimed, he would know I didn't bluff. The fact that we were having this conversation, after I'd already settled the matter, created no small amount of heartburn. He was right in that Uva Persa was weighing on my shoulders with all the unwieldy grace of an elephant, but the day would never come that I invited Como back into my bed. I never made the same mistake twice.

"No one will ever love you the way I do," Como said, his lips disappearing as his frown deepened into a scowl. "No one will understand your burdens as I do."

Como truly believed his own conviction and because he was a good man, I softened a little. "Perhaps," I conceded for the sake of his ego. "But I am not the woman for you. I would only bring you misery. Please, let us put this tiresome argument to rest and return to what we are truly good at together."

I would never beg but I didn't want to lose Como as a friend or as a trusted business ally. He'd been my right hand for so many years and I didn't want to lose him over something as stupid as misplaced affections.

After a long tense moment, Como jerked a short nod to indicate we could move on and I breathed a secret sigh of relief. Hopefully, this conversation was well and truly done. Moving quickly to business, I tapped the desk, saying, "I need to go over the contracts for the campaign. Would you please have them sent to my office?"

"Of course."

Grateful to be back on course, I left Como and headed for the grounds. I liked to be visible in all areas of production, from the business side to the agricultural. But when I walked the grounds, the fresh air tickling my nose, the cypress trees swaying in the breeze, I felt closest to Enzo.

My twin brother, my touchstone, was the one who'd been enamored with the winemaking business. He'd had so many plans, so many hopes and dreams.

It was Enzo who had first mentioned the legacy of the lost grapes. At the time, I'd listened to him talk about the possibility of resurrecting ancient varietals but it'd seemed a fantasy, something to dream about. Enzo had been sure that it was a possibility and he was going to try to make it happen when he was old enough.

But my brother never got the chance. When he died in an auto accident at sixteen, a part of me died with him. Twins share a bond that is hard to explain.

Enzo would've been a premier winemaker—his love for the business had been unparalleled. I was but Enzo's weak imitation, but I swore to his memory that I would never let Baroni wines fail. They would thrive in his honor.

Uva Persa would be our crowning achievement. Only Nonno knew what I'd been through to cultivate my secret vineyard, and he kept my secret, but the pressure to succeed was nearly crushing me.

Even after carefully selecting the property to grow the *tenerone*—testing the soil, checking for acidity and appropriate climate, tending to the vineyard as it finally yielded fruit—it'd taken three years for the wine to mature and it was finally ready for its debut.

So when Donato came around making offers, what he didn't know was that there was no amount I would ever accept. I would never shame Enzo's dream by selling—much less selling to an American.

Donato would just have to find another winery to purchase for his collection.

Castello di Baroni would *never* be for sale.

CHAPTER THREE

Dante

ALESSANDRA EXPECTED ME to leave the grounds. Given her curt refusal to entertain my substantial offer, it wasn't surprising that she gave me little thought after leaving me in the great hall.

But I wasn't ready to leave.

Maybe I'd play tourist and check out the gift shop. I needed to poke around, get a more accurate idea of what I was dealing with. I couldn't think of a better way to get information than playing the part of a tourist within Castello di Baroni walls.

With a final appreciative glance around the great hall—my father would dig the whole king of the castle vibe the room gave off—I headed for the gift shop.

It was easy enough to find, and I stepped inside with a friendly smile and a disarming disposition for the attractive woman manning the counter. Unlike my brothers, I wasn't one to use the Donato charm to get what I wanted, but I liked to win and I wasn't above using whatever tools I had at my disposal.

"Welcome to Castello di Baroni," she said with a sweet Italian accent and a welcoming smile. "My name is Mia. May I interest you in a sample today?"

"Pleasure to meet you, Mia. I'm Dante. What are you pouring?" I asked, feigning curiosity.

"Well, Dante, you're in for a treat," Mia said, retrieving a small tasting glass. "Today we have a bottle of Castello di Baroni's Chianti Classico. Our wines have been served on royal tables since the seventeenth century."

"That's quite a claim," I said.

"And completely verifiable," she said, eyes sparkling. "But once you taste our wines, you'll understand why Castello di Baroni is a premier choice for discerning palates."

I accepted the glass and swirled the dark burgundy before burying my nose to appreciate the notes rising from the glass. With a short smile, I took a sip. It was good. Not quite as good as the Riserva Alessandra had shared earlier but still quite good. It was easy to see why Castello di Baroni was a solid label.

My father would enjoy having the label in his collection.

But first, I had to bring it home. "Excellent," I said, smiling as I pretended to be in awe of the grounds.

"We offer shipping to anywhere around the world," Mia said, fishing for a sale. "Having a Baroni wine on the table is a guaranteed conversation starter."

"I can imagine," I mused, savoring the wine. I took a moment to peruse the shop, making sure my gaze returned to the large open window with the gorgeous view of the grounds. "Incredible. The history within these walls… I'm overwhelmed by everything."

She nodded, pleased that I was impressed. "Is this your first trip to Italy?"

"Actually, yes," I answered, stretching the truth a bit. I'd been to Italy for business but I'd never played the tourist. Most of my time in Italy had been spent in boardrooms or hotel bars. I'd spent precious little time enjoying the visual treats the country was known for. "I'm so glad I stumbled on this place. It's simply stunning. A working winery with such deep roots…pretty amazing."

Mia was happy to chirp on about her employers' origins, which I eagerly encouraged. The more I knew about my opponent, the better.

"Castello di Baroni has the distinction of being the largest winery in the Chianti Classico area as well as being one of the oldest working wineries in the region. Did you know that the original castle was built in the late thirteen hundreds?"

"Very impressive. All that history…if only these walls could talk, eh?"

Mia giggled. "Much intrigue and bloodshed. The Medicis were frequent guests and where they went, scandal followed."

I laughed along with Mia. "You should put that on the brochure."

"Oh, goodness," she said with a flirty smile. "Alessandra would never do that."

"And who is Alessandra?" I asked, feigning ignorance.

"Alessandra di Baroni. She is the winery's CEO and the only living Baroni heir."

"And does this Alessandra have no sense of adventure? I think playing up the Medici angle would be a sensational tourist trap. You'd sell more wine that way."

"We do things differently here at Castello di Baroni. It's not always about the sale," Mia said, politely chastising me for such a crass suggestion. I probably came off as typically American. I'd done enough traveling throughout Europe to know that Americans were often disdained for our lack of tradition or sense of ritual.

"I agree, the way you're doing things is better. Obviously, when you've been around since the thirteen hundreds, you've got a firm handle on how to succeed." I winked to show that I was capable of listening to subtle cues. She rewarded me with an approving smile. I sensed a deep appreciation for Alessandra, which was interesting. While Alessandra may seem the hardnose, she must truly value her staff as Mia wasn't about to say anything that threw her boss under the bus.

There was no one I would consider loyal in our employ. I had no doubt that any of the executives who sat in the boardroom at Donato Inc. would sell their own grandmother if it meant getting ahead.

That was just the nature of business. I didn't hold it against them, but I wondered what it would be like to be the recipient of Mia's brand of loyalty. A world without fake smiles, ass-kissing and backstabbing as the norm.

Right, like that place existed. Appearances were deceiving. For all I knew sweet Mia could be sleeping with Alessandra's father behind closed doors or embezzling from the company.

"Tell me more about the castle," I prompted, steering the conversation to ground where Mia felt more comfortable. "I find it all so fascinating."

"Oh, it truly is. The castle survived the devastation of World War II without so much as losing a pebble in her foundation, whereas other castles in the area weren't as lucky. Some say the castle is blessed."

"And here I thought castles were supposed to be haunted. Surely there are a few ghosts rattling around the stones. Please don't ruin all my European castle stereotypes."

"Perhaps one or two," she said with a conspiratorial wink. "There is a story about an old grounds-keeper who can be seen walking the vines from time to time, but he seems to be the helpful sort of ghost, not the scary kind."

"No wailing lady in white to be found?" I asked.

"Not that I've heard but you'd have to ask Alessandra. She grew up in the castle and if there's anything ghostly, she'd know."

I let that information sink in for a moment. "Grew up in the castle? Wow, that's not something you hear every day. The only people I've ever heard of living in a castle are the Windsors."

"Well, Windsor Castle is older than Castello di Baroni and impressive as well. Have you been?"

"Not much of a touristy traveler," I admitted. "But I see now that I've been missing out. I think I need to start seeing the world through a different lens, which definitely includes a few castle tours. I'm bound to find at least one with a wailing lady in white, right?"

"The odds are in your favor," she said, laughing. "Actually, you seem like someone who might be interested in a special event the winery holds each year to celebrate the harvest," she said, reaching beneath the counter to produce a five-by-seven invitation printed on thick card stock with gold filigree. "A man of your tastes might find tonight's event worth your while."

The woman was good. Without being obvious, she'd sized me up quickly and determined I had the pocketbook required for such an event.

I accepted the invite, flipping it over to read the details of the black-tie event. "Una Notte Magica," I murmured, and I knew I'd been given an excellent chance to learn more about Alessandra even if she didn't welcome me with open arms. "Will the Baroni family be in attendance? I'd love to meet the people behind such an esteemed winery," I said.

"Oh yes, it's a big event for the family. They take great pride in their annual event. It's a Baroni tradition and they are very approachable, very generous with their time."

Perfect. "Forgive my ignorance but…how does one family run this operation so seamlessly?" I asked, pandering to the woman's pride in her employer. "I'm surprised Castello di Baroni hasn't been snapped up by a corporation by this point."

"Oh no, signor, the Baronis are very close, very dedicated to keeping the business going privately and family operated as it always has been. Tradition is everything to them. They treat their employees like family, unlike those operations owned by bigger entities. We are very proud to be Baroni employees."

Ah, that explained the loyalty.

"That's amazing. American business could take a lesson in Baroni employment retention tenets," I said, playing along. "So, Alessandra is the sole heir? She handles all of this on her own? No other family to help?"

"No, sadly, it is only Alessandra Baroni running things. Enzo, her twin brother, died when he was young, and everything fell to Alessandra. But she has more than risen to the occasion, wouldn't you say?"

"Absolutely," I said, seeming impressed. "She must be a powerhouse. A real modern woman."

The woman giggled. "Oh yes, Alessandra is all that and more. She is bringing Baroni into the future even if her father is a little more reluctant to be so progressive. The wine industry is slow to change but Alessandra is a force of nature. She does not need anyone's approval to make the big decisions. We are all so proud of her and what she's doing."

Realizing she may have said too much, the woman straightened with a quick smile. "I talk of things that are of no interest to you. My apologies, signor."

"Not at all. I love hearing about the winery's history," I said, putting her fears to rest. I'd have to stop giving my younger brother shit for always using the Donato charm to get his way. I had to admit Nico was right, it was efficient. I smiled for Mia's benefit, adding, "Will you be at the event?"

She blushed and shook her head. "Not this time. I have other plans, unfortunately."

"More's the pity," I said, letting the innuendo drop between us before drawing a regretful breath and pocketing the invite. "Do you work on commission?"

Her cheeks pinked a little. "I receive a small bonus for sales," she admitted.

I grinned and tossed down my black Amex card. "Then, I'll need to buy a case of your Riserva. I know my father will go nuts over it."

She flushed with pleasure and nodded as she prepared the paperwork to finish the sale. I had the case shipped to my father with the simple message, "A preview of your newest obsession," and then with a smile left the gift shop with a plan forming.

I needed to get closer to Alessandra and this event tonight was just the venue I needed to make my move.

There were certain things in life that were irrefutable:

1) In spite of the recent spate of flat-earthers

squawking to the contrary, the earth was, in fact, round.

2) No matter race, religious background or gender, everyone had a price.

And finally…

3) Women couldn't resist a Donato in a tuxedo.

I chuckled at my private wisdom and headed for my hotel room.

CHAPTER FOUR

Alessandra

UNA NOTTE MAGICA was an event my family held every year to celebrate a successful harvest. We spent a lot of money to ensure the attendees remembered the Baroni name. It was advertising at its most obscene. I tolerated it because business was more than just making sure your product was superior, it was also about making connections within your community and circle of influence.

It just so happened my circle of influence comprised old white men stuck in their ways, and suffering a night of their condescending snobbery was a waste of my precious time.

However, I wasn't so foolish as to believe that I didn't need their influence, particularly with the launch of Uva Persa around the corner, so I would play the game a bit longer.

My best friend, Sophia Russo, zipped my dress as I held my hair up. "Suck it in," she advised with a laugh as she shrink-wrapped me into the black form-fitting gown. I squeaked a little as the final stretch of zipper found its home and I slowly let out my breath as I turned to face Sophia. Her smile was radiant, if not a little sardonic. She quipped, "I hope you didn't plan to eat tonight because not much else could fit in that dress."

"Of course not, I'm too on edge to eat anyway," I said, turning to put the finishing touches on my makeup. My thoughts should've been on tonight but my brain kept stubbornly throwing Donato into my mental theater, which was a fresh irritant to my already taut nerves. "If Alberico is there and tries to pressure me to dance with him, I'll grind my heel into his insole."

"His family expects you to marry him," Sophia said. "Your pedigrees match up. It's not a terrible idea, you know. He's not ugly and he stands to inherit a sizable fortune. Plus, his family descends from the House of Medici so he has royalty in his blood."

"Well, perhaps if the Italian monarchy hadn't ended in the forties that might be something to crow about. Today, it's simply colorful conversation and it means nothing. Besides, I'm not looking for a man to lend his influence. I've had enough of that nonsense and it's time to make a change."

Sophia sighed, shaking her head. "Always trying to change the world," she said. "Enzo would be proud."

Enzo had been Sophia's one true love. His death had brought Sophia and me closer and we'd been thick as thieves ever since. She was the one I could trust with anything. If things had turned out differently, it might've been Enzo and Sophia making this historic leap into new pastures for Castello di Baroni, but fate had played a cruel game, taking Enzo and leaving me to push for change.

"I hope so," I said, trying not to tear up and ruin my makeup. Enzo was my soft spot. I dabbed at my eyes. "Everything I do, I do with Enzo in mind."

"I know you do but this is your accomplishment," Sophia reminded me. "You push so hard in his memory that you overshadow your own talent. I've seen you do things that I'm not sure Enzo would've been able to handle."

"What do you mean?" I asked. "Enzo loved this business."

"Yes, and he was a dreamer. He loved the romance of the wine industry, not the business side of it. Sometimes I think because we lost him so soon we've idealized him. We can be honest about who he was without diminishing his character."

Enzo's memory was precious. Maybe Sophia was right. I did have a tendency to protect his legacy with a ferocity usually reserved for mothers and their children.

Sophia slipped her hand into mine. "But I do know that he would've been so extra proud of you for everything you've accomplished thus far. You're the reason Castello di Baroni remains top tier, not because the wine sells itself. Even if your father does not see this…I do."

I paused for a minute to gaze at Sophia with love. "You're too good to me, Sophia," I said.

She shook her head. "No, I only speak what I know to be true."

Sophia would never lie to me nor would she fill my head with flattery simply to play to my ego. "I wish Enzo had lived so you could be my true sister instead of simply the sister of my heart."

Sophia's smile warmed with love. "That's all I need." She released my hand and stepped back to give my dress a final perusal with a critical eye. Satisfied, she nodded, proclaiming, "Absolutely exquisite. It simply isn't fair to every man whose heart will explode upon seeing you."

I chuckled, my cheeks heating, but I quickly pointed out, "I'm not the only one who will turn heads. That white dress on you is nearly a crime. Perhaps Alberico will notice you instead of me."

Sophia's white gown was in stark contrast to mine but she wore it with grace and elegance. Whereas I was blessed with an overabundant bosom that made everything I wore nearly obscene, she was lithe and lean like a willow tree.

Sophia blushed, pushing a lock of her burgundy hair behind her ear, pink staining her cheeks. "You are a sweet talker. You're the one who steals the air in the room. No one will notice me the minute they see you."

"Nonsense. You're so beautiful. Enzo is surely smiling down at us both, but you in particular. I am sure he's staring hard enough to leave a bruise."

Sophia's breath caught as her smile deepened with soul-deep longing, and my heart hurt that Sophia would forever reserve that special place for Enzo. She was too young to willingly put herself on the shelf but Sophia was as stubborn as she was beautiful.

If soul mates existed, Enzo had been Sophia's.

But Enzo died so young. It wasn't fair.

Sophia was like a hothouse flower, stunning and fragile. She was incredibly beautiful but she lacked the fire that burned in my belly. Whereas I was loud and determined, she was quiet and kind, preferring a book and a glass of wine over a party. "Your Prince Charming is out there but you're not going to meet him in your sitting room," I playfully admonished. "You have to actually get out there and meet people."

"What am I doing tonight?" she teased. "Is this not going out?"

"Once a year doesn't count," I said. "And none of these old men are anyone I'd want you falling in love with. They are fossils—you need someone with spirit."

She laughed. "Maybe I'd like a fossil. Seems very peaceful. You're the one who craves adventure, not me. We both know that Enzo was wild enough for the both of us."

I pursed my lips. "Enzo would've wanted you to find someone, not pine after him for the rest of your life."

This was a conversation we'd had many times and just as before, Sophia shut me down quickly but sweetly. "We are not playing matchmaker tonight. You need to focus on what's important. Uva Persa is your crowning achievement and you need to make sure nothing stands in the way of its success, which means you need to play nice with the old cronies who run this industry."

Solid advice even if I wanted to argue the point. "Still, you're too young to be closed off like you are. It worries me."

She laughed softly, her brown eyes full of love. "You worry about all the wrong things. I'm happy just the way things are. Why would I want to risk upsetting the balance I have now? Some people are not meant to be paired up and that's okay. I'm happy."

Was I worrying too much over something that wasn't true? "I know how much you loved Enzo..." I said, my voice trailing, not sure why I was pursuing this topic when it wasn't the time or place. Maybe I was nervous and talking about someone else's problems took the focus from mine. Yes, that was it, and it wasn't fair to Sophia to draw the focus unnecessarily. "I'm sorry. You're right. I shouldn't try to force you into anything you're not ready for or interested in."

Again, Donato popped into my head. He would try again, I could feel it. He wasn't the kind of man who gave up easily. He was accustomed to getting his way and losing was a foreign concept to him. His arrogance was the last thing I needed to deal with right now. I double-checked my profile, twisting and turning in the full-length gown, assuring myself that I looked impeccable as befitting my place within Castello di Baroni.

"You're exquisite," Sophia assured me as if privy to

my internal dialogue. I graced her with a grateful smile and knew it was time to leave. I had a small apartment in Siena, the closest city to the family estate, but I also had living quarters inside the manor. Tonight, for expediency, I chose to stay in the manor so our walk downstairs to the grounds was easy, even in heels.

Sophia clutched my arm and inhaled sharply as the grounds came into view. We pulled out all the stops for this event. Catering to an old-world guard, stately elegance was the key. We hired a catering company to transform a section of the grounds into a magical place with fairy lights winding through the cypress trees and a full orchestra playing classics from various Italian composers.

"You always outdo yourself," Sophia said, awed. "Truly magical, my friend."

I smiled, appreciative of her praise, but I was already in work mode. My father broke apart from his cluster of friends to kiss me on both cheeks. "You are a vision," he said, beaming. "Your mother would be proud."

Mama had passed several years ago, leaving me as the sole female in the Baroni family. My father would never remarry but I wished he would so he would have something to focus on other than what I was doing with the business.

I loved him deeply but he was steeped in the old ways and resistant to anything that rocked the boat, which caused friction between us.

Mama had always been the buffer that kept Papa and me from ruining each other with our stubborn natures. I missed her so much. It seemed unfair that our family had suffered so much loss, but I wasn't one to cry about things I couldn't change.

I couldn't help but wonder, if it were Enzo coming to him with the idea of cultivating the lost varietals, would my father have jumped on the idea, calling it innovative and brave? But because it'd been me to make the suggestion, he'd considered the idea brash and foolish.

"Thank you, Papa," I murmured. "Everything came together well for tonight. I'm pleased you're happy."

"Very happy indeed," he said, his barrel chest puffing up with pride. "My daughter knows how to put on a beautiful event."

I smiled through my irritation. I did far more than put on a good party. I was single-handedly dragging Castello di Baroni back into the limelight, but I wasn't going to mention that. As Sophia said, my father liked to believe that Baroni wines sold themselves, that our reputation was all that was needed to push sales, but he was wrong.

Maybe at one time…but times had changed and the competition was far fiercer than ever before. If left to my father's plan, Baroni wines would've become irrelevant long ago.

"My…who is that?"

Sophia's sharp intake of breath drew my attention straight to Dante Donato walking into my party as if he'd been invited. Instant irritation warred with a grudging appreciation for the form he cut through a crowd. If he'd been stunning in a business suit, he was downright criminal in a tuxedo. I could fairly hear the ladies in attendance fluttering their lashes and staring hard enough to be considered lewd.

"Sophia, would you mind keeping my father company while I greet our new guest?" I said from between gritted teeth. I didn't wait for Sophia's answer, too annoyed to care that I was frowning as I approached Donato.

"I don't recall your name being on the guest list," I said coolly as I met Dante beneath the twinkling arbor. "Why are you here?"

His gaze caught mine and for a moment I swore my heart skipped an extra beat. There was something intense about the way his gaze held mine that I couldn't quite tear my eyes away. Normally, I was the one arresting people with my stare.

Sexuality was a weapon I freely used and made no apologies for, but suddenly I felt like the hunted instead of the other way around. I lifted my chin, ignoring my body's sudden warming, and gave him a pointed look. "I could have you thrown out," I told him.

"You could but that would be very ill-mannered of you," he said, a slow, sensual smile forming on his lips. "I was invited." He produced a gilded invitation and handed it to me as proof.

It was indeed an actual invitation. I frowned. "How did you get this?" I asked with genuine confusion.

"Is the *how* that important? I am here and I'm an invited guest so to throw me out would be incredibly poor form on your part."

He was right. I couldn't throw him out with an invitation in his hand and he was already attracting attention. Forcing a smile, I looped my arm through his and said, "Well, then, let me be the first to welcome you to Castello di Baroni's Una Notte Magica."

The minute our bodies touched I knew I should've thrown him out—because the immediate sparks between us were dangerous.

"Magical indeed," he murmured, a sexy half smile playing with his lips. "Let me guess, you created this masterful entertainment for this evening?"

"It is one of my many duties," I said, careful to keep my voice even and controlled, smiling as if I were pleased as punch to have him crashing my party. "Truly, I'm curious how you received an invitation. This is black-tie, invitation-only and I approve the guest list."

"Not my style," he said with amusement in his tone. "Suffice to say, I'm here and I look forward to an entertaining evening spent with good company."

I didn't like mysteries, much less mysteries perpetrated beneath my nose. My intuition tingled and I guessed, "Was it Mia?"

"And if it were? I would not have you punish her," he said, his voice firming in a way that sent shivers dancing down my back. "She is a dedicated and loyal employee."

"I wouldn't punish her," I said, annoyed that he thought I would do something so terrible for a small lapse in judgment. Mia had done no harm and probably thought she was helping in some way. "Let me guess, you charmed your way into gaining her ticket."

"Charm is something that comes to me naturally, but I can promise you it wasn't my intention to get invited. I didn't even know about tonight until she produced a ticket. However, I was happy to accept."

"And why is that?"

We paused, and he turned to regard me with open interest as he answered smooth as cream, "Because I couldn't think of a better way to spend my time in Italy than to spend it with you."

It could be a line but he didn't have a practiced way about him, and that caused my breath to quicken in the same organic way.

"I have no time for games, Mr. Donato."

Was that a slight catch in my voice, a subtle quaver that gave away the liquid heat building in my belly? God, I hoped not.

The chemistry between us prickled with intensity and I felt myself losing my edge, which was as dangerous as it was alluring.

I never lost my edge.

Until now.

"I really should've had you thrown out," I murmured as his head dipped toward mine.

"Probably," he chuckled, seconds before his lips closed over mine.

CHAPTER FIVE

Dante

Kissing her hadn't been the plan but I took opportunity where I found it.

But in all honesty, I'm not even sure when game play had dropped from my brain and my primal instincts took over.

I've never been struck by a woman's beauty, losing all sense of reason over a hot body and pretty face, but for a heartbeat, the only word I could muster to describe how I was feeling was—*struck*.

Struck by lightning.

Struck by lust.

Struck by awe.

And it was disconcerting as fuck.

That dress, clinging to every hill and valley of her lush body, her breasts high and practically spilling out like candy from a crystal bowl, did crazy things to my head—and other places.

Too many times I'd watched with scorn as men slobbered and made fools of themselves over beautiful women. I never imagined I might fall into the same trap, but in that wild moment I probably would've done anything to feel those luscious lips on mine for just a heartbeat.

The kiss ignited something deep inside me but somehow by the grace of God, I pulled myself back to reality and broke away.

This woman—lovely as she might be—stood in the way of my goal. Strategy was in order.

"Before you judge Mia too harshly, she did manage to sell me an entire case of your Riserva, which I had shipped home to my father in New York. I'd say she's a pretty good saleswoman."

Cheeks flushed, Alessandra smoothed her dress and nodded, as if trying to regain her mental footing. Her scent still lingered in my nose, citrus and a tease of musk that did terrible things to my ability to focus. She exuded sexuality without trying, moving with effortless grace, yet the roll and sway of her hips were a moving violation.

"Mia's job is not in jeopardy," Alessandra assured me, but she was still struggling to put what'd happened into perspective. Our kiss had rattled her. Good—because it'd rattled me, too, but I was better at hiding it.

Every woman I'd ever spent time with paled before Alessandra and I found my tongue sticking uncharacteristically to the roof of my mouth.

"I'm sure kissing me wasn't your sole intention for this evening. Why did you come here?" she asked.

Straight to the point, she pulled no punches,

which I found invigorating. Hell, everything about her excited me right now but I had my game face on. "As I mentioned, I've come to enjoy fine wine and finer company. To that end, the evening has already started off well." We were surrounded by people but it felt as if we were the only two in the courtyard. "Una Notte Magica…a fitting name. There is something magical in the air. Hard to believe how quickly you transformed the grounds from this afternoon into this wonderland."

"I wear many hats here at Castello di Baroni, the least of which is party planner." She stopped short and disengaged from my arm, turning to face me, all business. "I know what you're doing."

Hot boss lady. *I like it.* My brow rose with interest. "Oh? Pray tell. Please enlighten me."

"You've crashed my party for a reason. You're seeking some kind of leverage to use because you think our negotiations are ongoing, which they are not."

I shrugged. "Maybe I've lost interest in the winery entirely and I'm simply looking to enjoy a nice evening."

"I find that highly unlikely."

"And why is that?"

She lifted her chin, assessing me without apology. "Because you're the kind of man who doesn't take no for an answer. *Defeat* isn't in your vocabulary. Your arrogance—"

"Confidence," I corrected.

Alessandra narrowed her gaze. "*Arrogance* clings

to you like that tuxedo. You couldn't hide or disguise it if you tried. It's part of your DNA. Even if I told you a million times that you were wasting your time, that we would never sell, you'd still try to win."

Astute observation. I smiled, pausing to accept two flutes of champagne from a passing attendant, handing her a glass before saying, "The invitation was a bonus. Mia took pity on me for being new to Italy and gave me her invitation. Perhaps she thought I'd make a new friend or two." Knowing this would hit a chord, I made a point to gesture discreetly to the redheaded woman Alessandra had been standing with. "Perhaps with your friend…she's quite beautiful."

I wasn't disappointed. Alessandra's eyes flashed and she stiffened as she retorted, "She's not your type."

"How would you know my type?" I chided, amused. "You don't know me."

"You cannot kiss me and then make eyes at my best friend. Even for an American, that's low." Alessandra was quickly becoming my type but the game was afoot and it wouldn't work to show my hand too early. "Your purchase offer isn't welcome at Castello di Baroni and your attention isn't welcome with my friend Sophia. Please don't make things awkward by making me throw you out."

That hot-blooded protectiveness was alluring as fuck. My breath quickened as a slow smile followed. "Are you always this delightful to guests?"

"You are not my guest," she pointed out, sipping

her champagne, smiling gracefully to a passerby as we moved through the courtyard to end in a slightly darker section where there were less people. "You are an interloper trying to poach on my property for your own gain."

I wasn't going to gain any ground this way. If Alessandra had her guard up every time I was around, I'd certainly lose. I needed a new tactic. "I think we got off on the wrong foot. May we start over?" I asked.

She hesitated, wary. "You assume that I am interested in starting over."

"I respect your position as the head of a historic winery in an industry that is predominantly male-dominated. If I'm being honest, I'm a little in awe of how well you've managed to carve a place for yourself in this business. I came with an offer from my father, but to be honest, I really could not care less about purchasing your winery. My father is old and bored. Purchasing wineries is his new pastime. I agreed to make the offer but I find you far more intriguing than a bunch of grapes."

Alessandra opened her mouth as if to fire back a retort but thought better of it. "So you're not going to press me for more negotiations?" she asked.

"You gave me your answer."

"And you accept it?" she asked, openly disbelieving me. "Just like that. You give up."

"You want me to keep trying? I'm getting a mixed message," I said, biting back a smile. "There are easier ways to get me to call than to lead me on a wild-goose chase. I'd be happy to take you to dinner."

She blinked, her adorable mouth popping open again before she snapped it shut and narrowed her gaze. "Good. Then I won't expect to see you again, crashing my parties or skulking around my winery."

"I've never skulked in my life," I said, affronted. "I'm not even sure I'm capable of skulking."

That cracked a tiny smile from her. I wasn't used to being the jokester—I left that to Nico—but I enjoyed sparring with Alessandra. There was something satisfying about matching wits and finding myself challenged. "Perhaps not but the meaning remains the same. I'm not selling."

"You've said that, and I've heard you." I waited a moment before asking, "Out of curiosity…what drives your passion to hold on to the winery? Surely, there are less stressful careers out there. From what I've seen, Italy is still staunchly patriarchal when it comes to the wine business."

I expected her to shut me down but she surprised me with an answer. "It was my twin brother's passion. I honor him by keeping Castello di Baroni alive. In some small way, it's like having him here still."

The genuine emotion in her statement left no room for quips or jokes. Mia had given me accurate information but hearing it from Alessandra's lips further validated my gut instinct. Sentiment was difficult to negotiate around. Not impossible but it definitely raised the stakes.

I digested her answer, giving it the weight it deserved, then said, "So, now that we have settled our business disagreement, what do you say about dinner?"

It was a bold move but I was ready to put the chess pieces in play. All I needed was the queen to make her move.

Alessandra regarded me with interest, something in her beautiful eyes flickering in a way that made my groin tighten. I wanted her to say yes so badly that I felt myself holding my breath in anticipation.

"Dinner…"

The fact that she was considering it gave me a sudden thrill. "You know the best places in town, I'm assuming, and basically I'm a tourist in your country. Seems smartest to have a well-connected local to show me the hot spots."

She laughed. "You want me to play tour guide? I don't have time for that."

"I could make it worth your while. What if I paid you for your time?"

Alessandra's brow furrowed as she pursed her lips. "There you go throwing money around again. If I choose to show you around, it won't be because you've paid me."

"So you're considering it?" I asked, grinning.

"Of course not," she answered with a smile. "But I will consider dinner."

Yes! Success. I kept my triumphant smile to a minimum. "I'll put that in the win column."

"Don't count it yet. First, a few questions…"

"Like a job interview? I haven't had one of those in a while."

"Are you married or have a girlfriend at home? I don't want to deal with a jealous woman showing up on my doorstep."

"Over dinner?" I teased. "This better be the most amazing food ever made."

"I'm serious. It's happened before and I don't have the time for drama."

If she knew me better, she wouldn't have had to ask. I didn't keep entanglements. I preferred to remain unfettered by emotional attachments. My two brothers were shackled and I had no interest in following in their footsteps.

But I was happy to allay her fears. I took a bold step forward, entering her personal space. She didn't pull back. The blood roared in my ears as she met my gaze with a boldness of her own. I hungered for another taste of her kiss on my lips. The first kiss had been a shock to us both, a reaction to the magnetism between us. This time, I was going to make it happen with all the finesse I was known for.

I knuckled her chin, noting the soft, firm skin of her jawline. "I promise you, I am *very* single and I am not interested in changing that status—no matter how enticing the vision before me."

Her slow smile tickled me in private places. "Good. Then you may take me to dinner." *Yes!* I took the invitation her parted lips offered, sliding my mouth across hers, tasting that exotic flavor of Italian spice I knew I'd always remember, and thrilled at the bold dart of her tongue against mine.

Heat kindled between us as if the ember had always been there, waiting for the right spark to start a fire. Even if the kiss lasted only a moment, it left me aching for more.

She pulled away, her cheeks flushed slightly, saying with a devilish smile as she walked away, "Dinner only."

I remained rooted to the spot she left me. My lips tingled from her touch.

My cock surged to life, nearly splitting the zipper as every primal need known to man came knocking on my door, urging me to toss her over my shoulder and carry her off like a Viking.

"Dinner it is," I murmured, staring after her like a hungry wolf. "At least to start…"

CHAPTER SIX

Alessandra

I LEFT DANTE, my knees a little weak from our kiss, but I kept my back straight and my smile fixed. I would die before letting him know that his lips had stolen my breath.

God, how long had it been since I'd felt this wild need to sleep with a man? Too long. Castello di Baroni consumed my every moment from sunup to sundown, leaving little time for personal pursuits. I wasn't complaining—the winery was my passion—but the touch of a man who knew what he wanted and went after it wasn't to be ignored.

Dante said he was no longer interested in purchasing the winery. His story made a certain amount of sense—his father had been the interested party, not him. Dante had no vested interest in the winery and had been pursuing the sale only as a courtesy to his aging father. I understood familial loyalty and the urge to make something happen for their benefit.

If Dante was truly no longer interested in purchasing the winery, that made him no longer a threat.

Which made him fair game for my bed.

A quick look to my father revealed he'd missed my kiss with Dante, for which I was grateful. I didn't want to explain why a strange man was kissing me in the courtyard. Sophia, on the other hand, had seen everything.

I rejoined her, and she met me with a curious expression. She led with, "I have questions...so many questions..."

I laughed, leaning over to whisper so my father didn't overhear. "Would you believe he was in my office earlier today with an offer to purchase Castello di Baroni?" Sophia's expression mirrored my own at the audacity. "I know. I turned him away."

"And he shows up here? How did he get an invitation?"

"Mia gave him her ticket."

"Mia?" Sophia looked surprised. "Why?"

I shrugged. "Likely, he charmed her but she did manage to sell a case of the Riserva so I can't be too irritated with her. Besides, Mia is sweet and probably had good intentions at heart."

"You think she was trying to play matchmaker?"

I pursed my lips in thought. "Perhaps. I think she may be sweet on Como but he hasn't the sense God gave a goose to notice."

"Is he still trying to pursue you?" Sophia asked. "I thought you nipped that in the bud."

"I tried. He is stubborn." I drew a deep breath. "But I think I finally got through to him today."

"Let's hope. It was embarrassingly awkward to watch him pine after you," Sophia said with distaste. "And unprofessional. I'm surprised your father never noticed."

"Papa rarely comes to the office these days." For which I was also grateful. There was nothing more troublesome than my father meddling where he was woefully underqualified. Of course, there was no telling him that, so it was better for everyone if he puttered elsewhere in his retirement.

Sophia nodded but returned to Dante. "You kissed him. What's that about?"

"It just happened. I don't think either of us planned to. I have dinner plans with him tomorrow. The jury is out whether or not I will kiss him again."

That was a total lie. It was surprising lightning didn't streak from the sky and burn me to a crisp as soon as the words left my mouth. I could still taste Dante. My tongue darted along the seam of my lips and my heart kicked up a beat. "I plan to see if he truly means to drop this whole matter with the winery. I need him to feel comfortable."

Sophia gasped. "And you think an intimate dinner is wise? You don't even know the man."

"I said dinner, not marriage," I said, smiling at Sophia's concern. "It's been a long time since I allowed a man to treat me. I look forward to a night out with someone who isn't connected in any way to the wine industry."

"I can understand that," Sophia admitted grudg-ingly, but she still wasn't sold on the idea. "But an American? They're dreadfully uncivilized. They drink lattes after ten in the morning."

"Don't be a snob," I teased, nudging her with my shoulder. "We needn't hold that against him. He's actually quite entertaining with a quick wit."

And a mouth that made me think of things he could do with it that had nothing to do with food.

Sophia frowned as she queried, "Why did he want to buy the winery if he's not in the business?"

"According to his story, his family built the manor and owned the original winery. His father wanted to return the property back to the fold. I refused and he accepted."

"He did?" Sophia's brow rose. "Just like that? He folded that easily?"

I shrugged. "His reasons are his own. I don't care as long as he's not sniffing around my business." And regardless of what happened between us, I'd make sure that didn't happen. I cast a sly smile Sophia's way. "He's handsome, is he not?"

"He's quite handsome," she agreed with a frown. "But I'm not sure it's a good idea to see him again. A man like him doesn't admit defeat easily. What if he's trying to get closer to you to get information he can use as leverage?"

"I thought of that, but his explanation makes sense. However, rest assured, I won't let him have anything of value that he can use later."

Even as I swore to my friend that dinner was

the only option I was currently entertaining, I already knew I wanted to take him home after. Sophia wouldn't understand—she was quite old-fashioned about sex—and I didn't want her to stress unnecessarily over something that was simply about physical need. Sometimes I wished Sophia would just run wild and sow some oats, but that wasn't her style. I feared my beautiful best friend would die alone surrounded by cats if she didn't start breaking out of her comfort zone and actually meeting people.

Ah, well, that's a problem for a different day.

I tracked Dante as he moved throughout the crowd easily, garnering attention from every female as he went. Every so often, he'd send a smoldering look my way, which I boldly met. The chemistry between us was immediate and intoxicating. Even if Sophia was right and Dante was trying to seduce information out of me, it wouldn't work. If he thought I was some silly female who swooned and fell in love with a man of his stature, wealth and looks, he was sorely mistaken.

I ate men like him for breakfast.

Lesser men, I destroyed.

Speaking of, Alberico made his way toward me and I suppressed my urge to be rude and send him on his way. With my father standing so close, I couldn't possibly do something so obvious.

As it was, my father thought Alberico was a fine catch—which he might be, for someone else.

"Alberico," my father called out, pleased to see

ALEXX ANDRIA 55

him. "You are looking fine this evening. How are you?"

"I cannot complain, signor, particularly when the view this evening is exquisite," Alberico answered, sparing a hot glance my way. I enjoyed the heat in Dante's gaze but seeing it on Alberico made me want to find a floor-length coat. He grasped my hand and kissed it lightly. "May I say, you look incredible tonight, Alessandra…"

Ugh. Every time Alberico was around me, he practically drooled. How could my father not see that we were a terrible match? My skin fairly crawled when he touched me.

The stark difference between how my body reacted when Dante's fingertips grazed my skin as opposed to Alberico's was striking, and further proof—not that I needed any—that a Salvadori/Baroni union was never going to happen.

I allowed a tight smile and withdrew my hand, turning brightly to Sophia as I said, "Sophia, may I introduce Alberico Salvadori? How is it that two of my dearest friends haven't yet met one another?"

Alberico turned his polite attention to Sophia as it would've been rude to do otherwise, bowed and kissed Sophia's hand, as well. *"Bellisimo,"* he murmured. "It is a pleasure."

"The pleasure is mine," Sophia returned, casting a knowing look my way as I prepared my exit.

"Please, enjoy yourselves. I must see to the caterers as they should be getting ready to serve the entrée."

I left Sophia behind with Alberico, not the least bit guilty for serving up my best friend to the thirsty Alberico. They made a better couple than he and I, anyway.

I'd make it up to Sophia. For now, I had a party to attend and having Alberico throwing those looks my way was nothing more than a distraction and an irritant.

My father could wish our families to join but I wasn't on board with that plan.

Not ever.

Alberico wasn't a bad man—not in the least—but he was not for me.

That much I knew.

I didn't need a man. I needed a way to guarantee Uva Persa was a stellar success. Everything else was unimportant.

However, if I could squeeze in a few much-needed orgasms, I wouldn't hesitate.

Particularly, orgasms with a man who promised no strings attached.

CHAPTER SEVEN

Dante

THE PARTY HAD been enjoyable but I hadn't learned anything of value from circulating through the crowd last night. Those who didn't have a crush on Alessandra were jealous of her success. I wondered if Alessandra knew how many people thought of her as a threat to their way of life.

Mostly, crusty old men with old money—like my father—were highly critical of Alessandra, even as they enjoyed her hospitality, drank her wine and ate her food. Misogyny was alive and well, hiding behind the stately cypress trees and lyrical Tuscan artwork, and it teemed beneath the facade of polite conversation.

My respect level rose for Alessandra. To succeed in this environment was an accomplishment worth noting.

However, even if the party hadn't revealed much more in the way of information, I considered it a win as I'd convinced Alessandra to meet me for dinner, and that was the real prize.

Not to mention, the memory of Alessandra in that black dress had kept me awake all night. I tossed and turned in my hotel bed for hours before giving up any hope of sleep without first jerking off to release some pent-up steam.

I couldn't help but fantasize about peeling that skin-tight dress from her luscious curves and feasting on every soft bit of flesh my hands could touch.

In truth, I'd never come so hard by my own hand with such limited mental imagery, but Alessandra was a walking contradiction that I found intensely arousing.

For now, I needed to shelve those lustful thoughts so I could focus on the task at hand.

I walked into the rustic restaurant, the sharp tang of fresh herbs and spices permeating the small, intimate space as local diners enjoyed authentic Italian cuisine without the intrusion of tourists hoping for chicken Alfredo.

Alessandra insisted on meeting me and while I was punctual, she wasn't at the restaurant yet, which suited me fine and gave me a chance to form a plan.

I ordered a bottle of wine, knowing that the move would either impress or irritate her, and I was interested to see where I landed.

My server had just decanted the wine when Alessandra walked in. My body stiffened as I struggled to appear nonchalant but goddamn, if the woman were any hotter, she'd set things on fire by proximity.

She wore a long, flowing tunic-style blouse with an exposed shoulder, her hair tumbling down her

back, and jeans. It was an effortless look yet a su-
permodel couldn't have worn it better.

Our gazes met and the heat jumped but she deliberately paused before joining me at the table to greet
the chef grilling lamb in an open-floor-plan kitchen.

"Alessandra!" he exclaimed, taking the time to
kiss her on both cheeks, clearly happy to see her.
A sudden flush of jealousy caused me to shift with
discomfort but I held it in check. I couldn't discern
their conversation but it was over before it mattered.

I rose as Alessandra joined me, and I reached out
to pull her chair free. "An American gentleman? I
didn't know they existed."

"Tsk, tsk, Alessandra, your bias is showing," I
said, returning to my seat. It was a good thing there
were linen napkins on the table...I might need one
to mop up the drool. "You look lovely."

She accepted my compliment with a smile,
steepling her fingers as she perused me openly before returning the compliment. "You are quite handsome but then you know this. I am simply stating
what you hear on a daily basis and I'm not sure I
want to perpetuate your arrogance."

"The same could be said for you."

She shrugged, her gaze alighting on the wine.
"You ordered ahead?"

"I took the liberty."

Her smile tickled my insides. "We shall see if you
ordered wisely."

I poured two glasses and waited for Alessandra's
assessment. She took her time like a true connois-

seur, first burying her nose in the glass to inhale the bouquet, then taking an exploratory sip between those luscious lips. I had to drag my gaze to avoid from staring too hard.

"Good?" I asked, pleased my voice held. "Does it meet with your standards?"

Alessandra smiled coyly as she answered, "Franco always carries excellent wine. Why do you think I picked this restaurant?"

I laughed. "You didn't trust my instincts so you hedged your bets. Crafty woman."

Alessandra didn't deny my assumption but the amusement sparkling in her eyes was like a drug in my system. I wanted to know why she was single, why some lucky bastard hadn't snapped her up by now. By the standards of polite etiquette, jumping into relationship statuses was usually considered rude. I never played by the rules, so why start now? "Why are you single?" I asked, throwing it out there.

"Because I am not interested in marrying," she answered without artifice. "And you?"

"Because I'm also not interested in marrying. Seems we have a bit more in common than we thought."

She chuckled but graced me with a patronizing look. "Tell me why you came all the way to Italy when you could've made a phone call that would've yielded the same result."

"Because I thought a face-to-face was more effective," I answered. "I should've done my homework first. I confess, I thought buying your winery was going to be an easy win."

"And why is that?"

"Because everyone has a price and it's usually lower than they realize. The wine business is capricious and most don't have the capital to weather the bad years. The other wineries my father purchased didn't resist much once we made our offers."

"We would never sell."

"Yes, I've come to accept this."

"Have you?"

The open suspicion in her gaze kept me on my toes. She didn't trust me or my motives. Smart woman. "It's true I could've made a phone call to get the same information that flying over garnered, but the truth of the matter is…I needed a change of scenery. My older brother runs the family business, which leaves me to collect dust. I was bored and Italy sounded more exciting than what I was doing."

"Your father favors your brother? He doesn't value his sons equally?"

Her simple question unexpectedly hit a raw nerve. Instead of answering, I took the time to sip my wine, savoring the flavor before drawing the conversation back to the present. "How about this…let's not talk about our fathers. They aren't nearly as interesting as the two people sitting at this table. I want to know more about Alessandra. Let's start there."

I wasn't fooling her, but she didn't press the issue and I was grateful. I had issues with my father— ones I wasn't ready to discuss with a stranger, not even one as beautiful as Alessandra—but if I could bring home this win, perhaps our relationship would change.

My father wasn't a bad man, self-absorbed and selfish at times, but he was still my father and I had looked up to him my entire life.

"What would you like to know?" she asked, curious.

"Everything." That much was true. I was greedy for details and not entirely to find information to use as leverage. That alone surprised me. "You fascinate me."

"Shall we speak plainly?" At my nod, she said, "We share an attraction. We can play the social game, dance around the small talk that we both know is simply courtesy, or we can both admit that our attraction is merely physical and lead with that."

Annnnddd, my cock nearly split in two. I swallowed. Had I just met the female equivalent of myself?

"You'd be okay with just sex between us?" I asked.

"Now that I know you're not interested in pursuing the purchase of Castello di Baroni…yes."

The heat between us climbed. I'd never been so eager to feel a woman's skin beneath my fingertips before that moment. The giddy teenager I think never quite leaves a man's psyche, no matter his age, urged me to signal for the check and haul ass out of there. I held the urge back by the thinnest thread.

I swirled the remaining wine in my glass. "Maybe I'm not that into you," I said, talking total crap.

At that she grinned, readily calling my bluff. "Are you saying you're prepared to sleep alone tonight?"

"I didn't say that," I answered. "Italy is a place filled with beauty of all kinds. I'm sure I could find someone to warm my bed."

"Why settle for a mild flicker of heat when you can have a bonfire?"

God yes, why?

Fuck it. The seventeen-year-old in me was in charge. I pulled a wad of cash from my billfold and tossed it to the table. "You make a persuasive argument. Let's go, then," I said, taking the leap. She slipped her hand into mine, her gaze dancing with anticipation as we left the restaurant for my hotel.

We were playing an exciting game but I couldn't quite tell who was in the lead.

All I knew was that in the end…I was going to win.

CHAPTER EIGHT

Alessandra

DANTE'S BIG BODY pressed against me, his hands interlinking with mine as he drew my arms up over my head. We'd barely made it through the door when he was on me. His ferocity took my breath away. There was something savage about Dante—something primal—that spoke to me, whispered dirty things into my ear and left me weak.

My breasts strained against my bra, my nipples pearling behind the silk with an eagerness I shared. I was already wet and ready. His tongue stabbed into my mouth, daring me to resist. I met him with a savagery of my own. It'd been so long since I'd slept with such a virile man that I was eaten by sensual hunger.

Our tongues danced, sliding against one another, building the heat to a fever pitch. He released my hands to cup my face, drawing me close as he continued to plunder my mouth. I could taste the lingering wine on his tongue, could feel the masculine energy coming off him in waves, and I was drunk on it.

"You are the goddamn hottest woman alive," he said against my mouth before pulling away to rip off his shirt, revealing a hard, powerfully built chest with only a faint smattering of hair that trailed down his belly and beyond.

I sucked in a tight breath as my mouth dried. I so desperately wanted to taste his skin, to suck that manly nipple into my mouth and worry it between my teeth. I stripped as quickly, and within seconds I was back in his arms.

He hoisted me up and my legs went around his torso, his hands cupping my ass. I swallowed his groan, the hardened staff of his cock between us, as he carried me to the bed.

We tumbled to the mattress and Dante immediately opened my legs to gaze at the prize he wanted so badly. His eyes fairly glowed with desire, lust radiated from every pore and his cock bobbed as if seeking that wet heat. "Jesus, woman, is every inch of you perfect?" he asked before locking his arms around my hips and drawing my pussy to his eager mouth.

And Dante came at me with the same level of ferocity as his kiss—open, demanding, searing—putting his entire face into the job. He ate like a dog determined to put his scent on everything he touched. Dedicated, single-mindedly focused and damn good at his task.

"Oh, my God, Dante!" was all I could manage before frantic panting escaped my parted lips as his tongue, mouth and fingers worked magic, building

the pleasure until I was thrashing like a wild woman, desperate for release. He kept me dangling on that edge, pushing me until I was almost crying.

But I wouldn't beg and if he was waiting for that, he'd wait until we both died, even as I so needed my climax. My legs were shaking, my belly trembled and I was almost out of my mind but I wouldn't give in.

And then it happened. My body wouldn't be denied any longer and I crashed hard into an orgasm that left me locked in a paralyzed scream. Each sensation crested over me, squeezing the air from my lungs until I saw spots.

I sucked in a sharp breath, whimpering as my clitoris pulsed with ragged beats, echoes of the climax with each rhythmic spasm. "Dante," I said weakly, sweat dampening my hairline as he climbed my body to kiss me deeply. I tasted myself and I melted a little more.

I was always the one in control, always the one in command in the bedroom, but Dante had taken my power as easily as one took candy from a child. My bones were soupy inside my flesh and it was the most amazing feeling I'd ever experienced.

"You come like a fucking savage warrior queen," he said with a feral grin that spoke to my soul.

A ragged breath rattled out of my chest as I tried to recover but he wasn't finished with me, not by a long shot. The hunger glowered in his eyes and promised more as soon as I caught my breath, but he was so tightly wound, I knew my reprieve wouldn't last long.

Dante flipped me on my belly, hooked his hands at my hips and drew me toward him while holding my head down. "I want to bite that perfect heart-shaped ass," he growled but instead of nipping at me, the shock of his hand coming down across my cheeks sent a vicious thrill arcing through me. He rubbed at the reddened spot where his hand had connected, soothing the ache until his palm came down again. I cried out but I was wet.

The pain was a delightful shock that he countered with another soft, almost tender touch afterward. Then his lips grazed the heated flesh and I groaned with need. He rubbed his hand across my slit, sliding it up and down, smearing my wetness along my swollen lips, teasing my aching clitoris over and over. I was nearing climax again—all it would take was the slightest direct contact with that vibrating nub and I'd fall into another orgasm.

But he was the master tonight. His tongue played with the puckered rosebud of my ass, tickling, teasing, and I gripped the bedsheets between clenched fingers. He rimmed my ass with the same dedication as he had eaten my pussy and I died a million times. The pleasure scrambled my brain in the most delicious way and I was helpless to stop the sensations from wreaking havoc on every nerve ending. And then he slipped a finger inside, pressing against the sphincter, slow but deliberate. *"Yes!"* I cried. I was sloppy wet and I arched into his invading digit, pushing against him for more.

Anal play was something I enjoyed but rarely invited. So few got it right, but Dante knew how to play me like a finely tuned instrument. One finger, two fingers, his tongue, working me until I was mindless with all-consuming fire. Soft, mewling noises erupted from between my lips that transitioned to outright groans as Dante left my ass to push that thick length deep inside me.

He was built like a sturdy horse, thick and long, beefy and strong. I was filled to my limit, almost to the point of pain as he nearly bumped against my cervix, but I welcomed every sensation. The pleasure outweighed everything else as he drove himself into me, gripping my hips with hot hands, the sound of his guttural moans sending my arousal into a wildfire.

Just as I was climbing that peak again, he stopped and rolled me onto my back, placing one leg over his shoulder as he drove into me again, the force of his thrusts something almost brutal. My breasts bounced with every thrust and I squeezed my eyes shut as the pleasure jumped a notch.

"Look at me, baby," he growled, forcing my eyes to pop open. "I want to watch you as you come again and again."

I was so close and he knew it. My thighs were already trembling, that telltale flutter in my belly had already begun. Usually I chased an orgasm but not this time. It was chasing me.

I groaned, my entire body shaking. "Dante!" I cried out as I came again with a ferocity that left me reeling. Dante chased his own climax, gripping my hips as though I might escape if he didn't clutch at my flesh with desperate fingers. He pummeled my body with his, each thrust more savage than the next until it was all I could do to hold on. A wild, defiant flutter began low in my belly and I moaned, knowing what was coming.

I couldn't help myself. My body responded to Dante's cock like a trained animal, barking and doing tricks for a treat. I tumbled into another orgasm just as Dante found his.

"Alessandra!" My name on his lips as he cried out was an aphrodisiac of another level. Everything about Dante was hard and masculine. For the first time ever, I softened beneath a man's touch and it was both wondrous and horrifying.

I didn't know if I wanted to be softened.

I didn't know if I wanted Dante to be the one who tamed the beast in my heart.

But I did know that Dante was unlike any lover I'd ever had—and I was already addicted.

CHAPTER NINE

Dante

MY BREATH WAS ragged and my heart felt ready to burst, but I'd never been so sated in my life.

I rolled onto my back. I didn't have the energy to remove the condom as my cock slowly shrank from such a wicked workout. Something primal had erupted out of my consciousness and taken over, but it'd been the most incredible fuck in the history of humans fucking.

My chest heaved as I fought to recover. Alessandra was no less winded. I'd gone at it pretty hard. I knew she'd climaxed several times without having to ask—some things were impossible to hide. Even the most accomplished of actresses couldn't have pulled off that act.

Pride suffused my chest and a slow yet exhausted grin formed on my lips. Thankfully, Alessandra had her eyes closed. If she'd seen my shit-eating grin, my chances of a second round would've disappeared. The woman was the most prideful I'd ever known. It was a turn-on.

Hell, everything about her turned me on. Was that a problem? Not at all. It just made my job that much more enjoyable. I had zero issues fucking Alessandra raw all the while finding the leverage I needed to get her to sell.

But for now, I needed to catch my breath before I died.

With a grunt, I rolled over to toss the used condom, then rose to grab two waters from the mini fridge in my room. I handed one to Alessandra, trying not to stare hungrily at her beautiful breasts.

Waxing poetic on anything wasn't my style, but if Michelangelo had seen Alessandra's tits, he would've been painting those beauties on every single canvas in his dusty studio. I didn't have an artistic bone in my body and her tits were inspiring me to do something artsy.

She slugged the water, thirsty as I was. Alessandra dragged her hand across her mouth, her eyes sparkling with residual heat. "Hungry?" I asked. We'd skipped out on dinner. I could use some food before jumping her sexy little ass again.

"I could eat," she answered, rolling away to climb from the bed. She disappeared into the bathroom while I ordered room service. Then she reemerged wearing one of the thick bathrobes that were complimentary to the guests. She belted the robe and walked past me, a regal queen even though she barely reached my chest level. "What did you order?"

"Fresh fruits, bread and cheese, and a little wine."

"Perfect."

Yes, you are. I smiled, already itching to pull the robe from her luscious body, but I followed her lead and put on the other robe. I supposed I couldn't answer the door with my dick hanging out, so concessions had to be made. I joined her on the bed, lying on my side. "Do we commence with the awkward chitchat or how do we handle this?" I asked.

"I despise small talk."

"Me, too."

She graced me with an approving smile. "So tell me something of value...something of interest about you."

"Hmm...okay, I'll do my best to sound interesting."

"Of that, I have no doubt."

I settled more comfortably, my gaze drawn to the shadow of her breast peeking out from the slightly open robe. I dragged my stare away and tried to focus but my cock was already priming for round two and the food hadn't even arrived yet. "Well, I'm the middle son of a wealthy family. My oldest brother, Luca, runs the family company after forcing our father into retirement, and my younger brother, Nico, just got married so he's playing husband and father. Honestly, I can't imagine why he'd want to do that, but to each his own."

"I agreed with you there," she said.

"I knew there was a reason I liked you."

She laughed, the sound tickling my insides. "And it couldn't have had anything to do with these?" Alessandra opened her robe, revealing those glorious breasts, and I nearly swallowed my tongue. It was difficult to play the part of the suave, aloof gentleman when my cock was throbbing like a motherfucker.

My own grin widened as I answered, "They don't hurt."

"Are you and your brothers close?"

I paused, not quite sure how to answer that question truthfully. I didn't want to seem like an asshole but I wasn't that close to either of my brothers. We got along to a point, but I didn't understand or agree with half their decisions in life, so that often created friction.

As if sensing my turmoil, she shrugged and said, "Don't waste time thinking of a suitable lie. Be honest. Your truth doesn't affect me so there's no reason to play with your answer."

"I don't want anything bad to happen to either of them," I supplied with a short grin, but she knew I was dancing around the question. "Damn, hardballing me out of the gate. Okay, the truth? We're not close but we're not enemies. For a long time there was friction between me and Luca. My father had always groomed Luca to take over the business, even when I was better suited to run the company, and it created some resentment between us."

"Why? It's not your brother's fault that your father chose him over you," Alessandra spoke plainly, pulling no punches. "If anyone deserves your resentment, it's your father."

"Yeah, I guess that's one way to look at it." But I'd never felt that way.

Alessandra shook her head. "I see no other way to look at the situation. How can you see it differently?"

The urge to go on the defensive was strong. I didn't like that she saw through to my deepest insecurity. I admired my father's shrewd sense of business, that shark mentality that I emulated in my own business dealings, but he'd been a less than stellar father. It wasn't as if he passed out hugs on the regular. Not that I needed them—I wasn't twelve anymore.

"I admire my father's business sense and I've always looked up to him. He must've seen something in Luca that he didn't see in me." Ouch, that hurt even to let the words leave my mouth. Was this part of the act or did I actually feel that way? I wasn't sure. In my attempt to emulate my father, had I become too much like him? Cold and distant, even with my own brothers, like our father was with his sons? I mentally shook the thought away. "It's fine, though. I'm still part of the business and I don't have to deal with the headaches that the CEO does."

"So let me see if I have this correct—you came to Italy to deliver my winery to your father in the hopes of impressing him because you are always searching for his approval?"

When she put it like that, it sounded pathetic. I forced a grin even as I denied her assessment. "I was just trying to help the old man out and it involved a trip to Italy. In my book, that's never a bad thing."

Alessandra sighed, digesting the information before she said, "It seems silly to chase after a dream created in the clouds. If your father hasn't recognized your worth by now, he never will."

There was a slight sadness pulling on her words, as if she were speaking to her own situation... I wondered what that was about.

"What's your story, beautiful?" I asked, drawing the topic back to her. I needed to know what made her tick. I knew how to make her come like a banshee, but I couldn't exactly use that information to my advantage to press for a sale. "I can already tell your story is five times more interesting than mine."

But before she could answer, a polite rap at the door signaled the food had arrived. I jumped up to handle the details and returned with a cart laden with delicious fruits, bread, cheese and fragrant olive oil, as well as a nice white wine. We didn't bother sitting at the small table in the suite, just continued to lie in the bed like old lovers, comfortable in our skin and with each other.

Which, to be honest, was out of character for me. Sex was a physical need I didn't deny myself, but I didn't encourage hanging around and shooting the breeze, much less delving into deep, personal conversations. But with Alessandra, it was as if she'd kicked open the gates and strode right in as if she owned the place.

I didn't have time to question the situation. My actions at this point were reactive.

After sopping up a piece of sourdough bread with oil and crushed garlic, I said, "Don't think for a second that I've forgotten my question to you. It's your turn. Tell me about yourself and your family."

"I've already told you everything of importance," she said with a coy smile. "What else is there to know?"

"If your brother hadn't died…where would you be today?"

Her smile faded and she drew a deep breath as if she hadn't expected me to go there so quickly. "I don't know," she finally answered. Maybe she'd given this question some thought on her own and still came up with the same troubling answer. "I was different before Enzo died. He was the responsible one, I'd been carefree. His love for the business and our family's place in the history of winemaking was far deeper than mine. If he were still alive, I don't know, maybe I'd be working the business by his side or maybe I would've walked my own path."

Alessandra's brow dipped slightly and I regretted bringing up something that made her sad. The mood between us had shifted and I needed to bring it back to a manageable, lighthearted tone…even though I wanted to know more about her.

For now, it could wait.

CHAPTER TEN

Alessandra

How did Dante know to ask the one question that nagged at me in my quiet moments—the moments when my reflections had a tendency to turn to melancholy?

Enzo's death had been a cataclysmic event in our family, a nuclear bomb that'd shattered us into a million pieces in our grief. My mother never recovered. She died with a sad heart. My father tried to soldier on but I saw the echo of pain in his eyes every time he looked at me. Enzo and I shared too many features to ignore. Although my father would never say, sometimes I feared he wished it'd been me in that car that night instead of Enzo.

The luscious cheese soured in my mouth. I chased the bitter taste with a sip of wine, allowing the dry white to cleanse my palate. "Perhaps it was better to stick to small talk," I said, allowing a brief smile as I settled into the bed, my belly satisfied even if my mind was wandering down sad roads.

I never showed this side of myself, least of all allowed a stranger into my private theater, but I felt oddly safe in this space with Dante.

I didn't believe in love at first sight, even though my grandparents' love story had always been a favorite, but there was something about Dante that drew me in, despite all the reasons I should steer clear. Perhaps it was the stress of launching Uva Persa beneath my father's nose that made me reckless or needy, but I was acting in ways that were out of character.

Dante cleared our food and returned to the bed. It was late. I should go but I didn't move. I watched with unabashed appreciation for the tease of his solid male form beneath the robe. His body was just how I liked my men—rough, hard, thick and muscular— just enough savagery beneath that civilized veneer to hint at danger. Yes, Dante was all that and more. This was how obsessions started.

As if sensing my mood had shifted, Dante slowly dropped his robe, his cock already hard and ready. I sucked in a tight breath as my heart rate kicked up. He was something of an enigma. He wore a tailored suit like an aristocrat but he had the touch of a blue-collar man who didn't mind getting dirty.

The dichotomy of the two was a wild, heady combination that ate at my ability to think rationally.

He slowly pushed my robe down to reveal my shoulder, where he pressed a soft kiss that sent tendrils of tickling sensation tripping down my flesh. His lips blazed a sensual trail down my arm as he relieved me of my robe until I was naked like him.

Our bodies fit together perfectly, as if we were made for each other. I didn't subscribe to that nonsense but how else could I explain how easily he twisted me into a panting she-beast as pleasure ripped through me?

This time I wanted to be in control. I wanted Dante groaning and losing himself as I pleasured him at my leisure. I rose and pulled the belt free from my discarded robe. Dante arched his brow in question but his mouth curved in a sensual grin. "Get on the bed, spread eagle," I ordered as I took the belt from his robe, as well. I straddled his prone body, enjoying the warm press of his hard cock against the cleft of my ass as I tied his arms to the bedposts.

This was more what I was accustomed to—my calling the shots.

"Are you going to have your wicked way with me?" he said.

I grinned. "Something like that."

"I'm all yours. Do your worst."

"Oh, I will."

Instead of immediately sliding down his torso to suck his cock down my throat, I slowly ground my wet pussy along his shaft, coating his cock, giving him a nice preview of what he wanted most. He groaned immediately, his hips thrusting against me, trying to slide it in, but I just laughed at his eagerness. He wasn't going to get off that easily, not when he'd kept me on the edge for so long.

I rubbed the head of his cock against my slit, moaning a little as the tiny flickers of pleasure licked at my insides. He surged against me but I kept him just on the outside, close but not where he wanted to be, driving him crazy. I climbed his body and bracketed his face with my breasts. He reacted like a happy puppy, lapping at my nipples, trying to get as much of his mouth on my tits as possible. He groaned with frustration when I kept the hard tips just out of reach, giggling when he growled.

"You're killing me, woman," he said, and I graced him with a knowing smile. Oh yes, and I was about to make it worse. I kissed him hard, our tongues tangling and dancing as he strained against the belts holding him in place. The wooden bedposts protested as he pulled but I had no doubt they would hold even someone of Dante's size and strength. Then I slowly slid down to his hard and ready cock. I teased it with the dart of my tongue and he sucked in a ragged breath. "Oh God, Alessandra…" he moaned as I took the head into my mouth, using my tongue and hands to work his shaft.

The slight salty tang of him was like a rare delicacy. I lapped it up, sucking and swirling my tongue beneath the mushroomed ridge where all the nerve endings were bundled, reveling in the low moans and subtle jerks of his thighs.

I worked him mercilessly, driving him to the edge and then pulling back, leaving him frustrated and groaning, only to push him further, going to that utmost precipice and then slowing down so his orgasm danced out of reach.

"Sweet Lord, woman, my heart is going to explode," he warned breathlessly, sweat dampening his hairline as he practically begged me to let him come. I laughed and lapped at his balls, gently suckling the tender flesh until I finally took mercy on him and began moving on his shaft with purpose, knowing he would blow a load so hard I might choke on it.

"Ohhhh fuckkkkkk!"

Right at the moment I knew his climax was coming, I slipped my finger inside his ass and his hips rocketed, thrusting as he came, shooting down my throat in great salty gobs, leaving him bone-dry as he finished with a shudder.

I wiped my mouth and finished my wine as Dante went boneless on the bed, all energy sapped from his body. I gently lapped at the remaining liquid on his cock and he jerked with a moan. I climbed his body and untied him, then he promptly curled his arms around me, tucking me into the cove of his arms and cuddling me like I was a rare treasure.

"I'm fucking tired," he said with an exhaustion that couldn't be faked. I took pride in the fact that I'd worn out such a virile man.

I hated cuddling but…in Dante's arms, I'd make an exception.

Just this once.

But I wasn't spending the night.

CHAPTER ELEVEN

Dante

I AWOKE TO the sound of fabric rustling with a hurried quality. My eyes popped open and I found Alessandra dressing, scooping up her clothes with an air of distress. I rose and rubbed the sleep from eyes, still trying to wake up.

"What's wrong?" I asked.

Alessandra shimmied into her jeans and buckled her belt before answering with exasperation, "I overslept. I never oversleep. I have to go."

"Is Daddy going to ground you for missing curfew?" I teased but she didn't find the humor. I threw the covers free and strode past her naked to the bathroom, where I noticed with pride that her gaze skidded straight to my ass before she managed to drag it free. I took a piss, washed my hands, then went to last night's room service cart and grabbed a few leftover grapes before falling into a soft chair, naked as a jaybird. "So who's going to bust your ass for being late? Aren't you the boss?"

She stiffened. "Of course."

"Then who are you trying to impress?"

"It sets a bad example."

"Are you in a habit of showing up late?" I asked, popping a grape into my mouth.

"Of course not."

"Then let it go. Aren't you entitled to a little leeway?"

She cast a sardonic look my way as she grabbed her purse. "I don't know how they do things in America, but here laziness isn't celebrated. Thank you for the nice evening."

A *nice* evening.

It was then I realized she was going to leave without so much as a kiss goodbye after I'd rocked her world and she'd rocked mine. I couldn't let that happen.

Hell no. She was going to remember how good our bodies were together and that memory would stay with her all day long, which would set me up nicely for our plans tonight.

I caught her before her fingers could twist the doorknob, pulling her into my arms.

"What are you doing? I don't have time for this."

"You were going to leave without a kiss?" I asked, my gaze riveted by the plump pout of her lips, my brain stuttering for a moment on how exquisite those lips had felt wrapped around my cock.

She opened her mouth to respond but my lips found hers and she automatically leaned into me, her body melding to mine. She could play all she wanted but her body's response was pure honesty.

As was mine.

I wanted her in ways I'd never desired a woman. I'd been around the world and never found a woman as intoxicating as Alessandra. It was a game but it was also the most genuine emotion I'd felt in a long time, and I didn't want it to end. At least not until I was declared the winner.

Boldly, my erection rose front and center and I purposefully ground myself against her. The tiny moan that slipped from her lips was like a shot of heroin straight to my veins. I pushed her against the wall, where she connected with a sharp inhale as I quickly unbuckled her jeans and shoved them to her ankles. I lifted one foot free as she watched, her eyes wide and her breath shallow. I rose and rubbed her slit, seeking that sweet heat and damp core. "You thought you were going to leave before I could enjoy my favorite breakfast?" I growled against the column of her neck as she groaned. I slipped a finger inside her and her knees wobbled as she clutched at my shoulders. "Bad girl," I tsked before withdrawing my digit to rub her own wetness along her bottom lip. I leaned in to inhale her own musk as she trembled. "Now you have to be punished."

I went to my knees and buried my face between her folds, sucking in the sweet musk as my tongue went straight for that tiny nub hiding from view. I wasted no time in destroying that clitoris until she was panting and her knees were threatening to give out.

But before she could climax, I rose. Her mewl of frustration hardened my cock to stone but I wanted her dripping and ready. Wrapping my fingers in her long, dark hair, I held her tight against me, exposing her neck for my lips. I kissed a trail down the column of her skin, then abruptly bent her over the thick rounded cushion of the chaise longue. Without releasing her hair, I drove myself into her. My steady thrusts caused a shock wave that rippled through her skin, each ass cheek bouncing as I rammed myself into her through her orgasm with a wild grunt.

Alessandra took each thrust and groaned, her tits likely abraded by the cushion fabric as I rode her hard.

God, the sweetness of that pussy was beyond anything I'd ever known. A man could get attached to this kind of sex.

I could get attached.

Maybe I already was.

My climax came fast, nearly too fast. I pulled out in the nick of time before I spurted inside her, spilling on the small of her back. Panting hard, Alessandra groaned against the cushion while I staggered away to find something to clean her up. I returned with a small towel and wiped her back. I spun her around, grabbing her ass with one hand and her chin with the other, and stared into her dazed eyes. "That was a preview for tonight. Wear something short and tight. I want to see those gorgeous tits on display."

Yet even as my firm tone brooked no argument, I reached down to help her with her jeans. I felt the tremble in her body and I knew she'd be thinking about that orgasm for the rest of the day, which was exactly what I'd planned.

I kissed her softly—the opposite of how I'd fucked her—and then walked her to the door.

A slow, contented smile formed as I closed the door behind her.

Alessandra didn't know it yet but I'd say that negotiation went very well.

Very well, indeed.

CHAPTER TWELVE

Alessandra

I HURRIED INTO my office after a quick shower at my apartment and found Como glaring as if I'd just spat on the Turin Cathedral in full view of the archbishop. My plan was to ignore whatever was biting him in the ass and focus on the business at hand, but Como's thunderous expression warranted a conversation before the day was completely ruined.

"Is there something on your mind?" I asked, settling at my desk, turning on my computer. My thighs ached, reminding me of Dante, and my cheeks flared with heat as my breath caught. I cleared my throat when I saw Como watching me with full accusation in his eyes. Exasperated, I said, "Spit it out already, Como. We have work to do."

"You didn't come home last night."

"And you know that why?"

Como shifted in his chair, embarrassed. "Because I went by your place. I thought you might be hungry. I brought some of Mama's leftover linguine."

Como's mother was a fantastic cook. I graced him with a genuinely apologetic smile. "I'm sorry I missed it but I had a business dinner."

Not entirely a lie but not the truth either. I wasn't about to tell Como about Dante, though. The niggling sense that Como was writhing with jealousy in spite of our previous talk made me nervous.

"I didn't see any plans in your schedule," he said, frowning. "Who did you meet with?"

"Not important. It was nothing. If you're finished grilling me over my evening, I'd like to discuss some of the advertising campaigns getting ready to launch for Uva Persa."

"Are you seeing someone?" Como persisted.

"Not your business if I were," I answered, growing impatient. "Please remember your place, Como. You work for me, not the other way around."

"I care for you."

I tried not to show my exasperation and chose my words carefully. "I know you do. I care for you as well, *as a friend*. Please keep sight of that fact." At his crestfallen expression, I sighed and said, "Como, we are the best of friends. We should not let anything get in the way of that friendship. Besides, you are my right hand and most trusted ally in this new venture and I need you focused by my side. Please say that we can remain friends."

"I will always be here for you, Alessandra," he said with a stiff upper lip. "Even if you are set upon being foolish with that American."

I tried not to react. How could he have known I

was with Dante? Was it possible he or another colleague saw me kiss him at Una Notte Magica? Regardless, Como was the one being a fool. I cast a
short smile Como's way. "I would never be the one to
act foolish with anyone, particularly with my dream
on the line. Have you so little faith in me?"

"No, of course not. I believe in you and always
have," he said, his brown eyes warming. "You are
an incredible woman."

"Then stop treating me as if I were made of glass
and in need of protecting. I can handle my own affairs and that includes whom I choose to allow into
my personal time. I don't wish to visit this topic
again, am I clear?"

Como didn't look pleased but he nodded in understanding. Relieved to move on, I said, "Excellent.
Now, did we get the color scheme resolved for the
branding? I want the label to be perfect and we are
nearly ready to go to bottling."

Como nodded and produced an art sheet, which I
looked over, pleased with the new changes. "Thank
God," I murmured, breathing a sigh of relief that we
were able to make the changes before going to press.
"Tell Victor we are good with the changes. Go ahead
and roll with the labels." I returned the art sheet to
Como, adding, "Have you heard from La Pergola
and Paul Bucose?"

Como answered with a proud nod. "Both have
RSVP'd for the launch. They are excited to see what
all the buzz is about. Uva Persa is going to be the
hit of the season."

"Let's hope." I resisted the urge to chew on my nail, a bothersome bad habit left over from my childhood that had managed to follow me into adulthood. In order to give my new experimental wine a stellar push into the world, I was putting everything I had into the launch, which kicked off with an exclusive tasting with some of the most renowned restaurateurs in the world. While Castello di Baroni used to grace the tables of aristocrats, my wine would be the preferred choice for the new generation of important people. At least that was my hope and dream, but I was well aware that I was putting all of my eggs into one basket and it could all go crashing to the ground. I couldn't think about that possibility, not now. "Excellent job, Como," I praised, shoving my fears to the bottom of my thoughts. "We're all set for the launch, then?"

"Everything has fallen into place nicely," he agreed but then brought up another sticky subject. "When are you going to tell your father that you've started this new wine on your own?"

I licked my lips, hating the anxiety that single question produced. "When it's ready," I answered firmly but I knew I was stalling. My father was old school and even though he supported me with Castello di Baroni, I was fully aware that if Enzo had lived, I wouldn't be in the position of power I was now.

My father was old and simply didn't have the energy to run the winery as it should be and even though I was a woman, he would not suffer a stranger running our family business.

So that left me—the least intolerable option.

I drew a breath, hating that it hurt my heart, but my father would never change, just like I couldn't change the minds of those staunchly refusing to alter the formulation required for the Chianti Classico label. Innovation paled in the face of tradition and no one could see that it was turning the industry into a stale pond run by old men.

"Your father might surprise you," Como said, reading my mind. "Change comes slowly but it comes nonetheless. He is very proud of you."

I smiled, accepting Como's words in the spirit they were given if I didn't quite believe them. My father was still waiting to see when I was going to come to my senses and marry Alberico, which wasn't going to happen.

Sophia walked in, a welcome surprise. "Hello, love," she said, pressing a quick kiss on my cheek before settling in the chair opposite my desk. "Would you like to get some lunch today?"

Lunch sounded wonderful. Sophia was a marketing consultant, often working with wineries in the area, and it was always a treat when we could meet. I'd skidded out of Dante's hotel room before eating and I was famished. I checked my watch. "Actually, I could eat now. Want to see if any of the cafés are still open?"

"It's too late for coffee but they might have some

fresh *bruttiboni* left over from breakfast," Sophia suggested, rising. "Let's do it."

"Sounds good to me," I said, grabbing my purse, but I paused when I caught Como's frown. "Is everything okay?"

"I just think we need to go over some issues with the latest Chianti shipment, seeing as you came in late already."

"I think you can handle that," I said with full confidence. "And I'm starved. I'll be back in an hour or two."

I left Como dissatisfied with my answer but I wasn't happy with the way he was trying to micromanage me since Dante came into the picture. I really hoped Como came to his senses soon because his attitude was getting on my nerves—which wasn't good for his job security.

CHAPTER THIRTEEN

Dante

I RETURNED TO Alessandra's office at the end of the day, purposefully choosing the time so that she couldn't turn down my offer for another night spent with me.

I knocked at the entrance and received a scowl from the lanky man I assumed was her assistant, and a blush of surprise from Alessandra, which I thought only made her prettier.

"By my clock, it's quitting time," I announced, going to her desk to plop down in the chair. I cast a grin toward the frowning man and said, "Am I right? Aren't you ready to call it a day? Grab a nice bottle of Cab and put a pin in this workday?"

"May I help you?" the man asked stiffly. "This area is private. I'll have to ask you to return to the gift shop, where it's appropriate for guests."

Alessandra chuckled and said, "It's fine, Como. Dante is right. I'm ready to relax for the evening." She rose and gathered her purse but before I could crow with what felt like an easy victory, she said, "But I'm sorry, I already have plans with my friend Sophia tonight."

My brow went up as a slow smile tickled my lips. I knew she hadn't forgotten my directive from this morning. I also knew all I had to do was whisper in her ear all the dirty things I was going to do to her and she'd be wet enough to bend over her own desk. I let my gaze slide to her desk, then back to her. The sudden flush of her cheeks told me she knew exactly where my thoughts had gone, and that pleased me. But she was playing hard to get. That was fine...I liked to play, too.

I leaned forward, pinning her with my gaze, letting her know in no uncertain terms that I was going to get my way and she could either get on board or I'd carry her out on my shoulder. Hell, that sounded fun just because. "Have you forgotten this morning already?" I asked in a silky tone.

And then I sensed the tension in the room climbing and I found her assistant, Como, staring daggers at me. Before Alessandra could calm him down, he shut off his computer and left us behind.

I rose to find Alessandra giving me a dark look. "What?"

"That wasn't necessary," she said, shouldering her purse and moving around her desk. "You had no right to bring up our personal business in my place of work. Now I have to smooth his feathers or he'll be unbearable tomorrow."

But I grabbed her hand and pulled her to me. "Let me guess…he has a crush on you."

Her breath hitched but a smile threatened as our lips closed the distance. "A little," she answered before I sealed my mouth to hers, my tongue taking hers. Her little moan did terrible things to my cock. Within seconds, I was ready to put that desk of hers to good use.

I broke the kiss with a grin. "Can't say I blame the guy. If I had to work day in and day out with you across the room, I'd never be able to get any work done. Does he take a lot of bathroom breaks?" I teased.

She laughed and shook her head. "Como and I are friends, nothing more."

"Poor guy," I said, reaching around to squeeze her plump behind. "He doesn't know the joys of pounding this sweet ass."

She blushed and slid her hand down my front, finding my rock-hard erection. "I didn't say that, now, did I?" she returned coyly, and I was shocked. Alessandra chuckled and stepped away. "Just out of curiosity…where were you thinking of taking me tonight?"

I was still stuck on the image of that gangly man pounding away at Alessandra's luscious body, and I didn't like it. I tried to shake it off but there it was, a growing sense of jealousy that was both foreign and inappropriate. "Sleeping with your employees, huh?" I asked, squeezing her ass and tilting her hips to grind her against my cock. "Isn't that frowned upon?"

"Generally speaking," she agreed breathlessly. "Which is why I put a stop to it."

"But now he's got a crush on you and that's bad for business."

Alessandra bristled even as she angled her hot core against me. "That's not your concern, now, is it?"

"No, I guess it's not," I agreed, kissing her hard again before saying, "Cancel your plans. You're with me tonight."

I released her and she returned with a fair amount of sass, "What makes you think I want to spend another evening with you? Maybe I've had my fill and now I'm bored."

I laughed at the pure nonsense. "You want me. I could stick my finger inside you right now and find you dripping wet. You might succeed at bluffing other people but not me, sweetheart. Now let's get moving. We're going to be late."

"Late?" Intrigued, she followed me. "Late for what?"

I grinned as I answered, "A cooking class."

The key to gentling a woman was to always keep her guessing.

CHAPTER FOURTEEN

Alessandra

ADMITTEDLY, MY PLANS with Sophia were something we threw together casually in light of neither of us having anything to do that night, but I felt I ought to turn Dante down simply because he was getting too cocky.

Yet I couldn't bring myself to say the words. I liked his confidence, even though it bordered on arrogance—he wore it well. A shiver danced down my spine as I followed him to his car, not at all surprised at the luxury sedan waiting for him.

"Perhaps I'd like to drive," I said.

"You don't know where we're going," he said as he slid into the driver's seat.

I chuckled and took the passenger side. "Well, only because it's been a long day…you can drive."

"Thank you, Your Highness," he said drily, and we started down the long, winding driveway to the road. Dante found my hand, clasped it between his and kissed the back as he said, "You do know how close you were to being defiled on your desk, don't you?"

I thrilled at the imagery and wished he'd made good on his claim but instead, I smiled with wry amusement, if only to take him down a peg. "You have quite the imagination. What makes you think I would've been okay with that? I'm a businesswoman, not a call girl."

"All work and no play makes Alessandra a dull girl," he said.

I laughed. "Do you find me dull?"

This time it was his turn to blush. "God, no. You're the most intriguing woman I've ever met."

His genuine response surprised us both, but I needed to reclaim the power in this relationship. "Don't make a habit of showing up unannounced. You disrupted my workday."

"The workday was finished. You were probably just playing solitaire at that point."

"I don't play solitaire."

"No? I do. It's my favorite card game."

I smiled, shaking my head. "Tell me about this cooking class that I haven't agreed to attend."

"Ah, well, seeing as I missed taking you out, I thought, let's make dinner together, get our hands dirty and then feed each other. Sounded like fun—and maybe if you're lucky, we could hole up in a pantry somewhere and really get creative." He paused to glance at me. "You're Italian...you can cook, right?"

"That's offensive," I said, laughing. "But yes, of course I can cook."

"Good, because I'm not exactly Gordon Ramsay in the kitchen," he admitted. "You might have to do the heavy lifting. I can definitely open jars, though, if that's something that's needed."

"Then why are you taking me to a cooking class?" I asked.

"Because it seemed interesting, and for what I have planned after dinner…you're going to need your strength."

My breath caught as my heart rate sped up. It was too easy to remember all the delicious things he'd done to my body last night…and this morning. It was tempting to say, "screw the class, take me directly to your hotel room," but I held my tongue. A woman never gave up too much or else the power was gone. I was a master at controlling the men in my sphere but Dante was giving me a run.

"I am hungry," I said with a small smile as I pulled my phone from my purse and quickly dialed Sophia. I glanced at Dante as I said when she picked up, "Hey, sorry to do this last minute but I have to cancel."

"Cancel? Is everything all right?"

"Oh yes, everything is fine. I'll call you tomorrow, yes?"

Sophia's sudden sucked-in gasp revealed she was onto me. "You little she-devil, you're seeing *him* again, aren't you?" I'd told her more about Dante over lunch, and she'd slowly shifted from being concerned he was a threat—I'd convinced her I was well in control of the situation—to being excited for me. Before

I could answer, she followed with an immediate, "I want details first thing tomorrow!"

I laughed and said, "Okay, tomorrow. Bye, love," and clicked off. "I just canceled on my absolute best friend in the entire world, so this night better be amazing."

"I can't make any promises on the food, but I can say that by the end of the night you'll wonder how you managed to go through your entire adult life without me in it."

Oh, his confidence was astounding and so cheeky, but I liked it. "We'll see," I said. His head was already too big for his shoulders. It was a small wonder he fit inside the sedan.

We arrived at the place and went in. There was a modest group of tourists, no one local whom I could recognize, and Dante found us a kitchenette that we could call our station. I smothered a laugh that I was in an actual cooking class. It was such a touristy thing to do that I would never have imagined doing it, but I had to admit that Dante looked pretty good as he wound the apron around his waist, ready to get his chef credentials for the night.

"Tonight we are making fresh pasta with clams and sausage," the instructor said in English as he addressed the group. Appreciative murmurs rippled through the group and my stomach actually growled. "You'll find the pasta dough prepared at your station. Please remove the wrapping and prepare to make the linguine."

I smothered a laugh as Dante tried to feed the

dough into the pasta maker, cranking the wheel with an intense expression, as if he were determined to make the utmost perfect example of linguine ever created. Flutters erupted up in my belly even as I tried to smother the electricity that snapped and sparked between us.

His hands, so strong and sure, were gentle enough with the dough to keep the strands from snapping in two. I struggled to keep my thoughts on the food when all I could focus on was how those big hands had twisted me inside and out with pleasure. My flushed cheeks gave me away just in time for Dante to catch my gaze. He knew where my thoughts had wandered and his gaze heated. Our attraction to one another was a torch that burned between us and it was difficult to squelch.

Even when we were surrounded by strangers and preparing dinner. The simmer in his eyes reflected my own.

"Are we going to make it to the clams?" he asked in a low tone. In response, my tongue darted along my lower lip, my heart rate kicking up a notch. I didn't want clams or linguine. God, I wanted Dante, splayed out, cock hard and ready to ride, but I managed to drag my gaze away and busy myself with preparing the sausage. He chuckled and teased, "If you keep looking at me like that, you're going to be the main course."

My breath hitched and I fought a delighted smile as I said, "Careful, your dough needs tending."

The low rumble of his laughter tickled my soul.

And other parts, too.

This game was becoming very dangerous.

CHAPTER FIFTEEN

Dante

WHOSE BRIGHT IDEA had it been to do a cooking class? Oh yeah, mine. I thought I was being so clever when in fact, it'd been stupid. I should've just ordered room service so we could eat naked and then get back to worshipping each other's bodies. Because, let's be honest, neither one of us could care less about whatever the chef was teaching.

All she had to do was say the word and I'd take off with her, but the stubborn woman was determined to let this asinine idea of mine play out. She knew I was dying, that my cock was practically bursting through my trousers, and yet she danced out of reach with only a coy smile.

My gaze drifted to that fantastic behind—an ass that could make a grown man cry—and I choked down a groan and tried to focus. My hands had become impatient and my interest level had definitely waned now that I knew Alessandra wanted to leave as much as I did, but her pride wouldn't let her give in.

She was ten times any woman I'd ever spent time with and I was out of my depth. I craved the mystery and challenge Alessandra presented unlike any I'd ever known.

We finally finished and carried our plates to the lighted patio, where there was an excellent view of Siena as it quieted down for the night. The cobblestone streets were something out of a fairy tale, and the faint sounds of music somewhere filtered in on the wind. It was so fucking charming that I couldn't have planned it better. Yet all of that could've faded away and I still would've been entranced by Alessandra.

Her long dark hair begged for my hand, and those lips I wanted to ravish as I watched her carefully wind her pasta and savor the meal. Everything she did was flavored with an exotic sensuality that made other women seem basic. I roused myself from the spell weaving itself around us and forced light conversation for the sake of making it through dinner.

"Not bad, eh?" I said, fishing for a compliment without shame. "If business doesn't work out, I might look into opening a restaurant. Of course, my menu would only consist of one dish. Hopefully, no one minds eating clams and sausage every time they visit."

She laughed at my silly joke and I smiled, happy to be there with her. For a brief moment it was easy to forget that I had a mission and it involved taking her winery from her.

I pushed the thought away. "How was work?"

I asked, playing the dutiful date with a benignly thoughtful expression. "Anything exciting happen today?"

Alessandra deliberately placed a bite in her mouth, chewing slowly and swallowing before she answered. "I don't talk business outside of the office." Then she graced me with a slow, closed-mouth smile that did weird things to my insides. God, she was mesmerizing, even when she was shutting me down.

"Fine. Shall we talk about how I can't wait to rip those clothes off your body and turn you inside out with my tongue?"

Aside from the slight hitch in her breath, she revealed nothing. Her self-control was legendary. I was used to women trembling, practically wetting themselves to be in my bed.

Not Alessandra.

"Tell me about your life in the States," she countered. "Tell me about the real Dante Donato."

"What you see is what you get," I said, making a grand gesture, but she wasn't buying it. I chuckled, murmuring, "Tough crowd. All right, what do you want to know?"

"Just as I said…the real you. I want to know who Dante is when he's not putting on a show for everyone."

"What makes you think I'm putting on a show?"

"Something in your eyes. You're always thinking one step ahead, always trying to stay in front of whoever is behind you. I suspect it comes from always feeling passed over by your father. Am I wrong?"

I sat stunned. Alessandra was not only hot as hell but dangerous. She saw way more than I wanted her to, which could seriously screw up my game. The crazy part was, I wanted to answer. I leaned back in my chair, regarding Alessandra for a moment, trying to decide which route to go.

"See?" She pointed out, folding her napkin neatly onto her lap. "You're doing it now. Instead of answering from your heart, you are searching for the most strategic answer, the one that gives you an advantage. I can't imagine living life in this way. Seems exhausting."

"Who is the real Alessandra?" I fired back, not quite ready to bare my soul. "Who is Alessandra aside from the dutiful daughter who carries the weight of an entire legacy on her back with no help from her own father against the patriarchal bent of the established wine industry?"

Almost leisurely, she said, "I asked you first."

She wasn't going to give an inch and that aroused me even more. I took a measured sip of my wine before answering. "I'm a businessman, ruthless and calculated. I do what needs to be done when others hesitate."

"That's your father's influence. Who are you without the voice of your father pushing you to achieve more than anyone else?"

All pithy answers aside, I didn't know who I was without the drive to succeed, but I didn't think I wanted to know. "Does it matter? It's who I am now, and I like who I am."

"Do you?"

"Yes."

Our gazes locked for a moment. Why was she giving me the third degree? Was there something I was giving off that spoke to a vulnerable vibe? God, I hoped not, but the fact that Alessandra didn't shrink away from poking the bear only heightened my interest. Finally, she reached for her wine and said, "You asked who the real Alessandra is…" She paused as the heat built between us, the people around us fading from our view. Then, she leaned forward with, "I'm the same as you—driven, ambitious, ruthless." She sipped her wine and added with a slow smile, "And I like who I am, too."

CHAPTER SIXTEEN

Alessandra

I SHOULD'VE LEFT after dinner. My internal voice of reason cautioned, *don't go home with him*, and yet, that was exactly what happened.

And I wasn't sorry one bit.

I gasped as Dante nibbled my earlobe, whispering terribly dirty things—things that would make the good Catholic girl in me blush but thrilled the naughty adult—and I lost all control of my will and determination to stay in the power seat. There was something so overwhelming about Dante that stole my breath and blotted out reasonable thought, but I was hooked on whatever he was dishing out.

God, I was so hooked.

"You like that, sweetheart?" he murmured with a seductive growl that tickled my insides as he slipped a finger inside me, easing past my dewed lips to find the swollen nub hidden inside. I answered his rhetorical question with a low moan. He found my mouth even as his fingers gently coaxed and teased my clit before moving to strum my G-spot. His fingers were like magic. My hips rose, begging for more, but he kept me at the edge, his tongue playing with mine, all the while creating a symphony of sensation with only his fingers.

My climax danced out of reach as he slowed his tempo. He knew how close I teetered to the edge and yet he pulled back, a wicked grin curving his lips. "Not so fast, sassy one," he admonished, taking pause from my lips to suck a puckered nipple into his greedy mouth. I arched on a gasp as my womb pulsed and my heart rate jumped, my head bobbing from side to side as I mewled. My grasping fingers threaded through his hair and held him tight to my breast until I thought I might die from pleasure.

"Fuck me, Dante," I begged, too bound with need to care how I sounded. I would've crawled on hands and knees to be granted my release but he wasn't ready to give in so easily. He was going to make me work for it. He made his way down my belly, pressing tiny, lingering kisses down to my pubic mound. Settling between my thighs, he parted my damp lips before burying his face there, his tongue seeking and finding that swollen bit of tissue that when touched right would make me do anything without shame. His fingers returned even as his tongue teased and sucked, and if he hadn't been holding my hips in place, I would've bucked from the bed. "Dante!" I groaned with an edge of desperate impatience, so hungry for that promised pleasure. "Please!"

But his muffled laugh was further proof that he planned to torture me. Perhaps it was payback for not giving an inch at dinner, maybe it was simply his favorite game, but either way, when he slowed at the crucial moment, when he knew I was seconds away from tumbling into the abyss, I cried out with frustration. "Finish me," I demanded, my fingers curling in his hair, yanking hard.

His knowing laughter was the sexiest sound I'd ever heard. "My name on your lips," he said with a wicked grin, "sounds about perfect."

Sweat dampened my brow, my chest rising and falling as I practically begged. "Dante...I'll say whatever you want...just let me come!"

"Say pretty please."

I licked my lips. *"Pretty please."*

"That's my girl."

My private heart thrilled at the small endearment even as I knew it shouldn't, because it meant nothing. I didn't want it to mean anything but I was wet and desperate to lose myself in the shuddering waves of pleasure I knew he could give me, and I wasn't thinking clearly.

"I knew from the first time I laid eyes on you, I would learn how you taste, how you feel, how you climax so sweetly, but do you know what I *couldn't* have known?" Dante dragged his mouth across the sensitive bare skin of my pubic mound, sending a riot of goose bumps jumping to the forefront. "I couldn't have known how quickly I would come to crave all of those things."

I swallowed and closed my eyes, unable to speak, for he had returned to my clit, sucking and nipping, swirling his tongue in clever motions as his fingers strummed my G-spot, pushing me without mercy to that edge.

I couldn't hold back another moment. Each agonizing second without release felt like an eternity. *"Please, please...oh God, yes, Dante,"* I babbled, my breath hitching in my throat just as every muscle spasmed in a beautiful concert, nerve endings rapidly firing, leaving me breathless as I rode the wave crashing over me, drowning me in orgasmic splendor until I was left a weakened kitten, too spent to move, much less speak.

He climbed my body and kissed me deep. I tasted myself on his tongue, and it kicked my arousal back into gear even as I lay there stunned. "I love making you come," he confessed. "I've never been with a woman who loses herself so completely."

I smiled with exhausted amusement. "Yeah? Well, you're pretty good with your hands and tongue. Plenty of practice, I'm sure."

He shrugged, saying, "I never kiss and tell."

"Oh, a true gentleman?"

"I wouldn't go that far," he said, chuckling as he gently rubbed the firm head of his cock against my soft, damp slit. My breath hitched a little as he grazed the achingly sensitive skin of my clitoris, still pulsing like a dying star in its final moment. "But pleasuring you has become my favorite activity."

"Lucky for you—" I sucked in a tight breath when

he applied more pressure in just the right spot, catching a moan seconds before it popped from my lips "—I haven't bored of your attentions yet."

"Lucky indeed," Dante agreed, though his eyes sparked with wicked promise. I bit my lip, knowing that I would pay deliciously for that sass, and it was the anticipation that left me trembling. Rising above me, he opened my legs and slid between them, my legs going over his shoulders as he bent me with the pressure of his body against mine. I was bared and vulnerable, my pussy eager and ready to feel his length splitting me apart. "If you can walk by tomorrow morning…I'll have failed to leave an accurate impression of myself."

I didn't have time to laugh or tease before he pushed himself deep inside, impaling me fully. I groaned, quickly losing myself to the pleasure of being beneath him, completely under his control. I willfully succumbed to the all-encompassing sensation of being driven toward that edge without a finger on the wheel. It was raw and powerful, totally outside of my comfort zone and intoxicating.

Santa Maria, it was, dare I say, *addicting*.

And I wasn't ready to give it up.

CHAPTER SEVENTEEN

Dante

THE NIGHT WAS QUIET. We were both exhausted, lying in each other's arms, listening to the evening sounds from the open window, content to be naked and still, sweat drying on our bodies.

I'd never known such bliss.

For the first time in my life, I felt a sense of peace. Usually after sex, I was eager to send the woman on her way. Having another person in my space after they'd already served their purpose ruined it for me.

Not with Alessandra. Her body in my arms felt as natural as an extension of myself. Her scent on my body smelled like heaven.

Better than freshly baked beignets.

I wasn't going to allow anything to ruin this moment. There was plenty of time for that later. I wasn't going to delude myself into thinking this was anything more than two sexually aligned people doing what they did best, but I did feel there was something between us that, in another life, might've been something worth pursuing for real.

"Tell me about Enzo," I said, tracing light figures on her skin with my fingertip. "What was it like having a twin?"

She drew a deep breath as if speaking about her brother, even after all this time, was still painful. "Having a twin is like looking at a living, breathing extension of yourself. You cannot explain the connection to someone who hasn't experienced it. When he died, I felt it in my soul."

"What happened?"

"A car accident. He was pinned in the car. They worked to free him for fifteen minutes before they realized the steering wheel buried in his abdomen was keeping him alive. His internal injuries were so severe that the pressure was keeping his organs in place. The minute they freed him, he died."

Dante felt her pain as if it were his own. As if he'd been gut-punched. "That's awful," he murmured, holding her a little more tightly. "I'm sorry." Even though he and his brothers weren't close, he couldn't imagine losing one.

"My nonna said, 'Heaven must've needed its angel back because nothing would've kept Enzo from going home,' but that had only made me angry at God for a long time. He took my brother from me when I needed him here."

"What do you believe now?" he asked.

"I believe that bad things happen to good people and the only way to make some kind of sense of those things is to make sure they didn't die in vain. Enzo loved the wine business, far more than I ever did. He had a passion for the grapes that I had never understood until he was gone. I wish he were here to see his dream finally come true."

That tiny slip of information pricked my interest. "What dream was that?"

But she was done sharing that much personal information. "What about you? Are you truly happy chasing your father's dreams? What about your own? Surely, there is something you want that has nothing to do with the errands your father sets you on."

I laughed but inside I was asking the same question. I'd spent my entire life trying to please my father but always came up short. Frankly, I was tired of fighting the same losing battle, but as much as I wanted to wash my hands of his expectations, I couldn't quite manage to do it.

My own private shame, I guess. The need for my father's approval was my inherent weakness.

"I love what I do," I answered, not ready to go there. Donato Inc. wasn't just a company, it was an empire. We owned all kinds of business, from magazines to wineries, and we were constantly looking for our next big investment. Being at the helm of that was riveting. "I admire my father's tenacity and willingness to make the hard choices for the good of the company."

"You put a lot of importance on the bottom line, but *people* make up the balance of your company's worth."

I chuckled at her naive statement. "Sweetheart, as much as I enjoy your earthy sense of capitalism, what matters is what ends up in the bank at the end of the day. People are replaceable."

Alessandra pulled away, her scowl apparent in the moonlight. "You're wrong. People are not replaceable and you are a bigger fool than I realized if you truly believe that. Do you think for a moment I wouldn't give anything to have my brother back? To have him by my side as a team in this business? I would do it in a heartbeat. Wealth can be rebuilt. People cannot."

I realized my error and tried to make amends. "You're right. I spoke too quickly. That was in poor form. I would never try to imply that someone you loved could be replaced. I was speaking more to the workforce, not family connections. As much as I'm annoyed by both of my brothers, I love them and wouldn't want anything bad to happen to either of them."

I thought I'd done a pretty good job of patching my gaffe but her scowl had melted into troubled silence. I reached for her but she stiffened and pulled away. "Sometimes the words that drop from our mouths without thought are our true thoughts and feelings without the mask of polite expectation," she said.

I sat up, my frown matching hers. "That's bullshit. Sometimes we say things without realizing how insensitive it might sound but realize after the fact that we should've clarified."

But she shook her head. "Dante, you're wrong.

You've spent your life playing a part. How can you possibly know your own heart? You value nothing. You've been taught to reject anything that doesn't have a direct dollar value. What about love? How do you put a price tag on that?"

I should've tempered my tongue but the odd chord between us had set me on a reckless path. I'd never felt defensive about my views because I'd never cared about the opinions of others; but for some reason I cared about Alessandra's opinion of me. Her obvious disappointment sharpened my voice.

"Love is a social construct based on a chemical reaction in the brain," I answered. "I'd say, enjoy it while it lasts but don't do anything that will put your livelihood in jeopardy. Case in point, I tried to get my brothers to have their wives sign a prenup but they were too blinded by their feelings to press it. Now, when that chemical reaction fades and, heaven forbid, their wives decide they don't want to be married to them anymore, it's going to cost our family a shit-ton of money to be free of them."

"What makes you think their wives will tire of them?" she asked, shaking her head. "Love isn't so fickle."

"The current divorce rate would disagree," I returned smoothly. "Nothing is forever but death and taxes."

"You have a cold heart, Dante Donato," she said.

There was something about the quiet way she delivered her assessment that cut me to the core. It wasn't the first time I'd been accused of being cold but hearing it from her lips was something I wasn't prepared for.

I stiffened as I put distance between us. "I like to think of it as practical."

"Doesn't change what it is. If you continue on this path, you will end up bitter, angry and alone."

How many times had angry lovers thrown that very sentiment in my face? Too many, but this time I couldn't seem to laugh it off. "I'm flattered that you care about my future self."

"You make jokes but I'm not laughing. You are incredible in bed but you are woefully inadequate when it comes to being a human."

I sat up, freshly irritated. "Not many people would dare to say that to me."

"Why not? Because you are so important? Because you are wealthy? Because they are afraid of bruising your delicate ego?"

Probably all of the above. "Because I don't tolerate people disrespecting me," I answered.

"It's not disrespect, it's honesty. Maybe that's part of your problem. People are afraid to tell you what you need to hear. Surrounding yourself with people who will simply nod and tell you what you want to hear won't do you any good. We all need someone who is willing to tell us the straight truth if we hope to evolve."

Evolve? Once I'd dated a yoga instructor who charged crystals by the light of the full moon. She'd said something similar as I'd walked out the door, leaving behind her New Age bullshit and losing her number. "You've got your opinion and I've got mine. I told you I like who I am. My desire for improvement isn't as needy as yours."

"I am not needy." Her laughter at my veiled criticism made me feel small and petty. "I feel sorry for you. You're dooming yourself to a lifetime of disappointment. You can't pour from an empty cup. You seek validation in the all the wrong places."

"Says you," I muttered. When did this turn into a Dr. Phil session? I tossed the blankets aside and strode to the bathroom, needing a little space. Couldn't we go back to the wild monkey sex and forget all this psychobabble bullshit?

Things had been going so well. They say that when words make you defensive, they've struck a chord, possibly a little too closely to the truth. If that were true, Alessandra must've hit the bull's-eye because I was humming with irritation. I wanted to lash out, to prove her wrong, to show her that she was off base with her assessment, but I also didn't want to ruin what progress I'd made by popping off in anger. I needed to stay close to her if I wanted my hands on the winery.

Even as I thought it, I knew that wasn't entirely true. Something was shifting between us, and it confused the hell out of me. I didn't want to admit that I wanted to keep close for other reasons. Ones I wasn't willing to explore too deeply.

If I wanted Alessandra to trust me, I had to swallow whatever ire I was choking on and make amends. Washing my hands, I made a mental note to calm down and do exactly that, but as I exited the bathroom, my mouth full of pretty words meant to placate, I found the room empty.

Alessandra had left.

CHAPTER EIGHTEEN

Alessandra

I WASN'T GOING to stay with Dante after that ridiculous speech. I was surrounded by machismo in my line of work but hearing Dante cover his feelings with that same useless veneer was more than I could stomach.

I wanted him to be better than that, although I didn't know why. It wasn't as if I was hoping for some kind of future together but I couldn't explain how deep my disappointment went at his reveal.

My eyes stung with grit. I hadn't slept well after returning to my apartment. I blamed Dante. What was done was done, though. Time to march forward. I made it to the office early, thankfully before Como, and started work. I wasn't in the mood to listen to Como's jealous sniping at the moment.

But as luck would have it, Como called in sick, and I was grateful for the silence in the office. If I was perturbed that Dante hadn't tried to call, it was a mild distraction and nothing more.

It was nearing lunch when my nonno popped his

head in. I smiled in welcome surprise at my grandfather's unexpected appearance. I rose and pressed
a kiss on each cheek. "What mischief are you up
to?" I asked, my heart filled with love for the old
man. "Does Martina know you're out and about?"
My grandfather's nurse kept a sharp eye on him,
though they doted on each other.

"No, and I don't need you squealing on me either,"
he answered, his chin proud even as he leaned on his
ornate cane. "I came to enjoy lunch with my favorite
girl and I won't take no for an answer."

"I wouldn't dream of it," I said, smiling. "And
where are we going for lunch?"

"My favorite place, of course."

My heart swelled with pride and my eyes threatened to fill. I knew exactly where he wanted to go
and he'd likely already made all the arrangements.
My nonno might not be the spry young man he used
to be but he still managed to get things done.

I linked my arm happily through his and we made
our way out of the manor and onto the south side of
the vineyard, where Nonno had had a gazebo built
in Enzo's honor. As we approached the gazebo, I saw
that a full luncheon spread had been prepared and
set out for our arrival. I nudged his arm, saying in
a conspiratorial tone, "Methinks you have Martina
wrapped around your finger. There's no way you
managed all this on your own."

"I admit to nothing," Nonno said, his eyes twinkling with merriment. He waited for me to take my
seat before taking his own and I wished my nonna

was still here to enjoy luncheons like this with the man of her dreams. Their love story was something that always made me privately sigh, even if I didn't believe it could happen in today's world. Once settled, Nonno snapped his linen napkin across his lap and went straight to business. "The tasting is soon. Are you prepared, *patatina*?"

A small smile warmed my lips at the endearment. "Yes, Nonno. I am as prepared as I can possibly be without knowing the future. The private tasting went very well. I believe wholeheartedly that Uva Persa will have a huge impact on the future of Baroni wine but only God knows for sure."

Pleased, Nonno nodded and poured a crisp white into our glasses. He raised his glass with an affirmative jerk of his chin. "Then so be it. It is out of our hands. It will be what it will be."

I blinked back sudden moisture. My nonno's faith in me was humbling and terrifying. What if I failed? What if I let everyone down and this venture turned out to be foolhardy and ultimately sent our legacy tumbling into ruin? I swallowed the lump of fear congealing in my throat and forced myself to smile against the urge to cry. "I love this spot. It was always Enzo's favorite."

"Yes, the sun hits the vines perfectly. Enzo always had a love for the vines but perhaps not the head for business, unlike you, *patatina*."

I met my grandfather's gaze, chuckling ruefully at how terribly transparent I must be if he saw through

me so easily. "Is it so obvious that I'm afraid of fail-
ing us all?"

Nonno shrugged as if failure wasn't the worst
thing that could happen to a person. "You cannot
win if you don't first try, and to try you have to face
the reality that you might fail." Such simple wisdom
was my grandfather's hallmark, something my father had never truly grasped. He sighed as he poured
the olive oil and grabbed some bread to sop it up.
"Enzo may have had the vision but he never would've
gone against your father to plant his dream, not like
you. You are bold and aggressive, which is exactly
what the blood needs to survive in the new environment. It is not the same as when I was a young man,
nor when your father was young. This is not a bad
thing. Change is necessary to evolve, and frankly,
our industry has been suffering from rot for a long
time. Not enough nutrients in the soil to grow quality grapes. The wine suffers. You know this."

I did know this—I knew it by heart as it was an
argument I'd held regularly with my father when I'd
been trying to convince him to partner with me on
the new varietals. "What made you decide to take a
chance on me, Nonno?"

My grandfather smiled as if I were blind. "Why
wouldn't I? I am an old man. What chance do I
have to make a difference now aside from helping
those who might have the opportunity to effect real
change? You are that change, the new guard. I am
honored and privileged to be some small part of this
change. Besides, what am I to do with money? I can-

not take it with me and my needs are met so I might as well do some good with it while I can."

Why couldn't my father have been as wise? I smiled in return with gratitude as my gaze drifted out toward the countless rows of the recently harvested vines. Even as my grandfather's confidence buoyed me, a small snippet of doubt wormed its way into my head. "Nonno, why am I so scared? I know in my heart this is the right decision, but I still worry that I'm being foolish and my ego is in charge, which is never a good navigator."

"Bah, don't underestimate the importance of a healthy ego. You have to believe in yourself in order to take a big risk. My girl, let me ease your fears. I love you. I love you with all the breath in my body but if I hadn't believed in your proposal, I wouldn't have invested with you. It's that simple. Love is love, but business is still business."

I laughed. Once again, simple logic at its best. "True." But it made me think of Dante and how business was all he had, which felt incredibly sad. "Nonno...an American wanted to buy Baroni. I turned him down." Nonno wasn't impressed, which I knew he wouldn't be—as I told Dante many had offered and we always sent them away. But there was more to Dante and I needed to talk to someone about my feelings. "His name is Dante Donato. Does that ring a bell? He says his family built our manor in the thirteenth century. I have done the research and his boast is accurate. He offered an obscene amount of money for our winery. Of course, the money means nothing but it seemed curious timing given our new venture. Do you think he knew about Uva Persa?"

"Donato…" Nonno rolled the name on his tongue and his gaze narrowed in thought. "Yes, actually, the name is familiar. I knew a Donato long ago. Brash, boastful and with the worst taste in wine. You were right to send him packing."

I laughed. "Yes, well, Dante seems to have improved on his predecessor but he is still boastful." *And sexy, and one helluva a kisser.* I blushed privately, drawing a deep breath, but my nonno's eyes were sharp. I shook my head, stopping him before he could start. "I am not interested in Dante. Intrigued, yes, but nothing more than that. He entertains me."

"Ah, *patatina*, remember love happens when we least expect it."

I barked a short laugh. "Nonno, hush your mouth. The last thing I want to worry about is some man falling in love with me. I have enough on my plate."

He chuckled. "Have I ever told you the story of how I met your nonna?"

"Many times." My favorite story ever, but I indulged him. "But you can tell me again if you like."

"Well, she was the most amazing creature I'd ever seen. A radiant force of nature. Her dark auburn hair had flecks of amber left behind by the sun's kisses. Her dark eyes were like large pools of black glass and that mouth, well, it was magnificent."

I didn't want to think of my beloved grandparents getting dirty together, but appetites didn't spring from the ground. They had to come from somewhere and I could only imagine how my spirited Italian grandparents had been in their youth.

"Of course you fell in love at first sight. Nonna was jaw-droppingly beautiful."

"Yes, yes, but it was not mutual," Nonno shared, shocking me. This was not part of the story I knew. He shook his head. "No, she had no interest in me. None. In fact, she thought I was a selfish prick."

I was shocked. "No," I protested, unable to believe this version of my family's love story. "Nonna always talked about how she loved you."

"Yes, yes, later. She came to love me but I had to win her love. Of course, I did, but it was smart to woo her. I'd never had to put so much effort into winning a woman. It was good for me. Nothing easily won is worth having, that was the lesson I learned very early with your nonna. And boy, was she ever worth having." A wistful pause followed before he added with a soft smile filled with yearning. "I miss her every day."

Tears pricked my eyes. "Me, too. No one can make linguine like Nonna could, not even Como's mama and she's pretty good."

Nonno smiled with pride, knowing this was true. "Every single day I wonder why God took her from me. But it is not for me to question, eh?"

My grandparents were good, strong Roman Catholics. Nothing shook their faith, not even tragedy. I wish I had their conviction, their belief in something bigger than themselves. A part of me was still angry with God for taking Enzo so young even though I knew I shouldn't admit to something so blasphemous.

"I don't know, Nonno," I admitted. "I suppose Nonna would remind us that God works in mysterious ways."

He nodded, agreeing. "That she would. She was a good woman. Strong in her faith. Sometimes I am weak." He drew a deep breath, nodding in memory. "My point, beautiful Alessandra, is that sometimes love comes when we think we aren't ready, but God always knows when the time is right."

I wasn't religious—well, of course, I was raised Catholic but I wasn't a *good* Catholic by any means. Nonna, God rest her soul, would've been horrified by how few times I'd actually attended Mass since her passing. I simply didn't have time, but I could only hope God would understand and forgive my absence. "Well, I definitely don't have the time nor the interest in love, even though I do adore yours and Nonna's love story and I never tire of hearing it." Even with the shocking new details, I thought privately. "Besides, I am far too busy with the launch of Uva Persa to even fathom adding another complication. The idea even gives me gray hair."

"You like him. I can see it in your eyes, *patatina*."

I shook my head vehemently. "No, you see someone who is hungry," I replied, reaching for the bread and the fresh garlic. I winked as I scooped the garlic onto the bread, before sopping it with olive oil, saying, "Love, hunger—the same." Then, with great flourish, I enjoyed my mouthful.

Nonno took my cue and dropped the subject and we finished our luncheon. Nothing was more precious to me than spending time with my nonno. I could always count on him for snippets of wisdom or entertaining anecdotes; but even as I adored time with my grandfather, the contrast between my relationship with my father was a bittersweet one. Enzo's death had been so traumatic for our family, it fractured our framework so terribly that it was impossible to return to our original state. I feared I'd always wonder if my father loved Enzo more than me.

"Nonno, what if…" The words were stuck in my throat. Fear of the answer stopped me. I looked to my grandfather, my eyes welling against my control. He reached over and placed his gnarly, soft hand on mine, squeezing gently. I nodded, swallowing.

Some things weren't meant to be said. The weight of the question and the potential answer were equally crushing.

"Thank you for lunch, Nonno," I said, smiling against the flutter in my stomach.

He patted my hand before withdrawing with a warm smile. "Time spent with you is time well spent."

I breathed against the tightness in my chest. Perhaps I was wrong and the burdens I carried were of my own making, but the anxiety was always with me, particularly now that I was gambling our entire future on a bet placed by my heart.

CHAPTER NINETEEN

Dante

MY FATHER'S VOICE was sharp as he berated my progress.

"What's the problem?" he asked when I admitted I hadn't procured the winery yet. "Did you offer more money? I want that winery."

"We underestimated the Baroni family. They aren't interested in money. They have something that money won't buy—sentiment. We need a different plan."

"Sentiment? What is this nonsense? Ridiculous. You just haven't found their price. *Triple* the price. I don't care. I want that winery," he repeated, the deep baritone of my father's voice grating on my nerves. I'd always admired my father's ability to push past any obstacle, regardless of who stood in his way, but I realized in that moment, his bullheadedness wasn't always a virtue.

In this instance, I didn't see stalwart persistence, I saw an old, petulant man throwing a temper tantrum to get his way. I shifted against the uncomfortable vision and tried to explain.

"The daughter, Alessandra Baroni, is at the head of the winery and she won't budge. Her twin brother, Enzo, died when they were teens and she's holding on to the winery in his memory. There's no amount of money that will change her mind, which is why I said we need a different tactic."

"A dead brother? For fuck's sake, this is what happens when you let women be in charge. God forbid we ever let one become president. There goes the nation."

"Alessandra is more competent that most CEOs," I said, pushing back. It didn't sit well that my father insulted Alessandra when he didn't know what he was talking about. "She's very good at what she does."

My father's disgruntled, "Clearly, she's better than you if you couldn't get her to see our way of things" made me see red, but I knew it was foolish to let my father bait me. Sometimes I felt he said things just to see how far he could push me.

"What about back taxes, liens? Anything we could use to put some pressure on them to sell?" he barked.

Of course I'd already considered these options but when I did a little digging, I came up with nothing. What I didn't admit to my father was that I'd been relieved. I hadn't wanted to win that way—for the first time ever, the win wasn't everything.

Still, I knew that I had to come up with some kind

of plan or else my father would lose all respect for me. "I'm working on something. It takes some finesse. Just relax, give me some time to figure this out and you'll have your winery."

"Maybe I should've sent Luca," he grumbled, and I clenched my jaw to keep from snapping. It was always the same old fallback of pitting me and Luca against one another. It used to motivate me to work harder, but now it just pissed me off. Still, I hated to lose and I would bring home the win, if only to stuff it in the old man's face.

"Be patient. I'll get the damn winery," I said, my brusque tone shutting him down before he could grouse some more. "I'll be in touch." I clicked off and left the conversation, a juvenile part of me wishing I could slam the phone down in my father's ear instead of clicking off with such anticlimactic dullness.

A part of me didn't want to buy Alessandra's winery for my father. I wanted to see her thrive and succeed, to shove her success down the old cronies' turkey necks for trying to keep her down.

My father was just as bad as the old white men determined to keep things the status quo when change was sorely needed. To my growing discomfort, I was beginning to realize that my father was a misogynist and the fact that I never really noticed before told an even deeper uncomfortable truth about myself.

God, I was an asshole.

Sure, plenty of people had thrown that in my face but I'd never cared. Now, it seemed less of a badge of honor and more a cone of shame.

When you had money, sometimes certain truths didn't apply because you could always make a problem go away with enough cash.

Unless that truth was coming from the lovely mouth of a woman who had her own money and didn't give two shits about impressing you or assuaging your ego.

The world needed more women like Alessandra.

Ha! I'd never been particularly *Go Woman Power!* but I was feeling it right now. I couldn't imagine the bullshit Alessandra had to wade through to be successful in her industry.

But then I supposed all generations had to put their stamp on things. Luca had had a time of that, trying to change the way our father did business, but in the end he'd simply put our father out to pasture with a firm but polite, "Time to retire," and then did things his own way.

Luca had never suffered from the need to please our father, probably because our father had always given Luca the benefit of the doubt. It was a blessing Nico had never been burdened by an overabundance of ambition. Since he was the youngest of the three Donato boys, our father had rarely paid much attention to Nico or his antics. If anything, our father had simply chuckled with absentminded amusement whenever word of his youngest son's nonsense had crossed his desk.

It'd always been up to me to clean up Nico's messes, which was why I'd been bemused when he'd up and fallen head over heels in love with a single mom, of all people.

I didn't have anything against his wife. Lauren seemed like a decent woman, but Nico had been the last person on earth I'd ever imagine settling down.

And yet, he seemed happier than ever.

Happier even than that time I'd had to extricate him from the arms of three strippers after a drunken bender before the press had gotten wind of it.

He was a different man.

And, I couldn't believe I'd admit this, but he was a great father. He seemed to enjoy the hell out of being a dad to Lauren's son, Grady, and that was probably an important part of being good at it. At least, I imagine, not having any practical experience in the matter.

I used to feel secure in what I knew. My foundation was solid. Since coming to Italy, my foundation seemed less stable than I'd thought. Questions that I never thought to ask, feelings I never thought to have, were crowding into my head and heart, demanding an audience.

I'd started to think about why I wasn't close to my brothers, and I realized that perhaps I'd never *let* myself get close to them. Growing up, they had their roles to play. Luca, firstborn and beloved heir. Nico, the baby and the charmer. As a kid, I'd sometimes felt like I was living on the sidelines, struggling to figure out where I fit. Maybe deep down, I resented them for having found their place in our family, knowing where they stood with our father, while I'd always felt I had to earn mine.

I frowned, shaking my head. I didn't like this newfound sensation. I didn't have time for an existential crisis. For fuck's sake, I hated nothing more than people who had everything at their fingertips yet whined about how life was somehow empty.

My life was a fucking dream.

I had more money than I could ever spend in one lifetime, beautiful women fought to put themselves on my arm and my name was powerful enough to create a ripple of unease in negotiating circles.

But since meeting Alessandra, everything seemed less cut and dry than before. What was it about her that had me twisted up in knots? She wasn't the most beautiful woman I'd ever spent time with. Okay, maybe that was a stretch. She was a fucking goddess. Even though her body made me weak, there was something far more exotic about the connection I felt when I was around her.

It was…fucking cosmic.

Electric.

Heavenly?

I sighed, grateful I was the only one privy to the running dialogue. I couldn't let myself think that way. I didn't believe in true love, perfect families or happy-ever-after. I still thought my brothers were crazy to go after those things—that was one dream I'd never chase.

And neither would Alessandra, thank God.

I was glad she wasn't mooning after me, staring

at me with longing, trying to become the newest Mrs. Donato.

No, she was running her own empire and couldn't be bothered with mine.

I liked that.

Damn, I liked it a lot.

But my amusement faded quickly, my father's voice carping in the back of my mind, dampening any semblance of a rising mood.

Luca never understood how much pressure our father put on me to always be better, no matter the situation, but then I guess I never understood how Luca never gave two shits about our father's expectations. In my darkest moments, I envied Luca for having that freedom not to care.

As much as I wanted to tell my father to drop the idea of buying the winery, I knew I couldn't. I hungered for my father's approval in a way that never satisfied, no matter how hard I tried.

If I could deliver this piece of history that he coveted so much, he'd finally see me as the son I'd always tried to be.

If not…maybe I was playing a game I was destined to never win.

CHAPTER TWENTY

Alessandra

I WAS MEETING with Sophia and taking her to a blind tasting of Uva Persa so I could get her honest opinion on the blend. Even though it was too late to make any changes, I needed to know that I was on the right track to calm my nerves.

As far as Sophia knew, we were enjoying a girls' day and nothing more, but in truth I could use the distraction.

After my conversation with my grandfather, my thoughts had been tangled on a number of subjects.

Mainly my feelings about Dante but also my understanding of my grandparents' story, which I'd always believed I knew forward and backward until my grandfather's revelation.

It was strange how something so small could rock your world.

Sophia, charming as ever, wearing a lovely yellow sundress, climbed into my convertible, smiling as bright as the lazy autumn sun overhead. "You are too pretty to be spending your time with me but I'm selfishly happy to spend the day with my best friend," I said, smiling with love in my heart.

Sophia waved away my praise, as usual, with an offhand "You're blind" as she buckled up, and I wished for the thousandth time that Sophia could see herself as the rest of the world did. That wasn't a battle that would be won today. "Where are we going?" she asked.

"There's a blind tasting that I thought you might enjoy and I could use the change in scenery away from the office."

"Sounds wonderful." Sophia was happy to tag along. She was always down for a wine tasting. Sometimes I wondered if it helped her to feel connected to Enzo to stay within the wine world but then other times I felt I was probably reading more into it than a simple enjoyment of wine. "So, have you seen your sexy American lately?" she asked, casting a sly look my way. "He sure is handsome."

I didn't really want to talk about Dante—I was still angry from our last conversation together—but I probably needed to process what I was feeling before I exploded.

"Actually, I saw him the other night. Everything was great until the night disintegrated and I haven't seen him since."

"How did it disintegrate?" she asked, concerned. "Was he a brute?"

"No, nothing like that. He just pissed me off and I didn't want to be around him any longer."

"That sounds serious. What could he have said that would have upset you so?"

I considered my answer carefully. To reveal the true depth of my disappointment would be to reveal feelings I wasn't ready to accept. I was still grappling with the magnitude of how upset Dante had made me over something that really was none of my business. I wasn't sure how deeply I wanted to dig into that particular hole. "He is a very cold person. He said that he believed people are replaceable, and I find that type of thinking typical of an American and not very flattering."

Sophia chuckled. "Well, he *is* American. Perhaps we should not hold that against him because he cannot change that aspect of himself. Is it possible that you misunderstood his position?"

I laughed ruefully, remembering quite clearly how Dante's eyes had been devoid of emotion as he'd explained himself. "No, he was quite clear about how he felt. Dante clearly has issues with his father and I don't have the interest or the time to mess around with his personal baggage."

"I don't think he's expecting you to become his doctor but I know you two share a connection. If it didn't matter, you wouldn't still be mad."

I rejected her theory, insisting, "I'm not mad. I could not care less what Dante Donato does with his time or his life. He is simply nice to look at when I need distraction. I risk nothing when I say his body is sublime."

But Sophia called my bluff, saying, "I've never

seen you so taken with a man. You've always been so focused and single-minded with a narrow sphere of attention. Honestly, I'm glad to see you fired up about someone even if he is making you angry. Life is about more than just work and passion is something you can't manufacture."

I cast a sardonic look her way, amused that she was being openly hypocritical. "That is interesting advice coming from the woman who refuses to step out socially because she's holding a torch for someone who died a really long time ago."

Ouch. Perhaps that was a bit too savage. Sophia's amusement faded and the pain in her eyes made me feel like a toad. She blinked back tears and a small laugh escaped as she said, "That was harsh."

Oh, I was a jerk of the highest order but I'd already stepped in it, so I might as well be honest about my fears.

"I love you, Sophia. You are the sister I never had. But you are dying on the vine. Enzo would not have wanted this for you. You're too much of an amazing human being to spend your entire life stuck in one spot."

A surge of life flashed in her eyes. "It isn't that I don't want to move on. I simply haven't found anyone worth spending the time to get to know. I have very high standards and unfortunately there has yet to be someone worth leveling up in my eyes."

I chuckled at her explanation. "I would love to indulge you but I'm going to point out something you told me recently. As much as I loved my brother, I fear you may have elevated him to God status at this point. I know you loved Enzo and I will forever love you for loving him the way you do. But it's time to move on, sweetheart. It's time to find an actual man or woman, no judgment, who can make you happy as an adult."

"Do I not seem happy?" she asked, lifting her chin. "I have no complaints in my life. You cannot fix your life by focusing on mine."

"My life doesn't need fixing," I balked, wondering how she'd turned this back on me. "I'm very pleased with my life."

"You bury yourself in work and the only time you 'date' is to satisfy your physical needs. I'm not stupid or blind, Alessandra. You're using people to fill a void in your heart that no amount of soulless encounters can fill."

"Soulless?" I repeated, remembering the cataclysmic sex between Dante and me, and how it'd felt the furthest from soulless as anything could. What did that mean? Was there more between Dante and me than something physical? I wasn't ready to go there. "Just because I'm not looking to fall in love doesn't mean I'm just opening my legs for anyone," I said, affronted.

"I'm not saying that you are," Sophia said, softening. "I'm just saying that you're hiding from anything real and I don't understand why."

"If I am hiding, what are you doing?" I countered.

"I am remaining ambivalent," she answered with

a shrug. "If love finds me, wonderful. If not, that's fine, too."

"Love can't find you if you don't put yourself out there."

"For someone who claims to not believe in love, you sure are concerned with my finding it."

"Because I know you do believe in it," I said, but even to my own ears I sounded like a raging hypocrite. I gave up. I didn't know why I was picking at this subject when I knew it was a dead end. Besides, maybe she was right and I was being ridiculously one-sided. Resigned, I finished with a heartfelt "I just want you to be happy" and prepared to drop the subject, but Sophia had one more thing to say.

"I love you, too, Alessandra, and I will give what you're saying some thought. It isn't that I haven't dated. I just don't feel anything that would encourage taking things to the next level. Trust me, I would love to feel something for someone else. I would love to be able to move on. But it's hard to compete with what I had. Even if I was young, I've known what true love feels like. Accepting a substitute would be like eating paper after you've tasted filet mignon."

Sophia's response hit me hard. Here I was worrying about my best friend when she had things more figured out than me. If anyone had known a love like my grandparents, it was Sophia and Enzo. Further proof that it likely wasn't in the cards for me as I'd never felt so consumed by another person. Well, not until Dante, but there was absolutely no future there. The irony was astounding. Fate was a fickle bitch, wasn't she?

"I'm sorry I left you with Alberico the other night. I hope he wasn't too unbearable."

Sophia smiled. "He was quite pleasant, actually. He's a very nice man but I agree with you—he is not your match."

"Thank you," I said with a relieved sigh that I wasn't alone. "I wish Papa would see this, as well. It's becoming downright awkward every time Alberico comes around and Papa is pushing him toward me like a meat platter."

Sophia giggled. "Maybe you should just talk to Alberico, tell him your feelings."

I shuddered, imagining his puppy dog eyes being similar to Como's. "I'd rather not. He is a smart man, he'll figure it out. Eventually." I cast an inquisitive look Sophia's way. "So what did you think of Alberico?"

She shrugged but looked away to gaze at the passing scenery. "He was very polite. A gentleman, which is a nice change from the men I've met as of late."

"Yes, he is very polite," I agreed, wondering if Alberico and Sophia were a far better match than he and I ever could be. Alberico had a genteel sense about him that matched Sophia's refinement and while there might never be fireworks between those two, they would probably manage to make each other very happy. I would have to explore that possibility later.

We let the conversation end, content to finish the ride in silence as we chewed on our own thoughts. By the time we arrived at the tasting, we were both ready to put the conversation behind us.

No one knew at the tasting that the wine was mine. I had purposefully arranged for the bottles to arrive with fake labels and no one at the tasting room was aware that I was the owner of Uva Persa, nor did anyone know my voice as I had Como arrange the tasting.

As far as anyone knew, I was simply another person looking to enjoy a new wine in a beautiful atmosphere.

The tasting room was small, elegant and extremely stylish, as were the patrons. This wasn't a tourist trap by any means, and while I recognized a few faces, smiled in greeting to a few, they were all content to stay within their own groups to enjoy the day.

We accepted our glasses with plates of fragrant cheese and crackers and went outside to the terrace, which overlooked Florence. Old-world charm intersected with the hustle of modern life, and we toasted to our friendship.

Although trying to appear nonchalant about her reaction to the wine, I was watching so keenly it hurt to breathe. I sipped the blend, my taste buds reacting to the bold wine, tasting the ancient *tenerone* grapes and smiling above the rim with pride. "Well?" I asked, trying for a natural smile. "What do you think?"

Sophia's brow dipped in thought as she considered her answer, taking the time to really savor the flavor and texture, just as a true connoisseur would. Her opinion meant a lot to me, not only as my best friend but as someone who knew wine. "This is incredible," she finally said, yet seemed perplexed. "I can't quite put my finger on the blend. I've never tasted anything like this. This is a Chianti?"

I nodded, my excitement building. "It's quite unique," I agreed, pretending to ponder the blend. "Do you like it?"

Sophia's delight was like sunlight to my soul. "It's delicious. I love it." She swirled the liquid, inhaling the bouquet. "This might be my new favorite," she said before twisting around to see if she could find an advertisement for the label. "What is it called?"

"Um, I don't know. I've never heard of it," I lied.

"Well, it's fantastic. Mama would love this."

A weight fell from my shoulders and for the first time in a long time I felt I could breathe. It was true that Uva Persa could still fail, but somehow gaining Sophia's unwitting approval was the reassurance I needed to push forward with renewed vigor.

"Are you all right?" Sophia asked, her smile quizzical. "You have a funny look on your face."

I decided to come clean. "The wine is called Uva Persa," I shared with a smile. "And it is a secret project of mine under the Castello di Baroni label, but for today I have a fake label on the bottle."

Sophia's amazement made me giggle like a

schoolgirl with a crush. Her eyes widened. "I can't believe you never told me. Why is it a secret?"

I carefully set down my glass. "Five years ago I planted a secret vineyard with my nonno with *tenerone* grapes to create a new blend using ancient varietals, and this—" I gestured to the glass "—is the fruit of that labor."

"It's amazing," Sophia said, the admiration in her eyes making me blush. "I am always in awe of how incredible you are, but today I am speechless. How did you convince your father to do this?"

"I didn't. My father doesn't know. Only my grandfather and I invested. I put everything I had into this project, and using the Baroni label is going to either ruin us or send us straight into the future of winemaking. It's really an all-or-nothing venture and I'm terrified."

But Sophia knew just what to say to ease my fears. "I used to worry that Enzo would live only in our memories. Not so. He is here in spirit beside you, guiding you. This is right. You were right to take this chance. I believe in you and your vision."

Tears sprang to my eyes. I hadn't realized how much I needed to hear that validation, but the choking sensation as my throat closed was proof enough that I wasn't as tough as I liked to pretend. Sophia wrapped me in a tight hug and whispered, "I am so proud of you and I know Enzo would be, too," and I bawled openly.

So much for a dignified outing.

Oh well, it was worth it.

"And now I need a refill," Sophia announced, smiling with tears in her eyes as she went in search of the bottle, leaving me to wipe my face and collect myself. I watched her leave, my heart light except for the shadow of lingering fear that I still had one dragon to slay before I could fully celebrate.

I had to find a way to break the news to my father before the launch, which was approaching faster than I was prepared for emotionally.

Dante would say I am the boss, therefore I could make any decision I deemed appropriate for the business, but the Baroni family wasn't like Dante's.

We knew people weren't replaceable and hurting those we loved—even for decisions we deemed right—still left a mark.

I could only hope my father saw the promise of a new dawn instead of the sadness of a sinking sunset with my decision.

Sophia returned with a bottle and filled both our glasses to toast boldly, "To Uva Persa."

"To Uva Persa," I murmured.

Please don't fail me.

CHAPTER TWENTY-ONE

Dante

I HAD TO make amends with Alessandra. It wouldn't serve my purpose to have her scowling whenever my face popped up, but chasing after a woman wasn't my strong suit. Women usually chased me.

If she were an ordinary woman, I'd send an obscene bouquet of flowers in an effusive display of wealth and seemingly considerate attention to win her over, but Alessandra would find that gauche and annoying. Jewelry wasn't an option either. She had her own wealth, and she could buy her own trinkets.

The key to Alessandra was to keep her guessing, keep her on her toes—whether through bone-melting orgasms or unusual escapades, such as the cooking course—but a little groveling wouldn't be amiss.

No woman could resist the temptation of hearing a man say those fateful words "I'm sorry" or alternatively "I was wrong," so I'd go prepared to drop either of those bombs into the conversation.

Assuming she didn't kick me out of her office.

Or that sulking office assistant of hers didn't have me arrested for stepping foot on the property.

It was easy to see that her assistant was head over heels in love with her, even if she couldn't see it or tried to deny it. Lord help me if I was ever so stupid as to fall in love with a woman who wanted someone else.

I showed up at the manor and bypassed the common area reserved for guests and customers to go straight to the office quarters, but not before taking a moment to appreciate the sturdy architecture of the manor. Seeing as my ancestors put this block of rock together and it'd held up for hundreds of years, I took a certain amount of pride in ownership, even if our contribution ended almost as long ago.

Still counted.

I rapped on the doorjamb, peeked inside the office and found Alessandra, head down, dressed with an elegant casual style that could've come straight from the runway to this moment without losing a second in grace. God, she was beautiful. I must've lost myself for a moment but the moment was interrupted rudely by her assistant clearing his throat and glaring. "You seem to feel quite comfortable coming and going where you've not been invited," he said.

At that Alessandra glanced up and our gazes locked. I could tell she wanted to be angry—those twin spots of color flashing in her cheeks gave her away—but she wasn't going to add fuel to the fire because it was unprofessional. "Can I help you?" she asked, ignoring her assistant's jab. "I'm quite busy so if you don't have anything of importance to share, I'll kindly ask you to leave."

I caught her assistant's silent triumph and I wanted to laugh. The game wasn't over by a long shot. I always got what I wanted. Today, I wanted Alessandra to forgive me. "I missed you yesterday."

Alessandra's glare turned frosty. "I have work to do."

"Walk with me," I suggested, and her assistant muttered something in Italian that was probably very unflattering toward me. I pushed off the door frame and came in without an invitation. "Look, I'll do this right in front of your guy but I'd rather have some privacy."

"And what exactly do you feel you need to do that requires privacy?" she asked.

"Apologize," I answered with as much humility as I could muster.

Alessandra folded her arms across her chest with a small smile. "And what are you apologizing for? How you live your life is not for me to say. I could not care less how you conduct yourself."

"And here I thought we were going for honesty," I chided.

She shrugged. "I have no reason to lie. You mean nothing to me."

"Ouch. Well, I wasn't expecting to run to Gretna Green for a quickie marriage or anything but I did believe we shared some good times. Times I'd like to continue while I'm here."

At that, her assistant made a sound of disgust as

he got up and walked out. The knowing smile on my lips only served to compress hers to a fine line. She knew the problem with her assistant was one of her own making, but I wasn't going to bust her too hard on that score. "You are a pain in the ass," she said.

"But that ass, though," I said with a devilish grin that I knew she couldn't resist. That Donato charm was something of legend. Now I understood why Nico had never shied away from turning it on. "Don't try to tell me that you don't want to take a bite."

She cracked a small, grudging smile but Alessandra didn't cave easily. "While I appreciate your humor I have work to do and you just made my work that much more difficult with your little display."

"Maybe it's time to clean house," I said, shrugging. I could give two shits about her assistant's unrequited love pangs. "Not trying to tell you how to run your business but that seems messy." Her glacial expression told me she wasn't amused. I grinned in the face of her irritation. "Come play hooky with me," I said.

"Only you could misinterpret a plainly unwelcome vibe into something else," she muttered but I could sense she wanted to drop whatever she was doing and leave. I'd say that was a good sign but it counted only if she actually came with me. "Unlike you, I'm not on vacation. I have work to do." She paused, her gaze narrowing in question. "Out of curiosity, what did you have in mind?"

"A walking tour of Siena," I answered, my eyebrows waggling like an overeager tour guide. At that she laughed and my grin broadened. I had her interested. "You game?"

"I have an apartment in Siena. Why would I want to do a walking tour?"

"Because if you're anything like me, you've never played tourist, not even in your own city. You might discover things you never knew were interesting right beneath your nose."

I had her intrigued. "Siena is a beautiful place. I'm sure there are plenty of interesting places to discover," she admitted but then said, "However, I don't have time to entertain you. Find someone else to play tour guide."

I pulled a brochure from my pocket and opened it with flourish. "Ha! Our tour comes with a guide. All you need is good walking shoes. Personally, I'm intrigued by the eighteenth-century history and I've been assured that our guide is well versed in ancient history, so we should enjoy many unscripted anecdotes about life in ancient Siena. Now, doesn't that sound far more fun than whatever you're doing right now?"

Whatever she was working on had put a furrow in her brow. I could fairly see the tension in her shoulders. I wanted to work out those knots with my hands just for the excuse of being able to roam her body... and maybe get some information about the Baroni family business along the way. I needed to find a weak spot—anything I could, really—that would put me at an advantage to get her to sell. "It would be a nice change of pace," she admitted, almost to herself, but she wasn't about to stop. The woman had an admirable iron will. It was a shame my father was so intent on taking her winery. I had a feeling he would like her. Or they would shred each other to pieces. Either way, the display would be spectacular.

Alessandra leaned back in her chair, regarding me openly with amusement. "So, back home, are you this easily distracted? I can't imagine that you get much work done."

At home I was nothing like this. I was a workaholic. "No," I admitted. "I'm like you. I work from sunup to sundown. I rarely take vacations and I don't have a lot of friends." What had started out as a sardonic quip ended with stark honesty that struck a deep chord inside me. When had that happened? When had I lost all sense of balance in my life? Since being here in Italy, I'd actually enjoyed my downtime, taking a break from the work I was usually hardwired to do. Well, there would be time enough to return to the grind when I was back in the States. "But I'm not at home. I'm here and I want to spend every moment with you. Naked or otherwise."

Her cheeks colored and her teeth worried her bottom lip as she tried not to smile, but I could see through her. Maybe I should've just bypassed the walking tour and invited her to spend the day in bed. We seemed to have a lot in common between the sheets and there was little to argue when our mouths (and other parts) were otherwise occupied.

"You're impossible."

"I've been called worse."

She wasn't going to budge. Time to switch up strategies. "Okay, all kidding aside, I know it's probably too much to spring a walking tour on you at the last minute but it wouldn't hurt you to change the scenery for an hour or two, would it?"

"An hour or two?"

"Yeah."

"No, I suppose it wouldn't." She crossed her arms and regarded me with a subtle smile. "And what exactly did you have in mind to do for this hour or two?"

I had to think fast. "Actually, I'd enjoy a tour of Castello di Baroni."

She snorted. "There are guided tours for that. If you check with the gift shop they'll let you know when the next tour starts."

"I'm not interested in the tourist version. I want the family version."

"You aren't family."

"Maybe not but my family did build this place and, what can I say, I'm curious." I grinned. "Give me the private tour."

"You are so damn presumptuous."

"And persistent," I added for her and she laughed. "You know I'm right."

Alessandra sighed and closed her laptop. "Fine. One hour, nothing more."

I didn't even try to hide my triumph and when she tried to walk past me, I pulled her into my arms, holding her tight, immediately springing to attention the minute those lush curves settled against the hard planes of my body. "Should I admit that you're the hottest tour guide I've ever seen?" I said right before sealing my mouth to hers.

Her tongue met mine with an urgency that belied her casually annoyed attitude at my untimely intrusion into her day. I saw through her protests and felt with my body how she craved mine. We were the same, even if we were worlds apart geographically.

Which was why she would ultimately understand that there was room for only one victor in this game.

And it would be me.

CHAPTER TWENTY-TWO

Alessandra

HE HAD THIS way about him—something that twisted and turned inside my psyche, rendering me unable to say no, even when I should. That was all I could say in my own defense as I closed up my office with a short note written to Como and led Dante on a private tour of my family home.

Sometimes I forgot how the property must look to fresh eyes. For me, it was simply home but it was truly massive. The largest property in the Chianti Classico region, our property dominated the rolling hills and stretched for 1,200 hectares with vineyards and olive groves.

But not all of the manor was in great shape. We'd closed off sections of it for safety purposes as repairs were needed to make them habitable; however, it was a lower priority because our family wasn't as prolific as it once was and it simply wasn't needed.

However, there was a section of the manor that had always been a favorite play place for me as a child and it was still relatively safe, even though it wasn't in great shape.

Slipping my hand into Dante's, I led him down the curving stone staircase and toward the northern section of the manor. The front door looked straight out of medieval times with its metal bracing and old-fashioned key and lock. I unlocked it and gave the solid wood door a hard push as it groaned in protest. The smell of mildew and time tickled my nose and I glanced back at Dante with a beguiling smile. "Still want the tour?"

"Hell yes, this is fantastic," he said, surprising me with genuine interest as he took in the history of the architecture and the creep of decay. "How old is this section of the manor?"

"It wasn't part of the original build so we think it was built sometime in the eighteen hundreds, but records have been unreliable. Our best guess is as good as we can come to the actual timeline."

He nodded, running his hand along the wooden beams, marveling at how well they'd stood the test of time. "When was the last time someone lived here?"

"Well, actually, about one hundred years ago from what I understand. My father said his great-grand-father had preferred this wing and made it his personal space." I smiled, enjoying Dante's appreciation for the old wing. Some people might see nothing but a falling-down wreck but Dante saw what I had as a child, the charm of a bygone era. "My father had forbidden us from going into the north wing but, of course, Enzo and I took that as an invitation to explore. We spent many hours down here. It became our own private place. We cleaned it out as best we could and made it our little hideaway."

A layer of dust blanketed everything but you could see that modern children had once inhabited this space.

The old sofa we'd managed to pay some of the workers to carry down here, a table, some chairs, but there were no light fixtures or present-day conveniences. I smiled at the gas lantern still on the table. "Although, as much as we loved our space, we never spent much time down here at night. It's a little spooky in the dark."

Dante nodded with complete understanding. "This place is probably haunted as hell. Ever see a ghost?"

"Do you believe in ghosts?" I asked, amused. "You don't seem the type."

"Well, I'm a humble enough man to admit that there are probably things in this world that I can't exactly explain and I'm willing to leave them be if they do the same."

I laughed at the idea of Dante exhibiting humility. "*Humble* and Dante Donato seem incongruous."

He shrugged. "Hey, I like to err on the side of caution." His smile widened. "You didn't answer my question…see any ghosts?"

Only one.

My smile faded a little. "My brother."

"Oh, I'm sorry," he said, contrite. "I didn't mean to bring up sad memories."

"It's okay, it was but a brief moment, a flash and he was gone. I think he was saying goodbye in his own way."

"You weren't scared?"

"I could never fear my brother. He was part of me."

Dante nodded and folded me into his arms. I melted against his chest, inhaling the sharp spice of his masculine scent, and breathed deep. I would never tire of that smell. Dante's particular odor was something that turned a lock deep inside me, releasing something that I couldn't put my finger on but recognized as powerful.

His soft lips brushed against mine with a tender touch even as his strong knuckles gently caressed my cheek. Our tongues slid against one another as our bodies craved the heat only we could create.

In that moment, I wasn't the head of Castello di Baroni, shouldering the burden of an entire legacy, but rather just a woman needing the firm touch of a man who knew how to stoke the fire capable of burning me to ash.

"Dante," I whispered against his lips, gasping as his hands roamed my body, anchoring on my hips to draw me close. "I need you…"

I needed to feel him inside me, moving with me, pushing me to that ultimate release that I craved so deeply.

Dante obliged without so much as a blink, sweeping me off my feet and carrying me to the ages-old sofa, setting me down gently. I helped him shimmy

my pants from my hips and toss them to the floor as I
quickly ripped my blouse off to join them. In panties
and a bra, I relished the smoldering heat in Dante's
gaze as he devoured me from head to toe. When he
looked at me like that, I was the only woman in the
world. I shivered from the intensity, goose bumps
rioting along my exposed skin, inviting his lips to
follow.

Dante placed one leg over his shoulder as he nuz-
zled the damp heat shielded by the tiny scrap of lace,
inhaling my scent as he groaned with pleasure. "I
can't get enough of you," he admitted with a husky
growl that I felt in my belly. I gasped as he teased
me through the thin fabric, dancing around my pussy
lips, tantalizing my clit with just enough friction to
make me squirm without actually applying enough
pressure to bring me to a shuddering end.

Oh God. Hands down, Dante was the most tal-
ented lover I'd ever entertained in my bed but we
were evenly matched. As he continued to tease me,
I made a vow to make him squirm when I had him
in my mouth. I gripped his hair and pushed his head
toward me with an urgent, "Stop fucking around,
damn it!" and he chuckled at my frustration because
he was doing it purposefully.

"Just remember," I reminded him with a sultry
smile even as I groaned, "you will pay when it's
my turn."

"I'm counting on it," he replied with his signature
charm, but then he inched my panties down my hips
and feasted like a man dying of hunger until I was

left drenched, tumbling into multiple orgasms until I was weak as a kitten.

Dante kissed me hard, swirling his tongue against mine, tasting me as I tasted him, and my desire climbed once again, seeking his touch, the feel of his cock stretching me to impossible lengths until I sobbed with pleasure.

He pushed his length inside me, his hips flexing, his large hands capturing mine above my head, holding me captive as he drove himself deep. He filled me completely, so perfectly. I never believed in such nonsense until Dante. Our bodies were made for one another. A key and lock. A song of decadent pleasure rang out in my bones as he emptied himself into me, both of us shuddering with completion.

The oppressive heat from the room coated our lungs and sent rivulets of sweat rolling down our bodies. Dante climbed off me as he slowly stretched, his semiflaccid cock still oozing droplets of fluid. I rose and pulled him toward me, my hands bracketing his hips as I gently lapped at the salty drops. Dante sucked in a wild breath, his fingers threading through my hair as I tended to his cock, licking and tenderly sucking him dry, until he was thoroughly spent and nearly buckling.

"Fuckkkk," he groaned under his breath as I finished. "You're going to be the death of me but I don't mind." Dante flopped onto the sofa beside me, sending a cloud of dust swirling into the still air. He dispersed the cloud with a heavy wave of his hand as I laughed weakly. "We need to equip this place with

some amenities…like a well-stocked fridge with ice-cold water or beer. A fan would be nice, too."

"You aren't staying long enough to make this our own private booty-call break room," I said, reminding him that our time was finite. "Otherwise, your idea has merit."

He swiveled his head to regard me with something I couldn't quite define. "Maybe I'm ready for a change of scenery. Italy has grown on me."

I ignored the little flutter in my belly at his reply. I wasn't going to buy into that. Dante was a player and I knew the game. I probably shouldn't have brought him here, but I was in no danger of giving him more than I meant to. "Don't flatter yourself. You bore too easily. You, my handsome American stud, are a bad investment, no matter how well you can fuck."

To his credit, he didn't try to refute my statement but even as I knew I should dress and go back to work, I didn't want to leave just yet. It could be that he looked like a god lounging, cock out, sweat glistening, muscles hard, and I wasn't ready to put all that behind me to face a scowling Como and a mountain of work that pressed for my attention.

At least with Dante, all he wanted was my body.

And my body fairly purred at his touch.

Hell, all he had to do was look in my direction and I was wet.

"Seeing as your business in Italy is concluded, when do you plan to return to the States?"

He shrugged. "My schedule is flexible. For now, I'm enjoying playing tourist."

I laughed. "Yes, are you still planning to take the walking tour of Siena?"

"I don't know. What does your schedule look like?"

His persistence was admirable. "I told you I wasn't free to traipse about the city with you. You are the tourist, not me."

"Be honest, wouldn't you rather spend an afternoon playing tourist with me than stuck in the office on a beautiful fall day with that stick-in-the-mud assistant?"

He had a point. I would rather do anything with Dante, even take another silly cooking class, if it meant escaping the condemning looks from Como. I really needed to address that issue but with Uva Persa's launch so soon, I couldn't take the risk of Como doing anything out of spite that might wreck the debut. "What about you?" I asked, turning the focus around. "What are you avoiding back home? Surely, you have responsibilities that await your return."

He exhaled a heavy sigh and shoved a hand through his damp hair, leaving behind a rakish, rugged look that made me want to eat him all over again. "Paperwork. Meetings. Dull market-share negotiations. Honestly, nothing my brother Luca can't handle on his own."

"So why do you stay in your job?" I asked, curious.

"Because it's my family's business and we have a reputation to uphold. The Donato name means something where I come from."

I understood that pressure. Living up to the Baroni name was my own personal burden. "Are you happy?"

"Are you?"

We were two peas in a pod. Perhaps that was why we clicked so seamlessly. "I asked you first," I countered with a sly smile.

I expected a pithy answer but he came back with genuine honesty. "I used to think I was. Now I'm not so sure. Italy has made me question many things about my life that I was unaware were even issues."

"Such as?"

But that was as much as he was willing to share. He grabbed his jeans and slid them on, grinning with the shake of his head. "If we stay down here much longer, either we need to fuck again because I can't be around your naked body without needing to be inside it, or we will die from dehydration because it's hot as hell down here." He reached out his hand to help me up. I slipped my hand in his and he pulled me straight to his mouth. A long, lingering kiss nearly sent us at each other again, but he was right. It was too hot and I needed to return to work, no matter how reluctant I was.

We dressed in companionable silence but as he turned to climb back up the stairs, I tugged at his hand and we detoured to my private chambers within the manor.

I undressed again, shedding my clothes as quickly as possible, and he did the same as I drew him toward the shower.

His grin was everything I'd come to crave without even realizing I needed it.

Standing beneath the cool spray, our slick bodies sliding against one another, senses alive at every touch, returning to the office had become a distant thought but I no longer cared.

Honestly, at this point, I no longer cared about anything but the pleasure between us.

And I was going to enjoy it while it lasted.

CHAPTER TWENTY-THREE

Dante

I WAS ACCUSTOMED to wealth. I grew up surrounded by privilege—private jets, mansions, high-end resorts—but there was a different kind of money exhibited by European old money.

This castle, for example, was something out of a storybook. I wasn't too proud to admit that I was impressed and a bit in awe.

"What was it like growing up here?" I asked, lounging on Alessandra's bed, snacking on grapes and cheese. "You literally grew up in a castle."

Alessandra shrugged as if it were no big deal. "The same as anywhere I guess. Except we had more rooms to hide in when we played hide-and-seek." She snorted in memory, adding, "We actually lost Enzo once. Took a full day to find him. Our mother nearly had a heart attack."

I laughed, imagining a young Alessandra and her twin running like heathens around this massive place. "Did you have a nanny?"

"No, our mother was very hands-on. She didn't believe in handing off her responsibilities to someone else. We were very close."

"She's passed?"

Alessandra nodded. "Not long after Enzo died. I'm told it was a coincidence but she died a year after Enzo. I say it was from a broken heart but the doctors said it was an aneurysm. Extreme grief will do terrible things to the body."

I sobered. So much loss in her family. My brothers pissed me off and were annoying but losing either of them would devastate me. Alessandra had lost her twin and then her mother. I couldn't imagine how much that must've changed her in such a short time. "What was she like?"

Alessandra closed her eyes, a small smile playing on her lips. "Beautiful," she answered, reopening her eyes. "I look like her. Sometimes I think my father's grief is cracked open all over again when he sees me. He says each passing year I look more and more like her."

"Are you close with your father?"

She hesitated. I identified so hard with her. Parental relationships were complicated. At least they seemed that way for my family. She wiped her mouth with a napkin before answering carefully. "I love my father very much. He is a good man but he is resistant to change, and change is inevitable if you want to stay relevant in this economy."

I understood her answer. I'd had the same argument with my own father but it'd taken Luca pushing him out to make change happen. "Powerful men become powerful by doing things their way, but sometimes their way becomes outdated and they're unwilling to bend."

She nodded in agreement and seemed to frame her next question cautiously. "You seek to please your father yet he's not happy with your efforts, but you continue to try?"

"Isn't that the endless cycle of dysfunction that we all endure?" I asked, feeling philosophical.

"True enough."

I sighed. "At least your father trusts you to run the business."

Alessandra chuckled ruefully, admitting, "Only because I was the less offensive option. The business had always been Enzo's legacy until he died. My father was loath to let a stranger run the company so it fell to me. I was the lesser of two evils."

I sensed fear of inadequacy tugging at her words and it bothered me. She was a force of nature and if anyone couldn't see that they were fucking blind. "You're an incredible woman," I told her, leaning over to brush a kiss across her lips. "Don't let anyone take that from you. Not even your father."

"My father loves me," she returned with a smile, but she couldn't hide the sadness in her eyes. "Although, I know he would've been more comfortable with Enzo at the helm. It's not his fault, it's his generation."

I chose my words with care because I knew how much Alessandra loved her brother. "I didn't know

Enzo, but I can't imagine anyone doing a better job than you're doing right now."

I wasn't blowing smoke up her ass—I truly believed what I was saying. For a full moment, I was stunned at my own earnestness. Where had that come from? Why did it matter how Alessandra's heart ached at her father's blind stubbornness to see what was right in front of him? I didn't have a ready answer, at least not one that was honest, and that was disconcerting. What was happening to me? I swallowed the odd lump in my throat and rose to put some distance between us on the pretense of getting two bottled waters from the fridge. When I returned, Alessandra had composed herself and I was relieved.

Too much emotion swirling around was threatening to replace my testicles with ovaries. I needed to lighten the mood. Dropping back onto the bed, I smiled and said, "So about that walking tour…"

"Fuck off with the walking tour." Alessandra laughed and tossed a pillow at me, which gave me an excellent window in which to tackle her to the bed, pinning her with my weight. She smiled up at me, blinding me with her beauty. I couldn't imagine ever tiring of that exquisite view. My cock stirred at the promise of action, thickening against her thigh. She giggled as she glanced demurely south, where I was quickly hardening to stone. "Again? You've the stamina of a horse."

"Hung like one, too," I quipped with an exaggerated slant of my brow. Her peal of laughter warmed the dark places of my soul that I thought light would never penetrate. Who was this woman and where did she come from? Maybe in another life, we were married and happily growing old together. I rather liked the idea of waking up to her gorgeous face every day, even to the point of being wrinkled old raisins together. I kissed her again, framing her face with my hands, content to feel my lips against hers. I lost myself in the joy of her mouth moving against mine, our tongues exploring with abandon, as if we had all the time in the world to discover what made the other tick.

But we didn't have time. The clock was doing the ticking…

Fuck it, I wanted this moment for myself.

I'd spent my life hungering for my father's approval and the time would come fast enough where I had to deliver—and I would deliver—but I was claiming this time as my own.

Time with Alessandra.

It might be the only golden moment of true happiness I'd ever known, and I was going to be selfish about holding on to it for as long as I could.

I rolled Alessandra on top, my cock prodding with an urgency that I felt in my bones. I needed to be inside her. Her expression split into pure pleasure as she slid down on my cock, her body absorbing my length inch by inch. *"Dante,"* she groaned, music to my ears. *"Oh God, yes…"*

I pushed up, burying myself as deep as I could go, but I wanted to touch her soul. I wanted to be so deep inside her that where I stopped and she began was hard to determine. There was a desperation to my thrusts as I flexed my hips while she ground on my pelvis, taking her own pleasure. Her beautiful, proud breasts rose high with rose-tipped, pebbled nipples, begging for my hands and mouth. She fucked me with abandon, groaning as she chased her orgasm, demanding everything from me. Watching her come was an arousal in itself. Her fingers curled into my chest, leaving tiny scratches as she lost herself in the ecstasy etched on her face. Tensing, her walls clenched around my cock as she went rigid. Her head fell back as her mouth fell open on a soundless scream locked in her chest, before she tumbled forward in a heap. I gripped her hips and thrust against her hard and fast to find my own savage release.

I lost myself inside her, jetting in fast, exhaustive spurts that left me breathless.

God yes, this was heaven, I realized.

In another life, sweetheart, you were mine—and I was yours.

But not in this one.

CHAPTER TWENTY-FOUR

Alessandra

I WALKED INTO the office the following morning, my step light, a smile on my lips until I saw Como and realized with a sinking heart that Dante was right. I had so hoped Como would come to his senses and stop this nonsense before our working relationship suffered, but my hopes were quickly dying. "Good morning," I said, trying to start the conversation off nicely. He ignored my attempt with a stare of distaste.

Prior to arriving at the office, I'd stopped at a local café in the hopes of bridging the gap between us with a peace offering. The unfriendly scowl stamped on Como's face didn't bode well.

Ignoring his frosty expression, I set down his coffee with a "Can we talk?" delving straight into the discomforting topic. "I feel we need to clear the air."

But Como wasn't in the mood to be civil. "You're fucking him, aren't you?"

His blunt question shocked me into stunned silence. I struggled to keep my composure at his breach into my personal business. "How dare you talk to me of business that has nothing to do with you? Our friendship does not include such privileges, Como." I shook my head, fuming. "You are my employee. I do not answer to you."

I didn't want to lose Como as a friend nor as a trusted business associate but I was vibrating with righteous anger. Not only was his question inappropriate but it put me on the defensive when I had no reason to suffer the weight of his judgment.

I met Como's hot glare with one filled with disdain. "I am an adult and I don't have to justify what I do in my private time. Whom I'm spending my time with outside of this office has nothing to do with you. Perhaps you should spend less time worrying about things that do not concern you and focus more on your own personal life. If you didn't have your head so far up my ass, you might see what's right in front of you."

Como blinked in confusion. "What are you talking about?"

"You've wasted your time pining after me when a good woman has eyes only for you. Though now, I realize she deserves better. You're not the man I thought you were."

Como sensed the tables turning and must've realized the pit he'd fallen into, and that the freefall was going to kill him. "Alessandra, I only say these things because I care," he said stiffly, but I was finished listening.

"My mistake was tolerating your outbursts out of deference to our friendship and long working relationship, but you've killed whatever respect I had for you. Whom I see or what I do on my private time is my business. I don't need your approval—or anyone's approval for that matter."

"Not even your father?"

"What is that supposed to mean?" I cast him a sharp look. "Are you threatening me with something?"

"I'm just saying it's possible your father might not appreciate that his daughter is letting her personal life cloud her judgment with his wine business."

His wine business? "Watch your tongue," I warned. Como seemed bent on destruction. I fought to keep from slapping the attitude from his fool head. My fingers curled into fists. "You're out of line."

Como didn't back down. "Well?"

"Well what?" I returned with ice in my tone.

"How would your father feel about you fucking the man who came sniffing around only a few weeks ago to buy this winery out from beneath you?" he countered with a sneer. "I've never seen you act so foolish. For all you know, this man could be using you to get information about Uva Persa. This is why women are poor businesspeople. They let emotion rule their head." He shook his head as if he had the right to be disappointed. "You're making a huge mistake."

"The only person in this room making a huge mistake is you." I didn't want to prove his theory correct by ripping his head off for spouting such offensive shit, but my heart was thundering in my ears at my attempt to remain calm. "Dante has zero interest in Uva Persa. He doesn't even know about the new wine." I narrowed my gaze, adding, "All we do is have sex, we don't discuss personal things."

My vicious jab hit the mark. Como's face reddened and his breathing became short, looking as if he were ready to explode with rage. "He's a Donato. They are ruthless. He would say or do *anything* to deliver this winery to his father. He's hungry for a win. Can't you see that? You're just a prize to be won and this winery is simply the spoils of victory. A victory you're practically handing to him on a silver platter! Sergio deserves to know that his only daughter has doomed this place with her foolishness!"

"What do you know about the Donatos?" I hissed. "You speak as if you have some kind of firsthand knowledge of bad behavior."

"Perhaps not firsthand but I did some digging on my own. They are savage Americans and they will destroy your family's legacy," he insisted.

"You don't know what you're talking about," I said, seeing red. If I didn't get Como out of my sight I'd bury a wine bottle in his face. "Get out, Como. Get out and don't come back. You're done here. I don't want anyone working for me who thinks so little of my abilities. I have spent years building up this company on my own and to have you tear me down simply because you're jealous… I won't tolerate another minute of your presence. Get the fuck out!"

"Alessandra—" Realizing he'd screwed up, Como tried to backtrack.

"No! You've said your piece, now get out. I'll have accounting cut you your last check and mail it to you. Don't step foot on the grounds ever again."

Como's mouth thinned to a fine line as rage and hurt warred in his eyes. "Fuck you, Alessandra," he spat, sweeping his arm across his desk and sending everything flying, including the espresso, which splashed against the wall. He smirked at the mess, saying as he walked out, "Have fun cleaning up the ruin that is to come."

I shook as I tried to regain my composure. Would Como run to my father and tell him of Uva Persa before I had the chance? I cursed my cowardice. If I hadn't avoided telling my father about my investment, Como's threats would've meant nothing. But my avoidance had created a ticking time bomb and Como was holding the detonator. My father should hear about Uva Persa from me, not out of the spiteful mouth of a scorned man.

There was a chance he'd seek another form of retribution. Would he try to leak the launch of Uva Persa to the media or sabotage the event in some other way? There was little I could do to stop him, but I was prepared to take legal action if necessary, and I'd make sure security was tight on launch night. I hated thinking that way about Como, but after his threats, I had to do whatever was necessary.

I fought tears. Como had been my friend and my trusted ally. Would he betray me in such a way? Part of me refused to believe he could. Giant tears rolled down my face as I tried to make sense of what had gone so terribly wrong so quickly.

Dante's words rang in my head, the warning about mixing business with pleasure, and all I wanted to do was bury my head against his chest. Dante had been right. I never should've allowed anything to happen between Como and me all those years ago. What had been convenient for me had turned into something far more for Como and I'd missed all the signs.

The whole time I'd seen him as a work ally, he'd been working toward what he'd thought was a future together.

I could never love Como the way he'd hoped. I would never look at Como the way I did Dante.

Oh God, Dante. Was I falling in love with him? I didn't want to love Dante. I didn't want to acknowledge the deep sense of rightness that fit perfectly between us when were locked eye to eye, skin to skin.

This was the most awful thing in the world.

Falling in love was supposed to feel amazing, wonderful and magical.

But I felt none of those things. I felt scared, apprehensive, off-kilter.

What the hell kind of joke was this?

Dante didn't love me. He was enjoying a vacation fling and I'd been fine with that up until this moment.

What happened now?

Nothing.

My family's legacy was on the line. I didn't have

the luxury of playing out whatever was happening between Dante and myself. My gaze drifted to the launch plans for Uva Persa. With Como gone, I would need help.

There was only one person I trusted more than anyone else in the world.

I grabbed my cell phone and called Sophia, my hands shaking as I held the phone to my ear.

She answered on the second ring. Her voice was an instant calming balm to my ragged nerves. "Hello, love, are you okay?"

The words tumbled out in a pained rush. "I had to fire Como. He lost his mind over the situation with me and Dante. He became crazy jealous and left me no choice. I lost my partner right as Uva Persa launches in a week and I am freaking out. Please help me, Sophia," I pleaded, my throat closing as I trembled like a leaf. "I don't know who else I can ask."

Sophia didn't waste time pestering me for more details. She simply said, "I can be there in a half hour," and that was that.

"I love you, Sophia," I said.

"I know you do."

I shuddered with relief. Sophia was smart and she caught on quick. I had no worries that she'd be able to pick up where Como had left off, but I hated that I was taking her away from her own life to deal with the chaos of mine.

When this was all over, I'd do something extra-special for her. She certainly deserved the best and I aimed to give it to her—if I survived the Uva Persa launch.

Pushing a shaky hand through my hair, I went about the work of cleaning up the mess Como had created, wiping away the spilled coffee and trying to salvage what paperwork I could.

Finished, I rose and went to my desk, sinking into the chair as I closed my eyes, focusing on the end game.

Nothing would stand in the way of making Uva Persa an international success.

Not Como. Not even my feelings for Dante—which would have to wait until I figured out what the hell was going on with my heart.

I laughed through a sheen of tears and I knew everything was going to be okay.

One way or another.

CHAPTER TWENTY-FIVE

Dante

"I CAN'T BELIEVE I'm doing this," Alessandra said, shaking her head as if she'd lost her mind. "How in the hell did you talk me into a walking tour of my own city?"

"I make a very persuasive argument," I answered with a charming grin, standing with our group at the Piazza del Campo central meeting point. "Well, that and the fact that I've got you so twisted around my cock that I'll need a crowbar to pry you off so I can board the plane home."

"Get over yourself," Alessandra said, laughing. "But I have to say, I'm a little intrigued by the idea of seeing parts of the city that I've taken for granted."

I didn't care how we got to this place, but I was very happy that I managed to talk Alessandra into taking a day off work to do this tour with me. Frankly, I think a fair amount of divine intervention was involved because Alessandra had a lot on her plate and yet she was still willing to take a break and play tourist together.

And, what a sexy tourist she made. A wide-brimmed floppy hat shielded her pretty face from the sun and even though her white shorts weren't special in any way, the way she carried herself made what she wore seem like couture.

"What is it with European women that makes any-thing they wear look like the height of fashion?" I asked, appreciating the view. Alessandra laughed and dismissed me with a wave of her hand as if I were being dumb. "No, seriously. I've dated runway mod-els with less style than you dressed down for a day trip. I mean, you're wearing tennis shoes for crying out loud, and yet you look sexier than anyone else in this city."

Okay, maybe that part was over the top but it was also true. I could see only Alessandra. I tried to drag my gaze away—I was staring hard enough to burn a hole in her skin—but my eyeballs wanted to stay put. *God, what's with me these days?* It was like I didn't even recognize myself anymore.

Fuck it, I wanted to just go with the moment. Was that so bad? My hand curled over hers and I drew her in for a quick kiss before our guide started talk-ing to the small assembled group.

"Buongiorno!" the guide called out with a wide, inviting smile. "My name is Carlo and I will be your guide today. I hope you've worn good walking shoes because we will be using our feet for the duration of this tour."

I grinned, a smart-ass quip on my tongue, but Alessandra quelled my urge to spout off with a look.

I had to remember this was her town, not mine, and I needed to be mindful of her reputation. I would leave Siena behind but Alessandra would remain.

Although I was intrigued by the promise of learning about the architecture of the city, my main interest was spending as much time as possible with Alessandra.

Her hand in mine felt natural, right. "Are you ready to play tourist with the most handsome American in the city?" I asked.

"Good God, I'm not sure the narrow corridors can accommodate your swelled head," she retorted with amusement, her eyes sparkling. "But yes, I am ready. This should be fun, and if nothing else, I'll get lunch out of the deal."

I pulled her close and kissed her laughing mouth, promising, "I'd be happy to feed you my cock later if you're still hungry."

And just like that, we were the only two people there even as we were surrounded by the hustle and bustle of a known tourist trap; but I didn't care. I craved Alessandra like a bear sought succulent berries at the height of summer.

"You're impossible," she murmured with delight, squealing a little when I squeezed her round ass with both hands, pulling her against my cock. Her mouth tilted with a sensual smile as she added with just a hint of mischief, "But I like you that way."

"Good." I gave her a resounding kiss before releasing her to straighten my ball cap. "Let's do this. I'm ready to see what Siena has to offer. You and

I will continue our conversation later when we're both naked."

It wasn't an invitation or a boast, simply a statement of fact, and she knew it. The fact that she gave me no pushback told me that she was just as eager as I was to end up entwined in each other's arms, and that was enough to put the biggest grin on my face that had nothing to do with the tour.

Hell, at this point, I could be touring a sewage facility and I'd be just as happy. The tour began and we walked hand in hand as if we were dating. As if it was perfectly acceptable to be casually strolling down the lane together when in fact, neither one of us would've ever been caught dead doing exactly that with anyone else.

By the time we reached the museum/chapel of Owl Contrada, I felt comfortable sharing something that might potentially ruin the mood. Nonetheless, it was important to bring up. "Look, I'm probably way out of line but…that guy Como…I get a bad vibe from him."

Alessandra's happiness dimmed and she said, "Como is no longer with Castello di Baroni. I had to let him go. I fired him two days ago. I haven't seen nor heard of him since."

I couldn't say I wasn't relieved. There was something about the man that set my teeth on edge, and while I was willing to admit it probably had something to do with the fact that he was clearly into Alessandra, there was an obsessive quality to the man's attention that I felt was unhealthy. "I'm glad to see him gone," I said, being honest. "He had crazy eyes."

"I've known Como for a very long time. I won't talk badly about him," she warned, setting up boundaries, which I respected. I didn't need to run the guy into the ground but I was glad he was out of the picture. "He was hurt but he stepped over the line and I couldn't handle his interjections into my personal life any longer."

"He was jealous," I said. "Jealousy in the workplace is never a good thing."

"Indeed."

"I sense that it hurt you to let him go."

She nodded unhappily. "He was my right hand in everything. Especially a project that I've been working on for five years that is finally coming to fruition. Losing him a week before launch…it's a blow but I'll recover. My friend Sophia has agreed to step in and help."

My ears piqued with sudden interest. "Which project is that?" She'd hinted at this before but never completely shared. I sensed it was big enough to matter, which meant it could mean leverage for me. Alessandra risked a glance from beneath her lush lashes, hesitating. I charmed her with a smile. "Come on, do you really think I'm going to swoop in and try to steal whatever it is you're working on? I have no interest in your winery but I am interested in knowing what has you worried and stressed."

She laughed as if realizing I made a certain amount of sense. "To understand the magnitude of what I've done you'd have to understand the world I work in. We are in the Chianti business and in order to qualify for a Chianti Classico label, there are very strict guidelines in which we have to adhere. The rules are restrictive and have yet to evolve."

"And you want to challenge the rules."

"I think there's room for innovation and that by tweaking the rules, we could usher in a lucrative new world."

"Seems smart," I agreed, loving the way her eyes lit up when she talked with such passion. "So what is this secret project?"

Alessandra drew a deep breath, biting her lip as if torn between pride and excitement, and fear of sharing too much. I waited, hoping that my interested silence would push her to spilling—and it did. "I invested my own money in a new wine using *tenerone* grapes, an ancient varietal that had all but been extinct until recently. I put everything I had, along with my grandfather's help, into the new label, Uva Persa, and it launches next week under the Castello di Baroni brand. It's going to make or break our business."

"Uva Persa...what does it mean?" I asked, intrigued.

"It means 'lost grape,'" she answered, smiling with pleasure.

I knew she had a hit on her hands. I could feel it in my bones. A success of this sort would make wrestling Castello di Baroni out of the Baroni family's hands nearly impossible. If that happened I would have to face my father without his prize.

I swallowed, my supportive smile frozen. I didn't want to hurt Alessandra but Uva Persa succeeding... would mean my failure.

"That's pretty impressive," I said.

"I've done small tastings here and there, and so far it's been a huge success. Sophia tasted it for the first time, without knowing it was my label, and she raved about it."

"Does Sophia have good taste?" I teased.

"The very best," she answered with a resolute nod. "Sophia's palate is sophisticated. She and Enzo would've made a formidable team in the wine business."

I drew her to me so I could kiss her forehead. "That's pretty damn incredible," I said without guile. Why did she have to be so amazing? "I'm sure you have the next big thing on your hands."

"I hope so," she said, worrying her lip. "The truth is, my father was not supportive of my desire to cultivate the *tenerone*. He refused to invest with me. If it weren't for my grandfather, I never would've been able to put my dream in motion."

"Why didn't your father want to invest?"

"He is very old-school. He doesn't believe a woman can have such big ideas. If the idea had come from Enzo, he would've praised him for being innovative, but because it came from me, it was reckless and foolhardy."

I prickled at Alessandra's sharing. I couldn't imagine anyone treating her so poorly. She was a force of nature. The fact that her own father... Hell, this was a fight I knew too well. My father rarely took anything I said to heart either. "Sorry, but that's bullshit," I said with perhaps too much of an edge. At her sharp look, I added, "Look, I know you love your dad and he's probably a great father but if he's too narrow-minded to see what's right in front of him, fuck him."

Was I still talking about Alessandra's situation or my own? I wasn't sure, to be honest. Alessandra's slowly spreading shy smile warmed me in places that I hadn't known existed. She squeezed my hand in solidarity and we dropped the topic.

She'd finally shared something of incredible value with me. Alessandra trusted me.

Now the question was, what was I going to do with that information?

Did I find a way to exploit it or did I walk away, forgetting all about leverage and my need to please my father?

I didn't have an answer—but I needed to make a decision fast.

The launch might be my only chance, and that window was closing.

CHAPTER TWENTY-SIX

Alessandra

I TOOK A chance sharing my secret with Dante but I didn't regret my decision. With Sophia by my side and the launch around the corner, I was confident that nothing could throw me off on this venture. Besides, the more time I spent with Dante, the less I saw him as a threat. I was starting to think of him as much more than that.

"Did you really take a walking tour of Siena?" Sophia asked, incredulous. *"You?"*

I shared her incredulity, hardly able to believe it myself. "Yes, and you know, it was quite lovely. I've always taken for granted the beauty of the city. Seeing it through someone else's eyes really opened mine to the splendor that we are blessed with."

Sophia chuckled. "Okay, you practically have stars in your eyes. Are you going to try to tell me that you still don't have feelings for Dante? I mean, you can try but I'll see right through your nonsense so why bother?"

Sophia was right, I couldn't hide the fact that I'd not only come to care for Dante, but that I might be falling for him. I couldn't pinpoint the exact moment my feelings had deepened, but I knew yesterday's walking tour opened my eyes to more than just the beautiful architecture.

"It felt good to share with him my journey with Uva Persa," I said, shocking Sophia. "I know I haven't known him long but I wanted to tell him, and I felt I could. He's a good man."

There, I'd said it. I hadn't wanted to fall for Dante. I'd fought my feelings tooth and nail but some things were out of your control. Like when my nonna and nonno fell for each other. It was fate.

"I've never seen you so lit up. Your face is glowing. It's a good look on you," Sophia said. "I'm assuming that Dante feels the same?"

I shook my head, still trying to find my footing. "Well, I'm fairly certain he feels something for me. We haven't actually talked about it. We don't do too much talking when we are together." I frowned as I heard myself. "Which probably means that we should do some talking before things roll out of hand. I need to know if we're on the same page or reading a different book."

"Oh, I just love when you use metaphors," Sophia said, laughing. "Reminds me of university."

I chuckled but Sophia had drawn attention to a very good point. Dante and I hadn't talked about our feelings for each other in actual words. I felt our bodies spoke eloquently to one another but there was plenty of room for misinterpretation when basing feelings only on the strength of one's orgasms.

Oh goodness, just thinking of Dante's touch made me weak. *No, focus.* Words. "I'm supposed to meet him at his hotel tonight. I am thinking of inviting him to the Uva Persa launch. I'd love for you to meet him officially."

"I wouldn't miss it for the world," Sophia said. "But if he's not good enough for you, I won't hesitate to be honest."

God, I loved her. "You will adore him. He's dreadfully charming," I admitted. "Seems like a deadly skill. I'm sure he's left a swath of women in his wake."

I didn't want to be one of those women crying after Dante. If he didn't feel the same way about me, I wasn't going to chase him.

We attended to our tasks but my mind was elsewhere. It should've been with the launch—confident as I was, everything I'd ever cared about was tied up in the success of Uva Persa. Yet all I could think of was how Dante would react to my admitting that I had feelings for him.

Would he push me away? Would he laugh? Or would he admit that he, too, had fallen for me?

My ego assured me that Dante had fallen as hard as I had, but that kernel of insecurity planted by my father that I somehow wasn't good enough worried at my confidence.

By the time I left for Dante's hotel, I was a nervous wreck, which was unlike me.

I didn't like this uncertainty. I wasn't accustomed to feeling off-kilter or out of control. I prided myself on being in control of any given situation and I excelled at grabbing the upper hand.

Not so now, and I hated it.

I might've been a tad grumpy by the time Dante opened his room door, all smiles and sexiness, which became evident when I snapped, "I'm starving, please say you ordered food."

"Hello, honey, nice to see you," he said, grinning at my sour attitude. "The question is, do I fuck the bad mood out of you or just stuff your face first?"

I couldn't quite stop the smile threatening. Why was he so damn perfect? "Kiss me, you idiot."

"How can I resist?" Dante closed the distance and pulled me into his arms, sealing his mouth to mine. His lips were perfection, the absolute best combination of firm yet soft. I'd never noticed a man's lips before Dante's. His tongue touched mine, encouraging a dance, and I eagerly obliged. It wasn't long before the heat between us ignited and he was carrying me to the bed.

I knew I came to talk, to have a serious conversation, but it was so difficult to remember why it was better to talk first, have sex later when he was devouring my body and I was writhing in his arms, happily losing my sanity.

"I missed you today," he said against my thigh as he nipped at the sensitive flesh. "I couldn't stop thinking about how much I love fucking you. I got so hot and bothered I had to jerk off just so my cock didn't split in two."

"You poor thing," I said, sucking in a tight breath as he traveled toward my aching pussy. My slit was already damp and ready. "And did you come hard?"

"I'm surprised I didn't put a hole in the wall."

I managed a laugh before he descended between my legs, feasting on the tender flesh with the skill of a master. My fingers curled into the sheets, my breath coming faster as he worked me without mercy. I craved this release only Dante could provide.

He pushed me to that edge and I tumbled into my climax, crying out as I shook like a leaf in the wind. Without giving me a chance to recover, Dante flipped me to my belly and worked his cock between my cheeks, sliding his length inside me. I groaned as he filled me completely. There was always a bit of savagery in Dante's lovemaking that thrilled me senseless. He took complete control, even when I was riding him, and I found that incredibly sexy.

"Alessandra." My name exploded from his mouth as he came and I quickly followed with a second orgasm, rasping into the sheets as I drew great, big shuddering breaths. Dante rolled off me and we were both left breathing hard but sated. Dante rose slowly to get us bottled water, something I'd come to find very sweet of him, and gazed with unabashed interest in his naked body. He was magnificent. I accepted the water bottle and cracked it open, drinking deeply. I was wondrously relaxed. I didn't want anything to ruin this bliss. Perhaps our conversation could wait.

"Are you busy this weekend?" I rolled to my side to ask, loving how well formed and masculine Dante's body was. I could spend a lifetime staring at that body. Dragging my gaze back to his eyes, I smiled when he caught me adoring his manhood.

"Depends. What did you have in mind?" he asked.

"I'd like to invite you to the Uva Persa launch as my date. Officially."

"Officially?" he repeated, his gaze inscrutable. "You mean, I'm no longer your dirty little secret?"

I laughed. "Exactly. I think I can clean you up sufficiently to pass you off as respectable for an evening at least."

"That's a tall order."

"I think I'm up to the challenge." I shifted on the bed to sit up, sliding my robe over my body and tying the belt. "Do you want to be official?"

I'd thought to wait but the question came up organically so I figured I might as well just go with it.

His strained chuckle sent chills down my arm. This wasn't exactly how I imagined he would react. "What are we talking here?" he asked. "I live in New York, you live here in Italy. Long distance isn't really my thing."

I stiffened, hearing the rejection in what he wasn't saying. "Of course. I wasn't expecting you to relocate." But maybe I was, because the minute I said it, disappointment flooded my breast. I wanted him to want to be with me and if that meant relocating, I wanted him to jump at the chance. Maybe that was my ego speaking but my heart felt pretty bruised, too. "I simply asked you to be my date for the launch, not marry me."

"Good, because I'm not the marrying kind," he said, and I was quick to add my own salt to that dish with a snapped, "Neither am I, as you know."

"Glad we got that sorted out," he said, rolling from the bed to get something stronger than water. He poured two glasses of wine and brought me one. "Look, we've got a good thing going right now. Let's not ruin it with talk of official whatever. We're fantastic in the sack, and I say we keep doing what we're good at."

I smothered a laugh at the irony. Hadn't I said those very words to men who wanted to get attached? *Oh, fate was a bitch.* I sipped my wine. "Of course." But I didn't want to keep fucking just to pretend that we didn't feel more than just physical pleasure together. However, I wasn't going to act the part of the jilted lover, wailing and carrying on with a broken heart. The plan had been to stay the night but I didn't want to sleep beside him if we were just fucking.

Snuggling was off the table.

Sighing, I rose and began to dress. Dante's immediate frown gave away his surprise. "What are you doing? You said you were going to stay."

"Plans change."

"All because I said I don't want to relocate to Italy?" he asked, incredulous. "That's a little extreme, don't you think?"

"Don't flatter yourself. I simply don't feel like

playing house. We both got what we wanted and now I want to sleep in my own bed."

"Seriously, Alessandra?"

I smiled coolly as I dressed. "Let me know about the launch. If you're not interested in being my date, I will invite someone else."

"Wow, that was cold. I get the message loud and clear—I'm easily replaced."

I tsked and wagged my finger at him. "You don't get to play the victim. You stated your position and I respect it but I'm also not going to chase you, so if you have other plans I'll make my own plans, as well."

"I didn't say I wasn't going," he growled. "Are you seeing anyone else you'd consider inviting?"

"I'd say that's privileged information that doesn't concern you, now, does it?"

"Alessandra," he warned, his temper beginning to flare. Good. Served him right for trying to play me. "Knock it off. Yes, I'll go, but you're not leaving."

"Oh?" I was amused by his machismo. "And why is that?"

"Because you know damn well that you're going to sleep beside me tonight so stop playing games."

"I'm not the one playing games. We aren't dating. We are fucking. Thank you for making that very clear. I just needed to know the rules before going forward. Your clarification is quite appreciated."

"I didn't say we were just fucking," he said, irritated. "I just said…" But he'd boxed himself with his own words. I smiled when he realized he'd screwed himself and he was going to sleep alone tonight.

I left him like that.

As I said, and Dante would learn…*I chase no man.*

Even if I wanted that man more than any I'd ever known in my life.

CHAPTER TWENTY-SEVEN

Dante

I COULDN'T BELIEVE Alessandra had left.

My plans for the evening were shredded to shit all because I couldn't lie to her. I should've just played the part she wanted me to play, said whatever she wanted to hear, and everything would've kept moving along smoothly.

But I couldn't lie to her.

What future did we have together? None.

Why pretend otherwise?

My life was in New York, hers was here.

My father was expecting me to deliver Castello di Baroni. If I decided to make that happen, I would ruin any chance I had with Alessandra. If I didn't deliver the winery as expected, I could piss off any chance of ever gaining my father's respect.

I had shit options.

Now that I knew Alessandra's weakness, I knew I could exploit the situation to my advantage. Uva Persa was the fulcrum point for this entire operation. I could sabotage the launch, ruin her chances of catapulting the Baroni label into the future and crush Alessandra in the process.

My father would be proud.

So why did the idea make me want to puke?

To take this victory from Alessandra felt wrong on so many levels. My father wanted this winery on a whim. The only reason he was pushing so hard was because he was a bored old man who found the opposition stimulating. He wouldn't elevate Baroni in any way like Alessandra would. Under my father's hand it would wither and disappear, a legacy gone.

My father could not care less about the future of Castello di Baroni, he just wanted the bragging rights of returning a familial property to the fold. He wanted to be able to boast to his old cronies that he had a European castle in Italy.

All the money had gone to his fucking head. He needed a better hobby than just spending money for the hell of it. For the first time ever, I questioned what my family had been doing that was good for anyone aside from ourselves. This fucking existential crisis crap was getting on my nerves but I couldn't stop the questions that hounded me from all angles.

So what was I supposed to do? The answers weren't so clear. I'd worked my entire life trying to earn my father's respect and always come up short no matter what I did. What happened if I crushed Alessandra by delivering the winery to my father and he still treated me like shit?

I'd snap and kill him.

I'd like to say that was just talk but I had some unresolved rage when it came to my father. We all dealt with our childhood traumas differently. Luca had funneled his anger into making the Donato legacy something less distasteful. Nico chose to be a charming playboy until he'd met his wife, and now he was the consummate husband and father. Where did that leave me? Dangling on the thin thread of our father's affection, desperately hanging on for dear life.

Not the best place to be.

How long was I going to chase after the scraps of my father's attention?

God, it was pathetic.

But just as pathetic was dropping everything I'd ever worked for just to chase some pretty, exotic pussy, pretending that the fairy tale was real just because cannolis and espressos tasted so much better in tiny Italian cafés.

What was I even thinking? Moving to Italy? Becoming Alessandra's boy toy? Her arm candy?

I wasn't accustomed to being useless. I needed to work. There wasn't a place for me here. As much as I was quickly becoming absorbed by Alessandra, that was unhealthy. What I was going through was simple lust. I was infatuated with her body and her beauty. It would fade and then what? I'd have lost everything.

No, I had to stay the course. Even if the idea of crushing Alessandra hurt my soul, I would do it because in the end, nothing truly lasted anyway.

My stomach roiled at my decision. In defiant response, I downed my wine and poured a fresh glass.

I was a Donato. I wasn't like my brothers. I didn't believe in love and I didn't believe in throwing away everything that ever meant anything to someone over a temporary emotion.

Unlike a romantic comedy, real life sucked.

The guy didn't always get the girl.

Sometimes the guy screwed the girl over, left her behind in the wreckage and boarded a plane to go home to his empty life.

You said it...empty life.

All I had was my work and I'd ceased to be fulfilled by the thrill of the office a long time ago. I was an asshole because I was miserable.

There was a reason I found happy couples annoying—because I didn't have what they did.

It was jealousy.

Jesus, I was fucking jealous of what I couldn't have, what I pushed away and rejected.

Alessandra was the real deal. I could love her. Hell, I probably already did. I couldn't get enough of her, that much I knew.

But that didn't change my situation. I could be crazy in love with Alessandra and it didn't change a damn thing.

I had no place in her world.

So, the question was, did I walk away now without destroying her legacy, so my father couldn't get his grubby hands on her winery, or did I deliver what I was expected to because there was no future between us and clinging to what I knew was the lesser of two evils?

I didn't have the answer.

All I knew was I wanted Alessandra curled up beside me more than anything right now.

Fuck.

Sleep wasn't going to find me tonight.

CHAPTER TWENTY-EIGHT

Alessandra

I HADN'T HEARD from Dante since leaving his hotel room and the launch was tonight. In spite of my bold words, I hadn't invited anyone else. I didn't want anyone else on my arm. My nerves were stretched taut. I hadn't talked to my father about the launch, and I couldn't account for my hesitancy. All I knew was, each time I tried to gather the courage, I chickened out and pushed the task away. Now I found myself out of time.

Surprisingly, Como hadn't tattled on me, which I found curious. I thought if he was seeking revenge, that would be the route he'd go. Nothing had been leaked to the press either. I could only hope he'd had a sudden change of heart, and out of shame for his behavior, decided to simply leave me and the launch alone.

As a precaution, though, I had talked to security about making sure they spoke to me if he tried to get into the event tonight. I didn't hate Como—we'd shared too much—but life had a way of removing the people we'd outgrown, and I wasn't going to question what God had set in motion.

I said a prayer for Como's happiness and moved on. As if on cue, my nonno walked in, the signature sound of his oak cane hitting the hardwood floor ingrained in my mind. I smiled before even seeing him. A visit from Nonno was always a welcome respite, especially so when my nerves were drawn tight.

"Have you come to check up on me?" I asked.

"The launch is tonight. Are you excited?"

"Very." And nervous enough to vomit. "Are you excited?"

"I am proud," he said, resting his hand on the knob of his cane. "You have come very far, my *patatina*."

"I haven't told my father about the wine we are debuting. He thinks it's another campaign for the Classico Riserva."

He clicked his tongue and shook his head with amusement. "My granddaughter lives for the thrill."

"I'm not so sure about that. I'm just a coward who can't seem to find her tongue."

"You are no coward," he corrected me. "Bravery isn't the absence of fear. It's pushing forward in spite of the fear."

"So full of wisdom," I said, winking at my handsome grandfather. My heart swelled with love for the old man but I needed direction, not cute snippets. "Tell me what to do. I'm not sure how to handle this. Should I wait and let him discover our new wine when everyone else does or should I face the dragon and tell him now?"

Nonno chuckled, shaking his head. "I don't need to tell you anything. You know what the right decision is."

He was right. I hung my head, knowing the answer. I needed to give my father a heads-up before tonight. Worry ate into my voice. "But what if he's angry?"

Nonno shrugged. "Then he will be angry and then he will get over it."

So simple. Why couldn't I embrace my nonno's reasoning? My heart hurt along with my head. The fact was, I wanted my father's blessing and I was afraid I would never have it because he didn't think me capable of making bold decisions.

If I failed, it would only cement my father's belief that he was right.

If I succeeded, maybe it would turn the wheel in my father's head that change was good and not to be feared.

Or maybe he would cling to the hurt caused by my betrayal and never forgive me, no matter my accomplishment.

There were a lot of *maybes*.

My thoughts drifted unhappily to Dante, where even more questions tugged at my brain.

I wanted Dante more than anyone I'd ever known. It was a foreign feeling and it scared me. When I closed my eyes I saw him in my future. I wanted to laugh, cry, fight, make love—everything that made

up a full life—with Dante. I could accept no sub-
stitutes.

"You have that look in your eyes that your mind
is elsewhere. Is there something else you need to
talk about?"

I laughed. "Since when did you become a thera-
pist, Nonno?"

"It comes with age. Nothing else works but my
mind so might as well put it to good use."

"It's nothing," I said, annoyed with myself that
I was letting the situation with Dante get the better
of me. "Something I need to work out on my own."

Nonno's knowing smile made me feel transparent.
Was I really that easy to read? Or was my grandfather a mind reader of some sort? Drawing himself
up to his full height, he said, "Your father will come
around. As for the other man in your life, if he's worthy of you, he'll come around, too. If not, he was
never strong enough to stand beside you, my girl."

And with that, he smiled and promised to see me
tonight, wearing his best tuxedo and a proud smile.

My eyes pricked with emotion. Why couldn't life
be as simple a picture as my grandfather painted?

Maybe it was that simple and I was the one com-
plicating things. I was overthinking everything.
Anxiety had sharpened my worst edges and I was
cutting myself on the blades.

Nonno was right in all things. When my father
put me in charge, it was with the understanding that
I would make decisions he might not always agree
with, but that they were my decisions to make. I

used my own money to fund the *tenerones* and if
Uva Persa did as well as I thought it would, I'd make
my own fortune apart from the Baroni trust while
pushing the family business into a new world of pos-
sibilities.

I closed my eyes and said a prayer to Enzo for
his strength and his courage. "This is your dream,
brother," I murmured. "Help me to make it successful."

I waited for my heart to stop its frantic beating
and headed for my father's section of the manor.
He was retired but he enjoyed tootling around the
winery. Thankfully, he had a pretty set schedule so
I knew I would find him in his solar, enjoying his
caffe corretto—coffee with sweet *grappa*, or white
brandy.

True to form, I found my father and he smiled as
I entered. I loved my father fiercely but this conversation was likely going to test us both.

"Ah, my beautiful flower, how is my Alessandra
today?" He gestured to the empty seat and I accepted
his offer, sliding into the solid chair with a small
smile. "Every day you look more like your mama. I
am a lucky man to have such a beautiful daughter."
He snapped the newspaper shut and grasped his cup
to sip at his coffee. "Have you spoken with Alberico
lately? I thought you two looked quite nice together
at the fund-raising event, which by the way, went
very well. Well done, as always."

My father was never short on praise when it came
to my skills as a party planner, but he seemed to for-

get that I did far more to keep Castello di Baroni relevant. Well, after I broached the current topic dancing
on my tongue, all that would change.

Was I ready? I had to be.

"Papa, I need to talk to you about something regarding the party tonight," I said, catching his attention.

"Is it about Alberico?" he asked, hope in his eyes.
"He is a good match. I would enjoy seeing you and
him become a couple."

My mouth firmed with irritation. "Papa, you need
to forget about a match between Alberico and me. It
is not going to happen. No more talk of this. Please,
I need you to focus and listen to what I'm about to
tell you."

"Did he insult you in some way? Did he take lib-
erties?" My father was instantly ready to slay the
poor man whom only seconds ago he'd been hoping
to add to the family. If I hadn't been on edge about
the true conversation I came to have, I would've been
charmed by his protectiveness.

"No, Papa, he has always been the perfect gentleman," I said, assuring my father but added, "However, I am not interested in him and I never will be."

Papa chuckled with a resigned sigh. "I will not
push it any further. I only thought to help."

"I know, Papa," I said, forgiving him for his un-
fortunate matchmaking efforts. I did add for his benefit, "I do, however, think that Alberico and *Sophia*
would make a lovely match."

"Eh? Sophia?" Papa repeated, surprised. He

sipped his *caffe* in thought, mulling over the idea. It took only seconds for him to approve. He had come to love Sophia as if she and Enzo had already married and she'd become his daughter. "I should've seen this myself. Yes, Sophia and Alberico…much better suited for one another. We should host a dinner and invite them. Sophia doesn't get out nearly enough. This is good," he declared as if it'd been his idea. It struck me that perhaps I was doing to Sophia what my father had done to me when he tried to play matchmaker, but I was pleased he was open to the idea. I smiled, glad that was done. Now the bigger conversation remained.

"Thank you," I murmured, searching for the right way to bring up Uva Persa. The coward in me wanted to run but I respected my father too much to let him discover my venture with strangers. It was inexcusable I'd waited this long as it was. I couldn't wait a moment longer. "There is something else I need to discuss with you, Papa."

"What is it, sweetheart?" he asked, frowning with concern.

I swallowed the lump in my throat. "Do you remember when I approached you five years ago with my idea to plant *tenerone* grapes?"

Papa's frown deepened as the memory returned. "Yes. Why? Please don't tell me you're revisiting the topic. We have always made our way with Sangiovese. We are Chianti Classico and we need not mess with a winning formula. Besides, it's a foolhardy gamble. There is a reason why the *gorgottesco* and the *tenerone* fell into extinction."

The same old argument. "I planted them," I said, throwing it out there like a gauntlet, mentally girding my loins for the explosion that was likely to happen. "I invested my own money with the help of Nonno and planted *tenerone* grapes. I harvested them and the fruition of that experiment is what we will be launching tonight."

Stunned silence followed as Papa stared. "What?" Papa said, his mouth trembling as he processed what I'd admitted. The betrayal in his eyes killed me but I could not regret my decision, whether he believed it was foolhardy or not. "You disobeyed me?"

"I am not a child, Papa. I run Castello di Baroni and I do it well. I haven't been the child you believe I am for quite some time. I weighed the risks and presented my information to you, which you disbelieved, but Nonno believed the risk was acceptable and he invested with me." I reached across the table to grasp his hand. "Papa, it is good. The tastings have exceeded expectations. This is the wine that will put Castello di Baroni back on the royal tables as we once were."

His eyes watered as he stiffened his bottom lip. "You lied to me."

"I never lied," I corrected him gently. "I simply withheld the truth."

"The same."

"No, I wanted this to be a success and I wanted it to be my own. This is my chance to show you that I am the right choice—not the *only* choice—for Castello di Baroni's future. Even if Enzo were still alive, it would be me, not him, who would see this winery to new heights. You need to finally see me for who I am, not who I was."

I was taking a chance. Pushing my father to see me in my own light. To see the woman I'd become.

"Enzo was a dreamer, a visionary. He was the one who told me about the *tenerone* when we were kids. He wanted to see the ancient varietals return. I took his vision and made it happen." Tears pricked my eyes. I so desperately needed my father to believe in me. "And it's going to be successful, but I want your blessing. I can do this without you...but I don't want to."

A long moment stretched between us until the tension was enough to choke the air from my lungs. Papa pulled his hand free and rose stiffly. My hopes slowly sank as he said, "I'm sure you have work to attend to. You are, after all, a busy woman."

And he left me sitting at the table, alone and afraid that I'd just crushed my father's love.

Nonno said Papa would come around, but what if he didn't? What if the success of Uva Persa came at the cost of my relationship with my only living parent?

Wiping at my tears, I shoved my pain to the bottom of my heart and silently rose to finish preparing for tonight.

Papa was right in one regard—I was a busy woman. My doubts would have to wait.

CHAPTER TWENTY-NINE

Dante

I WASN'T GOING to attend the launch.

Seemed a dick move to show up after everything that had been said, but it seemed like an equally crappy move to bail. This was Alessandra's shining moment. I could fairly feel the tension in the air even though we were apart. I'd done nothing in the past few days except wander around Italy without her, soaking in the good weather and trying to enjoy the time away from work. And ignoring calls from my father. Alessandra was likely running herself ragged trying to make sure everything went as planned for her big night.

I couldn't fathom letting her face the highs and lows alone.

Which was how I ended up walking into the high-end gala launch, dressed to the nines, searching for the woman of the hour. I found her easily. My gaze stuck to her like a magnet drawn to metal. She took my breath away.

I would never tire of Alessandra in my sights. The floor-length white gown she wore clung to her soft curves while her dark hair curled in lazy waves down her back. Everything in me tightened with need and desire but it was pride that rose to the forefront. This was her accomplishment, her crowning glory. Uva Persa promotional posters hung gracefully from the walls while the tables glittered with crystals and beautiful accessories. Everything in the decor succeeded in entrancing the guests and enhancing the experience. The event, similar to the Una Notte Magica, swam with elegance and wealth. I was so damn proud of her.

I went straight to her, sliding my arm around her waist and drawing her to me. She gasped when she realized it was me and her gaze narrowed. "Can I help you?"

"I seem to remember being asked to be someone's date for tonight," I reminded her, my gaze going to her full lips, wishing I could taste her right there. "Have I already been replaced?"

I waited for a pithy response but instead she shook her head, admitting, "There is no replacing you, Dante."

Her answer tripled my heartbeat and I struggled to remain in control when I wanted to hoist her in my arms and find a dark corner. I leaned in to whisper in her ear, "You've done an incredible job. Uva Persa is going to be a shining new jewel in the Castello di Baroni crown and I can't imagine a more fitting queen to rule than you."

I pulled away and saw with quickening breath, her eyes glittered with tears. I smiled with a playful warning as I handed her a napkin, "Don't cry. You'll ruin your makeup."

"I am not going to cry," she retorted but carefully dabbed at the corners of her eyes. "What made you change your mind and come?"

"You."

It was the simplest answer and the most honest. "I spent the week going over in my head all the reasons why it made sense to catch a plane out of Italy before the launch but each time I tried to make the reservation, I couldn't follow through. I don't want to leave but I don't know what I'll do if I stay. I'm still in a quandary but I knew the right place for me tonight was here with you."

"Thank you," she whispered, her voice strangled with emotion. "I'm happy you're here with me. Happier than you could possibly know."

I was, too. Mindful of her makeup, I kissed her sweetly. I didn't care who was watching. Hell, I wanted everyone to see that Alessandra was mine. We'd figure out the rest later. For now, I wanted to stand by her side and watch her shine.

Alessandra's bright smile lit up my soul and I realized I could bask in that sunny light for the rest of my life and never miss a moment spent in the dark ever again.

"Looks like I'm missing more than a status report."

The dry retort of a familiar voice stopped me cold.

I turned to find my father staring at me and Alessandra, his gaze narrowed and speculative, and I wanted to have him escorted from the building before he ruined the first good thing in my life.

"Excuse me?" Alessandra puzzled, her gaze going between me and my father. "May I ask who you are?"

"This is my father, Giovanni Donato," I answered before my father could. "And I have no idea what he's doing here."

I couldn't believe he'd come all the way here. Normally, my father sent people to do his bidding, rarely doing the legwork himself. Retirement wasn't entirely a good fit on my father as of yet but Luca was firm in his dictate that our father wasn't to meddle in the business any longer, which only left him to meddle elsewhere. Was this another example of his thinking I couldn't get the job done myself? Not that I wanted to anymore.

"I'm checking on the progress of my newest acquisition. You haven't been returning my calls so I figured a trip to Italy would be a nice change in scenery. But now that I'm here, I can see why you've been occupied," he said, winking.

I scowled, hating how easily he made what Alessandra and I shared seem cheap and tawdry; but then I remembered, I had started out with a ruthless mentality, determined to win at any cost. I'd learned it from him.

Alessandra cooled as she shared a look with me before saying to my father, "You made a wasted trip. As you can see, we are celebrating the launch of Uva

Persa, a new wine by Castello di Baroni. And we are in no way interested in selling. I thought Dante had already told you as much."

"Cute presentation," my father said, dismissing her. "Where's your father? Let the menfolk discuss things further. I'm sure we can come to an equitable agreement."

Before Alessandra could lose her temper, I stepped forward, barely able to rein in my own. This was her night, I wouldn't let my father ruin it. "You weren't invited, Father. I'm going to have to ask you to leave. You shouldn't have come."

"I had to. Someone dropped the ball," he said as if I hadn't spoken. "I knew I should've sent Luca. Maybe even Nico."

I felt the jab in my heart but what hurt more was his casual treatment of the incredible woman who was the driving force of everything good in my life. That was when I lost it.

"You can insult me all you want but you will not treat Alessandra that way." I grabbed my father by the arm and for the first time in my life, forcibly escorted my father out of the room. My father was still strong and hale, but he was no match for me. Once free of the people, I turned on him, ready to unleash a lifetime of anger on his ass.

"You're an asshole," I said, seething. "I've done nothing but try to show you that I'm worthy of your respect but I've been going about it all wrong. I shouldn't be chasing your respect. You should see what's right in front of you and if you don't it's your loss." I stared my father straight in the eye. "I'm done seeking your approval, because you'll never give it. You're a bored, angry old man with nothing better to do with his time than make others miserable. At this rate you're going to die bitter and *alone*."

He barely flinched at my cold words. "I sent you to bring me this winery. You failed."

"You don't deserve Castello di Baroni. Alessandra has managed to turn a legacy into an empire and all you would do is tear it down when it no longer served your ego. You disgust me. Even if I wasn't in love with Alessandra, I wouldn't let you get your hands on Castello di Baroni. You don't have the depth of character to understand what a gift this place is."

I felt a weight fall from my shoulders. For so long I'd chased what I couldn't catch—my father's affection—and I was done running after something that should've been mine all along.

I finally understood what Luca and Nico had already figured out. We didn't need our father—our father needed *us*, and if he didn't realize this sooner rather than later, he would indeed die a bitter, lonely man.

"You can bluster all you like, threaten to cut me out, fire me, whatever. I have my own fortune, I won't starve and I'll be happier than you've ever known because Alessandra has shown me how a real titan in the industry makes things happen."

I expected my father to start shouting, to tear me down, anything other than the silence between us. Then he shocked me when he said, "You really love her?" And his gaze tracked beyond me. I followed his stare and found Alessandra standing behind me, listening, her mouth open in shock.

Without returning to my father, I looked her straight in the eye and answered with a resounding, "Yes," and Alessandra covered her mouth with her hands. "I really do."

"Then, you should do whatever it takes to be with her."

I returned to my father, surprised. "Come again?"

"It's about time you found your balls. I've been pushing you harder than Luca and Nico because you were the one with the hardest head. You're a lot like me. I knew the day you learned how to stand up to me was the day you were ready to be your own man, not just whoever I wanted you to be."

My father had been testing me? I couldn't rightly process what was happening. All I knew was that my world had tipped upside down several times in one minute.

"What do I need with another winery? They all start to look the same anyway." He nodded, gesturing. "Seems to me, you have some loose ends to settle."

I didn't know how to respond. My brain was on tilt. Everything I thought I knew was dumped on the ground. I wanted my father to explain but Alessandra came first. "We'll continue this discussion later," I managed, leaving my father to go to Alessandra. I took her trembling hands in mine, the worst case of stage fright threatening to reduce me to a babbling idiot. Did she feel the same? Was I making a fool of myself? God, I wanted to throw up.

"You love me?" she asked in a tremulous whisper, her eyes shining.

A dam broke inside me and everything I'd been holding back out of fear came crashing free. I nodded, finally able to admit what I'd been fighting. "I knew it that night but I didn't have the answers. I thought the best thing to do was leave but I couldn't. I don't know where I fit in your world but anywhere by your side is better than without you. I guess, if you're willing to give me a second chance, we'll figure it out together."

"What about your father?" she asked, risking a glance at my father, who was, oddly, grinning as if he were finally proud of me. What the hell kind of *Twilight Zone* episode was I in?

"I haven't a clue," I admitted, still reeling from the revelation that my father had been pushing me in a different way than I'd ever imagined, hoping I'd finally stand up to him. Here I was trying to earn his respect when the old coot would've respected me more if I'd told him to fuck off and stop being a dick from the start. My family wasn't normal. "I'm sorry he crashed your party."

She surprised me with a smile, gesturing magnanimously toward my father. "I know something about difficult fathers. We will figure things out." Then she slipped her hand in mine. "Come. We are about to unveil Uva Persa."

"Have I mentioned how much I love you?"

"I will never tire of hearing it," she said, rising to brush a kiss across my lips. "Let's get back inside. I don't want to miss my father's reaction when he sees how well the wine is received."

I smiled, more proud than I had a right to be of the woman I'd crossed an ocean to meet.

I never could've known that the love of my life would be waiting for me when I arrived.

I was a changed man—a better man—all because of Alessandra Baroni.

I finally realized why my brothers were blissfully happy.

They'd discovered that love was real.

And now, I had, too.

EPILOGUE

Alessandra

I SAT QUIETLY, calming my nerves in the spare moments before I was supposed to walk down the aisle to marry the man of my dreams.

I missed Enzo and our mother but I was happier than I ever thought possible.

I couldn't wait to start my life with Dante. Everything up to this moment felt like the practice run for what would become the real deal now. How silly I had been, believing that true love wasn't in the cards for me. I smiled softly, running my hands down the front of my gown, breathing carefully in the tight bodice.

My dreams had come true. Even dreams I hadn't known I wanted.

My father knocked lightly on the heavy wooden frame. I glanced up with a smile. "Yes, Papa?"

"May I have a minute?"

"Of course."

We hadn't spoken much since the Uva Persa launch. I knew he needed time even though it killed me to have this distance between us. His hurt had run deep but he would never miss the opportunity to walk me down the aisle.

He grasped my hand, his mouth working to produce the words that were strangled in his throat. I understood how he felt because I felt the same. "I've been wrong," he said, his bottom lip trembling. "All this time I never saw who you truly were. I was being a stubborn old man and I nearly cost you your biggest triumph by being hardheaded. I am so happy you pushed forward in spite of my stubbornness. You were right. Enzo was the dreamer, you were the one who was never afraid to take risks."

I struggled to hold back tears. I knew how hard it must've been for Papa to admit his own failings. My heart was bursting with love and relief. My papa had forgiven me!

"I am so proud of you," he admitted. "Can you ever forgive me for being so blind?"

"Oh Papa, there is nothing to forgive," I said in a rush of tears, wrapping my arms around his weathered neck. "I love you. I'm sorry I hurt you. I am so grateful you're here with me today. I could not do this without you."

"Dante is a good man. A better match than Alberico ever could've been. Now that my eyes are open I feel a fool for pushing you in all the wrong directions. If your mother were alive, she would've slapped a knot on my head long before now."

I laughed through my tears. "Yes, she might've."

He chuckled, adding, "And once again your intuition was correct. Sophia seems taken with Alberico, though I can see she is taking things slowly."

I nodded. Indeed Sophia and Alberico were a good match. I suspected I would be attending my best friend's wedding sometime next year but in the meantime, they were like two people from a forgotten era—courting politely and stealing chaste kisses in the garden. It was darling and I was so happy for my sweet Sophia, who was also my new right hand. She had seamlessly stepped in where Como had left off, and even improved upon a few of our operating procedures and advertising venues.

Papa regarded me with love shining in his eyes. "You are the most beautiful bride."

"Thank you, Papa."

His twinkle slowly returned as he straightened his tuxedo and gently wiped away the tears from my cheeks before offering his arm. "Shall we do this?"

I nodded, swallowing the happiest of tears. "Yes, I'm ready."

And I was more than ready for what was to come.

I'd spent my adult life pursuing professional respect yet had found something far more profound, the confidence to push forward without needing the permission of others.

I'd also found the love of my life in the most unlikely of places.

A lost grape had led me to find the future I'd always dreamed of having. I was ready to embrace whatever life had in store with Dante by my side.

Together, we would build empires; together, we were unstoppable.

* * * * *

COMING SOON!

We really hope you enjoyed reading this book. If you're looking for more romance, be sure to head to the shops when new books are available on

Thursday 21st March

To see which titles are coming soon, please visit
millsandboon.co.uk/nextmonth

MILLS & BOON